THE LOYAL SERVANT

EVA HUDSON

THE LOYAL SERVANT

First published 2011

For Jo CFQ

4 May 1979

Prologue

A sweet burning smell hit him at the door. He peered into the gloom.

'Are you in here?' he said.

He moved slowly into the room, the wooden floorboards cool under his bare feet.

'Hello?'

He stood very still and listened. He could hear someone breathing.

'Who's there?' he said.

He held out a hand and edged forward.

'Why've you closed all the shutters? What's going on?'

The sweet smell thickened.

'Is Stevie in here with you?'

No reply.

'Stevie?'

His toes bumped against the edge of the thick Persian rug, he continued to move slowly, tracing the edge of the rug with his feet until his eyes adjusted to the dim light. Two wing-back armchairs on the far side of the room had been moved from their normal position either side of the fireplace and turned so that the backs were facing the door. Above them a pall of smoke reached up to the ceiling.

'Have you seen Stevie?' he said.

He stopped, not wanting to get any closer to the cloying sweetness.

'Are you still pissed?' A voice drifted towards him from the other side of the room.

His head and stomach were heavy with a combination of brandy and champagne from the night before. 'No.' He blinked. 'Have you seen Stevie?'

'Stevie?'

'You were with him out at the pool.' Immediately he regretted mentioning it.

'Have you been spying on us?' A woman's voice. 'What did you see?' Her tone was accusatory, anxious. Maybe she always sounded that way. He didn't really know her. 'Well?' she said.

He clenched his fists and screwed up his face. 'Nothing... I didn't see anything. I just wondered if you—'

'We don't know where he is. Maybe he's left already.'

'I was going to share a cab back into town with him,' he said.

'Looks like he's gone without you, then, doesn't it?'

He started to back out of the room. 'If you do see him, tell him I've—'

'I wouldn't bother. I don't think he was that interested.'

He turned and retraced his steps, moving faster now than on the way in, and stumbled over a corner of the rug. He stretched out his arms, but there was nothing to grab. He slammed hard against the floor.

'Are you still here?' the woman said.

He scrambled to his feet and finally reached the door. He crossed the hall and ran into the long drawing room, tripping over the trailing ends of the dustsheets covering the furniture. He flung open the French doors leading onto the veranda and gulped as much air into his lungs as he could. The early morning mist clung to his bare skin. He turned, dragged a sheet from the nearest chair and wrapped it around his shoulders.

He walked slowly down the half dozen stone steps leading to the swimming pool and passed through the gap in the tall yew hedge, wrapping the dustsheet closer to his chest.

Twenty yards from the marble edge of the pool, he saw it.

A pale suspended mass. Perfectly still.

He threw off the sheet and ran across the strip of lawn, hurdling over upturned sunloungers. He launched himself from the poolside, floating in the air for a moment before crashing through the glassy surface of the water. He thrashed his arms and legs until he was close enough to reach out his hand and touch a pink-white shoulder.

The face was submerged, as if something had caught Stevie's attention on the tiled floor beneath. He heaved at the bony back and managed to turn him over.

Blank eyes stared up at him, the mouth gaping.

He cupped a hand under Stevie's chin and windmilled his free arm through the water, kicking his legs frantically until he'd dragged the body to the shallow end. He tried to call out, but there was no breath left in his lungs. He sucked in more air, gazing at Stevie's long golden hair fanning out around his head.

'Help!' The sound came out as a whimper.

He tried again.

'Help! Someone help me get him out of here!'

Today

1

Caroline Barber heard the distant warble of a phone just as she was soaping her hands. She grabbed a paper towel and rushed into the fourth floor lobby of the Department for Education.

Please don't hang up.

She skidded across the marble tiles, neatly sidestepped the hat stand she'd left propping open a set of double doors, and barrelled into the unlit office.

In the gloom she weaved expertly through an obstacle course of filing cabinets, finally reaching her desk just as her landline stopped ringing. *Bloody bugger.* She scooped up the handset, pressing it hard against her ear, in the forlorn hope the caller was somehow still connected. All she heard was a perforated dialling tone.

A voicemail message. *Already?*

She punched in the numbers to retrieve it and sank heavily onto her chair.

At 3:30pm that afternoon her opposite number in the Sheffield office had promised faithfully he would get back to her by the end of the day. She'd been waiting for his call ever since. She rubbed a thumb and forefinger across her eyebrows and closed her eyes. The automated voice at the other end of the line informed her that the message had been left at 6:47pm. She checked her watch: 8:15pm. How had she missed the earlier call?

'Hello Caroline, it's me.'

Not the voice she was expecting at all. Caroline braced herself, anticipating a long list of extra chores.

'I hope you don't mind. I just wanted to say…' Martin Fox's voice wavered, uncertain. 'That is, what I mean…'

There was a pause.

Caroline sat up a little straighter, curious to hear what was so important the schools minister couldn't have left it until the morning. The line seemed to go dead. A crackle of static then nothing. She was just about to hang up when she heard a sharp intake of breath.

'I want to explain. You deserve an explanation.' Another pause. 'I thought speaking to your answerphone would make it easier, and still I can't seem to find the right words…' He swallowed. 'Things are likely to get a little… fraught in the department over the next few days. I just thought I should warn you.'

Caroline heard him inhale and exhale slowly.

'I want you to know I have complete confidence in you and I know that even in the midst of all the… upheaval, you'll do the right thing.' He paused again. 'You're the only one here I feel I can trust.'

There was another pause, a short one, before the dialling tone returned, a steady continuous purr in her ear. Caroline blinked hard, and noticed for the first time her heart was pounding against the walls of her chest. She took a deep breath and tried to make sense of what she'd just heard. *Explanation?* He hadn't explained anything.

An email alert pinged from her computer and made her jump. Automatically she grabbed her mouse and clicked on the box that had appeared at the bottom of her monitor. She skimmed through half the message before realising it was identical to two she'd already received – an incoming email was being held overnight. Twenty-three years in the civil service and still everything came in triplicate.

She returned the handset to its cradle and replayed Martin Fox's message in her head. She'd never heard the schools minister sound like that before. So strange. So… strained. What was it he'd said about the department? She snatched up the receiver and dialled for voicemail again. This time she listened more carefully, concentrating on every syllable, searching for meaning in the spaces between the words. At the long pause in the middle she was suddenly aware of heavier breathing than she'd heard the first time round. Then she felt a hot blast of air against her cheek. She jolted out of her seat.

'For God's sake!'

'Anything interesting, was it?' The face of Caroline's least favourite security guard loomed into hers.

'Why must you always creep up on me like that?'

'The threat level is still *substantial.* We need to remain vigilant at all times. I'm just keeping you on your toes.'

Caroline replaced the receiver and let go of the breath she'd been holding.

'Well?' He pointed a nail-bitten finger at the phone.

'Personal,' she said, as abruptly as she could.

Go away, Ed.

'Don't mind me.' He straightened to a round-shouldered stoop and tucked a loose corner of shirt into his trousers. Caroline couldn't help noticing the button straining on his waistband. Automatically she pulled in her stomach and sat up straighter. Ed Wallis was probably the same age as Caroline, give or take a couple of years, certainly no more than

45, yet he always reminded her of someone her dad might have met in the Legion for a pint.

He sucked his teeth and glanced round the office. 'Still working in the dark, I see. I don't understand you.' He shook his head. 'It's not as if it's your electric.'

Please, just go away.

'Ah – looks like you missed one.' He nodded to the glassed-walled room at the other end of the office. An anglepoise lamp was burning a bright halo onto her boss's desk. She was sure she'd turned it off.

'Fancy a cuppa?' Ed peered into her face. 'I've worked up a serious thirst.' He held up a hand. 'Don't get up – I can pop the kettle on.'

'Bit busy actually.' Caroline pointed at her watch. 'Got to get on.'

'Oh. Shame.' He didn't move. 'What about a drink then, when I've finished my shift?'

'And what would your wife say about that?'

He tapped the side of his cauliflower nose with a stubby finger and winked at her. 'What the eye doesn't see.'

Good grief.

'It's criminal – lovely looking woman like you…' His gaze lingered on the scooped neckline of her jumper. 'Spending your evenings cooped up in this place. You should be out somewhere enjoying yourself.'

Caroline grabbed the first folder that came to hand and stood up quickly. 'Actually, I need to get this to the minister,' she said.

'Minister? You'll be lucky – they won't still be here. That lot'll be propping up the House of Commons bar by now.'

'Not all MPs are the same.'

He raised his eyebrows, his gaze anchored to the small amount of cleavage visible above the file she was clutching. 'I can take that up to the seventh floor. Which minister is it for?'

He made a sudden lunge towards the file and Caroline reared backwards, desperate not to let his sweaty hands get anywhere near her, and sent her chair crashing into the desk behind.

'All right!' he said, palms aloft. 'I'm only trying to help.'

'I need to speak to Mr Fox anyway.' She walked in a wide circle around Ed and hurried towards the exit.

'So, maybe see you in The Feathers later for a quick one?' he called after her.

In my nightmares.

Caroline stepped out of the lift on the seventh floor and walked slowly across the lobby, taking a moment to compose herself. She stopped and looked out at the central atrium beyond the floor-to-ceiling glass wall – a rainforest of palm trees and ferns. All the floors except this one and the one she'd just left were blazing in fluorescent light, even though the building was practically empty. Sometimes she wondered why she bothered switching off lights and powering down computers, no one else seemed to care.

Except Martin Fox. He still gave a damn.

She glanced at the folder she was clutching like a shield and loosened her grip, only then realising it was empty. Probably Ed had noticed. He never missed a trick. She shuddered at the thought of his lunging hands and turned sharply towards the double doors leading to the ministerial offices.

She edged forward in the dark, tracing a hand along tall cabinets as she went, all the while wondering what it was the minister had wanted to explain in his phone message.

Outside his office she hesitated. She looked down at the wrinkles in her jumper and tried to smooth them out. She tucked a stray strand of hair behind her ear, sucked in a deep breath and tapped lightly on the door.

No response.

She knocked again, more forcefully. 'Minister?'

Still no reply.

Light leaked through the gap beneath the door. She knocked again and levered down the handle.

'Martin?'

She pushed open the door and stepped inside. The file fell from her hands. Her heart lurched into her throat.

Martin Fox was slumped over his desk, one arm hanging limp by his side. His head was turned towards her, glasses pressing painfully into his nose, his eyes closed. Caroline ran to him and reached out a hand. Then she froze. Inches away from his face, her hand started to tremble. All the colour had drained away from his flesh, his lips had turned a bluish pink.

She stepped closer and forced herself to place two fingers on his neck. She couldn't feel a pulse, but his skin felt warm beneath her fingertips. She shifted her fingers, pressed deeper into his flesh.

There was no pulse.

She withdrew her hand and backed away. There was nothing she could do.

Martin Fox was dead.

2

'And did you touch anything?' The tall uniformed policeman towered over Caroline, a concerned look on his face.

Caroline shook her head. She was sitting on a hard plastic chair opposite the minister's open door. She'd been answering questions for a while. She wasn't sure how long. Long enough for the paramedics to come and go. Long enough for more officers to turn up, these ones wearing white paper suits with little hoods bulging from the back of their necks. They were in Martin's office now. What were they doing with him all this time?

PC Mills had explained a detective would need to ask her more questions when he arrived later. So many questions already, Caroline's head was spinning.

'You're sure?' the PC said. He wrote something down in his notebook.

A female constable handed Caroline a glass of water, she took a sip and handed it back.

'Sorry?' Caroline said.

The policeman crouched down to her level and looked into her face, his gaze soft and sympathetic.

'I know how difficult this is for you. But we really need to know if you touched any surfaces, picked anything up. We are looking at a potential crime scene.'

'Crime scene?'

'We can't rule anything out at this stage.'

Caroline swallowed a rising wave of nausea and forced herself to remember the moments immediately after discovering Martin Fox's body.

'Yes,' she said. 'Yes I did. I'm sorry. I—'

She was cut short by the sight of two paramedics at the far end of the office wheeling a gurney towards her. PC Mills placed a hand on her arm and squeezed. His mouth twitched into a sad smile. She smiled back.

'I touched Martin,' she said quietly.

She watched as the gurney squeezed through the doorway into Martin Fox's office. She closed her eyes for a moment, suddenly aware how heavy her arms and legs felt. She just wanted to go home. Pete and the kids would be worried sick. Her mobile was probably ringing non-stop on her desk three floors below.

'Where did you touch him?'

She forced her eyes open and sniffed in a breath, determined not to cry. 'His neck. But I couldn't feel a pulse.' She searched the PC's face for reassurance. 'He was warm.'

The police officer nodded, encouraging her to carry on.

'I couldn't remember what it is you're supposed to do when someone... when they... I called for the ambulance.' The inside of her nose was tingling, she sniffed again. 'So I touched his phone too.' She bit her lip and looked away. 'Four nines.'

'I'm sorry?'

'I had to get an outside line,' she said, distracted by the memory. She heard a clank of metal against wood and twisted her head towards the noise. The gurney was stuck in the doorway. Hemmed in between the metal rails on either side was a long narrow shape covered in a red blanket. Caroline heard the constable say something to her, but his voice was muffled and distant. She couldn't take her eyes off the gurney as the paramedics struggled to manoeuvre Martin Fox out of his room.

'Mrs Barber?'

'Sorry. I...'

She lifted a shaking hand to pull a strand of hair away from her face. She swallowed.

Finally the gurney was through the doorway, the paramedics hurried it along the office towards the exit.

'Do you think you can carry on?' PC Mills rested a reassuring hand on her arm.

Caroline nodded and forced her eyes open wide.

'Do you remember touching anything on his desk? Did you move anything? Take anything away? A letter, a note? Anything like that?'

'A note?'

'Well, in these circumstances... it's quite usual—'

'These circumstances?'

He nodded.

It took her a moment to realise what he was getting at. 'But you just said it was a crime scene.'

'I said we're not ruling anything out.'

Caroline shook her head. 'No,' she said. 'I didn't see a note.'

A woman in a white paper suit waved what looked like a plastic freezer bag under the constable's nose. Inside the bag Caroline could clearly see an envelope with her name and address written on it in fat, black marker pen. It was Martin Fox's handwriting. She gasped.

'My card!' She reached towards the bag as it was snatched away and stared at the retreating envelope. 'It's my birthday.' She watched the woman in the white suit stow the envelope in a large cardboard box. 'Next Tuesday.'

PC Mills frowned at her.

'Martin has a big calendar with everyone's birthday on it, you see,' she said, suddenly feeling the need to explain. 'He never forgets.' A sob burst out of her throat, catching her completely unawares.

'We might be able to get it back to you – when we've finished with it.' He watched his colleague as she slotted a lid on the cardboard box. 'Not in time for your birthday though, obviously.'

Caroline stood up and tried to peer into Martin Fox's office. 'Did you find a CD in there too?' She listed to one side, unsteady on her feet. Her legs gave at the knee and she thumped back down on the chair.

'A CD?'

'Martin said he'd make me a mix of his favourite tracks – for my birthday. It's the same thing every birthday and Christmas.' She sucked down a deep breath. 'I told him not to bother – I can't stand jazz.'

'So you were quite close to the deceased?'

Caroline frowned up at him.

'I mean the, erm… minister?'

'What?' Caroline was distracted by another white-suited officer carrying half a dozen padded envelopes from Martin's room, each in its own freezer bag. He stashed them all in the large cardboard box.

'Mrs Barber?' The PC leaned his head closer to hers.

Caroline tried to focus on his face. He'd stopped smiling.

'Can I go home now?' she said. Her cheeks were burning, her eyes stinging. She tipped back her head to stem an approaching tidal wave of tears.

'Just a few more questions, Mrs Barber. And then the DI, Inspector Leary, will want to speak to you. He'll be here soon.' He stood up and stretched his legs, shook a foot, circled it at the ankle.

'Do you have a tissue?' Caroline wiped the back of her hand across her nose.

The female officer handed her a man-sized square and Caroline blotted her cheeks. 'He's a lovely man,' she said. 'Everyone loves Martin.' She blew her nose.

'Mr Fox was your boss, is that right?'

'My boss? No...' She watched PC Mills cross something out in his notebook. 'He's an MP, the minister responsible for schools. I work in the academies division.'

The officer looked at her blankly, his pen poised. She let out a sigh. 'An academy is a particular type of school – part of Martin's remit. He's very keen on promoting the academies programme. So we work closely together – the academies division and Martin's team.'

'So would you say you knew the minister quite well?'

Caroline nodded slowly.

PC Mills scribbled down more notes, filled a page then turned to a fresh one. 'I'm really sorry to ask you this,' he said, crouching again, his long legs folding awkwardly beneath him. He cleared his throat. 'Have you noticed anything different about Mr Fox recently?' He spoke quietly, not quite making eye contact. 'Anything out of the ordinary? Out of character, maybe?'

Caroline shrugged. 'Out of the ordinary?'

The constable nodded. His cheek twitched.

She didn't know how to answer. She wasn't sure whether or not to mention the phone message. She couldn't really remember it. She let out a ragged breath, sucked in another.

'Was the minister at all...' the PC hesitated, '...depressed?'

'No! Martin doesn't get depressed.' The words flew out of her mouth with more force than she'd meant. 'He's just not the type.' She stared at a spot on the doorframe where the gurney had gouged a jagged line in the paintwork.

'Anything at all strike you as different about him?'

She shook her head. 'He's been stressed. It's a very stressful job,' she said. 'But no way would he...' She turned towards a low murmur of voices coming from the far end of the office.

'Ah,' PC Mills said. 'That's Inspector Leary.'

The constable gestured towards a short man in a flapping raincoat hurrying towards them. He was deep in conversation with another man who was dressed in a formal evening suit. It took Caroline a moment to recognise him.

'That's my boss,' she said.

PC Mills wrote something else in his pad.

'Jeremy Prior.' Caroline looked at Prior, but he didn't return her gaze.

'Another minister?'

'God, no. He's acting head of the academies division.'

'A civil servant.' Mills was still writing.

'Not exactly.'

The man in the raincoat glanced at the constable and tapped his watch as he made his way to Martin Fox's office. PC Mills flipped back a page in his pad. 'You were saying, just now, about the minister...' He stared at his notes. 'He was stressed.'

Caroline pinched her lip between her thumb and forefinger.

'In what way?' he said.

She glanced into Martin Fox's room and tried hard to remember the exact words of the answerphone message. *Trust* was the only one that popped into her head and stuck. Through the open door and the buzz of men and women in white suits, she caught a glimpse of the half-empty bottle of Teacher's and handful of small round pills that had spilled onto his desk. Inspector Leary was talking to one of the forensics people, his face set in a grim expression as he caught her gaze. She looked away quickly.

'I realise what you're trying to suggest.' She turned to Mills. 'But Martin's not... he's not...' She searched for the right word. 'A quitter,' she said eventually. 'Martin's not a quitter. There's absolutely no way he would take his own life.'

3

Angela Tate poured the last of the Three Barrels into a chipped mug and clinked china against her colleague's glass.

'To Jason,' she said and downed the brandy in a single gulp. 'Bloody stupid sod.'

'That's no way to speak of the dead.' Frank Carter rolled his drink around the inside of the glass.

'But what a ridiculous way to go. London is no place for pushbikes. Haven't I always said that? And don't get me started on van drivers.'

'It was a meals-on-wheels lady driving the van.'

'Why do you always get bogged down in the unimportant details, Frank? She still swerved right into him.'

'She was trying to avoid a motorbike on the wrong side of the road.'

Angela shook her head. 'Details Frank… details getting in the way of the real story.'

'Which is?'

'The age-old struggle between good and evil. And let me say right now, Frank, Jason Morris was an angel – a lovely, lovely boy.' She gazed at the empty desk on the other side of the open plan newsroom.

'He was 29, Ange.' Frank Carter pulled a crumpled pack of cigarettes from his pocket and peered inside.

'Exactly,' Angela said. 'A babe in arms.' She waved her empty bottle in the air before letting it slip from her fingers into the bin. She looked down at the shattered glass. 'You got any more booze?'

Frank crushed the cigarette packet in a fist and threw it on the desk. 'Don't you think you've had enough?'

'Listen, Frank, my mother has been dead and buried for some considerable time now – it's far too late for you to step into her shoes and start up the nagging where she left off.'

She got up and swerved across the office to her dead colleague's desk. She grabbed the top drawer of an under-desk console and yanked it hard. It shot out and hit her on the knee. She winced but managed to keep a yelp in check. A hiccup escaped from her mouth instead. The drawer was empty. She tried the drawer below. It pulled out a few inches then got stuck. Angela bent down and peered into the void within. She slammed it shut and tried the bottom drawer.

'God, they cleared out his stuff fast. His body's not even cold in the ground.'

'He was cremated, Ange.'

'Poetic licence. Wasted on a philistine paparazzo like you.'

'What're you looking for, anyway?'

'I thought young Jason might have had a secret stash of booze.'

She grabbed the top of the console and wheeled it over the uneven and stained carpet, back to her own desk. Frank scowled at her.

'What's that face for? The lock's busted on mine. Might as well grab this one before some other bugger does. I'm sure Jason would want me to have it. I was like a mother to that boy. He looked up to me.'

She shook the detritus from her own console straight into the new one, locked it and threw the pair of keys into her handbag. 'No one gets to rifle through my drawers now.'

Frank raised his eyebrows. 'I'm going to push off,' he said.

'And leave me to drink on my own? We haven't even had a chance to celebrate the *good* news. That's got to be worth another half bottle, at least. Come on, Frankie, it'll take my mind off poor young Jason's premature departure.'

'As we're all out of booze and fags, I'd say it was a good time to call it a night.'

'Where's your sense of occasion?'

Angela leaned sideways in her chair and grabbed a pair of shoes from under the desk. She crammed her swollen feet into them.

'Let's go to the pub.' She got up quickly and the room began to sway, lurching from side to side. Her stomach felt like it was moving to the same rhythm. She sat back down, gripped her head in her hands and waited for the motion to stop.

'Do you know,' she said, after taking a few moments to recover. 'I still have my copy of the *Standard* from November 1990?' She let out a noisy sigh. 'Should have been a public holiday, the day Thatcher resigned.' She slumped back in her chair and ran her fingers through her hair until they snagged in a tangle. 'Come to the pub with me. Go on, you know you want to.'

Frank grabbed his leather jacket from the back of a chair and squeezed his thick arms into the sleeves. 'Just one drink. And it better be a small one.' He picked up his camera bag and swung it over a shoulder.

'That's the spirit, Frankie.'

He started walking towards the door, stopped halfway across the newsroom and turned back.

'Do you still want me to cover that demo next week?'

'Remind me?'

'The thing at the building site in Catford. Only I was thinking of taking a few days off.'

She screwed up her face. 'You never take time off – are you moonlighting?'

'Do you need me or not?'

'Be good to get some half-decent shots – you never know, something might kick off.'

'And who's doing the kicking?'

'Oh just a few concerned parents and a handful of militant teachers.' She reached down for her bag and dumped it on the desk. 'Though I'm not convinced waving a 'Save our School' placard and collecting a few hundred signatures is going to stop the bulldozers moving in.'

'What's so terrible about a new school being built anyway? You'd think they'd be grateful.'

'It's not just a school though, is it?'

Frank put his hands in his pockets and pulled a face. 'Isn't it?'

'God, Frank – have you read none of my features?'

He rubbed a hand over his chin, looking like a man who wished he'd never asked.

'It's an *academy*. Repeat after me: academies are evil.'

'OK – got that. Let's get to the pub.'

Angela made another attempt at vertical, this time employing a more gradual ascent. Thankfully the room stayed still and the contents of her stomach remained motionless.

'Number one,' she said, sticking a thumb in the air. 'Academies are not accountable to the local authority.' She waved an index finger at him. 'Two: they headhunt all the best teachers from the surrounding schools.'

'What's wrong with—'

She glared at him and he took a sudden interest in his shoes.

'Three: they suck up cash that would have been distributed to other schools. Four...' Her mind went blank. 'Four escapes me for the moment.'

Frank held up his hands. 'Really, Ange – I get the picture. Just tell me what time to tip up and I'll take all the photos you want – you can save the rest of the lecture 'til then.'

She pursed her lips and stared at him through narrowed eyes.

'I promise you'll have my undivided.'

'Hah!'

She'd been digging away at the academies story for weeks now and come up with nothing of any real substance. No nice juicy scandal to make her editor sit up and take notice. He was beginning to lose patience.

'Come on, Ange – let's get that drink. My shout.'

Angela wrapped a scarf around her throat and shrugged on a raincoat, taking care to keep her head as still as possible. She edged gingerly around the desk and glanced over at Jason Morris's empty chair. 'Such a terrible waste. He had real talent, that boy.'

Frank looked at his watch.

'Do you know what he was working on?'

Frank shook his head. 'Why?'

'Thought I might be able to pick up where he left off.'

'Not content snatching a dead man's drawers, now you want to steal his work too?'

'I wouldn't take all the credit. It'd be my tribute to him.' She laid a hand against her heart. 'You really don't know what he was investigating?'

'If you don't know it's not likely I would, is it?'

Angela did her best to focus on Frank's face. 'I know how you lot like to gossip,' she said. 'Standing around all day waiting for a celebrity to flash an unsightly bit of cellulite at you.'

'Is that how you think of me?' He flashed her a smile. 'I'm deeply wounded.'

'You do know something, don't you?' She tottered over to him. 'Come on, Frank – cough.'

Frank held out his arms. 'Would I lie to you?'

'Whenever you get the chance.'

'All I know, it was all very hush-hush. But then that's the whole point, isn't it?'

Angela shook her head and immediately regretted it. The office pitched and rolled. 'Whole point of what?'

'Jason Morris was working undercover.'

4

The squad car had a strange smell about it. Stale tobacco mixed with stale sweat and a trace of sick. The sick was stale too, Caroline decided. Anything fresher and she would have been gagging. PC Mills was sitting with her in the back while his colleague, the policewoman whose name Caroline kept forgetting, drove her home.

It was well past 11pm when they left the department and the roads around Parliament Square were choked with traffic. Motorists hooted horns and flashed their high beams, quickly stopping when they spotted the police car. As they drove around the square, Caroline watched a peace protestor running along the edge of the grass, his t-shirt pulled right up over his head, as if he'd just scored a last-minute winning goal in injury time.

'Has something happened?' Caroline turned to the constable. 'We've not won a world cup in something that's completely passed me by, have we?'

PC Mills smiled and her and shrugged. The policewoman looked at her in the rear-view mirror.

'I can radio in and check for you,' she said.

'Oh don't worry – I'll find out soon enough.'

'If we have, it's a world cup that I've missed too – international tiddlywinks championships maybe?' Mills gave Caroline an even broader smile, flashing gums as well as teeth.

The policeman had been valiantly trying to keep her spirits up ever since he and his partner were given the task of conveying her home to Catford. Before she'd been allowed to leave the department she'd had to endure an hour and a half of questioning by the inspector. He'd asked exactly the same questions as the PC, but with none of the constable's bedside charm. By the end of her interrogation, Caroline felt as if she was a suspect.

Over Westminster bridge the traffic started to thin and the police car made faster progress south of the river. The sights of Camberwell and Dulwich whizzed past the window in a blur. In no time at all they were turning off Brownhill Road and into her street.

'You can drop me off here,' she said, hastily unbuckling her seatbelt. 'We can't go frightening the neighbours, can we?'

'Are you sure?' The PC frowned and peered out of the window.

'You can practically see my front door from here. It's not as if I'm going to get lost. Stay here and watch until I get inside, if you like.' Caroline smiled at him. 'I'm not giving Brenda from number 24 an excuse to gossip about me from now 'til Christmas.'

PC Mills jumped out of the car. He scooted round to her side and opened the door. Caroline grabbed his outstretched hand and hauled herself out. She looked up into his face. He was smiling his sympathetic smile again. He reached into a pocket and plucked out a business card.

'If you think of anything that may help with our investigation, or even if you just want someone to talk to about what's happened, call that number.' He handed her the card. 'Just ask for me.'

Caroline took the card and squeezed his hand; it was much warmer than hers. 'Thank you, constable, for being so kind. Goodnight.'

She waved at the policewoman and turned slowly up the street, taking small, deliberate steps, determined to make the short journey to her front door last as long as possible. She was enjoying the coolness of the air against her cheeks and the quiet of her road, knowing as soon as she got inside she'd be confronted with a barrage of questions. She'd managed a quick call to her husband just before she left the department, but hadn't gone into too many details. Not over the phone. Not when she felt she might tip into tears at any moment.

She reached the front gate and stared up at the first floor windows. Through the gaps in the curtains she could see all the lights were still on. Downstairs too. She hadn't anticipated the whole family would be waiting up for her. She hesitated for a moment, desperately wanting to be with them but not sure she could face another interrogation about what had happened. She wanted to scrub that final image of Martin Fox from her mind, not be reminded of it as she gave them a blow-by-blow account. She drew in a deep breath, letting the chill air fill her lungs, and exhaled slowly. She pushed open the gate and hurried up the path. When she reached the front door she heard her mother shouting on the other side.

'Pete! Coffee or tea? Or should I get you *another* beer?'

Caroline recognised that accusatory tone only too well. She fumbled in her bag for her house key, angry with her mother, but nevertheless worried how many four-packs Pete had chucked down his throat since he'd got in from work.

She closed the door quietly behind her and slowly slipped out of her jacket, managing to squeeze it onto an overstuffed hook on the coat rack. She dropped her bag next to Pete's mud-encrusted work boots and took another deep breath. She stood for a moment, just listening, half expecting one of the kids to somehow sense her return and rush into the hall and throw their arms around her. But the television continued to blare from the living room and her mother carried on clattering crockery in the kitchen at the other end of the hall. Caroline wandered towards the hiss of the boiling kettle and pushed open the kitchen door.

Jean grabbed a tea towel to blot her soapy hands and hurried towards her daughter, smiling broadly as if she hadn't seen her for weeks. 'Hello, love! I'm so glad your home.' She wrapped her arms around Caroline's neck and squeezed tight, rocking her gently from side to side. 'Isn't it wonderful?' she said.

Caroline unpeeled her mother's arms and stepped back, eyeing her suspiciously, wondering if she'd finally succumbed to some form of dementia.

Jean was still beaming. 'You know I think it's the best news I've heard since Thatcher was forced to resign.'

Caroline leaned towards her mother and sniffed. 'Have you been drinking?'

Jean shot her a disgusted look. 'I leave that to your dipsomaniac husband.'

'Oh Mum! Please don't start.'

'Well... I think you need to have a serious word. Maybe fix up an appointment with the GP. Something's not right.' She turned away and threw a teabag into a mug. 'Cuppa?'

Caroline was too weary to rise to the bait. She collapsed on a chair and laid her hands flat on the table. 'Can we take this slowly?'

'Do you want tea or not?' Her mother waved a pyramid of tea leaves at her.

'People have been making me cups of tea all night.'

'Oh that's nice, love. Where've you been?'

Caroline jerked upright. 'Didn't Pete tell you?'

'Of course he did. That's why we didn't wait to eat.' Jean dug the nail of her little finger into the gap between her front teeth, pulled it out and inspected it. 'We had fish and chips from that new place up the hill. Wasn't bad.'

'What *did* Pete tell you?'

'That you'd be late – later than usual.' She turned back to the kettle. 'You should speak to your union rep – just because everyone in your office is terrified of being made redundant doesn't give your boss the excuse to work you all like dogs.' She poured hot water into a mug. 'In your father's day they would have downed tools and walked out.'

'Didn't Pete tell you why I was late?'

Jean looked at her blankly.

Caroline jumped up and hurried from the kitchen back into the hall and shoved open the living room door. Pete was trapped on the sofa, pinned down by a sleeping eight-year-old boy. Claire was sitting cross-legged on the floor, playing absent-mindedly with the dog's ears, the dog thumping its tail rapidly on the rug as Caroline walked in. Both her husband and daughter appeared to be transfixed by a political correspondent on the BBC News Channel.

'Would someone mind telling me what the bloody hell is going on?' Caroline said.

Claire groaned but didn't answer.

'Pete – could you enlighten me? I can't get any sense out of my mother.'

'You don't know?'

'Well of course I know, I was right there, wasn't I?'

Claire snapped her head round to look at her mother. 'At Number 10? Really?'

'What are you talking about? I was at work. That's where it happened.'

'No it didn't. He was standing right there.' Claire pointed at the television screen. 'In Downing Street. I must have seen it about 20 times.'

Caroline lifted a hand to her forehead and let out a long breath. 'I don't understand what you're talking about. I wish someone would just explain—'

'He said he's resigned for personal reasons. To spend more time with his family. Does that mean he's been caught having an affair?'

'Who?'

'It's all over the news. How can you not know? Dur! Where've *you* been? God Mum, I think you need—'

Caroline shot her daughter a look. Claire stopped talking and bit her lip.

'Who's resigned?'

'The prime minister.'

'Why? When did this happen? Is it because of Martin?' Caroline kept an eye on the ticker at the bottom of the television screen.

'I just told you why. Who's Martin anyway?' Claire said. She unfold-ed her skinny legs and stood up, right in front of the television.

'Martin Fox,' Caroline said. 'The schools minister? Hasn't it been on the news?'

'All the news is about the resignation, has been for the last couple of hours.' Claire walked round her mother and headed for the door.

'Where are you going?' Caroline said.

'Bed. If that's OK? Now you're home it means I don't have to take Minty for a walk. Night.'

'No one's taken her out? What are you all, helpless?'

The dog padded over to Caroline and nuzzled a damp nose into her hand.

'Where's Dan?' Caroline looked at her husband.

Pete shrugged, not taking his eyes from the screen, one hand stroking his son's hair, the other lifting a can of Stella to his lips. Caroline snatched up the TV remote, jabbed the mute button and stood directly in front of him.

'Dan? You remember – your other son. Quite tall for his age, floppy hair, skinny jeans, occupies the airless pit next to the bathroom. Is he up there now?'

'He went out. Said he had to sort something.'

'And he's not back? For God's sake, Pete. It's after half eleven.'

Ben stirred on Pete's lap and he shushed him back to sleep. 'Keep your voice down, Caz.' He carefully balanced his beer on the arm of the sofa. 'It's not like it's a school night. You need to cut the boy some slack.'

Caroline rushed into the hall to fetch the phone. She was just punching in the number for Dan's mobile when the front door opened. Dan grunted at her and slammed the door. He was halfway up the stairs before she had a chance to speak.

'Dan! Where have you been? Do you know what time it is?'

Dan grunted again and disappeared onto the first floor landing. Caroline heard his bedroom door bang shut.

Pete came out of the living room with Ben draped over a shoulder. 'See?' he said. 'He's fine. No harm done. Bit of slack, that's all he needs.'

As they passed her, Caroline planted a kiss on the top of Ben's head and wished him a whispered goodnight. She chose to ignore Pete's comments. Now wasn't the time for another row.

She watched Ben's sleeping face until Pete reached the top of the stairs, then she hurried back into the living room. She stared at the television. The reporter had been replaced by a grave-faced secretary of state for education. William King was effectively Martin's boss at the department. Caroline watched as he walked slowly down a flight of steps towards a crowd of jostling reporters. His wife joined him and held tightly on to his arm. Caroline felt a rush of relief – finally someone was going to make a statement about Martin Fox's death. Camera flashes popped as photographers and journalists pushed forward. King raised his hands to quieten the crowd. Caroline grabbed the remote control and unmuted the sound. She held her breath.

'What's King got to say for himself?' Jean came in and stood next to her daughter, mug of tea in her hand. 'Slimy bastard. I've never liked the look of him.'

'I've been trying to tell you since I—'

'Shhh!' Jean said. 'Turn it up.'

William King cleared his throat and stared directly into the camera. 'My colleagues have done me a great honour,' he said. 'I only hope I can live up to the confidence they have shown in me.' His wife shuffled closer to him. 'I will endeavour not to disappoint them. And I will do my utmost to serve them, my party and of course, most importantly of all, the people of this great nation of ours. Thank you for your support.' He smiled into the camera. 'Goodnight ladies and gentlemen. I'll give you a full statement in the morning.' He turned and ran back up the steps, his wife trailing behind him.

Jean started to say something; Caroline laid a hand on her arm. They both stared at the television in silence. Caroline read the breaking news caption at the bottom of the screen three times before its meaning finally sank in.

...William King replaces Duncan Oakley as prime minister...

5

Caroline lowered her head and summoned all her strength to force a path through the television news crews and rabble of reporters blocking the main entrance of the Department for Education. As she struggled across the final few yards of pavement, digital recorders were shoved at her and journalists shouted questions just inches from her face. Finally she made it to the revolving doors.

The hubbub didn't subside once she was inside. There was a buzz of movement around the reception desk as security staff issued temporary passes to a long line of visitors.

She nodded at one of the receptionists who immediately nudged her colleague; both women stared at her as she turned away. She fumbled with her security pass at the barrier and headed towards the lifts, keeping her gaze on the floor all the way. She hadn't slept more than a couple of hours all night and each step was an effort.

There was a shout behind her. 'Hold up!'

Immediately she recognised the security guard's voice and flinched. Ed Wallis caught up with her and timed his steps to match hers. He jabbed her arm with an elbow.

'That was a turn up for the books, wasn't it?' he said.

Caroline ignored him and tried to quicken her pace. He lengthened his stride.

'I mean, if I'd started my round on the eighth floor and worked my way down,' he continued, unabashed, 'rather than setting off from the basement going up... or maybe if I hadn't stopped on the fourth to talk to you... well... who knows? I probably would have been able to save his life. Makes you think, doesn't it?' He blew out a breathy whistle. 'Fate, my missus says.'

They'd reached the lifts. Caroline hit the *up* button and stepped right back, putting a safe five feet between her and Ed and trying to keep an eye on all six lifts at the same time, ready to jump into the first one that pinged onto the ground floor.

'But I reckon he timed it deliberate like.' Ed still hadn't picked up on her body language and ploughed on. 'I bet he'd been watching my routine and planned it down to the last second.' He shuddered, his huge stomach undulating under the straining buttons of his shirt. 'To think you and me were in the building while he was doing that to himself.' He whistled again.

Caroline looked directly into his face for the first time. 'No one knows what happened.' Her heart was racing, sweat started to prickle under her arms.

'But you found him. You know what happened. You must have seen the pills... the booze.'

He was staring at her cleavage again. She yanked her jacket across her chest.

'Who told you about that?'

'There's not much happens in this place without me knowing about it.'

The lift doors nearest Caroline opened and she threw herself towards them. Once inside, she stayed near the threshold and turned back quickly to Ed, barring his way in.

'Well then,' she said as the doors started to close, 'you must know the police are keeping all lines of enquiry open.'

The doors slid shut and Ed's blotchy, flaky face finally disappeared. Caroline edged her way further in and punched the button for the fourth floor. She could feel her face flushing; aware suddenly the loud chatter of the other occupants had died down to a murmur. A few of them threw surreptitious glances in her direction.

'Nothing to see here,' she said. 'As you were.'

After a moment of embarrassed silence, the chatter started back up. During the painfully slow ascent to the fourth floor, Caroline heard at least two exchanges speculating about the possible links between Martin Fox's death and the resignation of the prime minister. Lying awake for most of the night, Caroline had gone through all the permutations and combinations herself. But as much as she tried to force a connection, there really was nothing to tie the two events together. Martin Fox may have been a member of Duncan Oakley's government, but they had never been close political allies. Caroline had always got the impression they tolerated one another for the sake of party unity. The theories she overheard in the lift were no more credible than the ones spouted by the overexcited callers to the radio phone-in she'd listened to while she made Ben his breakfast.

Finally the doors opened onto the fourth floor and Caroline pushed her way out of the lift and into the academies section. As she passed her colleagues, heads turned and conversations stopped mid-sentence. She felt their gaze follow her all the way to her desk. She dropped her bag onto the floor, peeled off her jacket and slumped onto her chair. She waited a moment before glancing up. A few of her team smiled back at her and quickly looked away, while others made a show of studying intensely absorbing paperwork. She reached for her phone.

'I didn't expect to see you here today.'

Caroline replaced the handset and looked up to see her line manager emerging from the kitchen, a packet of custard creams in one hand, a mug in the other. Pamela Redman hurried over to her, liquid slopping over the edge of her mug. Without waiting to be asked, she dragged a chair from a nearby desk. The hydraulic mechanism let out a short hiss of complaint as she sat down. She dumped her coffee and biscuits on the desk and leaned her head close to Caroline's. She pulled a sympathetic face. 'Are you sure you're up to it?' She rubbed her dimpled knuckles up and down Caroline's arm. 'Should you even be here?'

Caroline glanced round the office again. 'Does everyone know it was me who… who…' She had to stop; she could feel her throat tightening.

Pam nodded.

'Who told you?'

'I don't remember – everyone was already talking about it when I got in.'

Caroline cleared her throat, not wanting to risk speaking again.

'Are you OK?' Pam stuck out her bottom lip and tipped her head to one side. 'You do look a bit peaked. Maybe you should go back home.'

Caroline dragged over a pile of papers from her in tray. She started leafing through them. 'Too much to do,' she said.

'But you're probably in shock and you just don't realise it. Trauma affects people in different ways. You should be taking it easy.'

Caroline took a deep breath and said nothing. Pam leaned in even closer and gripped Caroline's arm.

'Was it awful?' She lowered her voice. 'You know – finding him like that?'

Caroline stared at Pam, her mouth dropped open. She shook her head.

'What?' Pam said. 'I'm only asking what everyone else is wondering.'

Still Caroline said nothing. There was nothing she could say.

Pam gathered up her biscuits and mug from the desk and stood up. 'Well, you know where I am if you need to talk to someone.' She pulled her mouth into the semblance of a smile. 'I only want to help.'

Caroline went back to sifting through her paperwork.

Pam sniffed loudly and walked away. 'Oh, I nearly forgot.' She turned back again, losing more of her coffee over the side of the mug. 'Jeremy wants to see you.'

Caroline glanced at the glass-walled room at the other end of the office. It was empty. An image of Jeremy Prior pacing up and down the office dressed in his dinner suit forced its way into her mind. She blinked hard as if that might make it go away. 'What about?'

Pam shrugged. 'He didn't say. I should warn you though – he's in a stinking mood.'

She watched Pam lumber back to her own desk and waited for her to sit down before picking up the phone. She tapped in the number for voicemail. After a pause the metallic voice told her she had 'no new messages'. Caroline let out an impatient sigh and waited. 'And no saved messages.'

What?

She went through the process again, with the same result. She was certain she hadn't deleted Martin Fox's message. She replaced the receiver and sat staring at the phone, trying to remember the sequence of events from going up to the seventh floor to see Martin to being ushered into the police car by the two officers. She hadn't been allowed back to her desk in all that time; a police officer had brought her her handbag and jacket. So what had happened to the message? She punched in the number for facilities management, telling herself there had to be a perfectly innocent explanation, some glitch in the phone system. While she waited for someone to pick up, she turned on her computer and monitor. She typed her details into the login box and the PC started the slow process of loading her system preferences. After a dozen or so rings her call was finally transferred to the voicemail system. She hung up.

The desktop appeared on her monitor and she quickly opened Outlook and scanned her long list of emails. She scrolled through the unread mails, opening each one and quickly judging whether or not an immediate response was required. After five minutes of firing off urgent replies she'd reached the bottom of the list. The message that was being held overnight hadn't materialised. She punched in the number for the IT helpdesk, fully expecting to be shunted into the voicemail system again, but the call was answered after only two rings.

Caroline explained the situation and the patient man on the other end of the phone informed her there was no email being held. Caroline asked him to check again. He did. No email. Not even any record of the other mails she'd received notifying her one was being held. The only explanation the man in IT could offer was 'user error', which Caroline interpreted as a nice way of saying she had either done something wrong or else imagined the whole thing. By the time she put the phone down she was almost convinced she had. She stared at her monitor. Four missing emails and a vanishing phone message. The man in IT confirmed no one else had reported a problem. It was just her. She screwed her eyes tight and opened them wide, straining to focus again on her monitor. Was it user error?

Her son was always accusing her of having a peculiar effect on technology. Dan insisted that whenever DVDs stopped playing, computers crashed or digital radio broadcasts sounded like they were being transmitted under water, it was because she had just walked into the room. Maybe he was right.

She thought about trying facilities management again, but just as she was reaching for the phone it started to ring. She noticed her hand was trembling. She clenched her fist and stretched her fingers before snatching up the receiver.

'Yes?'

There was a hesitation at the other end, then a bout of noisy throat clearing.

'Is that Mrs Barber?'

She didn't recognise the voice.

'I'm investigating the death of Martin Fox.'

Caroline sighed. 'I told you everything last night. Twice. Why do you need to speak to me again? What's happened?'

'I believe you were the one to find the body, Caroline. I was hoping you could give me a brief statement.'

'Who am I speaking to?'

'I erm…'

'Who is this?' she shouted into the phone.

'I'm calling from the crime desk at the Daily—'

'You're a reporter?' Caroline glanced up at her colleagues, who had stopped their work to stare at her again. She lowered her voice. 'How did you get this number?'

'Do you have a few moments to tell me how you felt at the time? How are you coping—'

Caroline slammed down the phone. She looked across at Pam and caught her staring back. Pam smiled her fake smile. Only someone inside the department could have leaked the number of her direct line to the press. She suddenly had an overwhelming urge to wipe the smile off Pam's face. She jumped up and marched towards her desk. Pam quickly picked up her phone as Caroline approached.

'I need to speak to you.' Caroline leaned over her colleague's desk. Pam held up a finger and continued to mumble something into her phone. 'Do you know who that was?' Caroline raised her voice.

Pam pulled her finger to her lips and spun her chair away from Caroline. Caroline let out a breath, waited a moment, then reluctantly retreated. She walked out of the office into the lobby and tried to control her breathing as she paced up and down. She stopped and looked out over the atrium. She'd worked with Pam Redman for years. Could Pam really betray a colleague as easily as that?

Four storeys below Caroline could see Ed Wallis manning the security desk, the bald patch at the back of his head gleaming white and shiny under the bright lights. Ed was a much more likely candidate. He wouldn't think twice about giving out her number. He looked up and Caroline quickly stepped away from the glass. Her gaze automatically shifted upwards to the ministers' floor and the small room overlooking the atrium at the far end. Immediately her eyelids started to prickle, and her breath caught in her throat. Beside her the lift doors sprang open. A man stepped out and smiled at her, shuffling to one side so she could get in. She took a step towards the lift without thinking, then hesitated on the threshold. A sharp-suited man she vaguely recognised held his finger on a button to keep the doors open and gestured for her to hurry inside.

'Going up?' he said and smiled at her.

She glanced through the glass towards Martin Fox's room. The man in the lift cleared his throat.

Of course.

Caroline stepped inside, relieved to have made a decision.

'Floor?' the man said.

'Seventh.'

Suddenly she realised exactly what she needed to do, amazed she hadn't thought of it before.

Angela Tate barged her way through the tight pack of photographers and reporters blocking the entrance of the Department for Education and tapped Frank Carter on the shoulder.

'Can I bum a fag?'

'What time do you call this?' Frank pulled a pack of cigarettes from his pocket and handed them to her.

'My body can't take as much punishment as it used to. You shouldn't have let me drink so much. Call yourself a friend...'

Frank shook his head and shoved his camera under an arm. He took a drag from the last few millimetres of his cigarette and threw the stub into the gutter.

'Anyway,' she said. 'I haven't just fallen out of bed.' Angela ran a hand through her hair. 'I've already been into the office.'

Frank concentrated on polishing the lens of his camera and stuck his tongue into his cheek.

'I have! I've been waiting for Evans to turn up.' She stared down at the cigarette packet, instantly going off the idea of a nicotine fix.

Frank stopped polishing and looked at her.

'I wanted to ask him about Jason's undercover op,' she said.

'You're not still banging on about that?'

'Aren't you even a little bit curious?'

'And what pearls of wisdom did our esteemed editor share with you?'

'Oh I left before he got in. He must have a hangover of his own. Bloody lightweight.'

'Still doesn't explain your tardiness.'

'The roads are a complete fucking nightmare. Because of the fire.'

Frank perked up. 'What fire?'

'Come on, Frank – how can you not know? I'm surprised you can't see the smoke from here. The whole of Waterloo's been closed off. The bridge too. Which has made Blackfriars and Westminster pretty much impassable. I had to get on a tube.'

'My God, Ange – public transport – that is desperate.'

'Shut up.'

She looked around at the surrounding reporters and TV news crews. 'Have I missed anything?'

'Bugger bleeding all. I'm thinking of packing up. No one's managed to get further than the front desk.'

A black cab pulled into the kerb and the throng surged sideways towards it. Angela stuck out her elbows to avoid getting crushed.

'Has it been like this all morning?' she shouted above the din.

Frank nodded. 'Every time a car pulls up. But it's never anyone important.'

Angela looked at the greedy faces surrounding the poor unsuspecting soul who had just emerged from the taxi. 'I can't work under these conditions.'

'Exactly the conclusion I came to an hour ago. All I've got are dozens of shots of camera-shy civil servants holding their hands up to their faces.' He scratched his head. 'I feel like a wildlife photographer disturbing their delicately balanced ecosystem.'

'If there's nothing doing, why are you still here?'

'I've been waiting for you to turn up.'

'I don't need a minder, Frank.' She dug an elbow into the ribs of the *London Tonight* reporter as he attempted to record a piece to camera, just to illustrate her point.

'I thought we might get a spot of late breakfast before I head off.'

'Please, Frank – don't mention the 'B' word. The way I'm feeling I don't think I'll ever be able to eat again.'

'Suit yourself.' He lifted his camera above his head and snapped a few shots of the man from the taxi as he disappeared through the revolving doors. 'Oh yeah,' he said, turning back to her. 'There was some nugget of news I wanted to impart before I left.' He unzipped his camera bag and squeezed the camera inside. 'Not sure I want to tell you now – the mood you're in.'

Angela planted her hands on her hips and waited.

He slowly zipped up the bag. 'Not five minutes ago there was a buzz going around the tabloid hacks.'

She edged closer to him.

'We've found out who discovered the body last night.'

'And?'

'Some woman called Caroline Barber. She's a senior executive officer, apparently.'

'Forget about her job title – did you get a picture of her?'

'Might have done – probably got the whole department recorded for posterity.' He waved the camera at her.

'This needs a more direct approach.' Angela slipped Frank's cigarettes into her jacket pocket. 'Honestly – if you want anything done properly...' She pressed through the crowd towards the entrance and turned round when she reached the doors. 'Are you coming or what?'

Frank raised his hand. 'I'm off to check on that fire at Waterloo.'

'Chicken!'

Once she was through the doors and into the reception area, Angela pulled a phone from her pocket and pretended to be deep in conversation. She paced up and down for a few moments, glancing around, checking the possible routes past security. She spotted a man carrying a briefcase who was making for a side door just to the left of the long reception desk. Without breaking her stride she followed him to the door and passed through right on his heels. On the other side she found herself in a narrow carpeted area, emergency exit to the left and a staircase leading to the first floor in front of her. The man with the briefcase headed left. Angela looked up the stairwell, the stairs disappearing in a giddying blur several flights up. She glanced back at the man she'd followed in, just as he slipped through another door. She hurried after him and discovered another flight of stairs leading down to the basement. She heard a shout behind her.

'Oi! What do you think you're doing?'

Angela hurried through the door without looking back. At the bottom of the stairs she was confronted with three more doors and no sign of the man with the briefcase. She hesitated for a moment too long.

'Stop right there.'

She turned to see a potato-faced security guard struggling down the stairs. By the time he reached her he was panting.

'I'm sorry,' she said, 'were you talking to me?'

'Where's your pass?'

'My pass? Oh... yes... it's just here... somewhere... I'm sure I put it...' Angela made a show of patting her pockets and checking her bag. 'I appear to have mislaid it. You won't tell will you?' She fixed her mouth into what she hoped was a winning smile and thrust her chest towards him.

'No one without a pass in the building. Especially not today.'

She peered at his name badge. 'Now come on... Ed – I'm sure just this once you can make an exception. I'm already late for a meeting.'

The guard scratched his chin for a moment and looked her up and down, his gaze coming to rest just above the plunging neckline of her shirt. He turned a fraction and glanced back up the stairs. Angela spotted the early edition of the *Evening News* sticking out of the back pocket of his trousers. She edged backwards towards a door.

'Who's your meeting with?' he finally said.

'Caroline Barber.' It was the first name that popped into her head.

'She never mentioned she was expecting a visitor when I spoke to her earlier.'

'You know Caroline? Oh well – if we're both friends of Caroline's – I don't see a problem. You can just let me get to my meeting.'

The guard was nibbling at a piece of dry skin on his bottom lip. He let out a long halitoxic breath. 'Nah.' He shook his head. 'Can't be done. I'm sorry; you can't just wander round the building without a security pass. We'll have to go back to reception and get you another one. I can phone through to the academies division from there and let Caroline know you've arrived.'

Academies? Now she really wanted to meet this Caroline Barber woman. Angela put a hand on his arm, lightly brushing her fingers along the wrinkles of his badly ironed shirt. 'Congratulations!' she said. 'You've passed.'

'What? What are you talking about?'

'The security test.' She smiled at him again. 'I'll make sure your supervisor receives a glowing report.'

The guard stood a little straighter.

'My paper does it from time to time. To all the major government departments. Especially at times of extreme stress and er... high security alert.'

'What paper is that?'

'The one you've got there. Would you like to make a comment about the shocking events of last night?'

He opened his mouth but hesitated, shifting his weight from one foot to the other.

'Were you by any chance actually in the building when the body was found?'

The open plan office on the seventh floor was busy with civil servants and management consultants, talking excitedly in small groups or crowding around computer monitors streaming Sky News. These people were standing not twenty yards from where Caroline had found Martin's body, *gossiping* about his death and the PM's resignation as if they were discussing the latest twists in a soap opera.

No one noticed her as she made her way slowly and steadily along the wall of cabinets she'd walked past in the dark the night before. Finally she reached the desk of Martin Fox's PA, the chair tucked neatly underneath. Caroline scanned the office – there was no sign of Consuela. A man at the adjacent desk was pecking away at his laptop and didn't look up as Caroline approached. A mobile phone sitting next to his elbow started to vibrate, and began working its way steadily towards the edge of the desk. He ignored it and continued typing.

'Sorry to disturb you,' Caroline said, a tremble in her voice she barely recognised as her own. Still he didn't look up. 'Do you know where I might find Consuela?'

Finally he stopped tapping and tore his gaze away from the laptop screen. 'Who?' The buzzing phone tipped over the edge of the desk and he deftly caught it left-handed, looking decidedly pleased with himself. He pressed a button on the mobile and tossed it back on the desk. 'I'm sorry – it's my first day. I'm still getting my head round all the names. Who did you say?'

'Consuela.'

'Is she one of ours, or KPMG?'

'No – she's not one of yours. Or theirs. She's a civil servant, Martin Fox's PA.'

'Martin Fox? What, you mean the bloke who—' A second mobile on his desk started to ring, he snatched it up. 'I've got to take this, it's really important… sorry.' He turned away from her and barked his name into the phone, looking anything but apologetic.

Caroline checked Consuela's desk – neither the monitor nor the computer was on and the normally overflowing in tray was empty. She slowly turned towards the minister's room, expecting to see blue and white police tape strung across a padlocked door. But it was wide open. She crept towards it. Memory of the police constable's words describing the little office as a 'potential crime scene' sent a rapid shiver across her shoulders. She stopped at the threshold, unable to enter, or even look inside.

Someone nudged her arm.

'Excuse, please.' One of the contract cleaners was standing next to her, the handle of a Henry vacuum cleaner gripped firmly in one hand, a bucket stuffed with bottles of spray disinfectant and dusters in the other.

Automatically Caroline stepped to one side and the cleaner manoeuvred herself and her equipment through the gap. Caroline finally peered into the room and couldn't believe what she saw. Apart from a set of empty bookshelves, a desk and a chair, the room had been completely cleared. She imagined dozens of little freezer bags, each one containing a small fragment of Martin Fox's office – the whole of his professional life reduced to bundles of polythene bags neatly tucked away in a stack of cardboard boxes.

The cleaner found a socket on the far wall and plugged in the vacuum.

'Wait!' Caroline ran across the room and grabbed the woman's arm. 'You can't clean in here. The police may need to search it again. For evidence.'

The cleaner tilted her head at Caroline as if she was staring at a lunatic. 'Supervisor say clean room. I clean room. You want to make trouble for me?' She looked down at Caroline's hand, still gripping her arm. Caroline let go.

'Who is your supervisor? I really don't think you should be doing this. There must have been a mix up.' She yanked the plug from the socket.

The cleaner let out a long sigh and shook her head, as if she had to deal with crazy civil servants all day long. She produced a mobile phone from a pocket in her overall and tapped in a number. When she was connected she rattled away in an eastern European language Caroline didn't recognise. The woman jabbed the phone towards her. 'Supervisor.'

The man on the other end explained slowly, as if he was talking to a small child, that his instructions had been given to him by the head of facilities management, who had received his orders directly from the permanent secretary.

'Are you sure?'

'I'm just doing what I'm told to do. We got special instructions this morning.'

'From the permanent secretary?'

'That's right.'

'But who instructed her?'

Caroline heard the man at the other end exhale, losing his patience with her.

'Maybe you should check with the police,' she said.

'I spoke to them this morning.'

'What?'

'You want to talk to the permanent secretary – fine, go ahead. She will tell you what I've told you. But in the meantime I need to make sure the room is cleaned.'

The cleaner reached out her hand and pointed to the phone. Caroline reluctantly handed it back. The incomprehensible chatter started back up, then the woman looked at Caroline and started to laugh. Caroline felt a wave of intense heat in her chest that started to work its way upwards. Suddenly she couldn't breathe. She backed out of the room, getting only as far as the door where she collided with someone coming in. She spun on her heels and was confronted with Ed's sweating face.

'When you weren't at your desk, I thought to myself, where's the one other place she's likely to be?' He spread his hands wide, damp patches blooming under his arms. 'And here you are. I think I should have been a detective.'

Caroline watched as he tried to suck in his stomach and pull his shoulders back. He failed on both counts.

'Got something to show you.' He produced a newspaper from his back pocket and waved it in her face.

'Latest edition – hot off the press.'

It was a copy of the *Evening News*. He proudly held it up, as if he was showing her something he'd personally handcrafted. The headline zoomed out of focus, as he pushed it closer to her face. The words were swimming in front of her eyes. Opposite the headline was a colour photograph of Martin Fox.

'Well?' Ed said. 'I told you I was right. Haven't you got anything to say for yourself? Maybe you could start with "Sorry, Ed".' When Caroline didn't respond, he shook his head in a mime of disappointment. 'I haven't been in this job, man and boy, without picking up a few things, you know.' He shoved the paper at her. 'I understand human nature. It's essential in my line of work. I know what makes people tick.' He tapped a fat finger against his temple.

Caroline took the newspaper from him and stared down at the headline, too confused to say anything, even to tell Ed to shut up. She looked back at the minister's office. The cleaner was humming to herself, ineffectually flicking a duster across the shelves of the bookcase. Caroline turned her gaze back to the newspaper. She was distantly aware that Ed was still jabbering away next to her. She stared at the headline, but the words made no sense.

MET RELEASE MINISTER'S SUICIDE NOTE

6

A Saturday morning children's television show flickered in the corner of the room with the sound down. Caroline sat on the sofa hugging a cushion with the curtains pulled shut and the lights off. She'd given up channel hopping after seeing the smiling face of Martin Fox burning out of the screen on a 24-hour news station. Right now a muted CBeebies was all she could cope with.

The hum of voices from the street filtered through the double-glazing of the living room window. The voices grew suddenly louder, in unison, the mumble building to a fresh wave of shouting. Then the garden gate crashed against its post and Caroline heard the dog let out a protective bark. A few seconds later the front door squealed open and slammed shut. The heavy tread of footsteps trundling up the stairs was closely followed by a scratching and snuffling on the other side of the living room door. Minty whimpered plaintively for a few moments then gave up. Caroline heard the dog's claws tapping against the wooden floorboards.

Sorry girl.

Caroline buried her face in the cushion and let out a little whine of her own. In less than 24 hours the press had discovered her work phone number and her home address, and had now set up camp on the other side of her front garden. She squeezed the cushion tighter until the noise from outside finally died back down to a low mumble.

If she ever found out who was responsible for leaking her details to the press... she pulled the cushion from her face. Even if she did discover their identity, what could she do? Report them to her boss? Jeremy Prior wouldn't take much interest in any name-calling. She was yet to discover why he wanted to see her. She shuddered – the thought of spending any time at all with the acting head of the division was bad enough, without worrying what he wanted to speak to her about.

The door leading to her mother's annexe at the rear of the house opened.

'My God, Caroline,' Jean said. 'It's like a bloody funeral parlour in here.' She marched over to the window and reached for the curtains.

'Don't, Mum, they'll all start gawping in again. They've taken enough pictures already.'

Her mother hesitated, still clinging on to the curtains.

'Just leave it, will you?'

Jean let out an impatient sigh and flipped on the overhead light. Caroline lifted the cushion to shield her eyes.

'You can't sit in the dark moping all day, Caroline.'

'Why not?'

'What good is it doing?'

'Please, Mum.' Caroline threw down the cushion. 'It's not yet 9:30. I think it's a bit early to assume I've turned into a recluse.' She saw Jean staring at her baggy dressing gown, and looked down to discover tea stains on her pyjama top.

'Have the children had their breakfast?'

'Don't fuss, Mum.'

Caroline would gladly have locked herself away in the bedroom, but when she left him, Pete was still dead to the world, snoring like a bear in a coma.

Jean sat down next to her and grabbed her hand. 'Are you looking after yourself?' she said.

'I'm all right. The kids are all right...' Caroline dragged her hand away and gripped the cushion again. 'Ben's at football practice, Dan's upstairs, no doubt exceeding our broadband limit, and Claire's just come back from walking the dog. I haven't given up parental responsibilities, I'm just not dressed yet. Is that suddenly a crime?'

'All right. Sorry I spoke. I'm just trying to help.'

Jean lifted a hand to Caroline's hair and started to drag strands across the parting, first one way then the other. 'You know, you should get a few highlights, disguise the grey.'

Caroline batted her hand away. 'Mum!'

'I'm only saying.'

'What? What are you *only* saying? And exactly how is it meant to help?'

'You can talk to me you know.'

Caroline squeezed the cushion in her fists, the foam inside forming hard ridges between her fingers.

'I know you always preferred to speak to your dad about things, but... well, all I'm saying is... I can listen too. Your father didn't have a monopoly on sympathy.'

Caroline bit her lip and felt a rawness in her throat. In that moment she missed her dad more than she could remember. She squeezed her eyes tight and tried to swallow.

'If you don't want to talk to me – what about speaking to your sister? I could give a call now.'

'It's the middle of the night in New Zealand.'

'It's 8:30 in the evening.'

'I don't want to worry Michelle with all this.'

'You've got to speak to someone. I know what you're like, bottling things up. It'll all come out one way or the other.'

'I… I just…' Caroline searched Jean's face. She knew her mother meant well, but there were some subjects she just couldn't broach. 'I'm fine,' she said eventually.

'You don't have to put on a brave face with me, love.' Jean squeezed her hand. 'Why don't I make us a nice cup of tea and you can tell me all about it.'

'Not right now.'

'I realise how difficult it must be when you think you know someone and they do something so unexpected, so… out of character—'

'Oh, Mum! You have no idea what it's like.'

'Tell me, then.'

'No!' Caroline unhooked her hand. 'I can't.' She leapt up from the sofa and made it as far as the door and turned back. 'I'm going to have a bath.'

Jean opened her mouth, but Caroline put up a hand to stop her. 'I just need to be on my own for a while. If Pete's not up in half an hour, give him a prod, will you?'

Her mother frowned at her.

'He's picking Ben up from football practice.'

Jean pulled a face. 'Will he be able to?'

'What are you talking about?'

'Won't Pete still be, you know—'

'What?' Caroline glanced towards the front door – the noise of the journalists was getting louder.

'Won't he be over the limit?'

Caroline was about to defend Pete but stopped herself. Her mother was probably right. He wouldn't be safe to drive. 'OK then – you pick Ben up.'

Jean raised her eyebrows.

'What have I said now?'

'A bit of gratitude wouldn't go amiss.'

Caroline dropped her shoulders and sighed. 'Thanks, Mum. I really appreciate it.' Each word was excruciating.

'When does Ben's football finish? Only I've got a campaign meeting at lunchtime. The whole gang's coming round.'

'Round here?'

'Make sure either you or Pete is in the land of the living by then.' She looked Caroline up and down. 'Or at least dressed.'

'They're coming here with that lot outside?'

'We could do with a bit of publicity.'

'God, Mum – you can't.'

Jean folded her arms across her chest.

'I work in the academies division. Martin was a pro-academies minister. Do you think talking to the press about your campaign to stop the academy being built down the road is likely to save me from redundancy? I'm hanging on to my job by the fingernails as it is.'

'It's not all about you, Caroline.'

Caroline rolled her eyes. 'I'm asking you nicely. Please have your meeting somewhere else. You can have as many meetings as you like when the press have lost interest in me.'

Jean harrumphed and pulled a mobile phone from her cardigan pocket. 'Last minute changes do not go down well.' She moved her thumbs deftly over the tiny keypad. 'They might find themselves another chairman.' She finished tapping out her message. 'The things I do for you.'

Caroline turned away and trudged up the stairs. On the landing she pulled open the airing cupboard door, reached behind a stack of folded towels and dug out the West End Final edition of the *Evening News* she'd hidden there the night before. She slipped into the bathroom and locked the door behind her.

For once the bath didn't look like a team of muddy rugby players had been using it for a fortnight. She put the plug in and turned on the hot tap. The water spluttered out in a trickle, Caroline watched it for a moment and collapsed onto the toilet seat. She looked down at the newspaper on her lap. Her eyes were stinging now. She blinked and a few drips of salty water sprang onto her cheeks. Just as quickly as the prickle in her bottom lids came, so it dissipated again. She looked down at the main headline. Martin Fox's death had finally made it onto the front page. The *Evening News* had reproduced the typewritten suicide note in full colour. She skimmed over it again – she'd read it so many times now she knew the lines by heart.

> To whom it may concern
> I cannot find the words to describe the shame I feel. Not for committing this final act, but for the one that drove me to it.

Caroline rubbed the heel of a hand into her eye. The inside of her nose was fizzing. She re-read the next few lines.

> *To my friends and family, I apologise. For any hurt or embarrassment these revelations may cause you. I'm sorry I have not been man enough to face my tormentors.*

She took a deep breath before moving on to the next paragraph.

> *I have therefore decided to take the coward's way out. The easy road. And I leave you to make your own way along life's rocky path.*

Hard as she tried, Caroline couldn't imagine Martin Fox writing those words. The longer she stared at them the more alien they seemed. It just didn't sound like him. But it was the next section that really convinced her the note couldn't have been written by the man she'd got to know over the last few years.

> *To my tormentors – worse than bullies in the school playground – I deny you your weapons of blackmail and extortion. I admit it here in black and white, for all the world to read.*
>
> *Yes, I am a homosexual.*

Caroline read the line again. She'd lost count of the number of times she'd stared down at those words. Martin Fox wasn't gay. She would have known. She read the last few lines.

> *Yes, I have hidden the fact from my family, friends and colleagues.*
>
> *Yes, I have been living my life as a lie.*
>
> *There, I have 'outed' myself. So whoever you are, do not trouble yourself with this matter a moment longer. I have taken away your power. You cannot hurt me now.*
>
> *I only wish there was some sense of triumph to be gained by thwarting your grubby little plan. In my final moments, all I feel is shame.*
>
> *M.T.F. 31 March*

The only other story on the front page was an editorial piece speculating on William King's new cabinet appointments. The piece on Martin Fox's death continued inside, but up until now Caroline hadn't managed to read beyond the contents of the note. She swallowed hard, peeled away the rapidly moistening top sheet and forced herself to look at the article on page three. The first line rocked her so hard she felt as if she'd been punched in the stomach.

There was a thump on the bathroom door, then another.

'Are you all right?' Jean said.

When Caroline didn't answer straightaway her mother banged on the door again.

'Caroline?'

Caroline leaned on the side of the bath and tried to breathe. 'What is it?'

'Are you crying again?'

'Please! Can't you just leave me alone?'

'You haven't told me what time I should pick up Ben.'

'Half eleven.'

Jean muttered something as she walked away. Caroline waited to hear her mother's footsteps on the stairs before she turned back to the newspaper.

Schools minister Martin Fox's suicide note was found unceremoniously stuck to the screen of his computer monitor with a lump of Blutak.

She blinked and read the sentence again. She stared at the words until they blurred into a thick smudge of ink on the page. She closed her eyes and forced herself to picture Martin Fox's office, the way it was when she found him. There was no note attached to the monitor. There was no note anywhere. What was it the police constable had said to her? She could see his sympathetic face, his big sad eyes staring into hers. Hadn't he asked her if she'd seen a note, or a letter? She tried to remember his exact words. He'd asked her if she'd moved a note or taken one away. Surely that could only mean the police hadn't found one. How could a room of forensics experts miss something like that?

Ever since Ed Wallis had waved his newspaper in her face, Caroline had assumed the note had been found in Martin Fox's desk drawer, or maybe even sitting in a printer tray somewhere on the seventh floor. The journalist must have made a mistake about its location. Someone should let them know. The *Evening News* would have to print a correction.

She threw back the bolt on the bathroom door and hurried into the bedroom. Pete shifted his position; a ripple ran across the muscles in his back. His head was turned to one side and his sleeping face looked peaceful and untroubled. He reached out a hand towards her side of the bed and groaned. She watched him for a moment longer, expecting him to wake. But his eyes stayed firmly closed and he let out a snuffling grunt. Caroline turned quickly to her bedside table and grabbed the phone. She scanned the first couple of pages of the newspaper and found the number for the newsdesk halfway down page two.

While she waited for someone to pick up, she read the next paragraph of the article.

> Detective Inspector John Leary would not confirm that the existence of a suicide note meant that the Metropolitan Police were not looking for anyone else in connection with the minister's death, and would only concede its discovery was 'significant'.

> DI Leary has however confirmed that the note was found attached to the MP's desktop monitor by an unnamed civil servant and that the person in question has been interviewed and eliminated from police enquiries.

Caroline was only vaguely aware of a voice in her ear.

'Hello? Good morning... *Evening News*, how can I help you?'

Caroline could think of nothing to say. The journalist hadn't made a mistake. After a few moments the tiny disembodied voice stopped speaking. Caroline hung up. Why would Leary make something like that up? She grabbed her handbag from the dressing table and shook out its contents. Buried at the bottom of the pile was the business card the police constable had given her. She snatched up the phone again and punched in the number for the Belgravia police station. PC Mills would probably have seen the article. He must have known since yesterday how inaccurate it was. And he must know by now that the man in charge of the investigation had lied to the press. Finally the ringing stopped and someone at the other end asked if they could help her.

'PC Mills please.'

'Just a moment. I'll put you through.' Hold music started to play. Caroline pulled the phone from her ear and hit the speakerphone button. As the Lighthouse Family track distorted through the tiny speaker, Pete heaved himself on to his side and moaned something incoherent. Caroline started to pace the room, the floorboards creaking noisily under her feet. As the music continued to play she thought of the young PC's sad smile, his open, honest face. He'd told her she could speak to him about what had happened. He'd seemed like one of the good guys – could she trust him? The music stopped and Caroline lifted the phone back to her ear, unsure what she would say to him.

'Hello?' It was the woman who'd answered the phone. 'I'm afraid PC Mills isn't on duty today. What is it concerning?'

'Martin Fox – the minister who—' Caroline stopped, unsure how much she should say.

'Can anyone else help? I can put you through to Inspector Leary, if you like.'

Caroline stabbed the call end button and stared down at the phone.

7

A Sunday morning jogger dodged around Caroline and muttered something as he went by. Minty growled a warning bark at him.

'It's all right, girl. He's just a silly man.' Caroline watched the jogger disappear into the next turning. 'In very silly shorts.' She turned through 90 degrees then looked down at a battered copy of the *A-Z*. She turned another 90, dragging the dog with her and tangling Minty's lead around her legs. She checked the nearest street sign.

'Looks like we've already walked past it.'

The dog let out a grumbling whine while Caroline untangled the lead. They hurried to the next junction and stopped on the corner of Martin Fox's street. Caroline looked up the road and saw three men standing on the pavement outside a house halfway up. Two of them wore flapping raincoats; the third sported a leather jacket, with a long-lensed camera strapped across his chest.

'More reporters.' Caroline sighed and the dog did too.

An hour earlier she'd forced her way through the few remaining journalists outside her own front garden. She ignored their questions and with her head down, a scarf wrapped tight over her unwashed hair, she ran Minty down the road. A couple of energetic souls followed her for a couple of streets, shouting incomprehensible questions at her, but even they lost enthusiasm for the chase when it became clear she wasn't going to respond.

Before she'd left the house, she'd told Jean she was taking the dog for a good long run in Mountfield Park, but instead of crossing the main road she hurried a disappointed Minty west along Brownlow Road to the train station. A train and two tube journeys later she found herself in a quiet residential street on the fringes of West Kensington. She looked down at Minty, whose tongue was lolling out of her mouth.

'Poor love, you must be parched.'

She slipped the *A-Z* back into her handbag and retrieved a half litre bottle of Evian. Caroline unstoppered the bottle and poured a little water into her cupped hand. Minty's tongue seemed to blot it up in less than a second. She poured out the remainder and the dog let out a little yelp. Caroline waved the empty bottle at her. 'All gone,' she said.

The movement was enough to snag a reporter's attention. He turned away from his colleagues and stared right at her. Caroline sank to her knees and pulled her scarf over her head. She managed to manoeuvre the dog to block the journalist's view. After a few moments crouching on the corner of an unfamiliar street in west London, hiding behind Minty, Caroline began to feel self-conscious and mildly ridiculous.

When she'd thrown on her coat and grabbed the dog's lead, making a pilgrimage to visit Martin's house had somehow seemed the right thing to do. She wasn't sure what she'd expected to achieve, but at least she'd felt she was doing something, not just sitting at home in a darkened living room driving herself mad. She stroked the dog's ears.

'What was I thinking, Minty, eh?' She glanced up at the reporter who seemed to have lost interest in her and was chatting to his photographer friend. 'What on earth was I thinking?'

She stood slowly and wriggled her toes, waiting for the feeling to come back in her feet. Her phone started to ring. She quickly silenced the squawking ringtone and turned away from the three men standing outside Martin Fox's house.

'Caroline, where are you?' Jean said.

'In the park.'

'Why are you whispering?' Jean sighed noisily into the phone. 'Do you want me to make a start on lunch?'

Caroline glanced at her watch. It was 11:05am. Jean was point making again. One year Caroline fully expected to receive a t-shirt from Jean for Christmas with the words *Unfit Mother* emblazoned across the chest. She took a deep breath before answering.

'I won't be much longer. I'll sort out lunch when I get back. Just leave it – OK?'

'Please yourself.' She hung up.

'Grandma Henderson is in a strop, Minty.' The dog looked up at her. 'What do you say? Shall we stay out all day?'

Minty pressed a wet nose into Caroline's hand and wagged her tail. Caroline turned back to the house as a beige saloon pulled up outside. The two raincoats and leather jacket climbed inside and the car accelerated away with a squeal of tyres.

'Come on, girl. This may be our chance.'

Caroline ventured further up the street, wondering as she went whether Martin might have hidden a set of keys under a doormat by the front step, or beneath a flowerpot in the shrubbery. She stared straight ahead all the way up the road, trying too hard to assume the pose of a casual dog walker. When they drew level, she finally glanced towards the house.

Her heart sank.

A uniformed police officer was standing sentry at the front door, arms folded behind his back, feet wide apart.

'Don't think much of our chances now, Mint.'

As Caroline continued to look at him, the policeman unfolded his arms and took a step down the path. Immediately Caroline dipped into a pocket of her jacket and pulled out a blue plastic bag. She shoved her hand inside and reached down to the pavement. Minty let out a confused grunt that would have done Scooby Doo proud.

'Sorry girl – just got to look busy.'

Caroline stood up and nodded towards the police officer before hurrying down the street. She reached the end of the road and shoved the plastic bag back in her pocket, the policeman's view of her obscured by a tall hedge in the neighbouring garden.

'I think we might be going home.'

Caroline turned to take one last look at the house just as a black cab pulled up outside. A long-legged woman emerged, dressed from head to toe in black. Untidy blonde locks escaped from the baseball cap pulled low over her forehead. The woman made her way to Martin Fox's front gate and into the garden. Caroline half jogged, half walked back up the street and reached the house just as the policeman was turning back from the front door, the mystery blonde woman having already disappeared inside.

'Who do you think that is, girl?'

Martin Fox never spoke about his family, even when he asked Caroline about hers. She knew he lived alone. So this woman was what – a relative? A friend? Caroline gazed at the house for a few moments before she realised the policeman was staring right back at her. She threw him a quick smile, carried on up the road and pulled Minty into a phone box on the corner. The dog whined and wrapped herself around Caroline's legs, trying to find enough floorspace to sit down. She landed heavily on Caroline's feet. After a few moments the glass walls of the kiosk started to steam up.

'We can't stay here.' Caroline bit her lip and peered through the glass towards the house. 'What do you think? Shall we go and see if we can speak to her?' The dog barked. 'It's worth a try, isn't it?'

Caroline pushed open the door and stopped abruptly. A dark green sedan was pulling up outside the house. The driver climbed out and ran round to a passenger door at the rear and opened it. Something about the cut of his suit made Caroline think he was a policeman. She let the kiosk door close and wiped clear a porthole in the condensation fogging up the glass. The driver ran to the other passenger door and yanked it open. A man stepped onto the pavement, tugging at the bottom of his jacket. Even through steamed glass at a distance of 50 yards, she recognised him as soon as he turned around. It was William King's chief of staff. Caroline supposed he was visiting to offer his sympathies on behalf of the prime minister. Another figure finally emerged from the roadside passenger door. He followed the Downing Street spin doctor along the path to Martin Fox's front door, finally turning as his companion said something to the policeman on duty.

Caroline backed away from the glass, stepping on Minty's tail in the process. She pulled her scarf over her head, hoping desperately Jeremy Prior hadn't seen her.

8

On Monday morning Caroline took the precaution of entering the department via the underground car park to avoid the remaining reporters still camped out at the front of the building. She took the service lift up to the fourth floor, and reached her desk to find a Post-It stuck on her monitor. The message was written in the neat script of Jeremy Prior's PA, Lisa. Caroline glanced at Lisa sitting behind her desk at the other end of the office. The poor girl had probably been there since 7am, waiting on Prior's every whim. The note on the bright pink square of paper informed her the head of the academies division would see her at *8am sharp*. She looked at her watch. It was two minutes to.

She wriggled out of her jacket and tried to ignore the tightening knot in her stomach. All of Sunday afternoon and evening she'd been unable to stop thinking about Prior and his visit to Martin's house. She could understand why William King's chief of staff would be there, representing both the prime minister and the party. If she was feeling generous she could even explain Prior's presence – during his six months at the department as acting head of the academies division he'd worked quite closely with Martin to help extend the programme – it was understandable he might want to express his condolences. But the fact that he'd arrived with King's right hand man didn't make any sense at all.

She looked up at Prior's office and saw him pacing up and down, a mobile phone jammed against his ear. The knot under her ribs twisted tighter as she hurried towards the wide glass-fronted room. She nodded to Lisa when she reached her desk and checked her watch, waiting until the second hand counted down to twelve. Prior was off the phone and sitting behind his desk. Caroline knocked and pushed open the door.

'One moment,' he said, without looking up. He moved a sheet of paper from one side of the immense walnut desk to the other, placing it precisely so the sides lined up with the edge of the wood. After a few moments he tipped his head in her direction. He didn't smile. 'Come, come. Shut the door behind you.' He gestured for her to sit down.

She lowered herself slowly onto an uncomfortable straight-backed chair and waited for him to speak again. He leaned his elbows on the desk and templed his fingers, resting his chin on the apex. He scrutinised her through narrowed eyes and said nothing. It was so quiet Caroline could hear her watch ticking.

'I know I don't need to impress upon you how serious a situation we find ourselves in,' he finally said.

Caroline tilted her head down a few degrees, not wanting to commit to a full nod until she had some idea what he was talking about.

'Very serious indeed.'

She tried to read his expression, wondering whether he was expecting her to jump in and pick up the conversation where he'd left it. But she hadn't survived in a government department for this long without learning some basic self-preservation skills. Generally, the higher up the food chain someone was, the more difficult they were to deal with. And Prior was more slippery than most. She wasn't alone in mistrusting him. He had been parachuted in on a temporary contract, without going through the normal recruitment procedures. His appointment was resented by most of the division. Though Prior's predecessor had been unable to make decisions and was quick to cast around for a low-ranking scapegoat when anything went wrong, Prior had gone too far the other way, making policy changes without proper consultation. So far he hadn't made any huge mistakes to blame on someone else. But it was only a matter of time. She was pretty sure he'd be as adept at dodging bullets as a regular Grade 6 career civil servant.

Uncomfortable as this prickling silence was, she continued to return his gaze without uttering a word. She'd seen colleagues reduced to tears by Jeremy Prior. She settled into her seat, prepared for a battle of wills, determined she wasn't going to be his next victim.

'Have you spoken to Pamela about it at all?' he said.

If? Caroline shook her head.

'Ah. I see.' He tugged at his cuffs, pulling the sleeves of his handmade shirt over his bony wrists. He straightened his tie. 'Information, Caroline. It's a precious commodity.'

Was he talking about Martin Fox? Caroline uncrossed her legs and leaned forward a fraction.

'That's why we have to take such good care of it,' he continued.

She folded her hands into her lap.

'And I'm afraid the division has fallen short. Very short.' He continued to stare at her. And she stared right back. 'Derelict in its duties,' he said. 'Missed the mark.'

Caroline resisted the overwhelming urge to remind him how well the academies division was working before he joined it, even without anyone at the helm.

'A CD-ROM has been misplaced.' He didn't shift his gaze. She got the distinct impression he was trying to gauge her reaction. 'A CD-ROM containing the personal details of 150,000 pupils attending schools in special measures.'

All weekend she had assumed he was going to speak to her about the events surrounding Martin Fox's death. A lost CD-ROM seemed like a massive anti-climax.

'And that's a problem for the division?' she said.

'I'm not sure you have grasped the severity of the situation. *Personal* details, Caroline.'

'How personal?'

'Name, age, address. Special educational needs status. Whether or not they receive free school meals. Attendance records, educational achievements.'

'Oh.'

'Precisely.' He leaned forward, placing his hands flat on the desk. 'This is highly sensitive information. The department cannot be seen to have a cavalier attitude towards this sort of thing.'

'Of course not.'

'Especially after the events of recent years. We can't have this disc turning up on the 5.55 to Dorking. Or a pub car park somewhere.'

'So the disc is... misplaced? In the sense of—'

'It simply must be located, and discreetly. The fact that it's missing cannot be made public.'

'Who had it last?'

He shook his head. 'It's not a set of keys or a ten pound note lost between the cushions of a sofa.' He sighed. 'The disc was locked in one of the secure cabinets.'

'But the information itself isn't lost, we still have it all on the network somewhere?'

'Of course we have the information. That's not the issue.' He clamped his mouth shut, the muscles in his cheeks bulged as he ground his teeth. 'We can't have some unauthorised individual getting their hands on it. Especially not the media.'

'Why was all of that "sensitive" information put on a CD-ROM in the first place?'

'It was requested.' He looked away for the first time. Caroline wondered if he was lying.

'Requested?'

Prior blew an impatient little snort down his nose.

'Who requested it?'

'The late minister for schools requested it.' He practically spat the words at her.

Caroline tried to keep her face blank. If Martin Fox had needed that kind of information he should have come to her. Maybe Prior was lying. She waited for him to look at her before she spoke again. 'If the disc was specifically created for the schools minister, surely it must still be in the department somewhere?'

'That's what we have to find out.'

'Have you checked with the police? They've taken all of Martin's things from his office. It's probably sealed up in an evidence bag at the police station.'

'Not according to the investigating officer.'

Caroline remembered the inspector in the untidy raincoat arriving on the seventh floor with Prior and recalled how chummy they seemed to be. The very same inspector who must have lied about the suicide note to the press.

'So you think it's still somewhere in the building?'

'As I said, that is what you need to find out. I want you and Pamela to initiate a thorough search. Formally interview everyone in the division.'

Caroline opened her mouth, about to object, about to remind him how busy she was already, but instead she just nodded. Now wasn't the time to pick a fight with Jeremy Prior about workloads, especially with a fresh wave of redundancies on the horizon.

'You simply must find that disc.' He dismissed her with an almost imperceptible flick of a hand.

Caroline stood up and turned towards the door.

'While we're on the subject of the schools minister,' Prior said.

Here it comes.

Caroline slowly turned back to face him. Prior was studying his fingernails.

'I didn't get a chance to speak to you the other evening.'

She said nothing.

'Such a terrible shock. So awful for you to... come upon him like that.'

Caroline leaned a hand on the back of the chair.

'Had Martin asked you to go up?'

Caroline tightened her grip on the chair back. 'I'm sorry?'

'Did he call you? Ask you to go up and see him?'

Was he testing her? Did he already know the answer? She decided it was too risky to lie.

'The minister did leave me a message earlier in the evening.' She swallowed. 'I can't actually remember what it was about, now. Events kind of overtook me.'

'Of course they did, of course.' Prior stopped scrutinising his nails and looked up. 'But is that how you found yourself on the seventh floor, because of his message?'

She thought about her desperate dash to the lifts, escaping from Ed and his sweaty hands. She looked Prior squarely in the eyes. Why was he even asking?

Think of something.

'It's a bit embarrassing, actually.' She stared down at her hands, bent white at the knuckles, clutching the back of the chair. She lifted her head slowly and stared back at Prior, locking his gaze in hers. 'I needed change for the machine.' She paused for effect. 'In the ladies'.'

He didn't react.

'I'd started my period, you see. A couple of days earlier than I was expecting.'

She continued to stare at him. Earlier and a lot heavier.' Still he maintained eye contact. 'Early menopause, the doctor thinks. It's called flooding.'

Finally he looked away and cleared his throat. But Caroline didn't feel like stopping.

'It's something you can't just ignore – I'm sure I don't have to spell it out… draw you a diagram.' She took a breath. 'And you know, Sod's Law – I didn't have the right coins for the machine. I had to do something.' She let go of the chair. 'I guessed that Martin would still be in the building, so I went up to his office to see if he could change a five pound note.'

Prior's face seemed to have lost some of its colour. He pulled his mouth into something approaching a smile that looked to Caroline more like a grimace.

'Well, thank you for your time. I'm sure I don't need to take up any more of it,' he said. 'Let me know when you make progress.'

Caroline frowned at him.

'In locating the CD-ROM.'

She nodded and was grateful to finally turn away. She marched towards the door, but something made her stop and turn back when she got there.

'Of course there is another possibility,' she said.

Prior leaned forward again.

'The minister may have taken the CD-ROM home with him.' She thought she detected the merest sign of a flinch, Prior's shoulders seemed to tense. 'Has anyone been to his house?'

Prior continued to stare at her, the muscles in his jaw flexing.

'Perhaps someone should make a visit,' she said. 'You never know – the disc could be in his study – just sitting in a drawer or something. Would you like me to go? It's a bit out of my way, but if you think it might help—'

'That won't be necessary.'

'Oh – you've checked it out already, then?'

He cleared his throat and reached for his desk phone. 'You concentrate on questioning the team here in the department. Let me worry about everything else.' He held the receiver mid air. 'If you'll excuse me?'

Caroline opened the door, keeping her eyes on Prior as she backed out of the room. He was already murmuring into the phone as if she wasn't there.

She walked back to her desk, her legs getting shakier with every step. She sat down and looked back across the office to Prior's room in time to see Lisa ushering Ed Wallis inside. He sat down on the chair Caroline had just vacated, his stomach resting heavily on the top of his thighs. Why did Prior want to speak to a lowly security guard? Ed said something and laughed. He leaned back in the chair and folded his arms. What was he telling Prior? It had to be something to do with what happened on Thursday night. Immediately the events of that night came flooding back. She remembered again the conversation she'd had with PC Mills about the suicide note. Ed glanced in her direction and nodded. She quickly turned away and grabbed her handbag from the desk.

After a few moments fumbling inside the bag she located PC Mills's business card and laid it on the desk. She stared at it, breathing slowly, trying to slow her racing heart, wondering again if she could trust the policeman with the kind face.

She had to trust someone.

Her call was answered swiftly and an efficient voice asked how she could help.

'PC Ralph Mills, please. It's urgent.'

Caroline heard the plastic tap of fingers on a keyboard.

'M, I double L, S?' the woman on the other end asked her.

'That's right.'

More tapping.

'I'm sorry. I've checked it three times now. Are you sure you have the right number?'

'I'm looking at the card he gave me right now. What's the problem?'

'There's no record of a Ralph Mills on the system.'

9

Angela Tate leapt out of the taxi and left her photographer to pay the fare. She pulled up her collar and picked her way along a stretch of uneven pavement towards a mass of bodies being hemmed in by a sparse cordon of police officers wearing bright yellow vests over their uniforms. Two or three 'Save our Schools' placards swayed in the strong wind and a faint chant calling for the sponsor of the academy's early demise wafted from the back of the throng.

The group had gathered at the entrance to a muddy building site – the proposed location for the *Frederick Larson Business Academy for Entrepreneurial Excellence*. A dirt spattered truck filled with hardcore was parked on the road outside, its hazards flashing, the driver chatting amiably with a policeman dressed in a waterproof cape that billowed in the breeze. Both men were sipping tea from steaming polystyrene cups.

Angela sighed. The policeman was too relaxed, the protestors too polite. She dragged a strand of hair from her face and tried in vain to secure it behind an ear, but the wind whipped it from its dock and plastered it across her mouth. Her heart sank as she watched the policeman throw his head back at some joke the driver had just told him. She'd seen these kinds of well meaning protests before – meek and unthreatening, and ultimately doomed to fail.

She negotiated her way around a random lump of reinforced concrete dumped on the pavement and scanned the crowd. She recognised a few faces from earlier demonstrations. The group comprised a couple of governors, a few parents with nothing better to do on a dismal Monday lunchtime and a handful of teachers who must have nipped out of school during the midday break. By far the largest contingent was a noisy rabble of OAPs clustered in a separate huddle. One woman was standing slightly apart from the rest. It took Angela a few moments to realise the woman had chained herself to the metal railings next to the main gate. Her spirits lifted instantly. She could see the headlines already. She glanced over her shoulder to see Frank Carter at least forty yards behind her, slowly pulling his camera from its bag and looping the strap over his neck. She gestured to him to hurry up and pointed towards the woman in chains, who just at that moment started hollering. Something about freedom of speech. Angela spotted the reason for her sudden outburst. A thickset man wearing a fluorescent vest was striding towards her wielding an enormous pair of bolt cutters.

Angela picked up speed, but very quickly ran out of pavement. She reared up at the edge of a wide strip of muddy earth separating her from the protestors. She took a tentative step onto the churned-up ground and immediately felt cold mud seeping into her shoe. Another step and both heels sank completely into the yielding clay. She kept her gaze fixed on the chained woman, who had started waving a walking stick, brandishing it like a sword, swiping and jabbing the heavy handle towards the approaching yellow-vested man.

'Don't come any closer,' the woman shouted. 'You fascist pig!' She lunged towards him. The walking stick narrowly missed the side of his head. He staggered back, losing his balance. The stick jabbed towards him again. He ducked and dodged, jerking his head sideways and back like a boxer. 'Where's your boss? I want to speak to Fred Larson. Get him down here.'

From this distance Angela could see the woman was younger than the rest of the group, early sixties at most. She seemed to have more energy than all the other protestors added together.

'Oi! Stop that!' The policeman who had been chatting to the truck driver threw his cup to the ground and sprinted towards the duelling pair, his waterproof ballooning behind him in the wind.

Angela tried desperately to lift her foot, wrenching a shoe from the ground. The heel stayed embedded in the earth, snapping clean off the sole. She pulled up the other shoe, it thwocked out of the ground intact. She limped as fast as she could towards the woman with the stick, glancing over a shoulder to check on her photographer's progress. He was lumbering up the pavement, his chest heaving, his legs moving in slow motion.

'For God's sake, hurry up, Frank! You're going to miss the money shot.'

The policeman in the waterproof slowed right down and stopped beyond walking stick swiping distance, holding his palms aloft.

'Come on now, love. Let's be sensible about this, shall we?'

The huddle of senior citizens gathered around the old woman and the policeman like a hungry gang of twelve-year-olds in a school playground, baying for blood.

'Stay away from me – Nazi!'

She pulled back the walking stick and thrust it forward and up in a wide arc. The handle accelerated past the policeman's nose, and knocked off his hat.

'Right that's it,' he said.

He charged towards her and made a grab for the circling three-foot baton. He snatched nothing but air. The effort rocked him sideways.

Finally Frank Carter caught up with Angela.

'You want to ease up on the pie-eating, Frank.'

The pensioner, a glint in her eye, swung the stick again, like a golfer at the tee and hit the policeman's hat ten feet in the air. It landed with a splash in a muddy puddle.

'You getting all this, Frank?' Angela said.

Two yellow-vested policemen broke away from the ragged cordon surrounding the other protestors.

'There's more where that came from.' The woman was screaming now. 'Don't think you can bully me – just because I'm old and frail.'

The police officer stepped in again. This time he reached for her arm, but she was too quick for him. The stick came crashing down in a diagonal swoop and only just missed his right cheek. He stumbled awkwardly and dropped to his knees.

For a moment the stick wavered in mid air, the woman stood motionless, her mouth gaping. A pair of liver-spotted hands grabbed the stick and passed it to a blue-haired woman nearby and in an instant it was absorbed into the crowd, melting away behind a wall of pink, wrinkled, entirely innocent faces.

The two policemen finally arrived and helped their colleague to his feet, one of them handed him his hat. He shrugged away their hands.

'Arrest her. And anyone else who so much as opens their mouths.' He turned away, brushing mud from his trousers. 'And get those bloody chains off.'

The man with the bolt cutters hesitated, keeping a healthy three feet between him and the woman. After a few moments two female constables appeared. The woman smiled at them and seemed quite happy to let them hold down her arms as the cutters chopped through the chains like scissors through bacon.

Angela hobbled over to join the little procession of two police-women and old age pensioner as they made their way to a waiting squad car.

'Would you like to make a statement?' Angela said as she approached.

'Who are you?' The woman looked her up and down. 'And what happened to your shoe?'

'Angela Tate, *Evening News*.' Angela waved her business card in the woman's face.

'Never read it.'

'Well, even so, we do have a very big circulation.' She forced a smile at the woman. 'Think how much all that publicity would help your cause.' She managed to reach around one of the policewomen and slipped her card into a pocket of the OAP's cardigan.

After a few moments they reached the police car and the woman looked into Angela's face. 'Jean Henderson,' she said. 'Retired. Widow. Mother of three, grandmother of five. Sixth on the way.' Her mouth softened into a smile. 'That the sort of thing you're after?'

Angela smiled back at her and nodded. She turned to one of the policewomen. 'Which station are you taking her to?'

'Catford.'

'I'll see you down at the station, Mrs Henderson.'

'Call me Jean.'

A policewoman pressed a hand on the top of Jean Henderson's head, flattening her soft curls, and pushed her under the door arch of the police car. She climbed in after her and pulled the door firmly shut.

In her broken shoes, Angela limped back to the entrance of the building site, just as the big truck of hardcore was reversing in. The remaining protestors had drifted away. Frank was scrolling through the images on his camera.

'Any good?' Angela asked.

'Dynamite. Assuming no more shock Cabinet reshuffles happen overnight, we might even get the front page.'

Angela slapped him on the back. 'Now we just need to find ourselves a cab.'

The last of the OAPs eased themselves into a waiting minibus. The driver was leaning on the bonnet finishing a cigarette. 'Maybe we can cadge a lift with that lot back to the High Street – we know they've got at least one spare seat.'

She glanced around the site and spotted a group of thickset men gathered around the entrance to a Portakabin. They were wearing suits beneath their high-visibility jackets and highly polished Oxfords on their huge feet. They had wires trailing out of their ears.

'Frank.' She grabbed his sleeve and pulled him towards her. 'Poke your long lens through the fence and get a few shots of the site, will you? Include that little bunch by the hut. Fred Larson seems to be taking security of his building sites very seriously these days. This lot look more like secret service agents than bouncers.'

She continued to stare at the incongruous huddle as Frank fired off a dozen or so shots. One of the men turned round and spotted them. He shouted something and started running towards them. Frank lowered the camera to his chest and held up his hands in surrender. Still the hulk charged at them, two of his colleagues joining the chase. Angela grabbed Frank's arm and dragged him away.

10

The catering trolley, laden with trays of curling sandwiches and plates of sliced fruit covered in cling film, rattled out onto the lobby of the fifth floor, leaving Caroline alone in the lift. She jabbed the '7' button and leaned back against the wall as the doors creaked shut. It was the first time she'd been on her own all day. She took a deep breath and caught a lingering whiff of egg mayonnaise.

At lunchtime Pam had insisted on walking her to Prêt and escorting her back again, telling her at least half a dozen times how tired and pale she looked, reminding her at every opportunity just how traumatised she must be feeling. Caroline knew Pam was still hoping for an unexpurgated account of last Thursday night and she was determined to reveal precisely nothing, switching the conversation back to their investigation into the missing CD-ROM.

Caroline glanced at herself in the mirrored walls of the lift, suddenly feeling as if she was standing in a department store changing room, exposed and vulnerable, waiting for Trinny and Susannah to pounce. Pam was right about one thing – apart from the dark purple circles under her eyes, the colour had completely drained from her face. Maybe she should have taken some time off. Certainly she felt as if she was running on empty, relying on strong coffee and sugary snacks to get her through the day.

She lowered her gaze and checked her watch, eager to focus on something other than her 360-degree reflection. It wasn't yet 4:30pm. She should still be able to catch Martin Fox's PA before she knocked off for the evening. After the unexplained disappearance of PC Mills, Caroline needed to speak to someone about the minister, and Consuela was the only suitable candidate. Throughout the day she'd left the PA countless phone messages and sent enough emails to be accused of spamming. All of them had been ignored.

After what seemed an impossibly slow ascent to the seventh floor, the doors finally slid open. Caroline rushed towards the widening gap only to discover a five-foot high metal cage blocking her exit. The cage was attached to a wooden palette and was full of office chairs. She grabbed the metal mesh with both hands and pushed, but the palette wouldn't budge. The lift doors started to close, then jerked to a halt, the sensors detecting Caroline's presence on the threshold. She turned her shoulder towards the palette and heaved with all her weight. Still it wouldn't move. She stepped back, holding a hand against the door as it tried to slide shut.

'Hello!' she called. She waited for a response. None came. The seventh floor was normally alive with activity at this time on a Monday afternoon. She listened carefully. The only sound above the rattling of the lift doors as they tried to shuffle shut was the permanent hum of the air conditioning.

Then she heard the ping of another lift arriving on the other side of the lobby.

'Hello!' She shouted louder this time. 'Can you help? I seem to be trapped.'

She was answered by the sound of huffing and puffing followed by the squeal of unoiled wheels.

'Hello!' she hollered again.

'All right – keep your hair on.'

That was all she needed. *Why did it have to be Ed Wallis?*

'I can't get out of the lift.'

'Is that you, Caroline?'

Caroline sighed. 'Yes. Are you going to help me or what?'

Ed grunted. 'I'm not sure I should with that attitude.'

Dear God save me from this man.

'Please Ed, I really would appreciate it.' She had to force out every single word.

'Put it like that…'

Through the stack of chairs and grid of metalwork, Caroline watched the security guard wander slowly to the other side of the palette and kick at something on the bottom. He tugged on the metal cage and the palette rolled gently away from the lift.

'There we are… no harm done,' Ed said.

Caroline glanced up to see an empty palette standing directly in front of the other lift.

'Did you park this one here?' Caroline straightened her jacket and fastened the top two buttons.

Ed shrugged.

'Bloody stupid place to leave it.'

'You shouldn't even be up here. It's strictly out of bounds.' He patted a hand against the name tag pinned to his chest. 'Authorised personnel only.'

'Authorised? What's going on?'

'Refurb.' Ed flashed a mouthful of stained teeth at her.

'This floor's only just been refurbished.'

'Well, they're doing it again.'

He started walking to the glass wall at the end of the lobby and gestured for her to follow him. He stopped opposite the double doors leading to the ministers' offices. The doorway was sealed with long sheets of black plastic taped along the doorframe.

'No one's said anything official,' he said, 'but we've got a sweepstake going downstairs.'

'What are you talking about?'

He leaned in close and blasted fried onion breath into her face. She backed away.

'Infestation. That's what's behind all this,' he said. 'My money's on rats. But I picked cockroaches out of the hat.' He lifted a hand to his head and started scratching. 'I won't see that fiver again. Mind you, we may never find out for sure – they're stripping everything out tomorrow.'

'They're what?'

'Stripping my arse – fumigating more like.'

'Those chairs in the palette, they were new this year. Where are you taking them?'

'To the pulping van parked round the corner. Have you seen it?'

Caroline shook her head, too bewildered to speak.

'It's in Abbey Orchard Street. You should take a look – watch it in action. Eats through everything like it's made of cotton wool. Amazing bit of kit.'

'But there's nothing wrong with the chairs.'

'I'm just following orders.' He placed a hand in the small of his back. 'Though I shouldn't really be doing this at all. Not with my sciatica.' He kneaded his fist into a fleshy buttock. 'What are you doing up here, anyway?'

Caroline hesitated. She didn't want to tell Ed about Consuela. She didn't want to tell Ed anything, especially not after his little chat with Prior.

'I left a file here the other day.' She ducked around Ed and marched towards the doors and inspected the plastic sheeting. She started to pick at the tape holding the sheets in place.

'You can't do that!' Ed squeezed his bulk between Caroline and the door, arms outstretched.

'Oh come on, Ed.' She feigned a smile. 'I won't tell if you won't.'

Ed narrowed his eyes. 'What's it worth to you?'

58

Caroline stopped what she was doing and frowned at him.

'If I *was* to let you in... how would you... you know... show your gratitude?'

'Oh piss off, Ed.' She turned back to the doors and tried to scratch the edge of the tape with a fingernail. 'Do you have a penknife?' she said. 'Or some keys? I don't want to a rip a great hole in the middle of it.'

'You can't go in there, end of. Health and safety. It's just not safe – all the floorboards are up.'

'There aren't any floorboards.'

'If you don't stop I'll have to call for back up.' He pulled a walkie-talkie from his pocket.

'Oh for God's sake.' Caroline stormed past him and hurried back to the lifts. She punched the *down* button and wondered at the effort someone was making to eradicate every last trace of Martin Fox from the seventh floor. She stabbed the button again as Ed appeared at the end of the lobby. He slowly folded his arms, clutching the walkie-talkie in one hand.

'Where have they moved all the support staff to, while they're doing the refurbishment?' she asked him.

He didn't answer.

'Please yourself. I'll find out from someone else. Maybe your line manager.'

He walked towards her, his puffy face breaking into a smile. 'There's no need to be like that.' He slipped the walkie-talkie back into a pocket. 'They're all over the shop. Wherever they could find a spare desk.' He stopped just inches away from her, she could feel the heat coming off him. 'It's been a logistical nightmare.'

Not what Caroline needed to hear. That meant Consuela could be anywhere, possibly even camped out in the building the department shared with the Department of Work and Pensions in Tothill Street.

'Why?' he said. 'You after someone in particular?' He moved a step closer. 'Maybe I can help, track them down for you.' He looked her up and down. 'Is it anything to do with, you know, what happened the other night?'

The lift arrived and Caroline gratefully slipped through the doors without answering.

After a walk around the block to try to calm her nerves, Caroline returned to the fourth floor to discover her section of the academies division was completely deserted.

As she got closer to her desk, she spotted a large bulky object sitting on top. She rounded a bank of filing cabinets to discover a baby's car seat, complete with baby, had been dumped between her computer and in tray.

A farmyard smell was emanating from the red-haired, podgy-faced baby. Caroline scowled at it. The baby scowled back. Then it started to cry. Quietly at first, building to a wail in a few short seconds. Caroline looked frantically around the deserted office. Why weren't her colleagues fawning over its cute little fat fingers and toes? Where was its mother? Who was its mother?

She stared into its reddening face, the cheeks glistening now with fresh-sprung tears. There was something very familiar about the way the baby's eyebrows bunched up towards its nose. It took a few more moments for the penny to drop. The baby was the spitting image of Tracy Clarke. Tracy had been threatening to show off her firstborn to the rest of the team ever since she'd left the maternity suite. This had to be her little boy. But where was Tracy? The crying ratcheted up another notch. Caroline took a step towards it. The baby gulped air into its tiny lungs then let out an unearthly scream. Thankfully the shriek was violent enough to bring Tracy out of her hiding place.

'Ohhh, chicken. What's all this nonsense?' Tracy hurried across the office, holding out her arms. 'Hey Caroline! Thanks for keeping an eye on him.' She snapped loose the straps restraining his fat little body, lifted him onto her chest with a grunt and bounced him up and down. The crying didn't subside.

'Mummy's poor little one. What *is* the matter?' She bounced him some more. 'I think it was meeting all of Mummy's friends, wasn't it poppet?' She smiled at Caroline. 'Must be a bit overwhelming, so many strange faces at his age.'

'Everyone's seen him then?'

'They've all said hello – haven't they, lovely boy? And now auntie Caroline wants to say hello too.' She shoved the baby into Caroline's arms. 'Say hello to auntie Caroline.'

The weight of the child shocked her; he almost slipped from her grasp. She pushed his ugly red face over her shoulder and found herself bouncing him before she knew what she was doing. The farmyard smell intensified.

Tracy grabbed Caroline's office chair and wheeled it towards her. 'Hope you don't mind me using your chair – it was the only one free when I got here.' Tracy pointed at the cardboard box full of office stationery and paperwork sitting on top. 'I wheeled my stuff up from the car park on it.'

'What is all this?'

'Just my work stuff. As I was coming in anyway, thought I'd kill two birds with one stone.' Tracy beamed at her. The baby had stopped crying. 'Look at you – you haven't lost your touch. He's as happy as anything now. How old's your youngest?'

Caroline felt the baby deposit a mouthful of something warm and lumpy down her back. 'Ben was eight last month.'

'God, the time goes so fast, doesn't it? Ever thought about having another?'

Caroline said nothing. She thrust the baby back at Tracy and found a tissue in her pocket to wipe away the slimy puree that was fast soaking through her blouse. 'Are you back soon, then?' she said.

'Only a few more weeks off. Not sure I can bear to be apart from this little angel, though. I know I'll be in floods the minute I leave the house.'

Caroline forced a smile at the little red-faced monster. She lifted the heavy box from her chair and deposited it on Tracy's desk.

'Cheers Caroline.'

Caroline pushed her chair back under the desk and reached for her phone, hoping Tracy might take the hint. She wanted to try Consuela again before she left for the evening, and didn't need an audience.

Tracy shifted the baby from one shoulder to the other. 'I just wanted to say, Caroline...' She was speaking in a whisper. 'About that terrible business, you know...' She looked towards the ceiling. 'On the seventh floor.'

Caroline picked up the receiver and didn't respond.

'Well... I mean. It must have been a terrible shock – what with you working so closely with the minister... are you OK? You know, in yourself?'

'I'm fine.'

'Only Pam was telling me how she thinks you should probably be at home, recovering.'

'It's nice of you to be concerned, but there's really no need.'

'OK – but you've got my number, yeah? Don't hesitate to call me if you need someone to talk to.'

'Thanks – but I'm absolutely fine. Really.' She hoped the words didn't sound as hollow to Tracy as they did to her. 'Talking of Pam, where is she? And everyone else for that matter?'

'Oh they're all still gathered round the telly.'

'Why?'

'We had coffee and cake – it's a shame you missed it. Though there might still be a slice left.'

'What's everyone doing watching television in the middle of the afternoon?' She glanced at her overflowing in tray. 'Haven't they got better things to do?'

'Well it's quite big news, isn't it?'

'What is?'

Caroline's mobile started to ring, she grabbed it from her bag and checked the little screen: number withheld. She hit the call answer button and held up a restraining finger to Tracy. 'Hello?'

An urgent voice the other end of the line asked her to confirm her identity.

'Yes that's me,' Caroline said.

'I'm calling from Catford police station.'

'What's happened? Is it one of the children?' Caroline swallowed back a queasy burn crawling from her stomach into her throat.

'No, Mrs Barber. I'm calling regarding your mother.'

'My mother? Has there been an accident?'

Tracy was staring so hard into her face, Caroline had to turn away.

'Mrs Henderson has been arrested.'

Caroline leaned against the desk. 'There must be some mistake.'

'No mistake, Mrs Barber – she'll be released shortly, but someone needs to collect her.'

'Have you tried my husband? Only I'm at work at the moment and—' She looked at her watch.

'Mrs Henderson has asked for you.'

'What happened?'

'We'll explain when you get here.'

The line went dead. Caroline looked blankly at the phone.

'I couldn't help overhearing,' Tracy said. 'Is your mum all right? Can I do anything?'

It took a moment for Caroline to respond. 'What? No, no I don't think so.' She picked up her bag and looped the strap over her shoulder.

'What you were saying before…'

Tracy frowned, and for a moment looked just like her baby.

'Big news, you said.' Caroline powered down her computer and monitor.

'I was hoping they'd bring Stella back… I still miss her, you know. She was the best secretary of state we ever had.' Tracy stared mournfully into the middle distance.

'We all miss her, Tracy… Can you just tell me what's happened?'

'Fancy foisting that waste of space from the cabinet office on us.'

'I don't understand… how is that big news? King's replacement was announced yesterday.'

'He's just trying to prove how popular he his. Making a big gesture. He's fighting a losing battle if you ask me.'

'Who are you talking about?'

'King – that's why everyone's glued to the box. We've got a personal interest, haven't we? He was here for nearly two years.'

'You're going to have to spell it out for me.'

'It's an unprecedented move, apparently. That's what the reporter on the telly said. He wants to get a mandate from the people. Something like that.'

'Please Tracy – can you just tell me what's happened?'

The baby started to mewl, the mewl started to build. 'I need to get this little one his next feed.' She bounced the baby up and down, patted a hand on his back.

Caroline grabbed Tracy's arm. 'Please Tracy.'

'All right!'

Caroline let go. The bouncing finally ceased.

'William King has just called a general election.'

11

The congregation stood for the final hymn and Caroline slipped out of the pew at the rear of the art deco chapel in Chiswick Cemetery. She edged quietly towards the heavy double doors as the assembled dignitaries did their best to sing the first few bars of *I Vow to Thee My Country*.

She'd arrived late at Martin Fox's service of remembrance, just in time to hear the final words of Rachael Oakley's eulogy. From the little she did catch, it sounded to Caroline as if the former prime minister's wife hadn't even met Martin Fox. After two hymns and an awkward psalm reading from Downing Street's new chief of staff, Caroline was ready to believe she was the only one in attendance who knew anything about the schools minister at all.

In the past week, while the media had become increasingly distracted by the shock general election, the inquest into Martin Fox's death was quietly opened and adjourned. An interim death certificate was issued by the coroner to allow the funeral to take place, and during a low-key press conference, Detective Inspector Leary announced the toxicology results wouldn't be returned for another three weeks.

In seven days Caroline had failed to track down either PC Mills or Martin Fox's PA, and wasn't sure where else to turn. The press had accepted the official line that the minister had committed suicide, and even the conspiracy websites seemed to have lost interest. She felt so alone in her conviction that Martin Fox's death was suspicious, that she didn't feel she could discuss it with anyone.

A plain-clothes policeman nodded as she approached and opened one of the large wooden doors just enough for her to squeeze through. She stepped into blinding sunlight and held up a hand to shield her eyes. As she adjusted to the glare, she could just make out a stirring in a small huddle of men gathered on the other side of the wide gravel path. The grey-suited chauffeurs all looked over at her, seemed to decide as a group she was no one important, and went back to their newspapers and cigarettes. For the first time since she was pregnant with Claire, Caroline suddenly craved nicotine, and for a moment seriously considered cadging a smoke from one of the drivers. She glanced along the line of dark limousines, shining in the sun like enormous black beetles. There had to be at least half a dozen, all ready to dispatch the great and the good just as soon as Martin Fox's body had been lowered into the ground.

A loud squawking started up in her handbag. She wrenched out her mobile and jabbed the answer key. She glanced left and right, unsure of cemetery etiquette, and hesitated before putting the phone to her ear.

'What is it, Mum?' She was whispering, but still her voice seemed disrespectfully loud. 'I can't really speak right now.' She hurried away from the entrance of the chapel and turned down a side path.

'I can see that for myself.'

Caroline reached the far side of the red brick building and stopped. 'What are you talking about?'

'Look towards the gates.'

Beyond the scrum of reporters and photographers hemmed in behind a rigid wall of police officers, Caroline saw a raggedy bunch of white-haired men and women. Her mother was right at the front, waving cheerfully at her.

'What do you think you're doing?' Caroline said.

'We heard a rumour His Holiness Frederick Larson has turned up. We missed him on the way in, but we've got three dozen Tesco Value eggs to pelt at his car when he leaves.'

'For God's sake, Mum – you can't do that.'

'It's all right – Marge gets them cheap. Some of them are already cracked.'

Caroline tried to keep her voice down. 'It's not funny, Mum. You were lucky to be let off with a caution last week. If you get arrested again—'

Mourners had started to make their way out of the chapel.

'Look I've got to go,' Caroline said. 'Promise me you won't do anything stupid.' The line went dead and she saw her mother make an exaggerated shrugging gesture before turning away.

At the head of the line emerging from the small brick building, Caroline saw a tall woman walking on her own behind the coffin. A curtain of black gauze obscured her face, but Caroline was almost sure it was the same woman she'd seen visiting Martin Fox's house in Barons Court. The other mourners maintained a respectful distance, presumably not wanting to intrude on the woman's private grief.

Caroline waited for the bulk of the cortege to slowly make its way down the path leading to the gravesite before she joined the tail end. She spotted Martin Fox's PA emerging from the chapel, dabbing her face with a black lace handkerchief. Consuela's face was pale and gaunt, the rims of her eyes and outline of her mouth looked as if they'd been drawn on with a thick red crayon. Caroline reached out and squeezed her hand. Consuela managed the dimmest of smiles.

'It was a beautiful service.' Consuela was whispering. She hooked her arm around Caroline's and they started up the path towards the grave. 'I thought the speeches were very touching.'

Caroline didn't want to disagree, so she nodded and kept her opinions to herself.

'It's a terrible tragedy.' Consuela's nose twitched and she dragged her arm back. 'Excuse me.' She grabbed her handkerchief from her sleeve, blew her nose and shoved the sodden square of lace in her handbag. She sniffed again. 'I can't believe what's happened.'

'Neither can I.'

'Of course – it must be even worse for you.'

Caroline flinched.

'Finding Martin like that.' Consuela stopped and lifted a crucifix to her lips and kissed the little silver cross. 'A terrible, terrible thing.' She tucked the cross under her sweater. 'I can't help thinking, if I hadn't left early that day... I might have been able to...' She shuddered and turned to face Caroline. 'You know, I've had nightmares.'

Caroline nodded and took a deep breath. 'I've been trying to speak to you.'

'You have?'

'You didn't reply to my emails.'

'I've been away – the doctor has given me something for my nerves.'

Can he give me something too?

'I wanted to talk to you about Martin,' Caroline said.

Consuela started walking again, this time more quickly. 'I haven't spoken to anyone about him.'

'Neither have I, not really. I just needed to ask you something.'

Consuela kept her head down as they approached the mourners gathering around the grave.

Caroline stepped in front of her on the path and laid a hand gently on her arm. 'Please.'

'I'm too upset to speak about it.'

'Can you just tell me how he seemed to you, before... before...' She screwed up her face. 'Had you noticed anything different about him?'

'Different?'

Don't make me spell it out.

'In his mood.'

She looked into Caroline's eyes and nodded.

'You did?'

'He seemed a little… irritable.'

Martin?

'He'd started snapping at me.'

'Did you tell the police?'

'I haven't spoken to the police. They arranged an interview, but then the day before, they just cancelled. They said they didn't need to see me anymore.'

'Did they say why?' Caroline had raised her voice.

Consuela frowned at her and held a finger to her lips. She gestured towards the group of mourners ahead of them. The vicar had taken up his position at the head of the grave, clutching a prayer book tightly in his hands.

The two women walked on in silence and joined an outer circle of mourners. Consuela clasped her hands together and closed her eyes.

Caroline scanned the group of mourners standing immediately next to the grave. Most of them she recognised from television news reports, but she couldn't put a name to every one of the faces. Just as her gaze rested on Jeremy Prior he looked towards her then quickly away. The head of the academies division was standing between the tall woman in the veil and William King's chief of staff. Prior muttered something to the prime minister's aide then dropped his head, his hands gripped tightly together.

Brought up as a card-carrying atheist, Caroline was unable to say a silent prayer of her own. Instead, she closed her eyes and made Martin Fox a promise. Whatever it took, she was determined to find out what really happened to him.

She opened her eyes, grabbed a tissue from her bag and quickly dispatched the few tears that had escaped down her cheeks. She blinked hard and stared at the pale wooden casket lying next to the grave.

I won't let you down, Martin.

She took a step back and glanced around the graveyard. There couldn't have been more than 50 or so mourners. It seemed a pitifully low turnout. Martin Fox had devoted over 25 years of his life to public service and only a handful of dignitaries and a few dozen colleagues had bothered to pay their last respects. Had any of his hard work really made a difference?

Caroline shook the thought from her head and continued to scan the meagre congregation, looking for people she recognised from the department. Right at the fringes of the scattered groups of twos and threes she noticed a man standing on his own. His hands were shoved deep into his trouser pockets and he was rocking backwards and forwards on his heels. There was something vaguely familiar about the way he moved. She continued to stare, trying to make out his features. He shifted his weight from foot to foot and pulled his hands from his pockets. Caroline breathed in sharply. It was the dark brown suit that had thrown her; she'd only seen him in uniform before.

The vanishing PC Mills had rematerialised.

'Are you sure this is a good idea, Ange?' Frank Carter stood on a collapsed stretch of chain-link fence, trying to hold it flat against the ground.

'You said yourself you weren't getting any clear head shots.' Angela Tate, clutching a bedraggled bunch of daffodils, picked her way through the grid of wire diamonds, the pointy toes of her boots snagging in the mesh every couple of steps. 'Think of this as a practical demonstration of the right to a free press.'

'We got great head shots at the demo and sod all good it did us. Bumped right off the front page.' Frank held out his hand, Angela ignored it. 'And clean out of the paper.'

'That was just unfortunate timing. A snap election pretty much trumps everything else.' She stepped onto the safety of the manicured grass beyond the broken fence and peered at the group of mourners assembled around the grave on the other side of the cemetery. 'We'll go the long way round and approach them from behind. Take as many photos as you can. I want to see which of these cynical old buggers actually sheds a tear.'

She pushed Frank in front of her as they traipsed over the damp grass, weaving in and out of stone angels and dark marble headstones. They stopped when they reached a tree less than 50 yards from Fox's grave.

'This is me, then.' Angela leaned a shoulder against the tree trunk, just wide enough to obscure her.

'You're not coming with?'

'Photographs first and questions later.' She looked down at the wilting daffodils and chucked them onto the nearest grave. 'Now if I lose track of you, we'll meet at the front gate, after the convoy has swept back out again.' She tapped a number into her mobile and the light on Frank's Bluetooth headset started to flash. Frank tapped the earpiece.

'Are you receiving me?' she said.

Frank nodded and rolled his eyes.

'I want a blow-by-blow account of everyone who's there. Just in case something happens to you. Or the camera.'

'What's likely to happen? What are you getting me into, Ange?'

'It's not war-torn Beirut. I'm sure you can handle yourself with a few security spods.' She shoved him in the chest. 'Well go on then!'

Frank broke into a stuttering shuffle, his camera bag swinging around his neck.

'Is that as fast as you go?' Angela hissed into her phone.

The photographer waved two fingers at her and carried on. She slipped behind the tree trunk, peering out every few seconds to check on his progress, her phone pressed against her ear.

'Who's turned up? Can you make them out yet?' she said.

'I can see King's missus, but there's no sign of the man himself.' Frank took a gulping breath. 'So the rumours of a surprise appearance were unfounded.'

'That's probably because I started them. Who else?'

'The former PM's other half is here too. Looks like the pair of them are trying to out Jackie O one another.'

'Who's looking the most tragic?'

It took a moment before Frank replied. 'That prize goes to a leggy woman wearing a veil – you can't get more tragic than a veil. She's being propped up by the vicar on one side and King's attack dog on the other. Any ideas who she is?'

'Might be Fox's cousin. His only surviving relative. Apparently she stands to inherit his fortune. Can't find out anything about her. Trail goes cold just over 12 months ago.' Angela reached into her bag for a notepad. 'Who else?'

'Your favourite academy sponsor Fred Larson's sitting in his wheelchair, right next to the gaping hole, Lady Larson behind. I hope she's put the bloody brake on – could be a double burial otherwise. Were you expecting him to turn up?'

'Hoping he might.'

Angela peered out from behind the tree, but couldn't make out distinct faces. She saw Frank creep closer to the huddle of mourners, snapping off shots as he went.

'Who else Frank?' She heard the photographer gulping down another breath.

'One of the deputy assistant commissioners from the Met in all his finery. Medals and everything. Can't remember his name. You probably know him.'

Angela tried to focus on the uniformed man and spotted something flash at the far side of the grave. It flashed again. Then more flashing beside it. It took her another moment to work out what it was – sunlight reflected off pairs of mirrored sunglasses as heads turned in Frank's direction. Then the heads and the sunglasses were on the move. Even from that distance Angela could see they weren't regular plain-clothes policemen, or even personal protection for Mrs King and Oakley. They looked more like eastern European weightlifters, their arms and legs bulging in borrowed suits. They looked, in fact, very much like Larson's men from the building site.

'Watch out Frank! Three heavies heading straight for you, two o'clock.'

Frank pulled his camera from his face and started to run. Angela could hardly bear to watch. His flabby arms and legs pumped as hard as they could, but the three thugs were gaining on him.

'Frank! Can you hear me? I think there's something wrong with the connection – there's a funny noise.'

'That's me! Can't breathe!'

'Thank God you're still there. Who else did you see, Frank?'

The wheezing got louder.

'Frank?'

'Jesus… Ange… dying here.'

More rattling breaths.

'Come on Frank!'

The thugs were almost on him.

'Hang a sharp right.'

Frank looked up. 'Too many… coppers.'

'Your choice Frank – murderous-looking bastards right behind you, or the uniformed regular kind in front.'

Angela ducked back behind the tree. The heavy breathing on her mobile stopped. 'Frank?' She glanced at the screen. He'd ended the call. She risked another peek from her hiding place. Frank was in the middle of the police line, already making conversation with one of the officers. The three Larson thugs were keeping their distance. She looked for others of the same ilk and counted half a dozen before she stopped. It seemed the academy-sponsoring entrepreneur was taking his private army to funerals now. That either meant he was getting seriously paranoid in his old age or he was genuinely under threat. But who had made the decrepit old bastard that twitchy?

As soon as PC Mills saw Caroline approaching, he glanced left and right as if he was looking for an escape route. After a moment he shoved his hands back in his pockets and pulled back his shoulders. The corners of his mouth turned up a fraction.

'I was beginning to think I'd imagined you,' Caroline said.

The police officer stopped smiling.

'I wanted to speak to you last week. I called the number on the card you gave me.'

'I didn't get any messages.' He frowned at her.

'You wouldn't have.' Caroline glanced at the main group of mourners. They were starting to drift back towards the chapel and the entrance of the cemetery. Out of the corner of her eye she saw PC Mills checking his watch. 'I didn't leave any,' she said.

'What did you want to speak to me about?'

'I didn't leave any messages because when I tried the number a second time they told me they'd never heard of you.'

'What? When was this?'

'Last Monday.'

'Ah.' He folded his arms across his chest. 'I wasn't there. I've been transferred.'

'The woman on the phone said there was no record of you.'

'Who did you speak to?'

'Does it matter?'

'Sometimes they get temps in.' He lowered his head. 'And between you and me they can be a bit useless.'

'She sounded competent enough to me.' Caroline scrutinised the constable's face. 'Transferred? On Monday?'

He nodded.

'Why did you give me your card then, if you knew you wouldn't be there?'

'I didn't – the job came right out of the blue. I've waited so long to be a detective – I was gobsmacked.'

'You've been promoted and you didn't even know it was coming?'

'Not promoted – I'm still a constable.'

'Didn't you ask why?'

He shrugged.

Caroline blew out a long breath and tried to assimilate the new information. It didn't make sense. 'If you've been transferred, what are you doing here? Presumably this isn't your case anymore.'

He looked at the ground. 'It isn't. This is my day off.'

'So why are—'

'It's a long story.'

'I'm a good listener.'

Mills sniffed and started to nibble at his bottom lip. He rocked back on his heels and gazed towards Martin Fox's grave.

'The minister's wasn't the first suicide I've attended, not by a long way,' he said quietly. 'The first dead body I ever saw was a suicide.' He breathed out and his chest heaved. 'I didn't get a chance to pay my last respects to her, so I try to get to the funerals of other people who've… you know…' His cheek twitched. 'I've been to too many over the years.' He rubbed both hands across his face. 'Occupational hazard, I suppose.'

Caroline had so many questions she wanted to ask him about Martin Fox, but now suddenly didn't seem the right time.

'Had you been in the job long, that first time?' she said.

'It was long before I joined the force.' He swallowed. 'Years before.'

'How old were you?'

'Twelve.'

Caroline automatically reached out a hand. He recoiled from her touch. 'She was my sister,' he said.

'I'm so sorry.'

'It was just the way you described it.'

Caroline frowned. 'I don't understand.'

'She was still warm when I found her. Just like you said, you know… about finding the minister's body. Brought it back.'

Caroline stared at the grave.

Mills sniffed loudly and puffed out a breath. 'I should go now.' He started to move away then stopped. 'What was it you wanted to speak to me about, when you called the station?'

Caroline hesitated, not sure she should broach the subject. 'I needed someone to talk to about Martin's death.'

The policeman sighed. He reached into a pocket and pressed a business card into her hand. It looked the same as the last one, except now instead of a Belgravia address, it gave details of a police station in Lewisham.

'You've crossed the river,' she said. 'Isn't it a bit downmarket, after Westminster?'

Mills shrugged. 'Give me a call on the new number. I can put you in touch with counsellors in your area. Post-traumatic support. I'm not really qualified to—'

'I don't want to talk through my feelings.' She put a hand on his arm. 'I want to talk to *you*. About the investigation.'

He screwed up his face.

Caroline withdrew her hand. 'That night – when you were questioning me, you asked me if I'd moved anything, do you remember? Anything like a note or a letter.'

He didn't say anything.

'Do you remember what I said?'

He nodded very slowly.

'Then how do you explain the suicide note that was leaked to the papers?'

He rubbed his face again. 'I saw the note myself.'

'What?'

'When I read the story in the paper I thought it was weird. It didn't make sense. I didn't remember a note at the scene. So I went and checked the evidence myself. And there was the note, plain as day.'

'But there wasn't a note – especially not stuck to the monitor on his desk. You know that.'

'We must have missed it.'

'I know what I saw.' There was a tremor in Caroline's voice.

'And I know what I saw in the evidence box.'

'So you think it's genuine?'

'Why wouldn't it be? What are you suggesting?'

'You didn't see a note at the scene. Neither did I. All your forensics colleagues managed to miss it too. Then suddenly one turns up?'

Mills's cheek twitched. 'Stranger things happen.'

'That's reassuring.' Caroline started to bite her bottom lip. She was getting nowhere.

'Look,' Mills said, 'I've really got to go.'

'Wait.' She laid a hand on his arm. 'You said yourself it was your day off.'

'Still…'

'Assuming for a moment the note is genuine, how far have you got in tracking down the blackmailers?'

'What?'

'If it's genuine, those blackmailers supposedly drove Martin Fox to take his own life. That's not just blackmail – that's manslaughter, isn't it? What are the police doing about that?'

'I'm working out of a new station now. It's not my case anymore.'

Caroline threw back her head and gazed up at the cloudless sky. She sucked down a breath. 'OK,' she said, 'what about your colleague, then – the woman constable? She's still on the case, presumably. I'll talk to her.'

'You can't.'

'Just give me her name.'

'She's not at work at the moment.'

'Why not?'

'She's off – long-term sick. She's done her back in.'

'What? When did this happen?'

Mills shook his head. 'Don't look at me like that. It's just a coincidence. You can't read anything into it.'

'When did it happen?' Caroline asked again, but had a feeling she knew the answer already.

'Same day I got transferred.'

12

Caroline wandered up Victoria Street from the station in a daze. Everyone else seemed to be hurrying in the opposite direction, banging shoulders and elbows as they rushed past, hurrying back to work after their lunch breaks. She got as far as the bus stop opposite House of Fraser and sank onto the narrow plastic bench inside the bus shelter.

She'd planned to go back into the office after leaving the cemetery, and catch up on the missed morning's work. But now she was less than ten minutes away from the department, the reality of sitting at her desk, desperately trying to concentrate while Pam fired questions at her about the funeral was making her stomach churn. She retrieved her mobile from her bag, called a colleague and explained she wouldn't be in until the morning. She felt better as soon as she slipped the phone back into her bag.

Moments later the number 11 arrived, which would take her to Charing Cross, where she could jump on a train to take her home. Right now the idea that she could simply close her front door on the day made everything just a little easier to bear.

She gazed blankly out of the window on the top deck, replaying the events of the morning over and over. The faces of the mourners lined up in her head and the memory of Martin Fox's casket being lowered into the ground seemed to repeat on an endless loop. She searched the surrounding seats for a discarded *Metro* or early edition of the *Standard*, anything that might distract, shift her attention to something other than Martin Fox. She spotted a copy of the *Evening News* on the seat opposite and reached across the aisle for it. Most of the front page was taken up with a photograph of the leader of the opposition, trying to look statesmen-like as he stared grim-faced into the camera. The launch of his party's manifesto apparently warranted front page headlines. Caroline read the first few lines of the accompanying article. William King's election announcement had caught the other parties completely by surprise. It was a miracle they'd managed to magic up a coherent election message at all in the space of a week. There wasn't much to distinguish one major party from another. The opposition's manifesto bore an uncanny resemblance to the current government's. The election would probably be won on personality alone. Caroline wasn't sure how most people felt about William King. He was doing well enough in opinion polls, but having worked under him at the department for the last two years, she couldn't muster any feelings of goodwill towards him. Thoughts of King inevitably turned to memories of Martin Fox and the funeral she was trying to forget. She quickly opened the paper and scanned the inside pages for entertainment news and celebrity gossip, desperate to take her mind off the events of the morning.

A series of shouts from the lower deck reverberated up the stairs, followed by the sound of heavy footsteps. She turned to see a boisterous gang of two teenage boys and three girls clatter down the aisle to the back of the bus. Immediately a distorted dance track crackled from one of their mobile phones.

'What you looking at, Grandma?' one of the girls shouted at her.

Caroline was tempted to fire back a withering reply but decided instead to rise above the insult. She turned back to the *Evening News* and skimmed over the stories, keeping half an ear on the insults being hurled her way from the back of the bus. She continued turning pages still searching for something to grab her attention. The picture at the bottom of page nine did just that. She stared open-mouthed at the colour photograph of her mother being bundled into a police car. She checked the headline at the top of page:

AN ACADEMY TOO FAR?

She'd just finished reading the first paragraph when a half-crushed can of Coke skidded up the aisle of the bus and came to halt by the seat in front of hers, fizzing sticky froth all over the floor. Caroline turned to see the five teenagers all staring at her with their chins up and arms folded. She puffed out a weary sigh and stood up.

'OK – whoever threw that can come here right now and pick it up.'

The kids looked at one another, barely suppressing their laughter and then stared back at her.

'I mean it.'

'What you gonna do?' The same girl who'd spoken before shouted at her again.

Not today. Please not today.

They were nudging one another now, clearly egging each other on. Caroline looked at the spent can of Coke as it slid under a seat on the other side of the aisle.

Not today.

She slowly sat down to the sound of clucking from the back seat. She turned once again to the article, willing the words to register and sink in, the noise from the teenagers getting louder all the time. The story didn't seem much more than an anti-academy rant, focusing on the delayed opening of a new academy in Hammersmith and the protests at the proposed site in Catford. Hence the photograph of 'Frail old age pensioner Jean Henderson.' Frail wasn't an adjective Caroline would ever have imagined being used to describe her mother. She carried on reading.

In the final few paragraphs the tone of the piece seemed to change. It switched from a condemnation of the principle of academies in general to a more specific and personal attack on the sponsor of the Catford academy. The journalist questioned Sir Fred Larson's motives for his charitable works, and suggested control of the curriculum in the two academies he'd sponsored so far might be at the root of his apparent generosity. Caroline scanned the rest of the story until one word jumped out at her. She tried hard to remember Larson's academy applications. She'd dealt with the proposal for his first academy in Dagenham herself. Like the new one in Catford, the first two were business academies – focusing on excellence in entrepreneurism. She couldn't recall any mention of deviation from the standard curriculum in religious studies. Or biology. She read the paragraph again.

Creationism? Really?

Her phone started ringing. She pulled it from her bag and saw the number had been withheld. It was just possible someone from the department was checking up on her, Pam most probably. She answered just before her voicemail kicked in.

'Mrs Barber?' A man's voice. 'This is Ralph Mills.'

Something in Caroline's gut flipped over.

'What's happened?'

He didn't answer. Caroline heard him exhale.

'Constable?'

'Nothing's happened. I'm sorry – I shouldn't have called you like this. I don't have any news for you about the minister. I'm not on the investigation… I did try to explain before.'

'What is it then?'

A shout went up at the back of the bus, followed by chanting. Caroline stuck a finger in her ear.

'I'm phoning to apologise.' He puffed out another loud breath. 'After we spoke I got in touch with someone from my old station – Belgravia?'

'Apologise about what?'

'I asked him to find out when your birthday card could be released – it was last week, your birthday, wasn't it?'

Caroline had to think for a moment. Tuesday had come and gone without much of a fanfare. 'Actually I'd forgotten all about it.'

'Seeing you today... I thought you might like—'

'When can I have it?'

'That's why I'm phoning... it's not a regular occurrence, but when there's so much evidence collected... mistakes can happen.'

'I don't understand what you're saying.'

'He couldn't find a record of your card logged on the system. I'm really sorry.'

'But I saw it being put into the box myself.'

'Like I say – sometimes these things happen. Put it down to human error.'

'Did your colleague actually look for the box itself? Isn't it possible it's in the box but not on the system?'

'Things just slip through the cracks sometimes. I thought I should phone you personally to apologise – no one else would even know about it.'

Caroline sniffed. She'd forgotten about the card, but now she'd been reminded it felt like another memory of Martin Fox had been erased. 'Could you ask him to check the box again?'

A sudden burst of shouting and swearing erupted from the back of the bus.

'What's going on there?' Mills asked.

'Just some stupid kids.'

Caroline turned to see a young girl, not that much taller than Ben, but probably Dan's age, had appeared at the top of the stairs. She was dressed from head to toe in black and purple, thick eyeliner under her eyes, her hair gelled into fierce black spikes.

'Please constable – can you ask him to check again?'

'I thought I'd explained – he can't – there's no record of your card because there's no record of the box.'

'What?'

'The box containing the envelope addressed to you, and all those other envelopes... it's gone.'

'You're not serious?'

'Like I say – it doesn't happen often. I'm really sorry.'

There was another shout from the back of the bus.

'Oi!' It was the girl with the big mouth again. 'Oi! Lezza! What d'you fink you're doing, sitting right up at the front? You're spoiling my view innit? Fuckin' ugly bitch.'

Caroline swallowed. She couldn't let it go this time. 'Look, detective, can I call you back?'

'I... erm... I shouldn't really be speaking to you at—'

Caroline hung up.

The mouthy girl shouted again. 'You should be sitting downstairs with the other weirdos.'

The young goth glanced over her shoulder towards the commotion and quickly turned back again.

'Yeah – you! Get off the fuckin' bus, yeah?'

Caroline stood up.

'Ooh, watch it – Granny's after us.'

Caroline got as far as the stairs when the bus lurched to a halt; she shot out her hand and managed to grab a handrail before completely losing her balance.

'Careful Grandma!'

'If anyone's getting off this bus it's you,' Caroline said.

'Whassat, Gran?'

'Come on!' Caroline walked towards them. 'Get up, all of you.'

'Ooh, I'm scared.'

'Off the bus – now!'

'Can't make me.' The loud girl stood up, her friends stayed seated, one of them pushing her forward, further into the aisle.

A burst of radio static blared up the stairs from the lower deck.

'Nice bunch of friends you've got there.' Caroline looked at each of them in turn until they looked away. 'Loyal are they?'

'What?'

'Do you even know the meaning of the word? Will they back you up when the police come?'

The teenagers started to fidget in their seats.

'That's right – the driver's radioed for assistance. The police should arrive any minute – lots of them in this neck of the woods.' She glanced out of the window – the bus had turned into Whitehall, the Houses of Parliament behind them.

The girl held her ground but didn't say anything.

'Now,' Caroline said. 'You sure you've got nothing on you that the police might be interested in?'

The teenagers glanced furtively at one another.

'You see, primarily they're geared up for terrorists round here. You could be arrested and taken away and no one would ever find out what happened to you. Shoot first and ask questions later – if you know what I'm saying. Do you remember what happened in Stockwell tube a few years back?'

One by one the two girls and two boys got to their feet and slipped around their noisy friend, heads hanging low. When they'd finally disappeared down the stairs, the shouting girl started up the aisle.

'Be-atch,' she said, leaning into Caroline's face as she passed.

Caroline followed her down the stairs and watched as she joined her friends on the pavement.

Someone started clapping at the back of the bus and the rest of the lower deck joined in. Caroline glanced at the other passengers and immediately felt heat bloom in her cheeks. She rushed back up the stairs and sat down as the applause died away. The tiny goth was staring at her.

'Cheers,' the girl said. 'Though I would have just ignored them – usually the safest bet.'

Caroline smiled at the girl, embarrassed, wondering why she always needed to plough in when anyone else would have pretended nothing was happening. She sat down. The newspaper was lying open on the seat, the photograph of her mother staring up at her.

What a day. As far as Caroline was concerned, it couldn't end fast enough. She ran a hand over her face and let out a long, defeated breath.

'Are you OK?' The goth girl was still looking at her.

'Oh, you know… I dare say I will be.'

'You look like you might throw.'

Caroline smiled at her. 'No chance of that – I haven't eaten anything all day.' She picked up the newspaper. 'Really – I'm fine.' She glanced down at the article and pretended to read, hoping the girl would lose interest in her. A few lines in the final paragraph caught her attention.

> *This is an honest and open request, Sir Fred. All we're asking for is an unequivocal public condemnation of creationism in the school curriculum. Families living in the catchment areas of your three academies deserve to know exactly what your position is. They need to know they can trust your intentions are honourable. They deserve the truth. Or is that too much to ask?*

She let the paper fall onto the seat beside her. The truth? They'd be lucky. Right now the truth felt as if it had been put on a high shelf, somewhere permanently out of reach. The facts surrounding Martin Fox's death were either being deliberately misrepresented or disappearing entirely.

Maybe the truth was too much to ask for. She glanced down at the page and saw the journalist's byline and a thumbnail photograph of a heavily made-up woman smiling up at her. Journalists didn't really know what was going on any more than she did. How could any of them realistically expect to uncover the truth?

Caroline looked out of the window. The bus had made it halfway down Whitehall and was crawling past the bottom of Downing Street. She pictured William King ensconced inside Number 10 and remembered his chief of staff standing over Martin Fox's open grave. Her silent promise to the schools minister seemed more impossible than ever. How could she promise to discover what really happened if the evidence was being systematically destroyed?

She glanced down at the newspaper again. Was it possible that this journalist could make a difference? Caroline flipped back through the pages and pulled her phone from her bag. She'd punched in the number she found on page two and was transferred to the newsdesk before she had a chance to change her mind.

'I hope you can help me,' she said as the security gates protecting the entrance to Downing Street disappeared behind the bus. 'I'd like to speak to Angela Tate.'

13

Angela Tate was late. Caroline checked her watch – over twenty minutes late. She looked out through the enormous window of an Italian restaurant on The Strand, just a couple of hundred yards from Charing Cross station and a quick escape route back home if she needed one.

She watched people strolling by outside, chatting and laughing, enjoying the early evening sunshine. Caroline scanned their faces. She was dreading seeing someone from work. There was just an outside chance a familiar face from the department might pop up, pop in and sit down right next to her. How would she introduce Angela Tate?

Have you met my new friend, the investigative journalist?

She looked around the restaurant at the handful of pre-theatre diners and thought about moving to another table, further from the window.

Five minutes later she was checking her watch again, aware it was becoming a nervous tick. The waiter stopped and asked if she wanted bread or perhaps a bowl of olives while she waited for her friend. She'd refused him three times already. This time she agreed to some focaccia with a little olive oil – anything to occupy her fidgeting hands. She glanced again at her watch. It was 6:50pm. She'd already waited a week to be granted an audience with Angela Tate; a few more minutes wouldn't make much difference.

The waiter delivered a small basket of bread and a shallow dish of bright green olive oil. Caroline broke off a corner of rosemary-crusted focaccia and was just stuffing it into her mouth as the door clanked open. She looked up to see a woman wearing a black raincoat and knee-length boots stepping confidently over the threshold.

'Don't get up!' she said, striding towards the table. 'Caroline?'

Caroline nodded and chewed fast.

'What are you drinking?'

She wasn't what Caroline had expected at all. The photograph in the newspaper was easily ten years out of date. The woman standing in front of her now, inspecting the half-empty bottle of San Pellegrino and screwing up her nose, had to be in her early 50s. The eye shadow and lipstick were just as thickly applied, but her blonde hair looked almost white under the restaurant lights.

'Oh I think we can do a little better than that.' Angela Tate waved at a waiter. 'Excuse me! Bottle of Pinot Grigio. Make sure it's not the cheapest.' She turned to Caroline and winked. 'Expenses,' she said and smiled.

Caroline let out the breath that had stalled in her lungs and managed to smile back.

Tate wrenched her arms free of her raincoat and slung it over a chair. 'Angela Tate.' She slid a business card across the table and sat down. 'But you worked that out already.' She pulled her chair closer to Caroline's and planted her elbows on the table. 'Did you want to order something to eat? I'm not really hungry. But feel free.' She looked at Caroline closely, unashamedly scrutinising her face.

Caroline felt a flush start in her neck and work its way upwards.

'Have we met before?' Tate said.

'I think I would remember.' Caroline sat a little taller in her seat.

'You know I'm sure we have.' Tate pushed the sleeves of her fitted black shirt up to the elbows and pulled a notepad and pen from her bag. The wine arrived and she waved the waiter away. Caroline put her hand over her glass before Tate had a chance to fill it.

'Just a small one, surely?'

'I'd prefer to keep a clear head.'

Tate poured herself a glass and knocked back a third of it, then refilled the glass almost to the rim. She looked at Caroline. She waited.

'Thank you for agreeing to see me.' Caroline glanced over Tate's shoulder towards the door.

Tate followed her gaze. 'Expecting someone else?'

'No. I just feel a bit—'

Tate smiled. 'This isn't something you do everyday.'

Caroline shook her head.

'Well – in your own time. You're my last appointment of the day.' Tate glanced at her watch and started to tap her pen against her notebook.

'I'm not sure where to start, really. Such a lot has happened in the last couple of weeks. I'm still finding it hard to come to terms with the fact that Martin's gone.'

Tate stared at Caroline and pursed her lips. 'Of course!' She jabbed the pen in Caroline's direction. 'You were at the funeral last Monday.'

'I didn't see you there.' Caroline felt suddenly exposed as if she'd somehow been found out.

'I wasn't exactly invited.' Tate took a long slug of wine and refilled her glass again. 'You were close to the schools minister then?'

'I worked with him quite closely.' Caroline cleared her throat. 'I'm part of the academies division.'

'Yes I know – you mentioned it on the phone... and Martin Fox was a great advocate of academies.'

Tate continued to tap the pen against her notebook. The sound was going right through Caroline's head and into her jaw, setting her teeth on edge. She lifted her hand to cover Tate's, holding the pen still.

'Do you mind?'

Tate looked surprised, as if she hadn't been aware she was doing it. Caroline removed her hand and poured herself a large glass of wine. She sank a mouthful of Pinot Grigio then proceeded to give Tate a blow-by-blow account of everything that had happened over the last fortnight, from Martin Fox's strange voicemail message to the lying detective inspector and missing box of evidence. She even mentioned her boss's appearance at Martin Fox's house. Tate raised her eyebrows, but carried on making notes without comment.

When she was finished, Caroline watched Tate puff out a long breath, staring down blank-eyed into her glass. She said nothing.

'Well?' Caroline said.

Tate reached a hand into her bag. She pulled out an unopened packet of Marlboro Lights and put them on the table then shoved her hand back in her bag, rummaged around again and retrieved a wallet and a lighter.

'They're in here somewhere.' Tate smiled and eventually fumbled out a blister pack of Nicorette. She punched two squares of gum through the foil, shoved them both in her mouth and started to chew vigorously.

'What do you think?' Caroline said.

Tate screwed up her face. 'These things taste like indigestion tablets.' She chewed for a few moments more, staring at Caroline. 'It's... well... it doesn't really amount to much.'

Caroline's heart sank.

'A deleted message here, a missing envelope there. It doesn't seem more than coincidence, circumstantial. Nothing really solid to get hold of.'

'But it all adds up, surely?'

'To what?'

'I'm certain Martin Fox didn't kill himself. I know that suicide note was fake.'

Tate stopped chewing. 'How can you know that?'

'He wasn't that kind of man – he wouldn't run away from his problems – no matter how big they were.' Caroline looked down at the packet of cigarettes. 'May I?' She picked up the ten-pack.

'Be my guest. I've given up. Again.'

Caroline ripped off the cellophane and tore open the packet. She shoved a cigarette between her lips and grabbed the lighter from the table. 'I gave up sixteen years ago.' She pushed back her chair. 'I've had a terrible craving for a week now.'

Tate plucked the cigarette from Caroline's mouth and crushed it into the remains of the focaccia. 'Sixteen years is fucking remarkable,' she said. 'Don't step back on that slippery slope. I've been there too many times. Before you know it you're skidding on your arse and sliding towards thirty a day.'

A waiter walked past and snatched the plate from the table.

'Look, I know what you must be going through,' Tate said. 'It's always a shock when someone does something so... out of character. It's natural that you'd look for another explanation.'

'Why does everyone keep telling me that?' Caroline raised her voice. 'I know for sure there wasn't a suicide note found at the scene and I know for a fact Martin Fox was not being blackmailed.'

She saw Tate stiffen. The journalist spat the ball of gum into a paper napkin and picked up her glass. She rolled a gulp of wine around her mouth as if it were mouthwash and swallowed. She held her pen over her notepad.

'How do you know?'

'Don't you think it's strange we've heard nothing from the police about their investigation into tracking down the blackmailers?'

Tate let out a little disappointed sigh and laid down her pen. 'They've not got an awful lot to go on, have they? Just a few lines in a note.'

'They could be doing something.'

'I've been digging around a bit myself, and I've come up with bugger all.'

Caroline sipped her wine, taking a moment to think. 'You've been digging around what exactly?'

Tate made a non-committal shrug of her shoulders.

'You've been poking around the minister's private life, isn't that what journalists do?'

Tate leaned back in her chair and crossed her legs under the table.

'I bet you haven't found anything to confirm Martin Fox was gay, have you?'

Tate just stared at her.

'It would have been all over the papers if one of your lot had managed to prise an ex-boyfriend out of the woodwork. But you haven't, so that makes a mockery of the blackmail story.'

'It proves nothing. He might just have been extraordinarily discreet. We haven't found any girlfriends either.'

Caroline felt her heart speed a few beats. She tried to catch her breath. 'There was no suicide note.'

'So you say. But it's their word against yours.' Tate drained her glass. 'And there's a lot more of them.'

Caroline shook her head. 'This is ridiculous. I don't know why I thought you might help me.' She pushed back her chair again and started to stand.

Tate put a hand on her arm. 'What is it you were hoping I'd be able to do?'

A sudden wave of fatigue spread through Caroline's body. She collapsed back into her seat. 'I just wanted you to help me get to the truth. I can't do it on my own. I thought with the weight of the *Evening News* behind me...' She looked into Tate's face, but couldn't read her expression. She shook her head. 'Oh God... I don't know what I was thinking.'

'There'll be a bit of press interest when the toxicology report is made public, then again for the inquest, but I can't really see what's left to investigate.'

'He didn't kill himself.'

'You're suggesting foul play? You really believe someone murdered the minister for schools at his desk?'

Caroline stared into her glass and nodded.

'If you had even a shred of evidence to back that up, I'd go at this like a bloody terrier after a rat. But everything you've told me is circumstantial at best.'

Caroline swallowed. She had one last card to play, one final piece of information. But she wasn't at all sure she could share it with Angela Tate. She watched Tate refill her glass. What kind of woman was she? In the past week she'd done some research and discovered Tate had won awards for her work in the 80s and 90s and generally seemed well respected among her peers. But did that mean she could trust her? Tate turned and caught Caroline staring at her.

'The suicide note.' Caroline blurted out the words.

'I know, I know – you didn't see it.'

'No!' Caroline took a breath. 'Not just that. I know the note was fake.'

The journalist made a sympathetic face.

'I know absolutely that Martin Fox wasn't gay.'

Tate narrowed her eyes.

'I've never told anyone.' Caroline buried her face in her glass, and then knocked back what remained of her wine. She waited a moment, hoping to steady the tremor in her voice.

'Last year Martin and I... we...' She sucked in a deep breath. 'We became close.' She spoke in a murmur.

Tate leaned closer. 'I'm sorry?'

'We were...' Caroline hesitated, the word sounded ridiculous in her head, she wasn't sure she could say it out loud. She tried again: 'We were lovers.'

Tate stared at Caroline, her lips slightly apart, her eyes wide. Caroline could almost hear the journalist's brain whirring.

'I see,' she said eventually.

'Do you? Really?' Caroline's legs felt weak, as if her bones were melting into the flesh. She couldn't have stood up now if the restaurant was on fire. Her hands were trembling. She clasped them together in her lap. She'd said it. The secret that she'd kept buried for over six months had finally burst out.

Tate's face pinched into a grimace. Her tongue traced a line along her bottom lip. 'For how long? How long were you—'

'What's that got to do with anything?'

Tate uncrossed her legs and sat up very straight. 'You said you were... close last year. When did it end?'

'Why would that have any bearing on what I'm telling you?'

Tate scribbled something in her notepad. Caroline grabbed her hand. 'You can't write that down. You can't use it! For God's sake.'

'Who ended it?'

'I'm not telling you any more.' Caroline leaned a hand on the table and struggled to her feet.

'Then why tell me at all?'

Caroline bent down so she was face to face with Tate. 'Because I thought you might actually start taking me seriously.' She grabbed her jacket from the back of the chair and picked up her bag. She gestured to the waiter for the bill.

'Don't go now.'

'Why not? You're obviously not interested in helping me.'

'I didn't say that. Please, Caroline – sit down.'

Caroline remained on her feet. 'So you will help me?'

'Please.' Tate pulled the chair from the table. 'You look like someone's punched the wind right out of you.'

Reluctantly, Caroline sat back down. She felt more like she'd been slapped hard across the face. Her cheeks were burning. The waiter arrived with the card terminal and Tate paid the bill before she spoke again.

'I was actually hoping we might be able to help each other.'

Caroline pulled her glass towards her. It was empty, but she didn't remember finishing it.

'Should I order another bottle?'

Caroline shook her head. 'Help each other how?'

Tate was scrutinising her again. 'I won't lie to you. Especially not after your...'

'Confession?'

'I was going to say revelation.' Tate smiled awkwardly. 'I didn't come here this evening because I wanted to hear what you had to say about Martin Fox's death.'

Caroline started to speak, but Tate held up a hand.

'I've read enough crackpot conspiracy theories online linking his death to the PM's resignation and the subsequent appointment of King to fill three Dan Brown novels.' Tate shook her head.

'Then why—'

'I came here because you work in the academies division. I need classified data only someone working inside the department can get access to. My motivation was based on naked self-interest. Pure and simple.'

Caroline stared into Tate's face, not quite believing what she'd just heard. She laughed. 'You're not serious?'

Tate laid her hands palm upwards on the table. 'Deadly.'

'You're asking me to steal confidential information from the DfE?'

Tate nodded, maintaining eye contact.

'Why would I do that?'

'To get to the truth.'

'What has that got to do with Martin's death?' Caroline searched Tate's face.

'At this stage, I can't be absolutely sure. But I won't be able to make a link between my academies investigation and the minister's death unless I have that information.'

Caroline shook her head. 'You're asking too much. You want me to abuse my position, in the vague hope something I give you will be connected to Martin's death?' She rose to her feet again. 'I can't do it.'

'I promise you I'll do whatever I can to find out what happened to him.'

'You could do that without asking me to jeopardise my career.'

'Like I said, naked self-interest. If I help you, you have to help me.'

Caroline drew down a long breath and slowly exhaled. 'I can't. You'll have to get your information some other way.'

'If I don't help you, who else can you turn to?'

'I'll find someone.'

'Good luck with that.'

'There are other journalists.'

'None who have my interest in academies. You have something to offer me. Quid pro quo.'

Caroline shook her head again.

'Time's running out,' Tate said. 'You said yourself Martin Fox's office has been emptied – the whole floor has been stripped bare. How long before any remaining evidence disappears?'

'Are you saying you agree that Martin's death was suspicious?'

Tate shrugged. 'I'm saying I need more information.'

Caroline closed her eyes and rubbed a hand across her face. Twenty-three years in the civil service. How could she betray the department?

'You're not doing it for me.' Tate just wouldn't shut up. 'You're doing it for him.'

Caroline started towards the exit.

'Please, Caroline. You can't just walk away.' Tate got to her feet and shouted after her. 'What would Martin want you to do?'

14

The unmade road disappeared into a rocky crater full of rainwater. Angela Tate skirted around the perimeter and leapt over the final lump of rubble, her raincoat flapping open to reveal eight inches of leg between the top of her boots and the bottom of her skirt. A lone wolf-whistle echoed around the muddy yard. She looked up to see a yellow-vested builder balancing precariously on an eight-foot high stack of house bricks. He made a clucking sound through puckered lips and only narrowly missed a palette of bricks swinging towards him on the extended platform of a forklift truck.

'You want to keep you mind on the job,' she shouted up at him.

'Can't get my mind off it, darlin',' he shouted back.

Years ago she would have told him where to shove his 'darlin', but these days she tended to save her feminist battles for more worthy causes. The load of bricks crashed onto the stack.

'Watch it, Roman!'

His voice was carried away by the wind as Angela picked her way through the slalom of breezeblocks and bags of cement to get to the main reception block. The building was really no more than an extended Portakabin. According to the glossy brochure she'd flicked through on the train, the structure in front of her was the 'international head-quarters' of Larson and Co. But in reality the cab from the station had delivered her to a glorified builder's yard in an Essex backwater. The only thing remotely international about it was its proximity to Stansted Airport, 30 miles up the M11.

She skipped up the concrete steps and pushed open the door to find a vinegar-faced receptionist sitting at a low desk on one side of a shabby little room. The woman continued to tap noisily on a computer keyboard, eventually glancing up when Angela was leaning over her desk.

'I'm—'

'Late,' the woman said, barely opening her mouth.

'The cab got lost on the way here.'

'It's highly unlikely Lady Larson will be able to squeeze you into her schedule now, Miss Tate.'

'But I'm only ten minutes late.'

'You can take a seat and wait – but you might be wasting your time.' The woman vaguely gestured to a row of vinyl-covered chairs lined up against a wall.

Angela peered through an archway opposite the entrance. 'Valerie Larson's office just down here, is it?' She took a step towards the long corridor.

'Please! Just take a seat.'

Angela hesitated in the middle of the room, contemplating a reckless dash down the corridor, bursting into the acting CEO's office and persuading her to 'squeeze' her in right now. The receptionist cleared her throat theatrically. Angela decided to give it ten minutes then reassess her doorstepping options. She grabbed a magazine from a chipped laminate coffee table and sat down.

After five minutes of flicking through a dog-eared copy of *Construction News* Angela's phone rang. Relieved to have something to do, she snatched the white Sony Ericsson from her bag.

'It's me.'

Angela peered at the number on the screen, worked out who 'me' was and held a hand over her mouth.

'What can you tell me?' Angela kept her eyes on the receptionist, who seemed to be glancing at her every few seconds.

'Nothing you want to hear. No one's admitting evidence has gone walkabout. They counted 32 boxes in, and there's still 32 boxes in storage.'

'What about the two disappearing police officers?'

'PC Mills's transfer to CID had been in the pipeline for a while and there's a medical report confirming the female officer slipped a disc.'

Angela sighed.

'Anything else you want me to check?'

'I'll let you know.' Angela turned away from the receptionist's prying eyes. 'Have you been paid this month?'

'Yep – no problems. Your paper's regular as clockwork. Wish I could say the same for my other clients.' He hung up.

Angela put her phone away, aware the receptionist was still looking at her. She got up and stood over the desk again.

'Could you buzz through to Lady Larson? Remind her I'm still here?'

'I can't do that,' she said. 'Lady Larson is expecting an important phone call. I have to keep the line free.'

'You're telling me there's only one phone line? Can't you just call her mobile?'

'Please take a seat.'

'How much longer will I have to wait?'

'I can reschedule for another day.' The suggestion of a smile flickered across the receptionist's lips. 'Lady Larson may have a window some time next month.'

'This is ridiculous.'

'Here at Larson's we take punctuality very seriously.'

'Not to mention your own self-importance,' Angela muttered under her breath. She was just turning back to her seat when the main entrance door flew open. A construction worker rushed in and almost knocked her off her feet.

'Jesus!' He looked her up and down accusingly, as if she'd just crashed into him, then promptly ignored her. 'We need a hand, Shirley. Can you come out to the yard? It's bloody awful this time...' He glanced over his shoulder at Angela and lowered his voice. 'We've got a... situation. Be good to have your...'

'Input?' the receptionist offered.

'That's it – yeah. Can you come right now?'

Shirley looked up at Angela, who was still on her feet.

'Don't mind me,' she said, backing away towards the line of chairs. 'There's at least three issues of *Builders' Monthly* I haven't had chance to read.'

The receptionist logged off of her computer and locked the first of three filing cabinets behind her desk. She grabbed a hard hat and yellow vest from a coat stand, and threw Angela a warning look before disappearing through the door.

Angela sat patiently on the uncomfortable vinyl seat for a minute or so before jumping up. She peered out into the yard and saw no sign of Shirley or the construction worker. The 'situation' must have been happening somewhere else on the site. She made her way to the filing cabinets and tugged on the top drawers of the second and third cabinets – they were both locked, just like the first. She scanned the desk. A neat pen pot stuffed with biros and perfectly sharpened pencils was the obvious hiding place for a spare key. Angela shook the contents of the pot onto the desk. No key tumbled out. She shoved back the pens and pencils, but couldn't manage to fit everything in, so scooped up the excess and dropped it into the bin under the desk. She tested the desk drawers. They too were locked. Shirley the receptionist was extra-ordinarily security conscious, which could only mean she had something worth hiding.

Angela grabbed her handbag from the chair, checked outside the main entrance again, then ventured down the long corridor. She ignored a series of closed plywood doors on either side and headed straight for the wide oak one at the far end. At head height the door was decorated with a large gold plaque, the words *CEO, Lady Valerie Larson* engraved in large letters. According to a company press release, Valerie Larson had officially taken over the reins from her ailing husband only last week. She certainly hadn't wasted any time making herself at home. Angela held her breath, listening for movement on the other side of the door. She reached for the handle and stopped. A loud ringtone erupted from inside the room.

'About bloody time!' The shrill voice of Valerie Larson permeated the thick oak.

Angela hesitated. If she pressed her ear against the wood, she'd be turning her back on the reception at the other end of the corridor. Her position would be completely exposed.

'For God's sake!' The voice rang out again.

Angela leaned her cheek gently against the door.

'This isn't good enough, Bill.' Valerie Larson sounded decidedly irritated.

'How many more favours are you expecting?' Her voice was getting louder.

Angela could hear castors rolling over the wooden floor, then heavy footsteps as Valerie Larson stamped around the room.

'You can't fob us off with that promise anymore. We've gone beyond that now. A line has been crossed. Do you understand me?'

The sound of footsteps got louder; Valerie Larson was just the other side of the door. Angela tensed and pulled away. She held her breath then heard the footsteps retreating.

'But can't you see?' Valerie Larson said. 'We're running out of time.'

Angela waited, five, ten seconds without breathing. There wasn't a sound. She risked leaning against the door again, but all she could hear was an occasional muttered 'yes', 'no', and the odd 'hmm'. Whoever was on the other end of the line had managed to cool Valerie Larson's temper. Angela took the opportunity to snatch a few breaths and relax her clenched fists.

A loud creak, followed by bang, echoed down the corridor. Angela turned to see the reception door swinging open, Shirley standing in the doorway, facing away from her, looking out into the yard. Angela stepped away from Valerie Larson's door, backing up a few feet towards the reception, keeping her eyes fixed on the woman coming in. Shirley started to turn. Angela looked left and right at the closed doors on either side of the corridor.

'What do you think you're doing down there?' the receptionist hollered.

There was nowhere to run. Angela swiftly turned and marched back towards Valerie Larson's office. She thumped the thick oak panel with one hand and turned the handle with the other and flung open the door. Valerie Larson spun around, her mobile phone still fixed to her ear.

'What the…?'

The room was lined with large wooden filing cabinets. A bank of CCTV monitors filled the wall space opposite a large desk at the far end. It looked more like a military control centre than the headquarters of a construction company.

'Lady Larson.' Angela moved swiftly into the room. 'I'm your 2:30!'

'Who let you in here?'

'Shirley had to leave – an emergency, I gather – she told me to come straight through.'

'Look, I've got to go.' Valerie Larson threw the phone onto the desk and glared at Angela. 'I don't have time for this now – we'll have to reschedule Ms…'

'Tate. Please, call me Angela.' She skipped neatly around the desk and held out her hand just as Shirley arrived at the door, trailing a security guard behind her.

'I'm so sorry, Lady Larson. She had no right to come—'

'Get her out of here,' Valerie Larson snapped at her.

'Surely you've got a moment?' Angela edged sideways, putting the sturdy desk between her and the approaching guard. 'Or perhaps Sir Fred could give me a few minutes of his time?'

'Out of the question!'

The lumbering guard was only a few feet away.

'How about a brief comment on your husband's plans for a radical curriculum at his new academy?'

A thick-fingered hand landed on Angela's arm. She tried to pull away, but the grip tightened. 'Unless you want to be up to your eyeballs in litigation, I suggest you call your thug off.'

Valerie Larson glared at her.

'Do you really want to worry your husband with legal action when he's so ill?'

Valerie Larson gave the briefest of nods to the guard. He removed his hand.

'Where was I?' Angela said, rubbing her arm. 'Oh yes – a comment on how creationism fits into the curriculum, for the good people of Lewisham, Lady Larson.'

'My husband's beliefs are nothing to do with you.'

A moaning siren started up in the distance.

'But they do concern a number of anxious parents,' Angela said.

The siren wail intensified.

'I have nothing to say to you. If you don't leave right now… Shirley – call the police.'

Angela stared right into Larson's face, not budging an inch. 'Sounds as if someone has beaten you to it.'

15

Pam was towering over Caroline's desk, coat buttoned, arms hugging her enormous bosom. 'Come on, I'll walk you to the bus stop.'

Caroline glanced at the clock: 6:02pm. Pam should have been long gone.

Pam reached over to Caroline's computer. 'Turn that thing off.'

Caroline hastily shielded the power button with her hand. 'I don't need babysitting, Pam.'

'Jeremy's asked me to keep an eye on you.'

'He's what?' Caroline glanced at her boss's office. It was empty. 'Really Pam, I'm perfectly OK.' She ran her fingers over the tiny rectangular bulge in her trouser pocket, checking the memory stick she'd borrowed from Dan was still there.

'Jeremy thought you might be difficult to persuade.'

He did?

'I'm under strict instructions not to take no for an answer.'

'Please, Pam.'

'I'm not listening.'

'I've got things to finish up.' *And documents to steal.*

'I'll wait.' Pam reached for a chair and wheeled it over next to Caroline's.

'OK then, maybe you can help.' Caroline pulled a thick sheaf of papers from her in tray and offered them to Pam. 'This lot shouldn't take us more than a couple of hours – if we work at it together.'

Pam's eyes widened. She held up a hand. 'I wouldn't want to mess up your paperwork and ruin your system.' She backed away from the desk. 'Promise me you'll leave before eight.'

Caroline watched Pam scurry out of the office. She waited another few minutes, calculating how long it would take for the lift to arrive and carry Pam down to the ground floor.

She had waited all day for the right moment, but every time she took the memory stick from her pocket, a colleague would wander over to her desk, or the phone would start ringing.

She glanced round the office, checking she was quite alone, and shoved the memory stick in the slot of her desktop PC. She stared at the little yellow light, flashing like a beacon, suddenly unsure about what she was doing.

The previous evening she'd arrived home feeling grubby after her meeting with Angela Tate. The guilt crept over her like an itch. She couldn't face Pete or the kids, convinced the confession she'd blurted out to the journalist about Martin would somehow show on her face. How could she ever have admitted it? *To a bloody journalist.*

The light on the stick stopped flashing and a new window popped up on her monitor. She took a deep breath, grabbed her mouse, opened up Explorer and quickly navigated to the academy division's directory on the departmental network.

A sudden noise startled her. It took a moment to recognise the shrill ringtone of her phone. She exhaled and grabbed the bleeping mobile from her desk. It was Tate.

'Is it done?'

Caroline glanced around the office again. 'I'm doing it now.' She hadn't meant to whisper. She heard people shouting on the other end of the line. 'Where are you? What's going on there?'

'Look, I've got to go. I'll call you later.'

Caroline threw the phone into her bag. She double-clicked a folder in the branching tree structure displayed on her monitor and drilled down to the 'expressions of interest' documents. All the correspondence from business people, education trusts and religious organisations that had ever taken an interest in founding an academy was stored here. It was the first thing Tate had asked for. Caroline dragged the folder over to the memory stick's window and watched the animated paper icon somersaulting across the screen. While it was copying, she moved on to all the specific documents relating to Fred Larson's three academies. Tate must have known there would be sensitive financial information in those files, the sort of details a freedom of information request would never uncover. The sort of information Caroline could lose her job over. She dragged across the Larson folder and sat back. That much data would take a while to copy. She took a moment to concentrate on her breathing and tried her best to unlock the tangled muscles in her shoulders.

A metallic clank echoed through the stillness of the office. Caroline pushed back her chair and rushed towards the direction of the noise.

'Hello?' she hollered through the door leading out into the lobby. Her voice bounced back off the marble and glass. 'Is there anyone there?' No reply. She waited a moment longer then let go of the door and hurried back to her desk, relieved to find everything as she'd left it. Her palms were moist.

Keep it together.

The copying process finally completed. Caroline moved on to the next two items Tate had requested: the financials for the construction of every single academy and the accounts for each one in its first three years of operation. Hundreds of academies had opened in the last ten years. The information for each individual academy was located in a separate folder. She opened another branch in the directory, drilled down to the first academy and found the sub folder containing the financial records. She repeated the process for the next academy, and the one after that. It was public knowledge that most academy projects went over budget, some by millions of pounds. Tate's request for a record of every balance sheet seemed a little extreme. Caroline scrolled down the list and decided there were just too many folders to drill down into each one. Instead, she dragged the folder containing the whole lot onto the stick. Tate could pick out the relevant documents herself.

Ten minutes later the last of the files copied over. Caroline rubbed her eyes. As far as she could remember, there were only two more items to find. One of them would be much harder to track down than the other.

Tate had asked for a list of nominations for honours going back five years. Nomination requests were handled by another division – not Caroline's area of expertise at all. She wasn't even sure she could get into that section of the network. In the last ten years no journalist had ever managed to establish an unequivocal link between academy sponsorship and the promise of knighthoods and peerages; it was unlikely Angela Tate could make anything stick, even with the information she'd asked for. Caroline decided to leave the nomination request until last and move on to the remaining item on Tate's wish list: procurement.

A phone started ringing at the other end of the office and Caroline jumped. It stopped and another started up on the next bank of desks. The system had been set to automatically divert incoming calls. Eventually it would transfer to her section. She grabbed her handset and punched in a number to pick up the call. She made the standard department greeting and waited.

'Hello?'

There was a crackle of static for a few moments followed by the dial tone.

What were they playing at?

Caroline checked her watch. It was much later than she thought. Ed Wallis would have started his rounds by now and could turn up at any moment. She hurriedly navigated through the directory to the procurement folder. Tate had asked for a list of all the companies who'd won academy contracts worth over £100,000, going right back to the beginning of the programme. Again, there was just too much information to sift through each folder individually, so she dragged the whole folder to the stick. The copying process would probably take at least five minutes to complete. Caroline settled back in her seat and watched the flying icon, still trying to relax and let her mind go blank as the little page spun across the screen.

Someone cleared their throat behind her. She closed her eyes.

She hadn't been quick enough.

'For God's sake, Ed! How many times do I have to tell you?' She spun round in her chair, ready to give the security guard an earful. But it wasn't Ed. 'Jeremy!' She forced a smile.

Suddenly the noise of the hard drive chugging away behind her seemed deafening. How long had he been there?

'I'm sorry,' she said. 'I thought you were someone else.'

'Clearly.' He was smiling, but the network of lines on his forehead bunched in a tangle between in his perfectly groomed eyebrows.

Caroline desperately wanted to glance back at her screen, to see what he could see, but didn't dare.

'Still burning the midnight oil, even in the run-up to an election?' he said.

'It's not that late!' There was an undisguisable tremor in her voice. 'There's still plenty to do.'

'I told Pamela to keep an eye on you.'

'She only left a little while ago. I practically had to shove her out the door.'

Prior lowered himself onto the edge of the desk behind hers and scrutinised her face. 'Still no progress?' He nodded towards her monitor.

'I'm sorry?' She felt a drip of sweat trickle between her breasts.

'The missing CD-ROM, Caroline. It is meant to be your top priority.'

'It is. That's why I'm here now – catching up on my other work.'

'It's been two weeks.' He folded his arms. 'I have to say, I am rather disappointed by your lack of results.'

'It's not for the want of trying. We've interviewed everyone in the division. Most people didn't even know it existed. There's no way they'd have a clue where it is now.'

'You can't believe everything people tell you, Caroline. Not everyone is as honest as you.' He smiled at her with one corner of his mouth. Or was it a sneer?

'It's really awkward,' she said. 'I feel like I'm interrogating my colleagues, accusing them of something. I'm sure none of them knows anything.'

'Pamela doesn't share your unstinting faith in human nature. She's quite convinced someone has screwed up and is covering their tracks.'

'But who would—?'

'I tend to agree with her. You should interview everyone again. You need to be a little tougher with them this time.'

Caroline drew in a breath.

Tougher? Why don't you interview them yourself?

'Whatever you think is best.' She stood up, hoping to completely obscure her boss's view of the computer monitor. 'I'll start first thing in the morning.' She folded her arms, mirroring his pose. 'I'm just about finished here.'

'Don't let me stop you.' He made no attempt to move. He dropped his head to one side and pursed his lips. 'Pamela's certainly right about one thing – you are looking very tired. What about taking a couple of days off. Recharge your batteries?'

Cheeky bloody bastard.

'I'm perfectly fine.' She pointed at her face. 'This is the result of three kids. It doesn't get any better with a good night's sleep, believe me.'

'Only trying to help.' He levered himself off the desk.

Please go.

'Taking more work home with you?' He nodded at the memory stick jutting out of the desktop computer, its little light flickering.

Caroline's stomach lurched. Slowly, she followed his gaze, feigning incomprehension, playing for time.

'Oh that.' She hadn't managed to sound as casual as she'd hoped. 'Just copying something.'

'Really? Not state secrets I hope?'

Her hands felt numb. She managed an unconvincing laugh. 'Hardly.'

For Christ's sake – think of something!

'Tracy took some photos of the baby while she was here. We all had a little cuddle and said cheese. I'm just copying them onto a stick so I can show my mum. They're too big to email.'

As he continued to stare at the stick, Caroline edged closer to her monitor, putting as much of herself between it and Prior as she could.

'I'd like to see them.' He took a step towards her.

'Sure – not right now though, if you don't mind. I really want to get going. Like you say – midnight oil and all that.'

He took another step and stopped, his face just inches away, his eyes burrowing into hers. 'I'll say goodnight then.'

'Yes – cheerio, Jeremy. See you in the morning. I'll come in early – make a start on that interviewing.'

She watched him walk slowly to his office. He threw her a look before he went inside. She let out a long, snagging breath.

Please God he didn't see anything.

16

Caroline closed the front door behind her and leaned against it. She looked down at her hands – they were still shaking. Minty bounded through the kitchen door and leapt up at her. She grabbed the dog's ears and pushed her back down.

'Not now, girl.'

Minty whined a complaint.

'Mum!' Caroline threw her bag on the hall table and wriggled out of her jacket. 'Claire?' She hurried to the kitchen, the dog trailing behind her. An envelope was propped up against the kettle, Jean's handwriting scrawled across the back.

> Caroline
> Left message with ditsy girl – Vera Vague? – in your office. Not convinced you'll get it. Your mobile's switched off.
>
> Last minute emergency flash mob call – I'll be back late. Don't wait up.
> Mum x
>
> PS Ben @ Thomas's for tea/Claire revising @ Louise's/Dan – don't know/Pete – yr guess as gd as
> PPS Minty prob needs walking

'Great.' Caroline yanked open the fridge and pulled a bottle of wine from the door. The dog yelped a non-committal bark. 'Just you and me, girl.' She poured herself a glass and sat down at the kitchen table. 'Drink first then W-A-L-K.'

Minty's tail thumped the floor.

'When did you learn to spell?' She grabbed the dog's ear and tugged it. 'Clever girl.'

Caroline took a sip of wine. It was harsh and acidic on her tongue. 'The first time I feel like getting properly drunk. Typical.' She emptied the glass into the sink and watched the dog disappear into the hall. Minty came back seconds later carrying her lead in her mouth.

'In a minute, Mint.'

She pulled the memory stick from her pocket and weighed it in her hand. It was warm. She placed it carefully on the table and pushed it away with an index finger. 'It's a big step I've taken, Mint.' She shook her head. 'A giant leap.'

The dog thumped her tail again in reply.

Caroline jumped up and fetched her handbag from the hall. She grabbed her mobile from the inner recesses and tapped in Angela Tate's number. The call went straight to voicemail. Again. She'd tried her three or four times on her way home from the department. She just wanted to talk to someone. Why wasn't Tate picking up?

'Bigger fish to fry – eh Minty?'

The dog whined. Then she barked and scampered into the hall. The front door opened and slammed shut. Caroline heard the unmistakable tread of a 14-year-old boy trundling up the stairs.

'Hello, Dan!' she hollered. 'I'm in the kitchen.'

Dan grunted something back and carried on up the stairs. She heard his bedroom door crash against its frame.

'And good evening to you too, dearest Mother.' She checked her watch – not yet 8:30pm. It was the first time Dan had got home before 10pm all week.

Minty nudged her lead across the floor with her nose.

'Later girl – I promise.'

Caroline left the dog in the kitchen, quickly climbed the stairs and stood outside Dan's bedroom, listening for signs of life. She tapped lightly on the door and stepped back, staring at the *Keep Out* sign. Above it was a bright orange Hazchem symbol that had replaced the yellow and black radioactivity warning. Maybe she could find him a *Biohazard* sign to add to his collection. God only knew how many new forms of life were growing in the trainers at the bottom of his wardrobe. She knocked again, more forcefully.

'Who is it?'

'It's me, Dan. Have you got a minute? Can I come in?' She heard another grunt, not unlike one of Minty's, and the door opened a crack.

'What is it? I'm a bit busy.'

'We haven't really seen one another for ages. I suppose I just wanted some intelligent conversation.'

'Isn't that what Claire's for?'

'Claire's out tonight.'

'So I'm second best, am I?'

'You know that's not what I meant.'

'Can't you speak to Gran?'

'Your Gran's out... flash mobbing. Can I not talk to my number one son without a major inquisition?'

'OK – as long as it's quick.' Dan walked away from the door but left it open. 'And painless.'

'Good grief, Dan. You make it sound like humane animal slaughter.'

'Whatever.'

Caroline stepped gingerly into the room, trying not to judge, trying not to breathe in through her nose. She lowered herself tentatively onto the edge of his unmade bed, clasping her hands together to resist the urge to plump the pillow and straighten the duvet.

'Are you OK?' Dan asked.

'Me? Course. I'm always OK.'

'You look a bit weird.'

'Thanks a lot.' She looked down at her hands and untangled her fingers. 'No. I'm great, me. I thought we could have a bite to eat together. What do you fancy?'

'Not hungry.'

'Well that's got to be a first. I wish I had a tape recorder, get that down on record.'

'If you're going to take the p—, the mickey, maybe you should just leave.'

'I'm sorry. You're not hungry – fine. I'll order pizza just for me then, shall I?'

Dan shrugged. 'I'm going out, anyway.'

'Out? You've only just got in. Where are you going?'

'Just out.'

'It's a school night. You can't go out again.'

Dan's mobile started to flash and vibrate on his desk. He grabbed the phone, stabbed it silent and shoved it in a pocket.

'Anyone important?'

'Private.'

Caroline bit her lip. 'Of course – I didn't mean to intrude.'

Dan started swinging on his chair, the central spindle creaking with every partial rotation.

'We should get some WD40 on that. I'll tell your dad.'

'Doesn't bother me.'

After her confrontation with Prior, all Caroline wanted to do was reach out to another human being. Connect with someone. She was beginning to think Minty would have been a better bet. 'So... what have you been up to? How's school?'

He shrugged again, turned back to his laptop and tapped out an instant message. Caroline tried not to read it, but couldn't stop herself peering over his shoulder anyway. He turned suddenly and caught her trying to make sense of the consonant-only words of textspeak. Her cheeks flushed instantly like someone turning on a two bar electric fire.

'I'm not prying – it's just a normal reaction, isn't it? To read whatever's in front of you.' She had a sudden, awful memory of Jeremy Prior trying to look at her monitor in the office. She sucked in a quick breath and tried to recover. 'The number of cereal packets I've read over the years while you ate your breakfast...' She smiled. 'I can tell you the mineral and vitamin contents of a Coco Pop, no trouble.'

Dan slammed shut the lid of his laptop.

'I'm really sorry – I honestly didn't see anything. I don't want you to think...' She sighed, the nervous energy she'd been trying to control finally leaking out of her. Her shoulders sagged.

'You sure you're OK?' Dan said, and placed a hand on her arm.

She looked down at his bony knuckles. She couldn't remember the last time he'd voluntarily touched her.

'I'm completely fine. Just a bit stressed at work. The usual. Bor—ring!' She got up, reckoning she shouldn't outstay her welcome if she ever expected to gain entry to Dan's room again. She knew a hug was out of the question, so she squeezed his shoulder as she walked past. He winced. She looked down at the small patch of flesh visible above the neckline of his baggy t-shirt. A purple and yellow bruise bloomed outwards from his neck.

'What happened?' she said, failing to keep the alarm from her voice.

'S'nothing.'

'Dan!'

'A rugby tackle – no bigs.'

'No what? And since when have you played rugby?'

He shrugged her hand away.

'Dan!'

Her mobile started to ring downstairs.

'Tell me how that happened.'

'It was an accident. I was just in the wrong place at the wrong time.'

'I thought you said it was a rugby tackle.'

'It was... it is. God Mum, drop it, will you?'

She hesitated at his door.

'If I find out you're lying to me, I'll...'

'What?'

She stepped into the hall, desperate to get to the phone before her voicemail picked up the call. She had to speak to Tate.

'I'll take your laptop away.'

'You can't do that.'

'Just watch me.'

Dan snatched his MacBook from the desk and wrapped his arms protectively around it. Caroline wagged a finger at him. 'I mean it, Dan.'

She ran across the landing and threw herself down the stairs, holding onto the banister rail, her feet skimming the edges of each step. She snatched up the phone and jabbed the answer button.

'Mrs Barber?' A woman's voice, but not one she recognised. Definitely not Tate.

'Yes, speaking.'

'Good evening, Mrs Barber. I'm calling from Mayflower Hospital.'

Caroline grabbed the back of a kitchen chair, her legs suddenly unable to support her bodyweight.

Please God let Ben and Claire be all right.

She swallowed. 'What's happened?'

'It's your mother, er... a Mrs Jean Henderson?'

Caroline closed her eyes. *Now what?*

'Hello... are you still there?'

'Yes, yes I'm here.'

'It's really nothing to worry about. But we will be keeping her in overnight. We would have called you sooner, but we've had quite a few casualties to deal with.'

Caroline took a breath. 'A few? I don't understand. Has there been a bus crash or something?'

'No – nothing like that.'

Caroline grabbed her bag and lifted the car key from the hook by the kitchen door. 'Mayflower Hospital did you say? I don't know it. Where are you?'

'Goodmayes.'

Caroline was still none the wiser.

'In Essex,' the woman said.

Essex?

She ran into the hall and yanked her jacket from the stair post just as Dan was clattering down the stairs.

'Where do you think you're going?' she said.

'I told you – out.'

'You can take Minty for a walk, then you're coming straight back.'

'I've made arrangements.'

'Well you can unmake them.'

'Hello... Mrs Barber?' Caroline had forgotten she was still connected.

'I'm sorry. I'm still here.'

Dan opened the front door.

'Hold it right there.' Caroline shoved a hand against the door and shut it again. 'Overnight, you said?' She slid between Dan and the door.

'Yes – perhaps you could bring her some night things, nightdress, toiletries, that sort of thing?'

'You still haven't told me what happened.'

'It's not clear at present.'

'But it's bad enough that she has to spend a night in hospital?'

'It's just a precaution.'

'Against what?'

Dan reached up a long arm for the door latch. Caroline waved her hand at him and mouthed the word 'laptop'. He stepped away.

'It's normal procedure...' The woman hesitated.

'What aren't you telling me?'

'Really – there's no need for you to worry. It's just something we always do with head injuries.'

17

By the time Caroline reached her mother's bedside, Jean was in the midst of an animated conversation with two police officers, waving her arms around, occasionally grabbing a uniformed sleeve when she wanted to make a point more forcefully. Her head was wrapped in a thick white bandage from her eyebrows to the crown. A lock of tinted blonde hair poked from an airhole at the very top. Caroline approached the little group and stopped at the foot of the bed. Eventually Jean paused to take a breath and spotted her.

'What are you doing skulking down there?'

Caroline inched up to the side of the bed and nodded and smiled at the two policemen.

'Did you see my note?' Jean asked. 'About Claire and Ben. Are they here?'

'Claire's picking Ben up from his friend's and taking him home.'

'Is that a good idea?'

'You know Claire. She's sensible. Besides, Pete'll be home soon.'

'Oh, has he left already?'

Caroline glanced at the police officers, put a hand over her mother's and squeezed. She lowered her voice. 'Pete's not here, Mum. I came with Dan. He's sitting in the car sulking, keeping Minty company. Do you want to see him?'

'Pete's gone home? Without even coming in to say hello?'

'No, Mum. You're getting confused.' Caroline glanced around the ward, hoping to spot a doctor to speak to. Her mother's injury was obviously more serious than they'd led her to believe.

'I'm *not* confused. I saw his van.'

'It must have been another white van – they do all look the same.'

'I've had a bang on the head, Caroline. I haven't completely lost my senses.'

Caroline let out a breath. This wasn't getting her anywhere. She lifted the bag she was carrying and waved it in front of her mother's face. 'I brought you in a few odds and sods. Should I get you something to drink? Are you hungry?'

'If you want to make yourself useful. You can get these lovely boys a cup of tea.'

The two constables smiled apologetically at Caroline, insisted they were fine and told her not to bother.

'I won't be much longer,' Jean said. 'I've just got to tell these nice young men what happened while it's still fresh in my mind. Amnesia could set in at any moment.' She turned back to the policemen. 'Now… what was I saying?'

Having been dismissed from Jean's bedside, Caroline wandered into the corridor. She spotted a man listing slightly on a hard plastic chair. It was one of her mother's cronies from the action group. What was his name – Alfred? Arthur? Something old-fashioned and vaguely royal. He saw her and tried to get up. He didn't quite make it. She sat down next to him.

'I saw it all,' he said, quietly. 'Shocking, it was. Just shocking.'

He seemed genuinely shaken, his face whiter than his hair.

'Are you all right?' Caroline said, putting a hand on his sinewy arm. 'Should I get a nurse?'

'Heavens no! I'm perfectly fine.'

'What about a cup of tea then?'

Caroline helped him to his feet and they progressed slowly to the little café concession by the main entrance. It seemed to take all of the old man's powers of concentration to put one foot in front of the other – he didn't have the energy to walk and talk at the same time. Caroline found herself filling the awkward silence with mindless small talk that didn't require any contribution from him.

When they finally reached the café, the woman behind the counter was wiping down surfaces, the metal shutter already pulled down half way. Caroline helped her mother's friend – Albert, it turned out – to a chair and approached the counter. The woman let out a noisy sigh and looked at her watch. Then she looked over at Albert who was smiling back at her.

'I should have closed five minutes back,' she said. 'Your dad not well?'

'My dad?' Caroline glanced at Albert. 'He's not…' The image of her father the last time she saw him forced its way into her mind. He died looking as thin and white as Albert did now, in a hospital not unlike this one. She managed to shake the thought free and cleared her throat.

'Actually we're here for my mum. She's in A&E.'

The woman smiled sympathetically. 'Falls can be really nasty at their age.'

108

'Oh it wasn't...' Caroline thought better of explaining how her mother was more of a street-fighting anarchist than a frail broken-hipped OAP, and just smiled instead.

'The coffee machine's off now,' the woman behind the counter said, 'but there's still tea left in the pot.' She looked at Albert again. 'He'll be wanting plenty of sugar, I'd imagine. Poor soul.'

'I do appreciate it.' Caroline got her purse from her handbag and the woman waved it away.

'You sit down – I'll bring them over.'

Caroline shuffled a chair closer to Albert's. 'What a fine mess!' she said. 'Arrested one week, hospitalised the next. What am I going to do with her?'

'She's just doing her bit. For the good of the community. We need more people like Jean in the world. It would be a much better place if we did.'

Caroline baulked at the thought of an army of Jean Hendersons storming barricades and overthrowing governments.

'I know she's very committed to the cause,' she said, silently wishing her mother had chosen a different cause entirely. She suspected Jean had latched on to academies just to wind her up.

The woman carried over two teas in cardboard cups and a couple of flapjacks on a tray. 'Near their sell-by date,' she explained, depositing the contents of the tray on the table. 'I have to shut up now, so just put the empties in the bin.' She gestured to a recycling point.

'Thanks again,' Caroline said, but the woman had already turned away.

'You were saying just now you saw everything.' Caroline ripped open the cellophane wrapper of a flapjack and took a large bite of oats and golden syrup. She hadn't realised how hungry she was.

Albert nodded slowly. 'It was an organised attack. I've seen that sort of thing before.'

'Really?' Caroline took another bite.

'I do have some experience. I was at Suez – '56.' He stared down at his tea, but didn't touch it. 'They came forward in a line, in formation, Larson's hooligans, hit out at anyone who got in their way. Pushed back the crowd either side of the road until there was enough space for Lady Larson to escape in her Rolls Royce.'

'And Mum got hit on the head in the confusion?' Caroline popped the last of the flapjack in her mouth and stared longingly at the other one.

'Oh it wasn't an accident. They went for her.'

'They what?'

'She's the most vocal protestor. It's part of the strategy – take out the leader of a group, and the group disintegrates. We used the same technique in the army.'

'Wait – are you saying one of the security people deliberately attacked Mum?'

Albert nodded.

'They hit her over the head?'

'Not exactly.' He picked up his cup, held it mid-air for a moment then put it down again. 'Two of them ran at her. She lost her balance and fell awkwardly, she hit her head on the way down.'

'Have you told the police what you saw?'

'I'm just waiting for them to ask me.'

'Perhaps I can have a word with them for you.'

'I'm not incapable.'

'No – of course not.'

Caroline stared into space for a moment, trying hard to take it all in. 'I had no idea she was going anywhere today. This all happened at Fred Larson's head office?'

'We didn't know ourselves until the last minute. There was a cancellation at the coach hire company – Jean knows the proprietor. He called her at lunchtime.'

Caroline blinked. Why couldn't her mother organise coach trips to Southend and Eastbourne, like any other normal pensioner? She took a sip of tea. It was so sweet it made the flapjack taste like a sugar-free health snack.

Albert shook his head. 'You put a thug in a luminous yellow vest, and suddenly he thinks he can do what he likes. They're animals.' He sniffed. 'If they've done any permanent damage to that dear sweet woman... they'll have me to contend with.'

It took Caroline a moment to realise he was still talking about her mother. It hadn't occurred to her before that Albert was quite so ardent in his admiration of Jean. Suddenly she felt defensive, seeing Albert in a completely new light. Not a harmless old man at all, but an insidious interloper. Her dad had been gone nearly five years, but it still seemed far too soon for some suitor to be sniffing around. She bristled, snatched the remaining flapjack from the table and shoved it in her bag. 'We should probably be getting back,' she said, and reached a hand under Albert's arm.

'I'm perfectly capable of getting up under my own steam. Thank you.'

She watched him struggle, leaning heavily on the table to lever himself up. She scooped up the teas and left them at the recycling point, the cartons too full to throw in the bin.

Caroline led the way back to A&E, slowing every few steps to allow Albert to catch up. Halfway down the corridor she stopped. A familiar figure dressed in a black raincoat and leather boots was hurrying through the exit. Caroline glanced over her shoulder. Albert was still a few yards behind her. Tempting as it was to leave him in the corridor, she retraced her steps and hooked her arm through his. He leaned his weight into her and they picked up pace.

Having safely deposited Albert on the chair where she'd found him, promising she would be right back, Caroline rushed out of the A&E department. An April evening chill had set in. She dragged her thin jacket across her chest and scanned the forecourt for Angela Tate. She spotted her standing at the edge of a huddle of uniformed paramedics and nurses, a cloud of cigarette smoke hanging in the air above their heads. She headed across the forecourt towards them.

'Gone back to the evil weed, I see,' she said.

Tate turned quickly and peered into her face. It seemed to take her a moment to make out Caroline's face in the gathering gloom and then another to register who she was. 'It's my first of the day.'

'Are you here for the same reason as my mother?'

'Your mother?'

'Jean Henderson – you interviewed her a fortnight ago. After she was arrested?'

'Yes, of course. How is Jean? She's a game old bird.' She looked Caroline up and down, as if she was comparing her to her mother and deciding she didn't measure up. 'I'd like to have a word with her, if she's up to it.'

'She's giving a statement to the police. And dealing with the effects of concussion. Did you see what happened?'

Tate took a long pull on her cigarette. 'It was all over so quickly.' She tilted her head back and exhaled, blowing smoke upwards from the corner of her mouth, narrowing her eyes. 'I didn't see anything I'd be prepared to testify about in court – put it that way. I wasn't in the actual melee itself.' She dropped the cigarette on the ground and stubbed it out, adding to the collection of butts already scattered across the concrete. 'Whereas Frank – my photographer – was right in the middle of the action. He got hit in the face. A few stitches, nothing serious. I think he quite likes the idea of a battle scar. No doubt he'll make up some story about being under enemy fire in Iraq or Afghanistan.'

The two women looked at one another for a moment and said nothing.

'I left you a message,' Caroline said.

Tate stuck a hand in her pocket and retrieved a phone, held it at arm's length, screwing up her eyes to focus on the tiny screen. 'Seems I have quite a few.' She shoved the phone back in her pocket and grabbed Caroline's arm, guiding her gently away from the group of medics. 'Did you get it?'

Caroline slipped a hand into the front pocket of her trousers. It was empty. A surge of panic rose up from her chest. She quickly patted all her other pockets before remembering she'd put the memory stick on the kitchen table. *Please God it's still there.*

'I don't have it on me now.'

'Oh.' Tate withdrew her arm from Caroline's. 'But you managed to get everything I asked for?'

Caroline let out a breath and looked down at her feet.

'Oh please don't tell me you didn't!'

'My boss caught me.'

'What?'

'I'm not sure how much he saw. I've been worrying about it all evening.'

'Great – that's all we need.'

'Do you know how much of a risk I was taking?'

Tate bit her lip.

'I could lose my job – or worse.'

The journalist pulled a pack of cigarettes from her bag and lit one.

'I copied everything except the honours nominations.'

'Great – only one of the most crucial bits of information.' Tate marched away.

'This isn't easy for me, you know.' Caroline shouted at Tate's back, waiting for her to turn round. Tate continued smoking her cigarette and ignored her. 'I'm not actually doing this for you.' She was determined to stand her ground. 'What's so important about the nominations anyway?'

Tate hurried back over to her. 'For God's sake keep your voice down.' She pointed towards the group of smokers, which now included the two policemen who'd been interviewing Jean.

Caroline waved at them and smiled, then turned back to Tate. 'I'm doing this for Martin.' She lowered her voice. 'What have you managed to dig up so far?'

Tate extinguished her cigarette under the toe of a boot. 'I've got a contact in the Met.' She kicked the stub away.

'Yes?'

'No joy – there's no record anywhere of your missing evidence. No paperwork, nothing on the computer system. And your disappearing policeman applied for a transfer into plain clothes ages ago.'

'If there's no record at all then it must go higher than Inspector Leary. Only someone with real clout could tamper with computer records. Don't you see? That's proof there's something really dodgy going on.' Caroline shuffled out of the way as a man on crutches hobbled past her. 'What's next then?'

'Next?'

'What else are you looking at?' Caroline asked.

'I haven't worked that out yet.'

Caroline shook her head. 'Haven't worked it out? You're not taking this seriously enough.' She looked Tate up and down. 'Don't forget – I still have the stick.'

Tate grabbed her arm. 'You can't renege on our deal now.'

'Can't I?'

Tate pulled Caroline closer. 'Don't you forget I know about your affair with Martin Fox.'

Caroline dragged her arm away. 'What are you saying?'

Tate let out a long breath. 'I'm sorry. That was out of order. Forget it.' She reached for another cigarette. 'What do you suggest I look into next?'

Caroline bit her lip and stared at the journalist. She should never have told her about Martin. *So bloody stupid.*

'It's all right – honestly – your secret's safe with me.' Tate lit the cigarette and drew down a lungful of smoke.

'Get your contact in the Met to take a look at the suicide note. It must have turned up a little while after Martin died. There's an outside chance the actual date it turned up was recorded on the system. That would at least prove it wasn't part of the original evidence haul.'

Tate puffed a cloud of smoke above her head. 'I'll get on to it tomorrow.'

Behind them the automatic doors slid open again and another casualty staggered through the exit. This man had a thick dressing taped to his forehead and his arm in a sling. Caroline dodged out of his way.

'Frank!' Tate rushed towards him. 'What have you done to your arm?'

'Dislocated shoulder. They've popped it back in, but it hurts like buggery, worse than it did before,' the man said. 'I'm drugged up to the eyeballs too.' He shoved his good hand into a pocket and threw a set of keys at Tate. She stuck out a hand and caught them without looking.

'You're gonna have to drive me home,' he said and started walking unsteadily towards the car park.

'I'll be right there.' Tate turned to Caroline. 'As you're here you might as well take this from me now.' She reached into her bag and pulled out a fuchsia pink mobile phone. 'It's untraceable. Pay-as-you-go. Use cash to top it up. My number's already programmed in. From now on don't call me on anything else.'

'Untraceable? What do you mean?'

'It's not linked to you so there's no need to worry about using it.'

'I don't understand.' Caroline took the phone and stared down at it. She flipped it over in her hand.

'It's just a regular phone.'

'I still don't underst—'

'It's standard procedure.'

Caroline frowned at her.

'Do you have any idea how easy it is to listen to people's voicemails? Just punch in a factory setting PIN and bingo.'

'Voicemails? But I don't see—'

'Using an untraceable phone is a precaution I take with all my government whistleblowers.'

18

Angela Tate sat down and stared at Frank Carter across the desk. 'Should you even be in today?' She jabbed a finger at him. 'You're not much cop with only one arm.'

Frank plucked at the sling wrapped right around his left arm and shoulder with his other hand. 'I can use it when I have to. Meantime I've got everyone running round after me, making cups of coffee; nipping out for fags; treating me to their last Jaffa Cake. It's all good.' He leaned back in his chair. 'Just don't tell anyone.'

'What are you up here for anyway? How is the picture desk surviving without you?'

'There's no one downstairs. No one to treat me like a returning war hero. I'm getting properly pampered up here.'

From somewhere under the desk a Nokia ringtone sounded. Angela leaned down to Jason Morris's console and tugged at the top drawer. It was locked. She searched frantically in her handbag for the key and found it right at the bottom, attached to its twin on a tiny silver ring.

'I don't know why I bother to lock this thing.' She fumbled with the lock. 'It's more trouble than it's worth.' She yanked open the drawer and snatched up the phone just as it stopped ringing. 'Bollocks. How long before I lose the keys and can't get the bastard thing open at all?'

'Give one of them to me. I'll look after it.'

Angela stared at him.

'What? Don't you trust me?'

'Promise me, no rifling.'

'Scouts' honour.' He lifted his bandaged arm and saluted with three fingers flat against his forehead.

'You were never a Boy Scout.' Angela threaded a key from the ring.

'No… but I once camped with the Girl Guides.' He let out a satisfied sigh. 'Got a lot of badges that weekend.'

Angela held the keys in her open palm and proffered both to Frank. 'Take your pick.'

He peered at the keys. 'They're not the same.'

'What?'

'The keys don't match.'

'No wonder I've been having so much trouble with the bloody lock.' She threw both keys in the top drawer, slammed it shut and started tugging at the handle of the drawer beneath. 'This place is falling apart. When was the last time a piece of rubbish office furniture was replaced?'

Frank started to wave at her.

'What's up with you?'

He pointed behind her.

'What is it?' She turned to see the editor marching towards her. He called out her name.

'Have you got a moment?' he said.

She looked down at the little screen on her pay-as-you-go mobile, waiting for the voicemail alert to bleep at her. 'Not right now, Dominic. I'm expecting an important call.' The screen faded to its energy save mode without making a sound.

'Yes. Right now,' he said.

She hit a speed dial option on the phone and waited.

'Did you hear me?'

Angela threw Frank a glance, which he refused to acknowledge. She mouthed the word 'coward' and listened as her call was transferred to Caroline Barber's voicemail. 'Of course I heard you,' she said. 'I'm just a little tied up at the moment.'

The editor plucked the phone from her hand.

'That can wait. I can't.'

'What the…?' She snatched the phone back and stood her ground.

'I want you in my office now.'

Angela folded her arms.

'Please?'

'Do you see that, Frank?'

Frank was making himself look busy, adjusting his sling.

'The magic word,' she said. 'Works every time.' She followed Dominic Evans into his office, where he gestured for her to sit down.

'Baby keeping you up, is it?' she said, and pointed to his face, his red eyes, the grey bags underneath. 'How old is it now?' She sat down.

'*Isiah's* four months.'

'Children are such a blessing, aren't they?' She crossed her legs and relaxed back into the leather chair.

Dominic Evans sat down in a chair on the other side of the desk, carefully adjusted so that despite his diminutive stature he could sit at a higher level than his visitors. Angela suspected he thought it gave him more authority, and the means with which to intimidate whoever was sitting across the desk from him. All it actually did was lift his short little

116

legs off the floor so they swung backwards and forwards like a small child's. Let him try his pathetic little power games with her. She was filing copy when Dominic Evans was still handing in his English homework.

'What can I help you with, Dominic?'

He rubbed both hands across his stubble and let out a tiny groan. Was it a word? Angela wondered whether or not she was expected to respond.

'I don't want you to think you've been singled out. I'll be talking to every permanent member of staff in due course.'

She sat perfectly still, waiting. She had a feeling a hammer blow was coming and she hoped it would be quick. And painless.

Evans blew out his cheeks.

Come on, you little rat – get on with it.

'You don't need me to tell you the industry's going through massive upheaval at the moment.' He grabbed the edge of his desk with both hands and wheeled his chair towards it. 'And I'm sure you know we're not immune.' He cleared his throat. 'We need to look at streamlining the operation. Make savings where we can.'

Here it comes.

Evans looked down at a printed table of figures sitting on the desk.

She didn't have time for this. 'Am I a liability or an asset?'

He looked up at her.

'Do I appear on the credit or debit side of that little balance sheet of yours?' Angela uncrossed her legs and leaned forward. 'I'm guessing the number-crunchers in accounts have been very busy.' She got up and leaned over the desk.

'Please sit down, Angela.'

'I'd prefer to stand.'

He blinked at her.

'Have they told you just how expensive it would be to make me redundant?' she said. 'Do you know how many years I've been here?'

'I'm sure you're going to tell me anyw—'

'Thirty years, Dominic.'

'Maybe it's time to take things a little easier.'

'So I am on the hit list?'

'Nothing's set in stone. I just wanted to sound you out – test the waters.' He studied the page of numbers for a moment. 'If you did agree to go now, the package would be much more generous than if you waited.'

'You mean waited to be dragged kicking and screaming from the building?'

Evans smiled. 'That I would give money to see.'

'I'm bloody good at my job. Does that count for nothing these days?' She shook her head. 'It's OK – I already know the answer to that.' She walked towards the door. 'If you're quite finished I'm going to get back to that award-winning work of mine.'

She'd opened the door and was halfway out before Evans spoke again.

'You really should give the redundancy package serious consideration.'

'Not interested.' She stepped into the corridor. 'I've got work to do.'

'What are you working on today?' he shouted after her.

She turned back. 'Actually, while I'm here...' She pointed at the spreadsheet on Evans's desk. 'Have you accounted for Jason Morris in your number crunching?'

Evans turned the sheet over so that it was facing blank side up.

'Can you at least tell me if you plan to replace him?'

'We're implementing a recruitment freeze as part of the rationalisation process.'

'You could have just said no.'

'Jason will not be replaced.'

'In that case, can you give me the copy he filed? I'd like to see if I can work some of it up into a story.'

'He didn't file any copy.'

'Really? None at all?'

Evans threw his arms wide. 'He was working undercover – he thought it might jeopardise his position.'

'OK then – I've done the odd bit of undercover work myself. Maybe I can pick up where Jason left off.'

Evans smiled. A slow wide smile.

'This is one assignment that would be beyond even your enormous powers of deception.'

The mobile phone bleeped in her hand.

'Why?' she said. 'What was Jason working on?'

'Morris had infiltrated the south-east chapter of England for the English. Have you heard of them?'

Angela shook her head. 'Neo-Nazis by any chance?'

'Pretty much. They're new. And a charming bunch they are too. They make the English Defence League look like the Women's Institute. I don't think you'd fit in, somehow.' He smiled again.

'Jason must have given you some idea where his investigation was going.'

Evans shook his head. 'He wanted to stay as deep undercover as possible.'

Angela started to turn away, trying to remember the last time she'd actually seen Jason in the office. 'Do you know who cleared out Jason's desk?'

Evans shrugged. 'The cleaners, I expect. Why?'

'Where did all his stuff end up?'

'I've no idea. Why are you so interested?'

Angela didn't bother to answer. She slammed Evans's door and hurried down the corridor.

Angela looked at the hastily written address on the scrap of paper and scanned the row of houses from the other side of the street. 22a Gloucester Terrace occupied the lower ground floor of the converted Victorian house two in from the end of the terrace.

She scooted between parked cars and hurried across the quiet road just off the main drag in Kentish Town. She peered down the steep asphalted steps leading to Jason Morris's basement flat and pushed open the squeaky gate.

Through the glass panels in the front door she could see a pile of unopened envelopes and fast-food flyers. She cupped her hands around her eyes and pressed her face closer to the glass. The coat rack next to the door was empty and through an open doorway at the far end of the hall she could just make out a torn curtain hanging from the rail above the window. She moved on to the large sash window to the left of the front door and strained to focus beyond the grime on the glass into what must have been Jason Morris's living room. A three-seater sofa was pushed up against one wall, its cushions piled on the floor next to it. Cables snaked out of the wall in the opposite corner above a stack of old newspapers.

'Excuse me?' A voice boomed in her ear.

Angela started and spun round. A compact Asian man, with a bald head and a neat beard, was standing at the bottom of the steps, frowning at her.

'Can I help you?' he said and moved closer.

'Who are you?'

'I could ask you the same question.' He studied her face. 'I'm the landlord. I live upstairs.' He pointed to a grander flight of stone steps leading up to the main door of the building.

'So you know the man who used to live here?' she said.

He nodded. 'Such a tragic story. He died.'

'I know. I used to work with him. Angela Tate.' She extended a hand.

'You work at the insurance company?' He shook her hand and looked her up and down, his gaze lingering on her legs.

Angela nodded and smiled, wondering just how deep undercover Jason had gone. 'I'm a... loss adjuster,' she said. It was the only insurance-related role she could think of. She gestured towards the front door with an upturned thumb.

'Do you know who moved his things out of his flat?'

'His parents. Though there wasn't much left by the time they arrived, of course.'

Angela glanced back through the living room window.

'Is that why you're here?' the man asked. 'For the insurance claim?' He peered into the living room too. 'The thieves took almost everything.'

Angela removed her notepad from her bag.

'Some of it was mine,' he said.

Angela scribbled *Jason – ROBBED!!!* on her pad. 'Just to confirm the details I've been given are correct, the burglary happened when exactly?'

'Last month. The 17th.'

'March 17th?' Angela wrote the date on her pad and underlined it.

The man nodded. 'Just the day after Mr Morris was killed.'

19

Caroline closed the door on an indignant admin assistant she'd just interviewed for the second time about the missing CD-ROM and hurried back to her desk. She found Pam poking through the cardboard box sitting on the desk next to hers.

'Why did Tracy bring all this rubbish back into the office?' Pam said. 'She should have had a proper clearout.'

'Maybe it's not rubbish.' Caroline pushed the box away from Pam's prying fingers. 'It's Tracy's stuff – nothing to do with either of us.'

'She might have tidied it away somewhere. It's an eyesore.'

'It's not in anyone's way.'

'Even so…'

'What do you want, Pam?'

Pam lowered herself onto the edge of Caroline's desk, the hardboard laminate bowing slightly in the middle. 'Jeremy told me he caught you at your desk last night.'

'Caught me?' Caroline felt a band of heat tighten across her chest.

'There you were, large as life he said – after I'd promised him I'd make you leave on time.'

Caroline glanced towards her boss's room and wondered again just how much Prior had seen. He was pacing up and down, gesticulating, a mobile phone attached to his ear. From the expression on his face, it looked like some poor soul was on the receiving end of a bollocking.

'I told him not to blame you,' Caroline said. 'What did he say?'

'Oh I'm not in trouble or anything. But he's told me not to let it happen again – I've got to keep an even closer eye on you, he said.'

Did he?

'Tell Prior he doesn't need to waste his time worrying about me.' She managed to force a smile. 'I'm always better when I've got lots of work to focus on.'

'You're sure?'

Caroline nodded vigorously.

'In that case…' Pam got up and smiled slyly at Caroline. 'You can take my place at the workshop session. It's bound to overrun, they always do, and I need to leave early.'

'Workshop?' Caroline was only half-listening, her attention drawn back to Prior jabbing an angry finger in the air.

'It starts in about half an hour.'

'What's it for?'

'Didn't you read the email?'

'Remind me.' Caroline continued to watch Prior working himself into a fury. He hadn't mentioned anything to her about the previous evening, but she felt like it was hanging over her, about to fall from a great height.

'It's for the new website,' Pam said. 'The schools workforce website. They've been banging on about the thing for ages. They want our input. Half the team's in with the techies now – *workshopping*.' She made speech marks in the air and pulled a face.

'What's wrong with the old website?'

She shrugged. 'It's not user-friendly enough, or something.'

'Why would anyone be interested in my opinion?'

'We're stakeholders, Caroline. Our opinions count. You really didn't read the email, did you?'

'I've got better things to do.' She grabbed a file from her in tray.

'But you will go in my place?'

'Are you asking me or telling me?'

'Please, Caroline.'

'OK – if it's that important. Do you want me to pass on anything – any *input*?'

'Tell them I'd really like a blue one.'

Caroline exhaled as Pam finally went back to her own desk. Prior was still on his feet and pulling open his door. He stopped at his PA's desk and Lisa quickly stood up. She followed her boss down the office and disappeared with him into the lobby. Caroline couldn't help but feel sorry for her. Lisa was permanently in the firing line. She glanced back at Prior's room, the door swinging wide. The phone on his desk started to flash. After half a dozen rings the call redirected to the phone on Lisa's desk. There was no one at that end of the office; no doubt they were in with the web developers providing their own 'input'. Caroline punched in the pick-up code on her phone.

'Academies, Jeremy Prior's phone.'

There was a pause the other end.

'Oh – hello, I was just about to hang up.'

The voice was familiar but she couldn't quite place it.

'I was after the man himself – is he there?'

'Would you like to leave a message?'

'I'm not sure it'd make much sense. Just tell him Greg from IT phoned. He can get me on extension 4-3-2-4. Tell him it's about the ticket raised this morning. Tell him it's urgent.'

'What's it concerning?'

Caroline grabbed a notebook and pen. She wrote her boss's name at the top of the page and underlined it.

'It's a bit sensitive. I need to talk to the boss – no offence.'

Sensitive?

'None taken – but you said it was urgent. Maybe I can help? Speed things up a bit?' *Find out what Prior is up to.*

There was another long pause.

'Who am I speaking to?' he said eventually.

Caroline glanced back at Lisa's empty desk. 'This is Lisa, Jeremy's PA.' She bit her lip. The words were out before she could stop them. She heard Greg let out a noisy breath.

'Actually, Greg, I put in that ticket request for Jeremy myself.' She grimaced.

'Right... OK... Tell your boss he needs to be a bit more specific. We're drowning in data here. Ideally, before he phones back he should prepare a list of specific terminals to monitor. The fewer the better. As it is we're recording activity on the whole floor – I'm not being funny, but it is a bit OTT.'

Recording activity?

'Between you and me, Greg, Jeremy can be a bit like that sometimes.' Her heart had started racing. 'Demands the impossible and wants it by yesterday lunchtime.'

'Yeah? I had a boss like that once.'

'Anything else I should ask him to prepare before he calls? Do you have a best practice procedure? An implementation strategy?' She could hear herself sounding just like a jargon-filled Powerpoint presentation.

'A list of keywords or phrases that trigger the monitoring would be handy – then we can lose the 24-hour surveillance.'

Caroline lifted a hand to her face. 'Got that.' She swallowed. 'As soon as he's back at his desk, I'll help him draw up a list and get back to you ASAP.'

'Sweet. Cheers, Lisa.' Greg hung up.

Caroline put the phone down, ripped the page from her pad and threw it in the recycling bin at the end of her desk. Then she sat very still and tried to control the queasy motion roiling in her stomach. She went through everything Greg had just told her. If Prior had requested the monitoring of every computer in the academies division, surely that meant he didn't specifically suspect her of anything? She glanced over at Pam, who was concentrating on dunking a custard cream into her mug. Monitoring Pam's PC activity wouldn't have yielded much data. A shudder crossed Caroline's shoulders as she remembered again the way Prior had been staring at her the previous evening. She shuddered again when the unfamiliar ringtone of the mobile phone Tate had given her blared out from her bag. She grabbed the phone and hit the 'call end' button. The last thing she wanted to hear was Tate nagging at her for the honours nomination files. It was too late now. She wouldn't be going anywhere near them. She retrieved the memory stick from her bag and slipped it into a pocket, suddenly feeling the need to keep it close. She checked left and right, just to be sure no one was watching. She was starting to feel as if she was under permanent scrutiny. She glanced up at Pam again, who just at that moment was looking in her direction. Keeping an even closer eye on her, as per Prior's instructions. Had Pam been poking through Tracy's stuff because Prior had asked her to? Caroline looked at the cardboard box she'd pushed into the corner of Tracy's desk. It did look like a lot of rubbish. She exhaled slowly, but the more she tried to relax the more she felt Pam's eyes boring into her. When she turned around she saw Pam buttoning up her coat. She gave Caroline a little wave and dragged her bag over her shoulder. Caroline watched her leave the office.

God she was getting paranoid. What was next? Suspecting her phone was being tapped? She lifted the receiver and listened to the dialling tone. She wasn't sure what she expected to hear. She put the handset back down and puffed out a breath. *Don't be so ridiculous.*

She got up and leaned on the back of her chair, stretching some of the tension out of her legs. She circled her head, one way then the other, then rolled her shoulders and shook her hands. She felt too twitchy to sit down. She wandered over to Tracy's desk and peered inside the cardboard box, wondering what Pam had found so interesting. A pen pot was sticking out of the top, crammed full of standard issue Bic biros with chewed lids and a set of Prêt plastic cutlery. Maybe Pam was right – Tracy probably should have had a clear-out. A Post-It note was stuck on the side of the pen pot, thick marker pen scrawled across it. Caroline turned her head to make out the words. Tracy had written *IMPORTANT* at the very top and underlined it three times. She scanned the other two lines. Completely flouting departmental security guidelines, Tracy had stupidly written her username and password on the Post-It. Prior would have a fit if he saw it. Caroline peeled off the yellow square and looked for somewhere in the box to conceal it. She was staring down at Tracy's login details as the pay-as-you-go mobile rang again.

Bugger off Tate! Get someone else to do your dirty work.

She blinked and gazed more intently at the words on the Post-It. She glanced at Tracy's computer then back down at the username and password – login details that couldn't be traced back to her. She couldn't do it… could she? At that moment the mobile phone chirruped in her bag as if Tate was answering her question.

Before allowing herself to think too deeply about the possible ramifications, Caroline reached over to Tracy's computer and turned it on. After a few moments the login box appeared. She quickly typed in the username and password from the Post-It note and hit enter.

Sorry Tracy.

20

Caroline stood at the living room window, watching for any sign of movement from the street beyond the front garden. Apart from the odd piece of litter getting caught in the wind, nothing stirred.

For the past three hours a combination of tiredness and worry had created some kind of wave machine in her stomach. Every now and then the foamy tip of a breaker reached as far as her mouth and left a bitter taste at the back of her tongue.

All afternoon she'd been fretting over logging into Tracy's computer, worrying what would happen when the information got back to Prior. But everything looked different now. Right now she'd gladly make a gushing confession to her boss and whoever else might listen to her. Anything to have Dan walk through the front door.

Pete had given up waiting and gone to bed just after 1am, trying to persuade her to join him. She'd stood in the hall and watched him trudge up the stairs, wondering how it was possible for him to even contemplate sleep.

When Dan hadn't returned home by 11pm, Caroline phoned his mobile and was diverted straight to voicemail. She'd been getting the same response at ten minute intervals ever since. She checked the clock on the wall above the mantelpiece again – 2:04am. She'd promised herself hours ago that if he hadn't come home by 2pm she'd call the police. She pulled the phone from her pocket, hit the call button and stared at the illuminated yellow screen. She tapped in the first nine and heard the thud of heavy footsteps coming down the stairs. The living room door opened.

'Come to bed, love.' Pete padded over to her. He must have pulled on a pair of boxers and a t-shirt in the dark – both were inside out. He held out his hand for the phone. 'Come on – I can't sleep without you beside me.'

'You can't sleep because your 14-year-old son is out on the streets somewhere.' She punched in the second nine.

'Please, Caz – give me the phone. You can bet your life as soon as you call the police he'll come home.'

'All the more reason to call them then.'

Pete snatched the phone from her shaking hand. 'Dan won't thank you for it – not when he turns up to a house full of uniforms. He'll be mortified.'

'For God's sake, Pete. Grow up! He's not some gangster trying to impress his homies.' She reached for the phone, Pete shoved it behind his back. 'He's a 14-year-old computer geek, with nerdy friends. They wouldn't even know where to go at this time of night.'

'He's probably just got carried away playing on one of his video games at his mate's house and lost track of the time.'

'We've called all his friends, Pete.'

'Maybe he's with someone we don't know.'

'And you think that's going to reassure me?' She ducked around his back for the phone. He pulled it away from her.

'He's not a baby, Caz. You've got to let him grow up.'

'He's got no street sense. What if he's caught up in some trouble on one of the estates?'

'He's got enough sense to steer well clear of anything like that. He's a bright lad.'

'He's 14.'

'He'll be fine.'

'How can you carry on saying that? It's the early hours of the morning – obviously he's not fine. Or he'd be right here.' She blew out an uneven breath. 'I hate to break it to you, Pete. But sometimes things aren't *fine*. I know you like to think everything will work out for the best.' She rubbed her eyes. 'But sometimes things are fucking diabolical.'

Pete snorted and muttered something under his breath.

There was a clank from the back of the room. Caroline turned to see the door leading to Jean's annexe swing open. Her mother stood in the doorway, swaying slightly, clutching a hot water bottle. 'I take it there's been no news?'

'Go back to bed, Mum. I'll let you know as soon as I hear anything.' She walked towards her and stretched out a hand. 'Give me that bottle – I'll put the kettle on and bring it in to you.'

'I'm perfectly capable of doing it myself.' Jean leaned her weight against the doorframe to steady herself.

'You only got home this afternoon. You shouldn't even be out of bed.'

'Right now I've got a military tattoo being performed in my head. I can be kept awake by marching bands just as easily sitting on the sofa with some company as lying on my own in the dark.'

Caroline hooked an arm under her mother's and led her to the sofa.

'Have you called the police yet?' Jean said.

Caroline looked at Pete, who was still hanging on to the phone. 'I'm just about to.' She helped her mother sit down, pushed past Pete and grabbed her bag from the hall table. She pulled out her mobile and the business card Ralph Mills had given her at Martin Fox's funeral.

The police didn't arrive for another five hours. When the doorbell finally rang, Caroline flew into the hall and dragged open the front door. Two uniformed policewomen, one tall and thin, the other squat and sturdy, stood on the garden path looking up at the first floor windows.

'What kept you?' Caroline said.

'Sorry, madam. Er... Mrs...?' the thin one said.

Caroline left the door open and walked wearily back to the living room. 'Come in if you're coming – and shut the door behind you.'

'We got to you just as soon as we could, Mrs...' the sturdy one added.

'Not a priority – is that it?'

The policewomen looked at one another but didn't answer.

'For God's sake sit down.'

The thin one perched next to Jean on the sofa. 'I'm Constable Jane Fellows and this is Constable Jane O'Brien.' She gestured to her colleague, who was busy dragging one of the dining chairs to the far end of the sofa.

'Two Janes?' Jean said. 'Doesn't that get confusing?'

'Not really, madam.' The thin one, Fellows, unhooked a notebook and pen from a pocket. 'And you are?'

'I think we've gone past the stage of formal introductions, don't you?' Caroline let out a breath and tried to keep her anger under control by digging her nails into the soft pads of flesh below her thumbs.

'Why don't you sit down, Mrs...'

'Barber! For Christ's sake. Is it so difficult to remember my name?' Caroline stood her ground. 'What's being done to find my son?'

'Please, madam. If you would just sit down. Then we can make a start.' O'Brien, the fatter one, reached up a hand and lightly touched Caroline on the arm.

'Make a start? What does that mean? Don't tell me you haven't even started looking? I gave all the details to the man I spoke to on the phone, hours ago. Why do you need to hear them again?'

The policewomen exchanged a glance.

'This isn't happening,' Caroline said.

Jean eased herself from the sofa. 'Why don't I make us all a nice cup of tea?'

'For God's sake, Mum! Putting the kettle on doesn't actually make everything better.'

Jean ignored her. 'Milk?' The officers nodded. Jean looked at the sturdy Jane. 'I'll bring the sugar bowl in – you can help yourself.'

The front door squealed open and shut again. Caroline rushed back into the hall. Pete was pulling off his jacket.

'Why have you come back?'

'I'm exhausted, Caz. I could barely keep my eyes open when I set off. I've looked everywhere I can think of.' He opened his arms. 'Come here, babe, let me hold you for a second.'

Caroline shook her head. 'The police have arrived.'

Pete dropped his arms to his sides and clenched his fists. 'That's progress at least.'

'I'm not so sure.'

Pete followed her back into the living room and they went through the painful process of repeating all the information Caroline had already given over the phone.

'Do you have a recent photo of your son?' Fellows finally asked.

'His name's Dan.'

The police officer looked down at her notebook and let out a barely suppressed sigh.

'I'm sorry – is it all a bit too tedious for you – remembering his name?'

'Come on, Caz, they're only doing their job.' Pete smiled at them.

'Some support from you wouldn't go amiss,' Caroline snapped back at him.

The policewomen exchanged another glance.

'Has Dan ever stayed out before without letting you know where he was going?' O'Brien had turned to face Pete.

'Never,' Caroline said. 'You can speak directly to me – I am his mother.'

There was a scratching at the living room door.

'Who let the dog out of the kitchen?' Caroline opened the door and discovered Ben standing in the hall, Minty by his side.

'What's going on?' he said, his eyes just starting to water.

'It's all right, baby. Why don't you go and see Gran in the kitchen. I think she might be making pancakes.'

'I'm not hungry. Where's Dan?'

Jean appeared at the kitchen door, her face greyer than it had been in the hospital.

'God, Mum – you look awful. Go back to bed.'

Jean held out her hand. 'Come on Ben – let's get some breakfast for Minty.'

Caroline coaxed him into the kitchen and shut the door. She went back into the living room and found Pete and the two policewomen standing over the dining table leafing through a family photograph album.

'I'm sure there's a recent one of him somewhere,' Pete said.

The blanket of tiredness that Caroline had been wrestling with all night suddenly seemed to engulf her. She sagged against the side of the sofa. The shrill ringtone of the pink pay-as-you-go mobile trilled from her bag on the sideboard. Pete and the two constables all turned and looked at her expectantly.

'Do you want me to get it, love?' Pete said.

Caroline didn't reply. The last person in the world she wanted to speak to right now was Angela Tate. Pete ran to her bag.

'Leave it!' she shouted at him.

'Don't you think—'

'It's a work phone – Dan doesn't have the number.'

Pete's hand hovered over the open handbag.

'Just leave it, Pete.'

The ringing finally stopped, to be replaced by violent banging on the front door.

'Thank God!' Pete ran into the hall as the last trace of strength Caroline had been clinging on to finally ebbed away. She knew before Pete reached the door that it wouldn't be Dan. Dan wouldn't loudly announce his return. If he'd forgotten his key he'd be mewling apologetically through the letterbox, too embarrassed to draw attention to himself. She heard the door creak open. Then a huge roar.

'Where is he?' an unfamiliar male voice bellowed down the hall. 'Let me get my hands on him – the filthy bastard!'

A spike of adrenalin propelled Caroline forward into the hall. Pete was squaring up to a ruddy-faced man who already had one foot over the threshold. A string-thin teenage girl was cowering behind him.

21

'... well anyway, as I say, give me a call ASAP and we'll arrange a time for the handover. Later today would be good.'

Angela Tate threw the mobile phone onto the large oak table in the corner of her living room. She ran her fingers through her uncombed hair and let out a grunt.

'Bloody amateurs. Want a job done right... Honestly Kinnock...' She blinked and opened her eyes wide. How could she keep forgetting the cat had died? She'd dug the hole under the apple tree herself less than a month ago. And how was it perfectly acceptable to think out loud when a mangy ginger tom was padding around the house, entirely ignoring her, but talking to herself now felt as if she was one short step from the Maudesly? She looked out of the window. She could just make out the wooden cross she'd hammered into the ground at the end of the garden. When did her eyesight get so bad? She shoved the heel of her hand in her eye and rubbed, then remembered she hadn't taken her make-up off the night before. She blinked again and hooked out a congealed lump of eye shadow from the corner of her eye.

Caroline Barber had been ignoring her calls for nearly 24 hours. The jibe Angela had made outside the hospital about her affair with Fox was a stupid knee-jerk response. She hadn't been thinking. As if a woman like Caroline Barber would succumb to an empty threat like that. That thought stopped in her tracks. A woman like what? She was so used to making snap judgements about people she hadn't taken any time to think about what Caroline Barber was really like at all. She looked at the phone and considered leaving Barber a conciliatory message. Maybe even an apology... A shiver ran up her spine and she wrapped her dressing gown a little tighter. Apologising was more likely to make things worse.

She peered into what was left of her lukewarm coffee. Her hand hovered for a moment over a half bottle of Three Barrels sitting next to the mug on the table. She checked the clock on the shelf. *Sod the bloody yardarm.* She emptied a couple of healthy measures into the mug and knocked back the fortified coffee in one. She'd never been sure what a yardarm was anyway.

The surface of the table was covered with copies of the photographs Frank had taken at Martin Fox's funeral. He didn't manage to capture all the main players, so Angela had supplemented the collection with a selection of standard publicity shots. Where she didn't have a picture she'd written a name on an index card and added that to the random collage of smiling or grim faces staring up at her. She pushed the photos across the table, creating little groups of twos or threes.

One group featured William King and Martin Fox, together with an index card with the words *Cambridge* and *DfE* scribbled on it. She thought for a moment: what else did they have in common? Both were public schoolboys, both had master's degrees... What else? Both got into politics at roughly the same time. She added notes to the card and moved on. Sir Fred and Lady Larson. Apart from running the business together and being married to one another, she could think of nothing else that linked them. But then that was probably enough. She scribbled down the year of their marriage – 1971 – and left a gap for the annual turnover of the company. She stopped. That was one piece of infor-mation Caroline Barber had to come through with. If she ever answered her bloody phone.

Floating on its own, right in the middle of the table, was a photograph of deputy assistant commissioner Sir Barry Flowers, the man in full dress uniform at the funeral who Frank hadn't been able to identify. What was his connection to Martin Fox? She pushed the photo closer to the one of the deceased schools minister but left a gap of a good six inches. On an index card she wrote *Knife Amnesty, London Schools.*

The first two-week amnesty had been a big success. Angela had written a feature about it herself. She remembered standing in the crowded assembly hall of a Brixton comprehensive when Fox launched the scheme four years ago. Barry Flowers had been standing beside him throughout. The amnesty had been so successful it was now part of every London schools' academic year, like sports day or the nativity play might once have been. She stared at the policeman's thin face, a tightly cropped grey beard covering most of it. Did William King have any connection to the deputy assistant commissioner? Angela placed a tentative finger on Flowers' photo, pressing very lightly, waiting for it to move by itself, like a Ouija glass. It remained perfectly still. She left it where it was and stood back to study her handy work.

What a bloody mess.

She reached for the photograph of Susan King and put it next to her husband's, just inches away from the picture of Fox. How well had the prime minister's wife known the honourable member for Cambridge East? Angela drew a large question mark on another card and inserted it between Fox's photo and Susan King's. Then she did the same thing with the photograph of the former prime minister's wife. On the day on the funeral, Rachael Oakley had won the Jackie O competition by a whisker – the huge dark glasses just swinging the vote in her favour. How close had she been to Martin Fox? Maybe Angela could ask Caroline Barber the next time she saw her. Whenever that would be. She glanced down at the lifeless mobile phone lying on the table. Maybe she should try her again. She really needed those documents. She had to have something concrete to show Evans. Convince him she wasn't wasting her time or the paper's money on the academies investigation. She had to prove to him and the board that the *Evening News* was better with her on staff than not. She sat down with a thud, the antique dining chair creaking under the sudden strain.

She was too young for the scrapheap, and definitely too old to start a new career freelancing. The thought of hustling for commissions sent a chill up her spine. Competing with hungry hacks half her age was not a prospect to dwell on. Her journalistic instincts were still as sharp as her elbows, but there was no way she could compete on price. The mortgage still had to be paid.

She sat back and scanned the collection of photos, then drew a line with an arrow at either end on another card and pushed it between the Larsons and Martin Fox, the academies programme being the obvious link. William King was also an advocate of academies, so she shuffled his toothy-smiled portrait closer to the Larsons. She focussed on the imperious expression on Valerie Larson's face, standing stoically next to her withered husband in his wheelchair. Angela knew she wouldn't get another chance to see either of them, not after what happened at Larson's headquarters. She reached for her notebook and skimmed through the few words she'd scribbled after the aborted interview. The words *favours*, *Bill*, *fob off*, *promise* and *running out of time* had all been underlined. Why was Valerie Larson running out of time? Was Fred Larson that close to death? Angela studied the photograph of him. He certainly looked as if he could shuffle off at any moment. She grabbed a pen and wrote *'Bill?'* across King's photograph. She sat back and stared at his picture.

Really?

Was it possible Valerie Larson could have been shouting down the phone at William King himself? What kind of demands could she have been making? The general election was less than three weeks away. Surely King had more important things to think about. Not one to rule out any possibility too soon, she wrote *Party Funding* in big letters on another card and centred it between all the major players. Sir Fred had made a generous contribution way back in '96, but hadn't donated anything since then. In fact he'd made no gifts to any of the major parties. Maybe he'd decided fence sitting was the safest way to prosper in business. She picked up the card again, staring as the ink seeped into it. Perhaps the donation wasn't even relevant. She felt as if she was running round in circles, endlessly speculating, with no real evidence to come to any proper conclusions.

She gazed at the index card linking the Larsons. Fred and Valerie had got married in 1971, when Valerie was just 21 and Fred was already approaching middle age. That meant that Valerie had spent the best part of 40 years, all of her prime, at the heart of the Larson empire. No wonder she was such a tough nut to crack. She would never say anything to damage her husband's reputation. Especially now she was running the whole operation.

Angela stared at the couple in the photograph. Valerie in her black skirt suit and neat pillbox hat and poor old Fred looking like some creature from a science fiction horror film – a gruesome vision of the future. Angela had seen photographs of Fred Larson from the 1960s. He'd been handsome once – he must have been quite a catch even before he'd made his first million.

She grabbed a fresh index card and sat with pen poised, not quite believing she hadn't thought of the idea before. She tried hard to remember the name she was after, but it stubbornly remained just out of reach, somewhere in the murky depths of her memory. Perhaps she'd never even known the woman's first name. In lieu of further research, she quickly scrawled across the blank card in big bold capitals:

THE 1ST MRS DeWINTER

A mobile phone ringtone started warbling on the other side of the room. Angela padded over to the bookshelf above the mantelpiece and peered at the half dozen mobiles lined up along the edge. She plucked the white Sony Ericsson from the collection.

'You're really earning your money this month, Sherlock,' she said and wandered back to the table, trying to work out what it was she'd asked her contact at the Met to find out.

'You haven't heard what I've got to say yet.'

'That bad, is it?' She glanced at the photograph of Martin Fox and remembered.

'I can't tell you anything about the suicide note.'

'What? You leaked it to us in the first place, you must be able to tell me something.'

'My source can't get access to the computer records. There's no way of checking when the note was logged onto the system.'

'Why not? You've never had any trouble before.' She started doodling on a blank index card.

'This is different.'

'It is?'

'All the case files on the system are inaccessible to anyone below chief superintendent level. They've been classified.'

'You're telling me they're top secret?'

'If you want to put it like that – yes.'

'And how often does that happen?'

The line went very quiet.

'Well?'

'In my experience? Never.'

'And who decides to block access?'

'Someone much higher up the food chain.'

'And you expect me to believe your network of helpers doesn't include an amenable chief super?'

'Even if it did I wouldn't ask. Those files are toxic.'

'Don't exaggerate.'

'I'm serious, Ange. If you want my advice...'

Angela stopped doodling.

'Don't ask any more questions. Turn right around and run as fast as you can in the opposite direction.'

22

The red-faced man continued to rage incomprehensibly on Caroline's doorstep for a good five minutes, spitting as he spoke, flecks of saliva collecting in the corners of his mouth. Net curtains had started to twitch across the road by the time he'd run out of steam. In the moment of calm that followed, while he was still getting his breath back, Caroline eased him over the front step and into the hall, deciding it would be easier to control him inside the house with two police officers on hand.

Jean stood in the kitchen doorway, Ben peeking from behind her dressing gown and Claire peering over her shoulder.

'Keep them out of the way, will you, Mum?'

'Who is he?' Jean whispered.

'I'm expecting him to get on to formal introductions at some point. Can you sort out breakfast? Claire – you're taking your brother to school this morning.'

Caroline turned back to the shivering girl still standing on her front step.

'Are you coming in?' Caroline asked. The girl shrugged. 'For God's sake.' Caroline wrapped her hand around one of the girl's bony wrists and tugged her into the house. 'Just through there.'

The man had positioned himself in the bay window. The girl shuffled over and stood behind him. He scanned the room. The red mist finally seemed to lift from his eyes as he noticed the two uniformed police officers standing at the far end of the sofa for the first time.

'Are they here to arrest him? No more than he deserves – dirty little sod.'

Caroline took a breath and glanced at Pete, who was pushing up his sleeves.

'Can we all take a moment to calm down?' Caroline said. She extended a hand to the strange middle-aged man standing in her living room. 'I presume by 'him' you're referring to Dan? I'm his mother, Caroline.'

The man looked at her hand, but didn't take it.

'The name's Reynolds,' he said. 'This is my daughter Kylie.' He jabbed a thumb over his shoulder at the cowering girl. 'As I'm sure you already know.'

Caroline smiled at her. She'd never seen the girl before in her life.

'Dan's not here Mr Reynolds. The police have come to help us find him.'

'He's done a runner? That's very convenient, isn't it?'

Claire appeared at the living room door.

'Go back to the kitchen.' Caroline made a shooing gesture with her hand.

'What? And miss all the fun?' She slipped past her father and squeezed between the two policewomen.

'Do you have some information that might help us locate Dan, Mr Reynolds?' The thin policewoman stepped forward.

'Oh I've got information all right.' He turned and snatched Kylie's thin arm in a hairy fist and dragged her in front of him. 'Tell them. Go on. Tell them what he did to you.'

'Oh my God!' Claire's voice went up an octave.

The young girl bit her lip and stared at the floor.

'Kylie! Tell them.'

Kylie swallowed and opened her mouth, but before she could speak her father jumped in.

'The filthy little bastard's got her pregnant.'

'What?' Caroline stepped forward and stared into the girl's face. 'Is this true, Kylie? You can tell us. We won't be angry.' She scowled at the quivering girl's father. 'Is it true?'

'Hah! This I have to hear.' Claire started laughing.

'This isn't a joke,' Reynolds said, pointing an accusing finger at her. 'You're as bad as your brother, you stupid little bitch.'

'No one speaks to my daughter like that.' Pete marched across the room and stood nose to nose with Reynolds. 'Apologise, right now.'

'Make me.'

Both police officers darted round the sofa and separated the two men.

'Come on lads, let's not make matters worse than they already are,' the chunky one said.

'For God's sake – all of you!' Everyone looked at Caroline. 'Dan is God knows where, anything could have happened to him and you're scrapping as if you're still in the bloody playground.'

There was a knock on the front door.

'Is that him?' Reynolds shoved the tall policewoman and got as far as the living room door before Pete grabbed him by the scruff of the neck and hauled him back. Caroline ran into the hall and flung open the front door. Ralph Mills was standing on her doorstep. He was dressed in the same brown suit he'd been wearing at the funeral.

'It's you,' she said and breathed a disappointed sigh.

'Oh... I take it that means he hasn't turned up yet.' Mills laid a hand on her arm. 'I'm sure he'll be back soon.'

Caroline shouted into the living room, 'It's not Dan.' Her voice cracked part-way through. She turned back to Mills and sniffed. 'You don't have any news?'

Mills shook his head.

'Why are you here then?'

'I've just started my shift; I got your message from last night. I just wanted to check up on you.'

Caroline stood to one side and Mills eased into the hall.

'Are the Janes still here?' he asked.

It took Caroline a moment to register what he meant. She'd been thinking of them as thin cop and fat cop for the last hour.

'You know them?'

'Not really.' He took a step down the hall.

'They are. Before you go in, I should warn you... there's been another development.' She glanced over her shoulder at the living room door. 'In fact, why don't we go back outside?' She led him into the front garden and closed the door to behind them. 'It seems my son has been busy proving how fertile he is.'

'What?'

'We've had an unexpected visit from the mum-to-be and her angry father.'

'Blimey.'

'Exactly.' Caroline rubbed her eyes. 'I really don't know what to think now. Maybe Dan's run away. But he wouldn't do that. I'm sure he wouldn't.'

'How long's he been seeing the girl?'

'That's just it – I never even knew he had a girlfriend. He's always been into his computer games and sci-fi programmes. I thought he was too nerdy to attract girls. Seems he's been doing a lot more than that.' She craned forward and glanced through the living room window. It didn't look like any punches had been thrown. 'I suppose I should go back in there. I'm hoping I might be able to get some sense out of the girl. There's just a chance she knows where Dan is.'

Mills nodded and started back down the garden path.

'You didn't mind me calling you, last night?'

'Course not.'

'I suppose I just wanted to get a friendly voice on the other end of the line, rather than some faceless operator. I wasn't sure whether to call 999 or not.'

'That's absolutely fine – I'm just sorry I wasn't around. I'm pretty much working office hours at the moment.'

'Thanks for com—' She was stopped by a sudden movement out of the corner of her eye, just the other side of the garden hedge. 'Is that you?'

Dan appeared at the garden gate. Caroline ran to him and held her hands to his face. 'What happened to you?'

His hair was matted with dirt and grease. A long graze ran across his right cheek from nose to ear. His jeans were ripped and his trainers caked in mud. He wriggled his face free and ducked around her and Mills and ran into the house. Caroline ran after him but he was up the stairs and on the landing by the time she reached the bottom step. She heard his door slam and the bolt slide across. Pete joined her in the hall, closely followed by Reynolds. The two policewomen grabbed an arm each and dragged him back.

'He's locked himself in his room,' Caroline said. 'I think we should let him stew for a few minutes, then maybe one of you should try and coax him out.'

The policewomen looked at one another and the fat one glanced at her watch. 'Actually, Mrs Barber, we probably need to be getting along now. Your son's back home. That's the main thing. Safe and well.'

'Safe and well? You didn't see the state of him. He looked as if he'd been attacked. You'll need to take his statement.'

'Why don't you speak to him when he's ready and he can come into the station to report any crime that might have been committed?'

'Might have been? His face was cut.'

The police officer turned to Reynolds. 'I think this may not be the best time for an adult conversation about your daughter's... condition, sir. Why don't you leave now and contact Mr and Mrs Barber later? When the dust has settled.'

'Just give me five minutes with him!'

The policewoman and her colleague gripped Reynolds tighter as he strained to pull away. They managed somehow to manoeuvre him down the hall and through the front door.

'Don't think you've heard the last of me, Barber!'

Pete raised his hands. 'Any time you like.'

'Kylie!' Reynolds shouted.

The girl kept her eyes on the floor and scurried after her father.

'Unbelievable!' Claire was punching a text into her phone as she ran up the stairs.

'Leave your brother alone!' Caroline hollered after her.

'I've got no intention of getting anywhere near him.'

Caroline was suddenly aware of a tugging on her sleeve.

'Is Dan all right?' Ben looked up at her, his big eyes close to tears again.

'Course he is!' Pete roared. He scooped Ben off his feet. 'Where are those pancakes your gran was making?'

Ben started to giggle, which made Pete tickle him even more. Caroline put a hand on Pete's arm. He twisted Ben over, threw him in the air and caught him by his ankles.

'I'm sorry about before,' Pete said. 'You were right – I should have taken it more seriously. I was a prat.'

'Again, again!' Ben's face was scarlet.

Pete swung him slowly from side to side like the pendulum in a grandfather clock. Ben giggled even harder.

Caroline smiled. 'I'm sorry too.'

23

This time it was Caroline's turn to be late. She'd watched the train pull away from the platform at Catford Bridge, missing it by a matter of seconds. Sunday service on Southeastern Trains being what it was, she then had to wait half an hour for the next one. She arrived at Charing Cross station sweaty and flushed and 35 minutes later than expected to find Tate browsing through a copy of the *Sunday Telegraph* near the entrance of WHSmith's.

Caroline tapped her on the shoulder and Tate jumped as if she'd been poked with a cattle prod.

'I don't have long, shall we just get on with it?' Caroline said.

Tate looked at her watch and raised her eyebrows.

'All right. I'm sorry I'm late. I've had domestic issues to deal with. Mum's holding the fort at the moment when she should be in bed.'

'How is Jean?' Tate carelessly refolded the paper and stuffed it back on the rack.

'She'll survive.'

The journalist held out her hand. 'I'm pressed for time too, as it goes.'

'Not here.' Caroline looked around the busy concourse.

'Where?'

'Let's walk.'

'If we're walking I need more cigarettes. I won't be a sec.'

Caroline watched as Tate inched closer to the front of the queue, her thoughts returning inevitably to the events of the last two days.

Dan had refused even to set foot outside his room since locking himself in. Reynolds, the grandfather-to-be, had phoned on Friday evening, a little calmer, and grudgingly apologised for his behaviour. Caroline wondered if one of the policewomen had had a quiet word when they escorted him from the house.

According to her father, Kylie was two months gone and had pointed an accusing finger in Dan's direction. But as Dan wasn't confirming or denying the charge, and hadn't even explained where he'd been all night, the only thing Caroline could do was agree to meet with the Reynolds clan later in the week and promise Dan's attendance. If he ever emerged from his room.

Tate stomped out of Smith's ripping the cellophane from the cigarette packet with her teeth. She followed Caroline out of the station and into bright sunshine. She dropped her sunglasses over her eyes.

'You do have the documents?'

They were 50 yards down Villiers Street before Caroline replied.

'I've got the memory stick.' She looked down at the journalist's neat handbag tucked under her arm. 'Where's your laptop?'

'Laptop?'

'To copy the information onto.' They'd reached Embankment tube, Caroline led the way straight through to an almost traffic-free Victoria Embankment the other side.

'I don't have a laptop.' Tate unhooked her bag from her arm and peered inside. 'Or a bloody lighter, it would seem.'

Caroline stopped. 'You don't have a laptop? Well that makes it a bit difficult then.'

'Christ – just give me the bloody stick.'

'The memory stick's not mine. I can't just hand it over.'

'Oh please.' Tate held out her hand.

Caroline ignored it and started wearily up the steps leading to Hungerford Bridge, grabbing hold of the handrail and hauling herself up. When she reached the top she navigated around a noisy group of French teenagers and waited for Tate to catch up. Tate had decided to push her way right into the middle of them. She hollered something in French and immediately half a dozen adolescent boys waved cigarette lighters at her.

'Merci, merci.' Tate took a long hard pull on her cigarette, waved to the boys and finally joined Caroline on the bridge.

'So this stick,' she said. 'Does it have the nominations stuff on it too?'

'Do you have any idea what kind of risks I took to get that information?'

'You know how much I appreciate everything you're doing.'

'I may have incriminated a colleague.'

'Sometimes sacrifices have to be made.' Tate sucked on her cigarette. 'Can I have the stick now?'

'I need to talk to you first.'

Tate exhaled and the wind blew a cloud of smoke into Caroline's face. The journalist's shoulders seemed to sag. Caroline clutched her handbag to her side.

'What have you managed to find out about the fake suicide note?'

'Fake? No one else seems to be questioning its authenticity.'

'Who? Who have you spoken to about it?' Caroline stopped and held onto Tate's arm. 'What did they tell you?'

Tate puffed out more smoke and tried to bat it away with her hand before it reached Caroline. 'Obviously I can't reveal my sources.'

'But what did they say?'

Tate plucked a speck of ash from her tongue and gazed out over the river. 'They didn't tell me anything.'

'Oh come on – they must have.'

The journalist lifted her sunglasses from her nose onto her head, trapping her flapping hair underneath. She looked into Caroline's face, started to speak then stopped.

'We had a deal,' Caroline said. 'You investigate Martin's death and I give you information.' Caroline squeezed her bag even tighter.

'We've still got a deal.' Tate eyed the bag. 'I don't want you reading anything into this. It might be standard procedure.'

'Please just tell me what you know.'

'The files have been classified with a high security rating. One of the highest. My source can't get access to them.'

Caroline took a moment to digest the information. She grabbed the side of the bridge and stared out at the horizon, her gaze settling on the dome of St Paul's.

'Who can – get access to them?'

'Only high ranking officers.'

'And you expect me to believe that's just normal procedure?'

'I'm not expecting anything – I'm just telling you what my guy told me.'

'He said it was normal?'

Tate hesitated, pulling on her cigarette. 'He's never come across it before. But then a government minister has never been found dead at his desk before either.'

Caroline grabbed Tate's arm and pulled her round so she was looking into her face. 'Do you truly still believe there isn't a massive cover-up going on?'

Tate shook her head and flicked what was left of her cigarette over the rail. The wind picked it up and it hovered in the air for a moment before falling. She watched it drop. Finally she turned back to Caroline. 'I don't know what to believe. Something about it is starting to make me feel uncomfortable.'

'Uncomfortable? The whole bloody thing stinks. You can't still think Martin committed suicide?'

Tate shrugged. 'It's still the most logical explanation. He died at his desk, for God's sake. If someone killed him, wouldn't they choose a dark alley somewhere? Or a quiet country lane?'

'The location doesn't make any sense either way. You could quite easily argue if Martin had been planning suicide he would have chosen somewhere he wouldn't be discovered so easily. His house... or... I don't know.... a deserted beach or a remote hilltop. He didn't kill himself. How many more times do I have to—'

'All right. Let's say he didn't. Let's say he was murdered.'

Caroline flinched.

'But that is what you're suggesting, isn't it? So... who do you think would want to kill him?'

Caroline squeezed her hands together. 'I have thought about it. I've thought about it a lot.'

'And?'

'Someone who wanted him out of the way, obviously.'

'And that someone managed to get into the department undetected, force a bottle of pills and half a litre of whiskey down his throat then disappear again without a trace. You really think that's possible?'

'If they were well enough connected, yes.'

'And have you come up with any likely assassins?'

Caroline inhaled before she spoke, anticipating Tate's response. 'The obvious candidate is William King.' She screwed up her face, waiting for the flack. It didn't come. Tate just raised her eyebrows and shook her head.

'Look at the sequence of events.' Caroline couldn't stop now. 'Oakley resigns – for personal reasons – Martin dies then King is made prime minister.'

'Listen to yourself. Do you know how much you're sounding like those bonkers conspiracy theorists? We've been through this already.'

'Yes, but it's different now.'

'Is it?'

'Now what's happened is starting to make you feel uncomfortable.'

Tate blew out an impatient sigh. 'I need another cigarette. Let's get off this bloody bridge.' She turned back the way they'd just come and headed towards the steps.

Caroline ran after her. 'Does it at least mean you'll do some more digging?'

Tate bit her lip. 'If someone somewhere is determined to cover this up, there's not a lot more digging I can do.'

Caroline pulled her handbag from her shoulder. 'Promise me you'll try.' She retrieved the memory stick, gripping it tightly, still reluctant to hand it over. 'Promise me.'

'I'll do whatever I can. There might be something on that stick that helps.' She reached out a hand. 'Have you looked at the documents yourself?'

Finally Caroline relinquished the stick and watched Tate shove it into her handbag. 'I've had a brief look at the public ones.'

'Public? What do you mean?'

'Some of the files I can't open, they're password protected. I've tried all the passwords we generally use in the division – the obvious ones like *password*, *admin*, *academies*. But nothing seems to work.'

'How am I expected to read them then?'

'I spoke to a techie at work about it.'

'What? I thought you didn't trust anyone at the department.'

'It was one of the external contractors working on the new website. He doesn't know me from Adam. Anyway, he told me they're usually pretty easy to get into. You just need some IT whiz to crack them open. They've got special software to do it, apparently.'

'Oh – and there was I thinking it might be difficult.' Tate shook her head and reached back into her bag. She pulled out a folded sheet of paper and handed it to Caroline.

'What's this?' Caroline started to unfold the sheet, careful not to let the wind catch it.

'The next batch of documents I'll be needing from you.'

24

Caroline tapped very lightly on Dan's door. 'Come on, love. Why don't you let me in and we can have a quiet little chat, just you and me. Like we used to.'

No response.

'Or maybe you could come downstairs and I can make some brownies. Do you fancy that? You can lick the spoon.'

Caroline had tried every other kind of inducement, appealing to his stomach was the only one left. She wasn't even sure she still had the recipe for brownies, let alone the ingredients. She heard a chair scrape across the floor.

'I'm not seven years old, Mum.'

His voice was quiet but close. He must have been standing just the other side of the door. Caroline pressed her hand against the wood. What had happened to her carefree little boy?

'You're never too old to lick the spoon,' she said. 'In fact you'll probably have to arm wrestle your dad for it. That's if Gran doesn't get there first.' She tried to inject a note of light-heartedness into her voice, but only managed to add an edge of mild desperation. She could hear him breathing.

'We can sort all this out, Dan. It might seem impossible right now, but believe me, it won't seem nearly so bad when you get a bit of perspective. Nothing's too big a problem that we can't fix it for you.'

'You can't fix this.' His voice was even quieter.

'Help *you* to fix it then.'

Dan made a noise deep in his throat, was it a laugh?

'Open the door and we can make a start. I can't fix anything talking through an inch and a half of wood.'

The door moved slightly, creaking against the doorframe, as if Dan was leaning against it.

'You don't understand,' he said.

'I will if you explain it to me.' She ran her hand along the grain of wood. 'Talk to me, Dan. It'll make things better – I promise.' She heard him sniff. 'We can sort it out together. The first step is telling me about it.' She leaned closer to the door. 'Dan?' He sniffed again. 'Would you rather speak to your dad?'

He made another indecipherable noise.

'Shall I get him to come and see you?'

'No!'

'OK... OK, love. Just you and me then. How about you open the door?'

'Talking won't fix it.'

'It's a start. We can come up with the answers together.'

'There aren't any.'

'Course there are. We love you Dan. Please let us help.'

She held her breath and listened again for signs of movement on the other side of the door.

'Did you talk to that bloke at work?'

'What bloke, sweetheart?'

'Don't call me that!'

Caroline puffed out her cheeks. 'Who do you mean?'

'He knew his problem couldn't be fixed.'

'Who are you talking about?'

'The one who killed himself. No one helped him, did they?'

'Martin?' She swallowed. 'But he didn't...' How much could she tell him?

'Why didn't you sit down with him and come up with some answers?'

'I didn't... no one expected—'

'He must have been so unhappy. Didn't you even notice?'

The door banged against the frame again and Caroline heard a thud on the floor.

'Dan? Are you OK?'

'Just leave me alone.'

'Are you OK? Dan? Tell me you're all right.'

'Go away.' He let out a sob.

'Dan? Open the door.' She turned the handle. 'You're not going to...? She rattled the door, turning the handle one way then the other. 'Dan – have you hurt yourself?'

He didn't reply.

'Unlock the door, Dan. Or I'll have to get your dad to break it down.'

'Leave me alone!'

'Dan I mean it!' She leaned over the banister and hollered down the stairs. 'Pete! Can you get up here?' She glanced back at the door. 'Now!'

A squeal of scraping metal was followed by a loud thunk and the door opened a crack. From the sliver of her son that was visible, she could just make out a red-rimmed eye and a moist cheek.

'Open it right up.'

He pulled the door wider.

'Show me your wrists,' she said.

He waved both arms in her face. 'Satisfied?'

She poked her head through the door and scanned the room, looking for sharp objects. 'Let me in.'

Dan stepped away from the door and hung his head low as Caroline checked shelves and window ledges, peering under the bed and across his desk. 'I don't want you locking yourself in again.' She backed slowly out of the room.

Dan slammed the door. Caroline heard the bolt slide across.

'Dan!'

Pete appeared at the top of the stairs. 'Where's the fire?'

'It's a bloody good job there wasn't one, the time it's taken you to get up here.'

'What's going on?'

'Your son's locked himself in his room.'

'How is that an emergency?'

'He's depressed. I'm worried what he might do.' She walked across the landing and started down the stairs. 'Is your toolbox still in the van?'

'It's in the shed. What do you want it for?' He followed behind her.

'I'm going to get that bloody bolt off his door.'

'The lad needs his privacy. Let him be.'

'You haven't seen the state of him. He could be doing anything in there.'

They'd both reached the hall. Pete grabbed her.

'Caz, wait! What are you saying?'

'I'm frightened he might hurt himself.' She plucked his hand from her arm.

'You don't seriously believe he'd do something like that?'

'I don't know what to think.'

'What did he say?'

'Do you really care?'

'Come on, Caz. I don't deserve that.'

Caroline marched into the kitchen and started rummaging in a drawer for the spare key to the garden shed. 'Have you even tried talking to him?'

'I'm the last person he'd want to speak to. We're not exactly the best of mates.' Pete rubbed both hands across his face.

'When did you two have such a major falling out? And how did I miss it?'

'He's a teenager, Caz. He's meant to hate his parents.'

'Speak for yourself.'

'He's growing up, that's all. Testing boundaries. It's natural.'

'Impregnating an underage schoolgirl is more than testing boundaries, Pete.' She slammed the drawer shut.

'Accidents happen. We know that better than most people.'

Caroline froze. *Please don't bring that up now.* She flung open the next drawer, scooped up handfuls of the contents and threw them on the work surface. 'Where is that bloody key?'

Pete put his huge hands round her waist and pulled her backwards, pressing her into him. 'He'll be all right, Caz. We were.'

'History doesn't have to repeat itself. We weren't still at school when it happened.'

Pete pressed his cheek against hers, his lips brushing her mouth. She closed her eyes. It would have been a relief to have someone else take charge for a change. She took a deep breath and tried to relax into his embrace. She couldn't. She twisted round and wriggled out of his arms. 'Not now.'

'When, Caz?' He held her hands in his, staring into her eyes for a moment, searching. What was he looking for? Whatever it was, he didn't find it. He let go of her hands and turned away. 'I'm going to the pub.'

Caroline watched him hurry into the hall and grab his battered leather jacket from the coat rack. 'The pub?'

'I need to get out.'

'Not today. Please.'

'Do you actually give a toss where I am?'

She followed him into the hall. 'I thought today, after everything that's happened, we could sit down as a family. Have a proper lunch together.'

'That would involve some effort on your part.'

'What?'

'I can't remember the last time you cooked Sunday dinner. We just don't do that any more.' He lowered his voice. 'Maybe if you were around a bit more Dan wouldn't be acting up.'

'What?'

'You heard.'

'Are you blaming me?'

'You're never here.' Pete struggled to get his arm in the other sleeve of his jacket.

'Do you think I want to be in the department all hours?'

He shrugged.

'God, Pete – you know how many times they've threatened us with compulsory redundancy. Would you rather I stayed at home all day and became the perfect housewife? I'd like to see us pay the mortgage then!' She leaned a hand against the wall, suddenly unsteady. She hadn't meant to shout.

'You know, I wouldn't mind giving that a try, see if the woman I married is still lurking in there somewhere.'

'And if I did, do you think you might be able to stay sober for more than a couple of hours a day?' She stepped between Pete and the front door. 'I suppose that's all my fault too.' She let out a breath.

'You don't know anything about it.' Pete reached round Caroline and grabbed the latch on the front door, pulling it open as far as it would go without hitting her.

'You can't keep running away – pretend things aren't happening.'

'Well it's the best strategy I've come up with.'

'I mean it. I'm asking you – please don't go now. Stay and help me with Dan.'

'He won't talk to me – you're better off on your own with him.'

He squeezed between Caroline and the wall without making contact with either and slipped through the gap.

'Pete!'

The door slammed shut. Caroline yanked it open again.

'Don't expect to get back in!' she hollered after him. But he was already through the gate. She closed the door quietly and let out a long, low sigh. How had they come to this? She closed her eyes and sank back against the door.

She heard a tiny snuffling noise. She opened her eyes wide and peered up the stairs, towards the sound. The snuffle broke into a sob. Ben was standing at the top of the stairs, tears streaming down his cheeks.

25

'So Dan did turn up for registration?' Caroline hurried towards the back of the queue at the coffee counter on the lower ground floor of the department. 'You're sure?' The signal of her mobile phone was cutting out. 'And he's in class now? I'm sorry?' The violent hiss of the espresso machine drowned out the school secretary's reply. 'Hello?'

'Caroline! Just the person,' Jeremy Prior barked at her from the head of the line. 'Let me buy you a coffee.'

Caroline froze then looked left and right, feeling just like a cornered animal. There was no escape. The phone was dead against her ear. She shoved it into her bag.

'Peppermint tea for me,' she said, desperate for a double-shot latte and almond croissant, but not wanting Prior to make any judgments about her. She smiled apologetically at the other people in the queue as she walked past them. A cardboard cup appeared on the counter, the soggy paper tab swinging from a string. Caroline picked it up.

'Thanks, Jeremy. Very kind of you.' She raised the cup to her lips and pretended to take a sip. It smelled just like toothpaste.

'Let's go back upstairs together, shall we?' He gestured for her to lead the way. 'Pam tells me you've still made no progress.'

'Progress?'

'Three weeks now and you've not turned up anything.' Prior lengthened his stride, darted around Caroline and pushed open a set of swing doors. 'I can't deny it – I'm disappointed.' As he let her pass through the doors he peered into her face. 'Very disappointed.'

It took her a moment to realise he was talking about the missing CD-ROM. 'I'm not sure what else we could have done,' she said. 'It's just not here. I've spoken to everyone again – got the thumbscrews out, just like you said – and still no one's admitted to knowing anything about it.'

They reached the lifts. Prior continued to stare at her as they joined a group of young men who looked like they were dressed for the beach rather than a government department. Caroline nodded to one of them, recognising him as one of the external contractors responsible for building the new website. The one who'd told her about cracking password protected files. *Please don't say anything.* She quickly turned away to discover Prior still hadn't taken his eyes off her.

'We could speak to everyone again,' she said, 'though I don't know what good it would do. I think we just have to accept the CD-ROM's just—'

'Not here!' Prior threw up a hand. Caroline instinctively flinched. He raised a finger to his lips and tilted his head towards the group of contractors. The lift doors opened.

'How are you, anyway?' Prior asked, smiling at her now, switching with some obvious effort, to small talk mode. 'Pamela tells me you didn't get in until lunchtime on Friday.'

Thanks Pam.

'Is everything all right at home? Is your son quite well? Dan, isn't it?'

How dare Pam talk to Prior about Dan.

'Teenage boys must be a dreadful worry.'

'My son is very well. Thank you for asking. Everything's fine.'

'Are you sure?' He looked into her face and pursed his lips. Was he actually displaying concern? She found herself smiling back at him.

'Home's fine, Dan's fine, I'm fine.'

'Mmm…' He looked her up and down. 'You're no good to me in the office if you're distracted by issues at home. I need you at the top of your game.'

Caroline closed her eyes for a moment. How could she have thought even for a second that Prior was showing some genuine sign of human empathy?

Prior said nothing more until they were safely out of the lift and into the academies section. He started back on the subject of the disappearing CD-ROM as if there'd been no interruption.

'As it has been three weeks, we feel a change of tack is required.'

We?

'A change of tack?' Caroline's throat was parched. She took a sip of her peppermint tea and immediately regretted it.

'Damage limitation is our top priority from now on. We can't let this get out. Not during an election. If it did the results could be catastrophic.'

They reached Caroline's desk.

'I'm sure you – of all people – will understand the importance of discretion.' Prior held her gaze.

What was he getting at?

'After the events of the last few weeks…'

Caroline shrugged.

'Pam tells me you were hounded by the press. You kept your own counsel. I admire that. I admire your *loyalty*, Caroline.'

She wasn't sure how to react. Was it a test? There was a teasing, sneering tone to his voice.

'But the election doesn't really concern us, does it?' she said, staring right back at him, determined not to look away first. 'Not as civil servants – we are meant to be completely neutral, after all.'

'Don't be so naïve, Caroline. How long have you been in the job?' He glanced away and ran his fingers through his lank hair. 'Whoever's fault this was,' he said, gazing around the office at her colleagues. 'Whichever member of staff was careless enough to misplace all of that sensitive information... well... the buck will inevitably stop with the new secretary of state.'

'But how can she be responsible for something that happened before she even started working here?'

The pay-as-you-go mobile started to ring in Caroline's bag. She ignored it.

'Don't let me stop you,' Prior said and pointed at her bag.

'It's OK – they'll leave a message.'

Prior waited for the ringing to cease before he continued. 'That's not the way it works – surely you know that? The press would demand a scapegoat. The current secretary of state would have to be sacrificed. That's just the way things are.'

He was making it sound like the outcome had already been decided.

'But if the story never gets out—'

'It can't. I'm going to call the whole team together.' He sighed, as if communicating with the academies division was a particularly irksome task. 'I will not tolerate leaks, Caroline. We must ensure everyone understands that.' He was staring at her again, his eyes burning into hers. He glanced towards his office. 'I have to go.'

Greg, the IT man, was standing outside Prior's door, chatting to Lisa. Caroline felt her heart thud against her chest. What if he mentioned the phone conversation? Lisa wouldn't have a clue what he was talking about. She probably didn't even know about the computer surveillance. Caroline stood rigid at her desk, half inclined to make a bolt for the door.

'I'm sure I don't need to impress upon you the importance of confidentiality.' Prior was still there, watching Caroline as she stared at Greg and Lisa. 'Caroline?'

'No – of course not.'

Prior turned away and marched the length of the office. He grabbed Greg by the elbow and steered him through the door.

The pay-as-you-go mobile started to ring again in her bag. She dragged it out and stabbed the answer button.

'Before you even go there, forget it. I just can't risk getting anything else for you.' She heard an inhalation of breath at the other end of the line. 'What about your digging? Have you discovered anything new?'

Caroline looked up to see Greg leaving Prior's room, head hanging low, hands shoved deep into the pockets of his combats. Prior followed him out.

'Well?'

'I just wanted to touch base.'

'Call me when you've actually got something to say.'

Prior had stopped at Pam's desk. He lifted a file from her in tray and let it drop, then scanned the office.

'I've got to go.' Caroline hung up and threw the phone back into her bag.

'Not more domestic problems, I hope?' Prior walked straight past her and sat on the edge of the desk next to hers. 'Is it your son?' He ran his fingers lightly over Tracy's keyboard.

'Nope – sales call.'

'Have you seen Pamela?'

Caroline shook her head. What had Greg told him?

'Well then, perhaps you can tell me.'

Caroline braced herself.

'When was the last time Tracy Clarke was in the office? Do you remember?'

She took a breath, determined to keep her voice steady. 'Tracy? Why?'

'Do you remember when she was last here?'

'Well, she was in with the baby. A little while ago.'

'And since then?'

Caroline could clearly see Tracy's box under the desk, just inches away from Prior's feet. 'I couldn't really say.' She smiled, her top lip stuck to her teeth. 'Is it something important?'

Prior got to his feet. 'I'll ask Pamela. Perhaps her memory is more reliable than yours.' He walked away, then after a few steps, he stopped and turned back. 'Are you sure your... difficulties at home aren't... impairing your performance?'

He made her sound like a world class athlete, or a highly strung racehorse.

'Quite sure.'

'Perhaps you should box up your things early. Take a couple of days off until the dust has settled.'

'Dust?'

'The removal crates are due to be delivered this afternoon. Pamela's organising it.'

'I'm sorry, Jeremy, you've completely lost me.'

'The office move.'

She shook her head.

'Your mind really isn't on the job, is it?'

Why did he keep saying that? *Bloody Pam.* What had she been saying?

'The whole floor is being refurbished. We're moving down to the second floor in the interim. The memo was circulated last Friday.'

'I didn't get a memo.'

'Perhaps it arrived while you were busy dealing with your domestic issues.'

'Why is the office being refurbished?'

'Why not?'

First the ministers' floor, now the academies division. Someone really was determined to eradicate any lingering trace of Martin Fox from the building. What could there possibly be on this floor that needed to be expunged?

'When is this happening?'

'Thursday and Friday.'

'During the week?'

Prior nodded.

'They usually organise moves for the weekend.'

Prior shrugged. 'Ours is not to reason why, Caroline.' He looked into her eyes and held her gaze for a good few seconds before he spoke again. 'We just need to obey orders.'

26

As soon as she walked through the archway and started to climb the stairs, the sounds and smells of Angela Tate's childhood not so much flooded back as seeped into her clothes and crawled under her skin. The stink of vomit and dog piss made her eyes water. She trudged up the concrete steps, hesitating at each turn of the stair, fully expecting a shadowy threat to emerge from every dark corner. On the second floor landing she picked her way through crushed beer cans and empty takeaway trays, ducked under another arch and back into daylight.

She walked slowly along the narrow walkway, peering through metal-barred security gates to check the number on each front door. Betty Larson lived at number 29.

It had taken Angela three days to track down Fred Larson's first wife. She'd eventually discovered an Elizabeth Mary Larson on the electoral register for Tower Hamlets. It turned out Betty had been born, raised and married without venturing outside Bethnal Green. She tied the knot with Fred in a civil ceremony at the town hall in April 1958. They got divorced in 1971, only a couple of months before Fred Larson married the 21-year-old Valerie.

Angela passed number 28 and reached a metal gate spanning the width of the walkway. Betty Larson's door was tucked into the corner of the landing on the other side. Angela stretched an arm between the bars, but the bell was well beyond her reach.

'Mrs Larson?' she shouted. 'Hello – anyone home?' She rattled the gate.

'Whatever it is you're selling, I can't afford it.'

Angela spun round to see a grey-haired woman in a petrol blue raincoat and thick support stockings struggling slowly along the landing towards her. A pair of large-framed spectacles covered most of the top half of her face; a rictus grimace spread across the bottom half. She was gripping the handle of a tartan shopping trolley, using it for support like a Zimmer frame on wheels.

'And if you're on a recruitment drive for the local church, you're wasting your time. I'm adequately catered for in that department.' She gestured towards a silver crucifix hanging from her neck.

'Mrs Larson?' Angela tried her best to switch on an electric smile.

'Who wants her?' The woman scanned Angela from head to toe. 'The gas board? Or our Saviour?'

'Neither, Mrs Larson. Can I call you Betty?'

'No you certainly can't. Who are you?'

Angela extended a hand as the woman reached the gate. 'My name's Angela Tate.'

The woman ignored the hand and dipped her fingers into the knitted bag strapped across her chest. 'Do I know you?'

'No...' Angela glanced down at the crucifix and considered making up some story about being sent on an outreach mission from the local diocese, but wasn't sure she could pull it off. 'I'm a journalist, Mrs Larson. From the *Evening News.*'

The old woman's expression tightened, her glasses slipped down her nose a fraction. 'What do you want with me?'

Angela broadened her smile. 'I'd like to speak to you... to get your opinion.' She glanced over Betty Larson's shoulder at the front door beyond the gate. 'Can I come in?'

'Is it about the gangs coming onto the estate?'

Again, it seemed the easiest thing in the world to just say yes and inveigle her way into the old woman's flat with a lie. But Angela hesitated, letting the woman's gaze penetrate hers for a moment too long, and she found herself compelled to tell Betty Larson the truth.

'No, Mrs Larson... it's something else.' She looked towards the front door again. The paint was flaking from the wood, the mortar crumbling between the brickwork surrounding it. How could a multi-millionaire knight of the realm let his first wife live out her days in a shithole like this? 'I'd like to talk to you about your husband.' Angela braced herself for the fallout.

'Fred? What makes you think I'd want to talk about him?' She slotted a chunky key into the lock and pushed open the gate.

'I'm doing a profile on him.'

Betty Larson narrowed her eyes. 'He's not dead is he?'

'No! It's not an obituary.'

Angela thought she heard a little sigh of disappointment issue from Betty's mouth.

'I've got nothing to say.' The old woman retrieved the key and struggled to manoeuvre the tartan trolley through the gate.

'Let me help you with that.' Angela grabbed the handle and started pushing.

'I can manage!' Betty Larson yanked the bag back and shoved it down the landing. 'Just like I manage every other day.' She slipped through the gap and pushed the key back into the lock.

'Please, Mrs Larson. Just a quick chat. Ten minutes, that's all.'

'I have nothing to say about him.'

With the gate closing in her face, Angela's journalistic survival instinct finally kicked in. 'He has plenty to say about you.' She couldn't help herself.

Betty Larson's hand was still on the key, she'd turned it only halfway in the lock. 'Does he?'

Angela nodded, hoping to achieve the right mix of sincerity and sympathy in her expression.

'What, exactly?'

Angela glanced back down the landing. 'I think perhaps we should go inside to discuss it.'

She was through the front door, down the hall and into the living room in a matter of seconds. Betty Larson sat her on an uncomfortable settee and told her to wait while she 'put away her perishables'.

Angela perched on the edge of the 1950s-style three-seater, the hard wood frame pressing against her thighs through the thin cushions. She scanned the sparsely furnished room looking for clues to Betty Larson's personality. Apart from a crucifix on the opposite wall and a couple of framed photographs sitting at the far end of a dark brown sideboard, there was nothing to betray the woman's secrets. She was beginning to doubt Betty even had any. The room was scrubbed as clean as a nun's cell, the faint aroma of mothballs permeating everything, as if the upholstery on the settee and the grim velvet curtains at the window had been sitting in a charity shop for too long.

Betty Larson reappeared five minutes later wearing a drab beige coverall, a tray of tea things in her hand. She shuffled to the coffee table next to the settee in a pair of old-fashioned carpet slippers that looked two sizes too big. Once she'd deposited the tray, she slowly made her way to the window and opened it wide.

'You've brought in the smell of cigarettes with you.'

Angela smiled apologetically.

'I can't abide them.' She thumped a hand against her chest and let out a cough thick with congestion. She lowered herself into an armchair next to the settee.

'It's a terrible vice, I know. I've been trying to give up.'

'Sometimes it takes more than will power alone to resist temptation.' Betty glanced towards the crucifix on the wall.

'Indeed.' Angela reached for the teapot.

A scrawny hand slipped over hers. 'It needs to brew.'

Angela shifted position, trying to get comfortable, and failed. She got to her feet.

'What's Fred been saying?' The old woman peered up at her, the thick lenses of her glasses enlarging her eyes alarmingly.

Angela sucked in a breath and walked towards the window. Two storeys below a handful of children were chasing one another across a rubbish-strewn playground. She exhaled and turned back to Betty.

'He's been telling me all about...' She groped desperately for a subject. 'About your divorce. The reasons your marriage ended.' All Angela knew for sure was that they were divorced by mutual consent.

'He told you about that?' Betty Larson sat very upright, her hands clasped tight in her lap. 'He had no right to.'

Angela wandered across the room, hoping desperately Betty Larson wouldn't press her on the details. 'I'd like to hear your version of events. For the sake of balance.'

Betty Larson was staring into space, gripping her hands together even tighter.

Angela had a sudden flash of inspiration. 'He's writing his memoirs, you see. If you speak to me now, you can make your side of the story public before he does.'

The old woman's head had started to shake, as if she'd developed a sudden tremor. 'Story? My private life isn't part of some story.'

'That's not how most people will see it.'

'But that isn't right.'

Angela leaned a hand against the sideboard and glanced down at the framed photographs. 'I'm afraid private lives sell newspapers,' she said, and looked more closely at the two pictures. An old sepia image featured a man and a woman in Edwardian dress. The woman was seated in front of the man, holding a baby wrapped in a long lace shawl. The other photograph was much more recent. Judging by the fashion, it must have been taken in the early 80s. It was a head and shoulders shot of a young man with a prematurely receding hairline and perfect white teeth. 'It's better to get the truth out there first. Believe me.' Angela picked up the picture frame. 'Who's this?'

'Be careful with that.'

'He's very handsome.' She angled the photo towards the window.

Betty was struggling to lift herself out of her armchair. 'Put it down!'

Angela returned the frame to its spot on the sideboard and held up her hands.

'I'm sorry – I didn't mean to upset you.'

The old woman made it to her feet and shuffled towards her. She pulled a handkerchief from the pocket in her apron, snatched up the frame and polished the glass.

'Freddie always took a good picture.' She stared down at the smiling face. 'The only thing he inherited from his father.'

Angela swallowed, temporarily lost for words.

Fred Larson Jr? How had he never come to light in her research? Fred and Valerie Larson were childless. Recently, in the light of his ill health, there had been much speculation about who would inherit the Fred Larson fortune when he finally died. If that photo was taken in the early 1980s, young Freddie would be in his mid to late 40s by now. Yet never had there been any public acknowledgment that he even existed. Was Fred Larson *ashamed* of him?

'This is your son?'

The old woman nodded, her gaze distant again. She opened a drawer in the sideboard and took out another portrait of the same man. He was much younger in this one, a teenager dressed in a smart blazer and school tie.

'His teachers were so proud of him.'

'I expect you are too. He's a credit to you.'

'Fred left us before Freddie was even born.'

'It must have been very difficult for you at the time.'

'We weren't alone – my faith gave me strength.'

Angela studied both photographs of Freddie Jr. He looked nothing like his father, or even his mother, but still there was something vaguely familiar about him. 'And Freddie still lives in the area?' She struggled to keep the excitement out of her voice.

Betty Larson's shoulders sagged, she seemed to visibly shrink.

'How often does he visit?'

The old woman laid both photographs face down on the sideboard. 'I don't see him as much as I'd like.'

Behind the thick lenses of Betty's glasses Angela thought she saw the suggestion of a tear. The old woman turned away.

'I think it's time for you to leave.'

God, not now, we're only just scraping the surface.

'Don't you want to tell me your side of events – just how difficult it was for you – bringing up a child on your own in the 60s?'

'I've already told you – I had my faith.' She shuffled across the room and stood to one side of the living room door.

Don't shut up shop, come on, Betty.

'What about Freddie?' Angela reluctantly joined her at the door. 'Shouldn't he have the chance to speak out?' Angela frowned, realising in that instant Freddie Larson Jr could have spoken out at any time in the last quarter of a century. Why hadn't he?

'What did Fred tell you about him?' Betty was scrutinising her with those enormous eyes again. Angela hesitated, unsure which way to spin the next fabrication.

'To be honest...' She swallowed. 'Sir Fred didn't say an awful lot about him.' She snatched a breath. 'I got the impression he was...'

'What?'

'It seemed to me as if he's ashamed of his son.'

Betty's mouth dropped open. She leaned her weight against the wall.

'Are you OK – can I get you anything? A glass of water?' Angela hooked an arm under Betty's and forcibly guided her towards the settee. She sat her down, poured out a cup of inky tea and added three sugars to it. She handed it to Betty. The old woman took a sip then, with trembling hands, put it back on the table.

'He promised Freddie he wouldn't mention the problem to anyone.'

Problem?

Angela pulled a face and nodded as sagely as she could. 'Actually, I think he was relieved to be able to talk about it.'

'To a journalist?'

Angela shrugged. 'People like to confide in me.'

'But that was one of the conditions. He agreed to pay for Freddie's treatment just so long as no one found out about it. But he thought it was all right to tell you?'

'I'm a good listener.' Angela sat down and poured herself a cup of tea. 'Between you and me, Mrs Larson, I was quite surprised that Sir Fred was ashamed of his son's...' She was really groping in the dark now. 'His... condition.'

'You can't really blame him, I suppose.' The old woman let out a long sigh. 'It is a mortal sin.'

Angela fidgeted on the uncomfortable settee. 'Isn't it more a sickness?' She felt as if she was running out of guesses in a game of twenty questions. 'Shouldn't we really be feeling sorry for Freddie?'

'But the medicine they give him is just as bad as the filth he was injecting into his veins. It's still opium isn't it?'

Angela quietly pushed her business card onto the table and leaned back on the settee. She exhaled, not trusting herself to speak. She had an urge to punch the air. After a moment she cleared her throat. 'I'm sure the treatment will be successful. I expect you're praying for him?'

'Every day. But the treatment won't cure the reason he became addicted in the first place. I pray every day that he can rid himself of that sin too.' She turned to Angela. 'I suppose Fred was too ashamed to talk to you about that.'

'Actually, he did touch on it... briefly.' She wriggled forward on the thin seat cushion. 'Would you like to comment on it?'

'You would love that for your story, wouldn't you?'

'I... I just want a balanced account – like I said before.'

She looked into Betty's eyes and saw a shutter go down. It felt as if the temperature in the room had dropped a few degrees. Betty Larson struggled to her feet.

'I'll see you out.'

27

Caroline pushed open her front door, stepped inside and wearily unbuttoned her jacket. Her arms were heavy and her fingers numb, she fumbled with each button. The adrenalin she must have produced over the last 72 hours would probably have been enough to revive a three-day-old corpse. Right now it felt as if she'd completely exhausted her supply.

By the time she'd left the office, facilities management still hadn't delivered the moving crates. She'd planned to stay until they arrived, to make a start on packing, but Pam had practically prised her from her desk, telling her she was under strict instructions from Prior to make sure she left early. With Pam watching over her, Caroline had reluctantly gathered together her bag and jacket at 3:30pm, convinced more than ever that something was brewing and it was somehow related to the computer surveillance and the academies division move. Anything might be spirited away from the fourth floor in her absence.

She wriggled slowly out of her jacket and resolved to get into the office as early as possible the next morning. She still might be able to save some vital piece of evidence that was destined for the shredder. She shoved her jacket on the banister post, too tired to fight with the coats on the rack by the front door, and made for the clank and rattle of crockery coming from the kitchen. She pushed open the door, expecting to see her mother overexerting herself, but discovered Dan instead, squeezing a fat worm of mayonnaise over a sandwich filling that seemed to consist of an entire deli counter's supply of ham and cheese, with a handful of cheesy puffs piled on top.

'No wonder you never want your dinner,' she said and kissed him on the cheek before he had a chance to duck away.

'I'm growing.' He laid a hand on the top slice of bread and leaned on it until mayo oozed from the sides. 'It's important to get sufficient protein and fat in my diet.'

'Can I put in a good word for vegetables?' Caroline flipped on the kettle and retrieved a mug from an overhead cupboard. 'How about a nice tomato to go with that? Or a bit of lettuce?'

Dan pulled a face and headed towards the door, sandwich in one hand, can of Coke in the other.

'Where's your gran?'

'Having a lie down.'

'Good. I'll pop in and see her in a bit.'

'Whatever.'

'I was hoping we could have a little chat. Just you and me.' Caroline threw a teabag into the mug and tried to sound casual. 'Talk about… you know, things.'

Dan stopped before he reached the door. He didn't turn round. 'I don't want to talk about it.'

'You're going to have to at some point. The problem won't just go away through wishful thinking.'

Dan slouched into the hall.

'We all need to sit down and discuss what's going to happen next.' The kettle hissed noisily on the counter, Caroline flicked it off. 'Did you get a chance to speak to Kylie at school today?' Caroline shouted after him. 'How was she?'

'Mum! Can you just drop it? It's none of your business.'

'Oh I think it is. You're only 14. Your business is my business.' She could hear her mother saying much the same thing to her, 25 years ago. She shuddered. 'I didn't mean that. I'm sorry.'

Dan stomped to the stairs. Caroline ran after him.

'We will need to talk, Dan. Why not start now, when it's just the two of us?'

Dan ignored her and started up the stairs.

'Dan! Don't walk away while I'm talking to you. You still haven't told me where you were all night on Friday.'

'Please Mum – not now.'

'But what happened? Who were you with? Did you get into a fight?'

He disappeared onto the landing. Caroline heard his bedroom door slam shut.

Another triumph of good parenting. Well done you.

She trudged up the stairs and hesitated when she reached his room. What was the best way to handle this? She tried to remember what her mother had said to her so that she could avoid making the same mistakes.

Through the door she heard the tapping of fingers on keyboard. Dan seemed to be much happier instant messaging complete strangers than talking to his own family. Sometimes she thought she'd have a better chance communicating with him if she invented a screen name for herself and lurked in his favourite sci-fi forum. Maybe it wasn't such a stupid idea. There had to be a way of connecting with him. What she needed was something that didn't involve eye contact. Some activity where they could sit and chat while they were occupied doing something else. Preferably involving something techie. She stood for a few moments, just listening to the rapid whirr of fingertips on plastic, waiting for inspiration to strike.

Of course.

She ran downstairs, collected her laptop from the living room and hurried back to his door. She thumped her free hand against the wood.

'Dan?'

The rattle of the keyboard coming through door slowed for a moment.

'I'm sorry I've upset you, love. I didn't mean to. It was really dumb of me, especially as I need your help.'

The typing ceased.

'I need to ask you a favour. I've got a computer problem that could really do with your input. I'm sure you could solve it for me in no time. I've been struggling with it for days.'

'What is it?' His voice was indistinct, his mouth probably crammed with cheesy puff sandwich.

'It's a work thing. If I don't get it sorted I could be in serious amounts of trouble.' She knocked on the door again. 'Do you think you might be able to help?'

After a few seconds of silence the door creaked open a crack.

Several cups of tea and half a packet of chocolate digestives later, Caroline was still sitting next to Dan, watching her son's fingers blur over the keyboard of her laptop. He only used the first two fingers of each hand and his right thumb for the spacebar, but Dan's typing speed must have been twice the rate she notched up on the Pitman secretarial course she completed when she wasn't much older than he was now. He stopped at intervals to attend to the pinging of instant messages on his own laptop. As he typed his replies his forehead puckered and the corners of his mouth turned down in an exaggerated scowl.

'I remember when I used to speak to my friends on the phone. Or even meet up in the Wimpy for a gossip and a banana split,' Caroline said after one of Dan's prolonged bouts of messaging. 'I do hope I didn't pull a face like that. We used to have a laugh.'

'What – back in the dark ages?'

'Who are you talking to? Would I have met any of them?' She glanced at his screen. '*The Boss*? Which one of your mates is a Springsteen fan? Should get him together with your dad.'

165

'God, Mum! It's private. Do you want me to help you or what?'

'Won't say another word.'

She sat quietly for another five minutes eyeing the open packet of biscuits on the desk, desperately trying to resist helping herself to another. To avoid temptation, she twisted the wrapper tight shut and reached over Dan, putting them on the far side of the desk, well out of grabbing distance. As she sat back down she noticed a scrap of paper with an 0800 number scrawled across it, the initials 'CL' written underneath. It wasn't Dan's handwriting.

'What are you looking at now?' He stopped typing and turned round to face her.

'You know me and biscuits – I won't be happy until I've hoovered up the lot.'

Dan got out of his chair and looked across the desk. He spotted the paper scrap and glanced back at her. He plucked it off the desk, together with his mobile phone, and stuffed them both in a pocket.

'How are we getting on anyway?' Caroline said. 'Making progress?'

'Can't really tell you that.' Dan clamped his bottom lip tight between his teeth. 'Might be another five minutes, or another five hours. You could just leave me to it.'

'Not sure I could, actually – given it's a work thing – you know, confidentiality rules and all that.'

'What? Are you telling me it's top secret? Where you work?'

'Less of the sarcasm, thank you. You'd be surprised what passes across my desk. All manner of classified information.'

Dan snorted and started typing again. 'If you're staying you might want to get something to read.'

'I'm fine as I am.' She made an effort not to glance towards his pocket. An 0800 number? She tried to remember the other digits, but the glimpse had been too fleeting. Who was 'CL'? The company whose number it was, or the person who'd written the note? She resolved to check the last landline phone bill; it was just possible Dan had called the freephone number using the home phone.

'So… how's school?' Desperate to keep him talking, she plumped for the safest subject. Everything else seemed to be out of bounds.

He shrugged.

'Played any big matches lately?'

'What?'

'The rugby – how's your shoulder?' She lifted off her seat a fraction, trying to get a better look. Dan immediately pulled the collar of his shirt up.

'I know you didn't want to go to the doctor's after last Friday, but you might have done yourself some serious damage. Why don't you let me take a look?'

Dan shoved back his chair and stood up. 'I'm not sure we're going to have much luck with this.'

Caroline let out a breath. She'd pushed him too far. God knew how many more unexplained injuries he was carrying. 'If you were having trouble at school...'

He stared down at her, his face contorting the way it used to when he was a toddler, just before the tears started to roll. As much as it pained her, she pressed on. 'You would tell me, wouldn't you? Or if not me, a teacher?'

Dan marched across the room, folded his arms and stood facing the wall.

'If someone's been threatening you...' She had a sudden vision of Reynolds spitting and swearing. He was no better than a school bully. 'Kylie's dad hasn't... If he's so much as laid a finger on you... Dan – has he hurt you?'

Dan blew out a noisy breath, but didn't say a word.

'Dan? You can tell me, you know. I won't go round there all guns blazing.'

'You don't know what you're talking about,' he said quietly.

'Tell me, then. Don't leave me on the outside.'

He turned slowly towards her, rubbing a hand up and down his arm.

'What's wrong with your arm?'

'It's nothing. Drop it.' He was closer to tears than she'd realised.

Caroline held up her hands. 'OK, OK.'

'I'm not leaving you on the outside. It's just that...'

Come on Dan, you can do it.

'I mean...' He screwed up his face, took a step forward and lifted his arms from his sides. For a moment Caroline was convinced he was going to embrace her. She smiled and walked towards him.

Her laptop let out a loud ping.

'Tell me what's wrong Dan.'

He turned away from her to look at the laptop screen. It was too late. The moment was lost.

'That means it's cracked the password.'

'No, I meant—'

'Excellent!' He sat back down and expanded an Excel spreadsheet so that it filled the screen. 'Is this what you were expecting?'

Caroline slumped into her seat and stared at the small text until it gradually stopped swimming in front of her eyes. She nodded slowly.

The heading at the top of the sheet: *Contractors,* didn't come as a complete surprise. It was, after all, a document taken from the procurement folder. The first column was headed *Name of contractor* and each cell below contained the name of a company – again, hardly earth shattering information. The names ran in alphabetical order, from AB Containers at the top to Davis Electricals at the bottom of the screen. Caroline grabbed the mouse and scrolled down a few dozen lines. She'd still only got as far as the E's and the F's. A few of the companies were listed more than once. She checked the heading in the next column: *Academy.* That explained the repetition in the first one – government approved contractors were likely to work on more than one building project. She couldn't understand why someone had gone to the trouble of password protecting such uncontroversial information. She was obviously missing something. She scanned the remaining columns. The third was headed with a pound sign followed by three zeros, which presumably would be the total worth of each contract. The amounts ranged from a few thousand to a few hundred thousand pounds. As each academy cost around £25 million to build, these amounts weren't particularly out of the ordinary.

'Was it worth the bother?' Dan said. 'You look disappointed.'

'It all looks pretty standard stuff.'

'No state secrets then?'

She shook her head.

The next column contained a list of names, surname followed by initials. The one after that was headed *Severity* and contained numbers, mostly eights, nines and tens. Caroline traced a finger along a row. *Fisher Logistics, Cuckmere Arts Academy, 20, Rogers, B, 10.* Her finger stopped underneath the heading of the final column.

'*User error, Y, N?*' Dan read out the heading for her. 'What does that mean?'

Caroline looked down the final column. A 'Y' had been entered in every cell. 'I've got no idea.'

Dan took over the scrolling and the rows shot up the screen, like speeded up credits at the end of a film. Caroline had to look away, to stop herself feeling sick.

'One hundred and... 74 entries.' Dan frowned.

'What is it?' Caroline said. 'Now you look disappointed.'

'VL Construction?' He pointed to the bottom of the screen. 'Isn't that the name of the company Dad works for?'

28

Angela Tate dumped her bag on the desk and collapsed onto a chair. She slowly eased off first one shoe, then the other. Three toes on her left foot and two on the right were bleeding through her tights. She held her breath and carefully pulled the nylon away from the skin. Sudden tears sprang into her eyes.

She had walked from Sadler's Wells to Holborn before finally managing to flag down a cab. Her shoes hadn't been designed with pavement pounding in mind. But then neither had her feet. She pressed a tentative thumb into the ball of her left foot, then pushed it deeper into the flesh. She massaged anti-clockwise for a couple of minutes, reversed direction for a couple more, then switched to the other foot, sniffing back the tingle in her nose and dabbing her eyes free of moisture.

She threw the offending footwear into the bottom drawer of Jason Morris's console, slammed it shut and dragged her handbag across the desk. A handwritten note had somehow attached itself to the bottom of the bag. She unpeeled it from the leather and held it at arm's length. She could only just make out her editor's tiny initials at the bottom. Dominic Evans wanted to see her. He'd struck through 'at your earliest convenience' and written 'ASAP' and underlined it three times. Angela screwed the paper into a tight ball and tossed it in the bin under her desk.

Jumped up little sod.

She retrieved her notebook from her bag and flicked through it until she reached the two pages she'd scribbled on at the Family Records Office in Clerkenwell. She'd tried as best she could to duplicate the format of the original ledger, even drawing the boxes around each entry as she copied them onto the page. The official copy of Freddie Larson's birth certificate she'd ordered wouldn't arrive for another two weeks. In the meantime she would have to make do with her hastily drawn facsimile.

Betty Larson had visited the register office to record the birth of baby Freddie a month after he was born. His full name was Frederick Joseph Larson. Betty must have allowed herself a little creative licence when describing her estranged husband's occupation. Fred Larson was

169

down as *Building Engineer*, when in fact at that time he would have been no more qualified than the other hod carriers he worked with. Angela suspected Betty had wanted to give the young Freddie something to aspire to, though God knew what story she'd spun over the years when her son had asked difficult questions about his father.

Daddy abandoned Mummy when you were still in her tummy.

Maybe she hadn't explained at all, or told him his father was overseas. Angela often thought her own upbringing had left much to be desired, but Freddie's story was in a different league. She shook her head as she stared at her scribbled notes.

The meagre facts contained in her reporter's pad were all she knew for sure about Freddie Jr. It wasn't much, but the mere fact of his existence was a hell of a lot more than she could have hoped for before meeting Betty. With both the Mrs Larsons offering very little in the way of information about Sir Fred, she decided tracking down his son had to be her next priority. Freddie Jr might just open up a wormhole into the Larson empire, big enough for her to work with a pencil and eventually make a large enough opening to crawl through. All she needed to do now was locate the middle-aged drug fiend.

She switched on her iMac, pulled open the top drawer of the console and dug around in the pile of chewed pen tops, dog-eared pads of Post-Its and half-empty cigarette packets looking for her glasses. All she managed to unearth was a dried up mascara wand, a lipstick in a colour she hadn't worn for years and an unexpected pack of flavoured condoms she must have bought when the panic about AIDS was at its height in the mid 80s. She supposed they must have exceeded their best before date over a decade ago and shoved them in the bin.

She continued to sift and sort through the rubbish she really should have cleared out and discovered the useless key that had been attached to the console key ring, together with a leaflet about pensions she'd meant to read while it still made sense to make contributions.

But still no sign of her glasses.

She yanked the handle of the middle drawer but it only yielded a couple of inches before stopping.

She turned to her computer and opened a browser window ready to set the font size to maximum, grateful she no longer had to trawl through at least half a dozen editions of the *Yellow Pages* to find what she was looking for. She typed 'Drug Rehabilitation Centre' into one search box and 'London' into another, hit 'Go' and sat back as the page reloaded with a very long list of almost 200 results. She narrowed the search area to 'Tower Hamlets', scribbled down the names and numbers of the half dozen or so results then repeated the process using 'City of

London' as the catchment area instead. Then she spent the next 20 minutes trying to wrangle information from tight-lipped receptionists, getting precisely nowhere.

'Why can't you tell me whether or not he's a patient of yours? For God's sake – confidentiality has got nothing to do with it. He's my brother!' She slammed down the phone and slumped back in her chair.

'He ain't heavy, he's my bro-o-o-ther.'

'Oh shut up, Frank.'

Frank Carter grabbed her shoulder and squeezed. 'God – feel the tension in those muscles.' He squeezed tighter. 'Since when have you had a brother, anyway?' He unfastened his hand just before Angela had a chance to dig her nails into it and sat down at the desk opposite hers. He started whistling The Hollies hit.

'How's *your* shoulder?'

'Almost completely healed. Thanks for asking.'

'Good – you can get me a coffee then.'

'How did I not see that coming? Must be losing it.' He got up. 'Black two sugars?'

'Just black – I'm trying out a new brand of sweetener.'

'I don't know why you bother. Nicotine patches, sugar replacements... You're in perfect shape.'

Angela narrowed her eyes. 'What are you up to? Do you owe me money I've completely forgotten about?'

'I mean perfect shape for someone of your vintage. Obviously.' He shoved his hands in his pockets and wandered away whistling *The Girl from Ipanema*.

'Piss off!'

Angela turned back to the phone and punched in the number for the switchboard and asked for the IT department. While she waited to be connected, she glanced down at the list of rehab clinics, thick lines of ink striking through the ones she'd already tried. Only another page to go. She was doodling a climbing rose around the name of the next one on the list when a gravelly voice barked into her ear.

'Yo! You're through to Nick in IT, how can I help?'

'Yo... Nick – I spoke to your colleague earlier. There are some files I need decrypting.'

'The password protected ones?'

Angela sat up a little straighter. 'Yes – have you managed to open them up?'

'No chance.'

'What?'

'Takes a while, well... it will take a while as soon as we make a start.'

'You haven't even…' *Jesus.* 'How long will it take?'

'Can't tell you that. What you've got there is a piece of string scenario.'

'You must be able to do better than that.'

'It's not exactly a top priority. Give us a call in a few days.'

'Days? I don't have a few days!' She slammed down the receiver again.

'They're not really designed for that sort of abuse,' Frank Carter murmured into her ear. He clattered a steaming mug down on her desk so hard the coffee slopped over the edge.

'Christ, Frank!'

'Don't take whatever it is out on me!'

'It was just a simple request for a cup of coffee and I only asked for it to stop you whistling.'

'My whistling has been greatly admired over the years.'

'I bet.' Angela mopped up the pool of coffee as best she could.

'Oh, by the way, I saw Evans in the corridor – he wants to see you quick smart. What have you been up to?'

'Well he can just piss off.'

'Dare I ask…' Frank stayed on his feet, shifting his weight from foot to foot, no doubt ready to make a swift exit if he had to. 'How is the evil academy exposé shaping up?'

'Let's not go there, if you want to stay in possession of your vitals.'

Frank made a show of cupping his crotch. 'Maybe I can help?'

One of the mobile phones trilled in her bag. She stuck in a hand and plucked out the vibrating white Sony Ericsson.

'You took your time.' She turned away from Frank.

'You're lucky I'm calling you at all.'

'Don't start on about "toxic" files again. This is a completely different investigation.' She glanced over at Jason Morris's empty desk. Someone had stolen his chair. 'This is just a road traffic accident and a burglary. Meat and potatoes stuff for you, right?'

'You'd think.' The line went very quiet.

'What is it?'

'I can't do any more poking around for a while. It's getting too uncomfortable.'

'Are you going to tell me what you've found out about Jason Morris's break-in or what?'

'No can do.'

'Why not?'

'I don't know what it is you're involved in, but you should really consider getting yourself out of it as fast as you can.' Another pause. 'Look, I really can't say anymore.'

'You can't just—' The line went dead. Angela stared at the phone as the screen faded. It was beginning to feel as if every door she tried to inch open was being slammed in her face. What was it about Jason's files that had caused such an extreme reaction?

She turned round to see Frank gazing at her.

'Boyfriend trouble is it?' he said. 'Can Uncle Frank help?'

'That makes you sound like such an old letch.' Angela reached under her shoes in the bottom drawer and retrieved a large brown envelope. She pulled out a bundle of photographs and index cards and waved them in the air.

'OK, Frank – if that was genuine offer before... Maybe you can provide a fresh perspective. God knows I'm getting nowhere.' She padded over to the empty desk on the other side of the office and carefully placed the various photographs with their corresponding index cards across the surface, in the same groupings she'd decided on previously. 'I'm trying to link the various runners and riders,' she said. 'Make connections between them. I promise any suggestions you make won't be shot down in flames. At least not straight away.'

Frank peered at the clusters of headshots and cards. 'These are the shots I took at the funeral.'

'Mostly, a few library photos to fill in the gaps.'

He walked round the desk, brow furrowed, breathing heavily through his mouth. Angela recognised this as Frank's concentrating face. Eventually he pointed to a collection of photographs with no label. 'Who's this bunch of dodgy characters?'

'Miscellaneous. All the faces I couldn't put names to.' Angela scribbled on a blank index card and placed it beneath the group.

Frank craned his head to read it. '*Unidentified*. That's really helpful, thanks, Ange.' He stared at the photos more closely. 'I don't even remember taking half of these.' He picked one up. 'You wouldn't want to meet him on a dark night.' He turned the picture around so Angela could see it. 'A face only a mother could love.'

She peered at the bald man with the sunken cheeks and dark circles under his eyes. There was something about his expression that looked familiar. Maybe. The curve of the eyebrows? She snatched the picture and laid it back down on the desk.

'Oh God – it's not someone you know, is it Ange? An ex-boyfriend or something? When I said about a dark night—'

'Shut up, Frank!' She held a hand over the bald pate, halfway up the forehead, and squinted at the image. It wasn't possible, was it?

'Seriously Ange, I'm sorry. I'm sure the fella's got a lovely personality.'

'I thought you were trying to help.' Angela sifted through the other unidentified photos and found another of the same man. In this one he wasn't exactly smiling, more pulling back his lips and baring his teeth. The effect was no longer dazzling, but he still seemed to have a full set and they were perfectly straight. She slid the first photo next to the Larsons and squinted again. Was there a slight resemblance now where she hadn't seen one before? She grabbed another index card and scrawled *Freddie Jr* across it.

'What?' Frank looked from the card to Angela.

She nodded.

'You're kidding me – a secret son?'

'From his first marriage. I only found out this morning.'

'From a kosher source?'

'Does his own mother count as kosher?'

'Fair enough.'

'I've even been to the records office to check the story out.' She pointed to the photo of the sunken-faced man. 'Say hello to Frederick Joseph Larson.'

'You think that's definitely him?'

'In the photos I saw this morning he had more hair and more flesh on his face.' She picked up the picture again. 'If I was a betting woman, I'd put a monkey on it.'

Frank whistled.

'But I don't remember anyone getting anywhere near the Larsons – God knows you were chased away swiftly enough by his henchmen when you got too close.'

'Do the pair of them not get on then?'

Angela shrugged. 'Not sure. According to the first Mrs Larson...' She smiled a wry smile. 'You may not believe this... but according to Betty, Sir Fred's been paying for his son's drug rehab treatment.'

'No! This story just gets better and better. I'm surprised you're not doing cartwheels. I thought you weren't getting anywhere. This is dynamite stuff.'

'Don't get too excited, Frank. I've still got to find the heroin-addled waster.'

'Ah.'

'Can you run me off a few copies of his picture, and any others you might have taken of him?'

'Sure.' Frank looked at the other groupings of photos and cards. 'You reckon he never made contact with his old man at the funeral?'

'Not as far as I remember.'

'So assuming this is Frederick Larson the second, why would he be at the funeral at all, if he wasn't with his dad?'

'That's what I've just been wondering. The only other explanation is that he was paying his last respects to Fox.'

'How likely is that?'

'Freddie would have to have been pretty close to Fox to get through the security checks.'

'We found a way in.'

'But not as far as the graveside.' She gathered up the photographs and hurried back to her desk.

'What's happening now?' Frank followed her across the office.

'I'm off to the library. I could spend days trawling the internet and Lexis Nexis looking for a connection between Fox and Freddie Larson. I haven't got days. It's time to call in the cavalry.'

'I thought the powers that be ditched the librarians years back.'

'Last time I checked, Rita was still ruling the roost with an iron fist on the second floor.'

'Rita?'

Angela nodded.

'Alberta Einstein still works here?'

'You should try calling her that to her face.'

'She'd love it.'

The landline on Angela's desk started ringing. She glanced at her watch – it was nearly 6pm, going home time for civilians. She'd have to hurry to catch Rita still at her desk. She snatched up the receiver.

'Tate!'

'This is Aleesha in IT – you left some files with us.'

'It's OK – I know the score. I've got days to wait—'

'That's why I'm calling. We've opened them.'

'You have?'

'I took on the job personally. I'll email them to you now.'

'Thank you – I'll put in a good word with your boss.'

'I am the boss.'

'Oh… well done you.' She put the phone down.

'Progress?' Frank said.

'Maybe.'

Angela took the stairs down to the second floor, the stone steps cold under her stockinged feet. She reached the library and spotted Rita standing over her desk at the other end of the room.

'Just the woman I'm looking for,' she shouted.

Rita stared over her half-moon glasses and narrowed her eyes as she watched Angela approach, and glanced down at Angela's shoeless feet. She plucked her coat from a stand and threaded her thin arms into the sleeves.

'How do you fancy the role of superhero?' Angela reached the desk.

'Superhero I do every day between nine and six. You can even find me wielding my superpowers most lunchtimes.' She tapped the slim gold watch on her wrist. 'Six-oh-one. I'll see you in the morning.'

'That's the thing Rita – time is a key factor here.'

Rita pursed her lips. Recently applied lipstick had seeped into the lines around her mouth. She started to button her coat.

'It's Evans. He's really putting me under pressure. Making it almost impossible for me to do my job.' She exhaled a defeated breath. 'He's looking for any excuse to get rid of me. If I don't get this story to him first thing tomorrow… well, that could be it.'

Rita stopped buttoning.

'You must know what it's like at the moment. They're pushing out the old guard as quickly and as cheaply as possible.'

Rita didn't respond. Angela soldiered on anyway.

'Which means trying to make my life as uncomfortable as they possibly can. That way they make it my decision to leave.'

Rita was nodding her head now, almost imperceptibly.

'Saves a lot of money if I jump.'

'What does any of this have to do with me?'

Come on, Rita, where's your sense of comradeship?

'Tomorrow morning is an impossible deadline. I can't do it alone. Evans has made it quite clear if I don't deliver I'll be writing the horoscopes and compiling the quick crossword this time next week.'

Rita picked her spectacles from her nose and tucked them away in a case, shutting it with a crocodile snap.

'Believe me, I wouldn't be asking if it wasn't so critical. My career is literally hanging in the balance.'

'Not *literally*.'

Oh come on, you pedantic old witch!

'You know what I mean. You've lost how many staff in the last couple of years?'

Rita glanced around the office let out a quiet groan. 'Tomorrow morning?'

Angela nodded. 'First thing.'

Rita unbuttoned her coat and wearily hooked it back over the hat stand. 'I can't make a habit of this.'

'Of course not.' Angela wanted desperately to smile but managed to keep her face straight.

'What exactly do you need?'

'To establish a connection. Between two people who on paper at least shouldn't even know one another.'

'What kind of connection?'

'That's just it – I'm not sure.'

Rita handed Angela a notepad and pen. 'Names, ages, professions, education, spouses, children, places of birth, current location.'

'Anything else?' Angela regretted the slightly sarcastic tone as soon as she saw Rita's expression.

'I'll let you know.'

She wrote down all the concrete facts she had and gave Rita a quick summary of everything she'd discovered about Freddie Larson. Then, after a few minutes watching the librarian trawl through God knew how many records, public and otherwise, she decided her time would be better spent making enquiries of her own. Rita was quick, but there were only so many pages one woman could scan in 60 seconds.

Angela logged on to the computer at the next desk, fired up Entourage and found the email the lovely girl in IT had sent her. She opened the first attachment – an Excel document – and quickly scanned the single worksheet. It didn't look like the sort of information anyone would bother protecting.

'Rita?'

The rattle of rapid typing ceased for a moment.

'Do the following categories, grouped together, mean anything to you?' She leaned back from the screen to stop the words swimming into one another. If only she'd found her glasses. '*Name, Severity, User Error.*'

'Severity of what?'

Angela shrugged. 'It's a number between one and ten.'

'Ten being the most severe?'

'Not sure.'

'Are there any 1s?'

Angela scrolled through the spreadsheet. 'No – the lowest is seven.'

'What options are there in the *User Error* category?'

'Yes or no. They're all yeses.'

'So a name, then a measure of how serious something is, then whether or not it was their own stupid bloody fault.'

'Could be…'

'Any other categories?'

'Company name, name of an academy and a figure in thousands of pounds.'

Rita pushed her spectacles up her nose. 'Haven't a clue.'

'How's it going with you? Made any progress?'

'Are you sure Frederick Joseph Larson actually still exists?'

'That bad, is it?'

'Unsurprisingly, I've unearthed plenty of info on the honourable member for Cambridge East.'

'But nothing on Freddie?'

'Could Larson be one of Fox's constituents?'

'I doubt it. As far as I know he lives in London.'

'Has he always lived here?'

'I would presume so. Certainly born in London and most probably living here now.'

'He didn't go away to university?'

'University?' Angela thought about the photographs Frank had taken at the funeral. Going away to prison was a more likely scenario. 'Given his current recreational activities, I'd guess he's always been a bit of a waster. I certainly can't see him sticking a three-year degree course.'

'So he could have dropped out?'

Angela shrugged and once Rita went back to her typing, she returned to the spreadsheet. Without expecting any positive results, she entered all the column headings from the spreadsheet into Google. The first page that came up offered a list of health and safety links. She changed the search criteria to include the name of a company from the first column and the words 'health and safety'.

'Hah!' Rita said.

Angela looked up to see the librarian's face had cracked into a smile. In fact, it looked to Angela suspiciously like a self-satisfied grin.

'As you suspected,' Rita said, 'Freddie Larson doesn't seem to have excelled academically.'

'Shame – it was definitely worth a try, though.'

'I'll say – as *I* suspected, he dropped out after only a year of study.'

'You've found a record of him?'

'The lists of alumni usually include all students enrolled at a university, not just the ones who graduated.'

'Right... OK.' Not having set foot within the hallowed halls of higher education until she doorstepped a lecherous lecturer at Southbank Poly in 1984, this was news to Angela. 'But how did you find him so quickly? There must be thousands of Unis to check.'

Rita was smiling again. It was unnerving. 'But only one college attended by Martin Fox.'

'You're not serious.'

'Deadly. Frederick Joseph Larson attended Newton College, Cambridge during the academic year 78/79.'

'And was that the same time as Martin Fox?'

'There would have been an overlap – yes. Fox completed his History of Art MPhil in 1980.'

Angela jumped up and ran to Rita. She was just about to throw her arms around the librarian's neck when she saw the look of horror on Rita's face. 'That's brilliant Rita.' She punched her gently on the shoulder.

'Don't get too excited. We only know they were at the same place at the same time. It doesn't mean they actually knew one another.'

'What was Larson studying?'

'Oh you'll love it. Can you guess?'

'History of art, same as Fox?'

'Try again.'

'Really – I give up.'

'Something dear to Fox's heart.'

'Just tell me, Rita, for God's sake.'

Rita pursed her lips and tilted her head.

Oh go on – make me beg. 'Sorry.'

'Politics.' There was a triumphant ring to her voice.

'Who would have thought? Are there any contact details?'

'Not without a user account.' Rita turned off her computer.

'We can't stop now!'

'You wanted a connection – I found you one. I do have a home to go to.'

'Yes – sorry… thanks Rita. I do really appreciate it.'

As Rita put on her coat, Angela returned to her page of search results. She clicked on a link for the website of a West Midlands newspaper and quickly scanned the story. A labourer had died on the construction site of a new academy. To avoid a court appearance the company in question had agreed to a 'substantial but undisclosed' sum in compensation. She searched again, changing the company name for the next one on the spreadsheet. The top result was another newspaper link, this publication based in Suffolk. Again, the story was about an accident at an academy building project, but this time the case never made it to court because the charges were dropped.

'I'll say goodbye then.' Rita was standing over her. Angela had forgotten she was still there.

'Yes – goodnight. And thanks again,' she said without taking her eyes from the screen.

She repeated the search procedure with all the other companies listed on the spreadsheet. When she'd finally finished, 14 deaths, 11 maimings, 32 severe injuries and 117 serious injuries later, she reached for the phone.

29

Tate had phoned just as Caroline was getting ready for bed. She wouldn't normally have answered, but the call came through on her own mobile, from a number she didn't recognise. Tate then hung up and immediately called her back using the pay-as-you-go phone.

Caroline listened to most of what the journalist told her in a daze, all she could really think about was the fact that Pete worked for one of the companies on the list. One of the unscrupulous, feckless, court-dodging organisations, and all the time he never said a word about any of it. Never said a word about two fatalities and three serious injuries at his firm. How could he go on working for a company like that?

She'd put the phone down and made herself a cup of tea. Then sat at the kitchen table and watched it go cold. She couldn't stop her mind racing with everything Tate had told her. The health and safety records of all the companies on the list were appalling. In the course of her job she'd met a lot of the project managers in charge of the construction work, even visited a few of the building sites. On every occasion, everything seemed well organised and properly administered. The companies wouldn't have made it onto the list of government approved contractors without meeting the highest health and safety standards. Something somewhere had gone seriously wrong with the vetting procedure.

She got up and emptied and refilled the kettle again. While she waited for it to boil she wiped down the counter tops and cleaned the sink. By the time it had boiled she'd gone off the idea of tea and started to tidy the contents of the kitchen drawers. She was doing everything on autopilot, going over the facts again and again. She'd asked Tate to tell her specifically about VL Construction, but hadn't told her why.

According to Tate, the company Pete worked for had escaped court appearances for all the cases listed on the spreadsheet and hadn't even paid out any money in compensation to the injured workers or the families of the two men who had died. It was suggested at the time that the accidents were caused by sloppy work practices and institutionalised corner cutting. But nothing had been proved.

Pete wouldn't have just turned a blind eye to that kind of company-wide negligence. His firm must have been keeping him in the dark. She checked the time. It had just turned midnight and Pete still wasn't home. There were so many questions she needed to ask him.

She fretted for another 25 minutes before hearing his key scrape against the lock in the front door. She hurried into the hall and watched him stagger over the front step, blinking at the bright light.

'Do you know what time it is?' Caroline closed the door as quietly as she could behind him.

He swayed towards her. She put her hands against his chest to keep him upright.

'I must have lost track.' He laid a big hand over both of hers. 'It's OK, Caz — I'm not Cinderella — I can survive after midnight without turning into a rat… or whatever it is.'

'Have you been drinking all evening?'

She could see him trying hard to focus on her.

'Come with me.' She slipped her hands from under his and turned back to the kitchen.

Pete shuffled along behind her, exhaling beer and whiskey fumes. She sat him down at the kitchen table and flicked on the kettle, then spent the next 20 minutes watching him drink a mug of strong black coffee and a pint and a half of water. He drained his mug, swallowed the two paracetamols she'd pressed into his hand and pushed back his chair.

'I feel much better — thanks babe. Let's go up now, shall we?'

'We need to talk.'

He rubbed his hands up and down his unshaven cheeks and let out a low moan. 'Talk?' He stood up quickly and lurched sideways, grabbing the edge of the table. 'I'm not going to make much sense right now. Let's talk in the morning.'

'I've been waiting for you to come home.'

Pete smiled and opened his arms wide. 'And here I am. Can we leave it for now?' He tugged at her sleeve. 'I promise never to stay out this late again. OK?' He stared at her with bloodshot eyes. 'Whatever else you want to talk about can wait a few hours, can't it?' He pulled up his sleeve and stared long and hard at his watch. 'Bloody hell. It is late. I've got an early start in the morning.'

'Maybe you should have thought about that before you went to the pub.'

'Please, Caz. I've got to get to Maidstone before eight.'

'Sit down.'

'For fuck's sake.' He collapsed back onto the chair and buried his head in his hands. 'I really need to get to bed, I just—'

'What's in Maidstone?'

'What?' He emerged slowly from his hands. 'Work – work's in Maidstone.'

'Tell me about it.'

He rubbed his eyes. 'You do pick your moments. Why'd you want to talk about my work now? You've never taken an interest before.'

'This Maidstone job – would it be the Mote and Medway Business Academy, by any chance?'

'How'd you know that?'

'How many other academy building projects have you worked on?'

He shrugged. 'I don't know... I don't keep count.'

'And you never thought to mention it to me?'

He screwed up his face, trying to understand, as if she'd asked him a particularly testing question. 'Why would I?'

'For God's sake, Pete. I work in the academies division – don't you think I might have been interested? Why didn't you tell me?'

He shrugged again. 'You never asked.' He eased himself off the chair, carefully negotiated the edge of the table and made it as far as the fridge. 'I'm going to bed.'

'We have to talk, Pete. It can't wait.' Caroline struggled to keep her voice down, aware her mother was asleep in the next room.

'I'm sorry I'm so late. I'm sorry I'm so drunk. What else do you want from me?'

'I need to know...' She took a breath. 'Did you know the men who died working at your firm?'

'What?' He was struggling again to focus on her. 'How do you know about them?'

'Were they friends of yours?'

'Why are you asking me about this now?'

'Because I've only just found out. Did you know them?'

Pete nodded and closed his eyes. He swayed sideways and leaned into the fridge.

'And were you working with them when they died?'

He opened his eyes and dragged a hand down his face. 'I was on site.'

'Did you see what happened to them?'

'Please, Caz – I can't talk about this now. I don't feel up to it.'

'Why didn't you tell me about it at the time?'

He sighed. 'You wouldn't have understood. I know what you're like – everything's black or white in your book.'

'What's that supposed to mean?'

'We can't all be as perfect as you.'

'What are you saying?'

Pete swallowed and traced the tip of his tongue over his cracked bottom lip.

'Answer me, Pete!' Her heart was thumping.

'There was nothing I could do.'

'You were there, when they died?'

He nodded. 'I'd been telling them for years something was going to happen. No one took any notice.' He ran a hand over his head. 'You can't save that amount of money with no consequences.'

Caroline blinked. 'You knew they were cutting corners?'

'How could I not know? Work in the same firm that long and you become part of the furniture. They talk about all sorts of stuff in front of you like they don't even notice you're there.'

'Men have *died*!' She couldn't catch her breath. 'How can you live with that on your conscience?'

'Live with myself? You call this living? Why do you think I've been drinking myself fucking senseless most nights?'

'How could you just stand back and let it happen? Why didn't you report them?'

'Yeah, well. Maybe it's not as simple as that.'

'It's always as simple as that. A choice between wrong and right.'

'See? You and your moral high ground. Don't stand there and judge me. You don't know anything about it.'

'I don't know because you never bloody talk to me. If you could just—'

There was a noise from upstairs. A moaning in the floorboards

'You've woken the kids,' she said.

'That was me, was it?' He walked to the back door and leaned his forehead against the glass.

'Pete... it's not too late. You can still do the right thing.'

'And what might that be?'

'Go to the police. Tell them everything you know.'

'You've got no fucking idea. And what do you think would happen to me then?'

'You'd find other work.'

Pete let out a long slow breath – his whole body seemed to shake. He turned back to face her. 'Don't you get it? It was just as much my fucking fault as anyone else's.' He thumped a hand on his chest. 'Me! If I go to the authorities, I'd be grassing myself up as well as Larson's.'

'Larson's?' A breath caught in her throat.

Pete looked at her for a moment. 'You didn't know I work for Larson's?'

'You've never actually said.' Caroline put a hand on the kitchen counter to steady herself. Angela Tate hadn't mentioned that. Was it possible she didn't even know?

'*VL Construction*?' he said. '*Valerie Larson* Construction. All Larson's companies are registered offshore. Some tax dodge or something.'

'How could it have been your fault as much as theirs?'

'Lose concentration for a second and bang!' He slapped his hands together. 'Andy. Really young bloke, couldn't have been more than 23, 24.'

Caroline remembered seeing an Andrew Brown listed on the spreadsheet.

'They don't train them properly anymore. Don't even give them hard hats. Supposed to provide their own.'

'What happened?'

'I was supervising him. But I got called away. Some other balls up about to kick off, wrong mix of cement for the concrete foundations.' Pete screwed up his eyes, as if he was trying to banish whatever image his memory had conjured. 'I got back to him, five, ten minutes later. A forklift had backed right into him. He didn't hear it coming. He was wearing earphones, stupid bloody sod. On a building site!'

'How was that your fault?'

'I was responsible for his safety.'

'But that would all have come out at the inquest, exactly who was responsible. You would have had to explain everything – the lack of training, the missing safety equipment.'

'Yeah, well, I didn't.' He pinched the top of his nose. 'Fred Larson himself had a little chat with me. Made it quite clear what was expected.'

'He asked you to lie?'

'There wasn't anything else I could do.'

'Pete! For God's sake – what were you thinking?'

'I had no choice.'

'Of course you did.'

He turned away. 'He's very well connected, old man Larson.' He dragged his fingertips across his scalp. 'I'd be propping up a flyover in no time if I didn't go along with him.'

'That's ridiculous – he's not the Mafia.'

'You've got no fucking clue.'

A door creaked open upstairs.

'A mother's son dies in your care and you lie about it out of some misplaced sense of loyalty? Worried you might upset your employer? What about the other man who was killed? Did you lie about him too?'

'I'm going to bed.'

'No you're not!'

'There's nothing more to say. I've got an early start.'

'How can you go on, day after day, working for that company?'

'Drop it, Caz. I don't want to talk about it anymore.'

'Did you lie about the other death?' She thumped a fist against his chest. 'Was that something else you agreed to cover up?'

'You'll never understand. There's no point even trying to explain.'

She thumped him again. 'You mean I'll never understand that my husband's a coward?' She drew her hand back again and he caught hold of her wrist, gripping it tight in his fist.

'Don't you ever call me that!'

'Why not? It's what you are.' She tried to pull her hand away, but his grip tightened.

'I mean it, Caz.'

'Let go of me!' She struggled against his grasp. 'What have you turned into?'

Pete released her hand. 'I'm sorry I can't live up to your standards. But you know what? Nobody can.'

'Get out,' she said quietly.

'I've been trying to.'

'Get out of my house.'

'What?'

'You heard me. I don't want you anywhere near the kids.'

The kitchen door flew open. Ben stood in the doorway, his face flushed, his eyes brimming with tears. He ran to his dad and threw his arms around Pete's thighs, squeezing tight. Pete twisted awkwardly and stared at Caroline, an imploring look on his face.

She ignored him and bent down and kissed the top of Ben's head. 'Ten minutes,' she said. 'I'll pack you a bag.'

30

On Tuesday morning Caroline had to pick her way through piles of empty plastic packing crates to get to her desk. No sooner had she put her bag down than Pam appeared like a giant sprite hovering over her.

'They finally arrived.' Pam gestured across the floor.

'Did we need this many?'

'There's a lot of stuff to pack.' She put her hands on her wide hips and surveyed the office. 'All the filing cabinets are being cleared.'

'We're not taking the cabinets to the second floor?'

'God no! We're getting brand new ones.'

'And these ones?'

'Crushed in the big crusher parked round the corner.'

Caroline tried to shake the intense feeling of déjà vu from her head.

'Most of the files are going into deep storage up at Runcorn. The rest of it's getting dumped.' Her mouth twitched into a tight 'O'. 'Bugger – the confidential waste sacks haven't arrived. Can you chase facilities management for me? Only I'm up to my eyeballs at the moment.'

That's why you're chatting to me, presumably. Caroline sighed.

'Are you OK?' Pam squeezed Caroline's arm. 'I tell you to go home early and put your feet up and you come in the next day looking more knackered than you did before.'

'Thanks Pam.'

'No offence... I'm just saying...'

'I didn't sleep that well.'

'You should look after yourself better. Do what I do – put yourself first once in a while.'

'Thanks for the tip – I'll make sure I ignore my kids in future.'

'There's no need to be funny.'

Caroline pushed a couple of crates out of the way and sat down. 'What's the plan? Are we packing last thing tomorrow afternoon – try to minimise the disruption?'

'No – that's the great thing about the latest plan.' Pam beamed at her. 'We don't actually have to lift a finger. Bishop's Removals are coming in to do the packing for us. Isn't that fantastic?'

'But who's going to decide what goes into deep storage and what gets dumped into confidential waste?'

'A team of management consultants. Hand-picked by Jeremy. They're starting first thing in the morning.'

'How much is that costing?'

Pam shrugged 'Jeremy's dealing with that side of things. And he's offered to oversee their work himself. Saves me having to stay here 'til God knows when.'

Caroline switched on her computer. 'So you're saying we don't have to pack at all?'

'Jeremy decided it would be more efficient.'

'So why are we overrun with plastic crates?'

'Last minute decision, yesterday evening. I couldn't postpone them.'

Did you even try?

Caroline opened the bottom drawer of the pedestal under her desk. It was crammed with all manner of rubbish. She didn't feel entirely comfortable about some burly removals man going through her personal things.

'What if I want to do my own packing?'

'Jeremy's told me to insist it's left to the professionals. We've got better things to do, he said.' Pam skirted around a crate. 'Well, that's you completely up to date.' She stopped. 'I forgot to ask. Have you got any idea why that tall bloke from IT is in with Jeremy?' she said, pointing to Prior's room.

Caroline turned to see Greg being shouted at by a gesticulating Prior.

'Only Jeremy's been like that for at least five minutes. He'll burst a blood vessel if he carries on.'

'I wouldn't know, Pam. Why don't you ask him?'

'I don't like to pry.'

They both watched the silent scene unfold for a few moments until Greg emerged from the office looking shell-shocked.

'Another computer cock up, I expect.' Pam clucked her tongue against her teeth.

Prior came out of his office and said something to his PA. She jumped up and followed him back in.

Finally Pam set off for her own desk. Caroline watched her nod to Greg as he passed. He carried on towards the exit, without acknowledging her, his movements stiff, his expression blank.

Caroline could only assume Greg had been updating Prior on the surveillance operation. What had he said to make Prior react so violently? She looked back at Prior's office and saw Lisa looking down at the floor, her shoulders shaking, her chest heaving.

What is he saying to her?

Lisa finally returned to her desk and sat down, wiping her face with a tissue. Prior peered out of his office and Caroline quickly turned back to her computer, hoping he hadn't seen her gawping at him. Her mobile started to ring. She plucked it out of her bag, saw it was Pete calling and stabbed it silent.

Pete had left the house less than eight hours ago and he'd phoned her at least half a dozen times since. Eight hours ago she'd had to prise Ben's arms from Pete's legs, telling him his dad had to go away for a few days. She shoved her mobile in a drawer and logged on to her computer. As ever the start-up procedure cranked through the motions of retrieving her system preferences. It seemed to take even longer than usual. Was that because the IT department was monitoring her PC? She stared at the screen for a while and decided watching would only slow it down even more, like a watched kettle stubbornly refusing to boil.

She opened up her bottom drawer wide and peered inside. So much of this stuff could be thrown away. She glanced up to make sure Pam wasn't on her way over and lifted out a handful of old magazines and glossy departmental brochures. She sorted them into two neat piles on the desk. The next layer of detritus down contained more useful items: a spare pair of tights, a unopened packet of Elastoplast, a box of man-sized tissues and a small zipped bag of painkillers, from co-codamol through to Anadin. In the event of a headache or raging period pains she'd be well sorted. She quickly shoved all of it into the nearest packing crate and moved on to the remaining rubbish lurking at the bottom of the drawer. This was stuff she hadn't seen for months. Wedged right at the back was a folded Paperchase bag. She reached in a hand, curious to see what was inside – trying to remember when she'd bought a birthday card and forgotten to send it. As soon as her hand closed around the bag and she felt the outline of a slim square object, she remembered exactly what was inside. She placed the bag gently on the desk and glanced across the office to check Pam wasn't looking in her direction.

She sucked down a deep breath and removed the cards and CD from the bag.

She turned over the two birthday cards Martin had sent, both still in their envelopes. The CD had been a gift from him the previous Christmas – more jazz she couldn't bring herself to listen to. With shaking hands she opened the accompanying Christmas card and read the message inside. Martin's lengthy and excruciating apology triggered the memory of their one evening together so vividly, she couldn't quite catch her breath. It all came flooding back at once: the drunken cab ride to the hotel, the giggling at the reception desk as she signed them in as

Mr and Mrs Smith, Martin lurking next to the lifts wearing dark glasses and a hat pulled low over his forehead. She screwed her eyes shut and saw the champagne cork bursting out of the bottle and hitting the ceiling. Then both of them collapsing onto the bed in fits of laughter.

Stupid bloody cow.

The next part was less distinct, the most embarrassing moments expunged from her memory. She did still have a vision of herself naked under the covers, but she didn't remember taking off her clothes, or being undressed by Martin. She shuddered. She hadn't forgotten what happened after that. She could recall every humiliating second of their hurried grope in the dark. The awkward fumble between a rapidly sobering schools minister and a 40-something civil servant. Wife. Mother of three.

What was I thinking?

The back of her chaired rocked.

'I thought I told you to leave all the packing to Bishop's.' Pam was almost level with the desk. 'What have you found lurking in a drawer?' She kicked the pedestal. 'Caroline Barber... you're blushing!'

Caroline grabbed the cards and CD and shoved them onto her lap under the desk.

'Oh come on – share! Is it something rude?'

Caroline gripped the little bundle tighter. 'It's nothing – just a couple of Valentine's cards from Pete. He sends them here, the daft apeth.' She forced a grin. 'He doesn't want the kids to know what an old romantic he is. Or my mum – she'd rib him something rotten.'

'Sexy cards from your hubbie – no wonder you wanted to pack your own crate! You are a dark horse, Caroline.'

You have absolutely no idea.

'Go on – just a little peek.'

Caroline sat rigid.

'You're no fun.' She started to walk away. 'Oh yeah – I came over to tell you, don't bother ordering any waste sacks. They've just been delivered.'

Caroline nodded and smiled, gave Pam the thumbs-up, all the while feeling her throat tightening. When Pam was out of sight she stuffed the bundle on her lap back in the paper bag and shoved that into her handbag, resolving to keep her bag close for the rest of the day. The pay-as-you go ringtone sounded from inside. She hooked out the phone.

'It's not a great time. Can it wait?'

'Good morning, to you too.'

Caroline opened Outlook and scanned her emails. 'I'm serious, I've got a lot on my mind at the moment.'

'Haven't we all.'

Caroline heard Tate sighing theatrically.

'Following up from that health and safety information I gave you yesterday,' Tate said.

'I can't talk about that in the office. It's not... safe.' Caroline glanced over her shoulder towards Prior's office. She saw Tracy Clarke going through the door. *Oh my God.* First Greg, then Lisa, now Tracy. Caroline's breath stalled in her chest.

'Are you still there?'

'What is it?' She couldn't take her eyes from the scene unfolding in Prior's office. Prior gestured for Tracy to sit down. Tracy remained standing.

'I'm trying to find out a bit more about those organisations on the spreadsheet. So far I've not come up with much.'

Caroline bit her lip, wondered for a moment whether she should tell Tate about the Larson connection.

'Actually, I'm hoping you can do a bit more probing for me,' Tate said. 'I need you to search your system, see what information the department might have on file about the companies.'

'I already told you – I'm not doing anything else for you. Not until—'

Tracy was still on her feet, Prior standing just a few inches away practically squaring up to her.

'Please Caroline. I've got a really strong feeling this might be the key to the whole thing. What if Martin Fox knew about the dodgy firms and was about to expose them? Wouldn't that be a reason to silence him permanently?'

'Are you finally admitting...' Caroline glanced quickly around the office to see who might be listening. 'Foul play?'

'That's what we're trying to find out, isn't it?'

Caroline looked down at her keyboard. Should she trust Tate? She looked back at Prior's room. Tracy rushed to the door, her head bowed. She ran out and headed towards the exit. Prior was staring through the glass. He made eye contact with Caroline. She stared right back for a few moments then returned to her computer and quickly navigated to the F-drive. She entered the term 'VL Construction' and limited the search to the academies procurement directory. She hit the enter key and waited.

'Caroline? Are you still there?'

By my fingernails.

A pop-up window appeared on her screen. She read the error message and re-entered the search term and clicked the search button again.

'Caroline?' Tate shouted down the phone.

'Wait a second!' She tried a third time. 'I can't help you,' she said quietly.

'But we're so close. I promise you, I will do my utmost—'

'Not *won't* help you. I *can't* help you.'

'Why? What's happened?'

'I no longer have access to the academies directory.'

'I don't understand.'

'I'm staring the alert box right now. Permission has been denied.'

31

Time hadn't been kind to Dennis Watson in the years since Angela Tate last worked with him on the *South London Press*. As he lounged on yellow waterproof seat cushions at the other end of the narrow wooden boat, she couldn't help noticing the greasy strands of thinning grey hair smeared across his scalp. His teeth were mostly blackened by nicotine, and the skin around his nose and mouth had a purple flush to it, as if the network of fine veins covering his face had burst their banks.

'Do you think if they'd known we only had a handful of A-Levels between us, they would have let us hire a boat?' she said.

Dennis Watson sucked languorously on his cigarette. 'Punt. You speak for yourself. I've got a 2:1.'

Angela wobbled dangerously, rocking the punt from side to side, before steadying herself by driving the pole into the soft earth of the riverbank. 'A 2:1! What in – bullshitting?'

'History, if you're interested.'

'Did you buy it online from a dodgy college in America?'

Watson blew a perfect ring of smoke into the air. 'I'm a graduate of the Open University.' He screwed up his face. 'It happens to be a highly respected institution.'

'Not quite on this level, though is it?' Angela nodded towards the twin spires of King's College just coming into view.

'There's no need to belittle my achievement. Do you want my help or not?'

Suitably chastised, Angela hung her head low and concentrated on not ploughing into the other boats on the River Cam. She glanced up at their occupants. Privileged didn't really cover it. Cambridge was another world.

Dennis shifted on his cushions and the punt rolled alarmingly. He was holding his cigarette stub vertically between finger and thumb, looking for somewhere to stub it out. Angela decided it was probably time to make for dry land.

They decamped to the nearest pub with a decent beer garden and a view. Watson came back from the bar with a pint of dirty-looking beer and a small Pinot Grigio, condensation dribbling down the outside of the glass. He shoved a wooden spoon with a large '11' felt-tipped on the paddle end on the table.

'I took the liberty of ordering us a couple of ploughmans – on your tab,' he said and creakily hoicked one leg over the seat of the picnic table, which lurched sideways as he sat down.

'Steady on, Den. I feel like I'm still on the water.' Angela lifted her glass and gulped down the first inch of wine. 'Cheers!'

Watson proffered his packet of cigarettes. She refused and wriggled a shoulder out of her jacket to reveal three nicotine patches covering the top of her arm.

'Are they working?'

'I'll let you know when I've finished my second glass.'

Watson unbuckled the canvas bag at his feet and pulled out a bulging file, newspaper cuttings spilling from the edges.

'Now… I can't let you keep these.'

'Wow – real cuttings. I haven't seen cuttings for years.'

'Are you taking the piss? I don't have to help you – you might do well to remember that.'

'All right, Den! Don't get your Y-fronts tangled.' Angela held up her hands. 'I am grateful. Have I mentioned that?'

'Yeah, well, gratitude is all very nice, but it doesn't pay the bills.'

'I've already told you – we'll get you some kind of payment sorted. I'll have a word with accounts.'

'It's not just about the money.' He looked away and stared into the distance.

Angela knew what was coming next.

'How about a credit?' he said. 'Maybe a joint byline?'

'You drive a hard bargain, Dennis.' She smiled at him. 'Joint byline it is.'

'It better be.' He glanced at her, an accusing look in his eyes.

'I've said haven't I?'

Watson opened the file. The sections of newspaper were yellow and curling at the edges. He tried to smooth them flat. The wind picked up suddenly and whipped a couple of loose pieces into the air. Angela snatched them before they flew away.

'Maybe we should adjourn inside?' he said.

'That'd be a real shame. It's so much nicer out here.' Angela leaned down and grabbed a few pieces of flint from a nearby flower border and anchored the clippings to the table.

Watson sniffed out an irritated breath. 'I've compiled all the stories from August '78 to September '79, just to give us a bit of a safety buffer either end of the academic year. I've only brought you the hundred or so most interesting stories, to keep it manageable.'

'A hundred?' she spluttered into her glass.

'Still overreacting I see.' He shook his head. 'I've whittled it down to a hundred – I can email you the headlines of all of them if you want – but I'm actually only going to talk you through my top five.'

'How have you rated them?' She grabbed a paper napkin from the dispenser on the table and dabbed her mouth.

'Relevancy, importance of story and length of coverage were all factors.'

'You're sure you can't just let me take the file?'

'Do you want the benefit of my invaluable local knowledge or what?'

'Won't say another word. But before you get started, how about another drink?'

Angela returned from the bar armed with another beer for Watson and a small glass of white wine for herself.

'OK,' he said, 'the top five, in no particular order—'

'Oh Dennis, I'm disappointed. I thought you were going to do a proper rundown in an Alan Freeman style.'

'Shut up and listen.' He drained his first pint, sediment and all, and spread five newspaper clippings over Angela's side of the table, placing a restraining lump of flint on top of each one. He pointed to the one on the far left. 'Right, first up is a drink driving case. Lecturer from Newton College ploughed into a bus stop while under the influence.'

'I can see the connection to my major players – Newton's the right college, but I'm surprised it made it into the paper at all. Was it a slow week?' Angela peered at the yellowing clipping.

'A 16-year-old girl was standing at the bus stop at the time. She died in the ambulance on the way to hospital.'

'Christ. What happened to the lecturer?'

'Got off on a legal technicality. Had a very high-powered lawyer representing him.'

'Still can't see why you think it warrants a mention. Did the lecturer actually teach Fox or King?'

'Nope.' Watson was looking decidedly pleased with himself. 'I can do better than that.'

'Go on.'

'The hotshot lawyer who got him off also represented Fred Larson in a compensation case brought against him in the early 80s. The lawyer got Larson off using a legal loophole.'

'The lecturer had the same lawyer as Larson?' She picked up her glass.

'The lecturer was Freddie Larson's tutor.'

She planted her wine back on the table without taking a sip. 'You think Freddie asked his father for help?'

'Looks that way.' Watson lifted the piece of flint from the clipping and returned it to the flower border. He put the section of newspaper back in the file.

Angela scribbled a quick note in her pad. She had no idea Fred Larson was in touch with his son when he was studying at Cambridge. Betty Larson hadn't given that impression at all.

Watson slipped another cutting from the file. 'Next one is a missing teenager. 19-year-old...' He quickly scanned the text. 'No, wait... 18 – Stephen Cole. Doesn't return home after a daytrip to London. Parents report him missing the next day. He's never stayed away overnight before without letting them know where he was.'

'And he was an undergraduate at Newton College too?'

'No, a local. He worked in the students' union bar.'

'Frequented by Fox, Larson and King.'

'Very probably.'

'Why's it in your top five? Seems a bit thin to me.'

Watson started on his second pint of beer. He shook a cigarette from his packet and lit it. Angela pressed a hand against her upper arm, trying to get a bit more mileage from her nicotine patches.

'It came out during the investigation that the lad also worked at another bar in the city.'

'So?'

'A gay bar. It was one of your keywords. I was paying attention.'

'You think Fox might have known him?'

'I'm just saying it's a connection – however *thin*.'

'Point taken. I promise not to jump down your throat again.'

Watson sucked on his cigarette for a few moments, and stared blankly at the cloud of smoke. He took his time tidying away the flint paperweight and clipping, the cigarette dangling from his lips. Angela had the feeling he was enjoying himself. Here she was hanging on the every word of a washed up hack who couldn't stick the pressure in London, so ran away to the provinces. This was probably the closest he'd got to a big story in years.

'The next one you're going to love, I had planned to save it 'til last, but I just can't wait.' He extinguished the cigarette in the ashtray, still a good inch of smokeable tobacco beyond the filter. Angela stared long-ingly at it. Watson picked up a cutting and waved it in the air. It was the biggest of the five and the only one with a photograph. Angela could just about make out a figure clad in dark clothes giving a Nazi salute.

'Right – April 1979 and the run up to the general election. Actually, before I start with the meat of it, I should probably give you a little of the background. What do you remember about the National Front in the 70s?'

'A bit. I covered the Lewisham riots for the paper. Actually – we both did, as I recall. I was desperate to get a better angle on it than you.'

'Always so competitive. I suppose that hasn't changed, even now.'

'Nothing wrong with a bit of healthy professional rivalry.'

'Who's in your sights these days?'

'Well obviously, no one can hold a candle to you, Dennis. It wasn't the same after you left.'

Watson snorted a laugh.

'I mean it! My competitive drive has long since abandoned me. These days I'm concentrating all my efforts in clinging on to my job by my cuticles.' She drained the last of her second glass.

'That bad? It's pretty rubbish out in the sticks too. So many work placements. Even on a local. I can't compete with a 22-year-old doing the job for nothing.'

'Don't get me started on that particular festering open wound – we'll be here all fucking day.'

'Fair enough.' He looked down at the clipping and took a breath. 'So, anyway… in '79 there was a policy within the NF to field as many candidates as possible at the general election as a show of strength – but they'd lost a lot of support to the Tories. Maggie's tough stance on immigration went down very well with your casual right-wing bigot. Consequently the National Front lost all their deposits – it practically bankrupted them.'

Angela stifled a yawn, hoping Watson would finish his history lesson and move on to the main event.

'The National Front candidate here in Cambridge was the focus of a few Anti-Nazi League demonstrations. At one particular event at the town hall there was a major scuffle and a couple of coppers were hospitalised. Over twenty arrests were made.'

'Well I know neither King nor Fox have ever been arrested, so I suppose you're going to tell me Freddie Larson got done for standing up to fascism.'

Watson nodded. 'He was indeed arrested.'

'Convicted?'

'Cautioned.'

'Shame – a nice juicy custodial sentence would have suited me.'

'Ah – but that's not the story.' He looked her in the eye and smiled. Then he picked up his pint and gulped down a third of it.

'Come on, Dennis. Don't dangle a tidbit like that and snatch it away again.'

'Freddie Larson was not on the side of the angels.'

'Not on the… you're kidding me. He was a member of the NF?'

'Not officially, but as good as.'

'Bloody hell. No wonder Daddy Larson has kept him hidden from public view – a junky *and* a Nazi.' Angela reached for her glass and discovered it was empty. 'Your turn – I can't take the piss with expenses. And find out what's happened to those ploughmans.'

Watson carefully extricated himself from the picnic table.

'Can you get me a list of everyone else arrested at the time?'

'You don't ask for much, do you? That's something that hasn't changed in the last 30 years.'

While Watson was at the bar Angela read all the cuttings about the NF rally and the other two stories Watson had singled out for her. One was a brief report about a rare 16th Century painting by an Italian artist she'd never heard of. According to the piece, the work of art went missing from the refectory of Newton College during the summer of '79. Freddie Larson had already been sent down by then, so she assumed it was irrelevant. The other article was much more interesting. In the aftermath of the Jonestown mass suicide in November 1978, a copycat event took place at Newton College. Eleven students were discovered unconscious in an undergraduate common room, having taken overdoses of barbiturates. All the students were brought back from the brink except one young economics graduate studying for his masters. It was revealed at the subsequent inquest that the reason he never regained consciousness was in all likelihood due to the fact he had also ingested half a bottle of whiskey.

32

The hand dryer roared for a few moments, the door clanged shut and Caroline exhaled. She'd been hiding in a cubicle in the ladies' loos on the lower ground floor for the best part of an hour. She checked her watch for the hundredth time. Her colleagues would all be long gone by now. She decided to wait another few minutes, just to be safe.

At 6:50pm she made her way back up to the fourth floor, flicking off the overhead fluorescents whenever she passed a light switch, relieved to see the office was deserted.

She took a few deep breaths and waited for her heart to stop repeatedly hurling itself against her ribs. The long line of filing cabinets stretched from one end of the room to the other. There was no way she could check them all. Instead, she decided to head straight for the procurement section and the drawer labelled *T-Z*. She pulled it out slowly and flinched as it squealed against its rollers. Instinctively she glanced around the office, checking again she didn't have company. She blew out her cheeks and flipped through the hanging files until she reached the V's. The swinging cardboard folders went straight from Vancouver Holdings to Vulcan Structural Engineers. Nothing for VL Construction. She slammed the drawer shut and tried to remember another company from the spreadsheet, but the only names that came to her were those of the men who had died at Pete's firm. Since she'd found out about them, she felt like she'd been grieving, even though she knew nothing about them. But each man would have been someone's son, probably someone's sweetheart.

She paced up and down the narrow aisle of carpet between the cabinets and the row of desks, hoping the physical activity would help jog her memory. Something beginning with... D. She turned towards the beginning of the alphabet and opened the *D-F* drawer. She flipped through the D's, hoping a name would jump out at her. None did, but in the process she remembered *Davis Electricals* from the first column of the spreadsheet. There was no file for that company. Reluctantly, she reached into her bag for the mobile phone Tate had given her. The journalist answered after a single ring.

'Tell me you got your computer access sorted.'

Caroline took a breath. 'I haven't spoken to anyone about it yet – I don't want to draw attention to myself.'

'Then why are you calling?'

Caroline quickly explained where she was and what she was doing, and Tate, after recovering from her initial disappointment, read out the names of another half dozen companies from the beginning of the list. Sure enough, the corresponding files were missing from the cabinets.

'It looks like they got to the records before me,' Caroline said, slamming another drawer shut.

'They?'

'Whoever. Files don't just get up and walk.' She turned towards her desk and spotted a collection of three or four confidential waste sacks heaped up next to the photocopier. 'I really feel as if...'

'What?'

'It feels like it's all slipping through my fingers.'

'I'm still working through the first batch of documents you gave me – I'm sure I'll find something useful soon.' Tate was obviously trying to sound upbeat.

It wasn't working.

'But that won't get us any closer to finding out what happened to Martin.' Caroline walked over to the cluster of orange sacks by the copier and prodded one with a toe. A rectangle the size and shape of a folder appeared under the thin layer of plastic. 'I've got to go,' she said. 'Sorry for disturbing you.'

The tops of the sacks were tied in half-hearted bows. Caroline quickly loosened one of them and plunged a hand in. She pulled out a slim hanging file and opened it. Empty. She checked a second, and a third. They too had lost their contents. The other three bags contained more empty files. She was too late. The censors had got there ahead of her.

In the gathering gloom she glanced up at Prior's office. He had to be behind the cleansing operation. But who was giving him his instructions? First the computer surveillance, now the office clearout. Authorisation must have come from higher up the food chain. For a moment she thought she glimpsed movement behind the glass. She froze, just watching, holding her breath. Then exhaled. There was no one there.

For God's sake, get a hold of yourself.

She swallowed and shook her head. She should leave before paranoia properly set in. She glanced round the office again. The packing crate lying on her desk was open. When she'd left it the flaps had been closed.

She dumped her bag and checked inside the crate. All her stuff seemed to be there, but it had definitely been disturbed. She slammed the lid shut. Someone had been poking through her things. Pam? Prior? She dragged the crate onto the floor and stacked another one on top. As she leaned on the desk to get up she spotted Tracy Clarke's forgotten cardboard box shoved right underneath the adjacent desk. Given Tracy's stuff looked like junk, if Caroline didn't pack it into a crate for her it would doubtless end up in the crusher with all the other rubbish.

She got to her knees and scrabbled under the desk. As she reached for the box, the sudden memory of Tracy's ashen face emerging from Prior's office stopped her in her tracks. A spasm of guilt jabbed like a stitch beneath her ribcage. She took a deep breath and waited a moment for it to pass then grabbed a corner of the box and heaved it onto the desk.

Still nestling in the corner of the box, just where Caroline had shoved it, was Tracy's pen pot. She lifted it out and found the Post-It note with Tracy's login details. She snatched the yellow square of paper, screwed it into a tight ball and shoved it in her pocket.

A faint squeal sounded from another part of the office. Caroline strained to listen, holding her breath. The noise stopped as abruptly as it started. It was impossible to tell which direction it had come from. She stood motionless for a few more seconds, but there was nothing to hear.

Bloody paranoid.

She dragged a plastic packing crate across the floor and decanted Tracy's stuff until all that remained right at the bottom of the box was a hairbrush, matted with Tracy's frizzy hairs, and an old copy of *heat.* Caroline screwed up her nose and, pinching the very end of the brush between finger and thumb, threw it quickly into the crate. As she picked up the magazine something fell out and clattered back into the box. It wasn't like Tracy to leave a freebie inside a magazine. Caroline grabbed the CD case and angled it towards the window to catch the last of the daylight filtering through the blinds, expecting to discover it was some awful compilation album. But the CD inside was blank except for a few handwritten lines in black marker:

Primary & secondary pre-Ofsted:
Pupil records
CONFIDENTIAL

Caroline edged closer to the window and read it again. It was Tracy's handwriting. She'd circled the word *confidential.* Caroline swallowed. The missing CD-ROM. Tracy must have had it for the whole of her maternity leave. Caroline quickly slipped the CD-ROM back into the pages of the magazine, shoved the magazine in the crate and stepped back.

She stared at the crate, unable to move.

The squealing noise sounded again, louder this time. Caroline glanced over her shoulder in the direction of the noise. It stopped again. Her gaze was drawn magnetically back to the contents of the crate and the magazine resting on top.

If she presented Prior with the CD-ROM now, how would she explain where she found it? Tracy was already in enough trouble because of her. But she couldn't just leave it there, pretend she knew nothing about it. Before she had time to consider the consequences, she scooped up the magazine and the CD-ROM and shoved both in her handbag. Then she flipped closed the lid of the packing crate and hurriedly slapped on a label and scribbled Tracy's name on it in block capitals.

She stepped back and gazed down at the crate, already questioning whether she was doing the right thing. Her heart was racing; she could hear it pounding in her ears.

Then she heard another noise, just a little way behind her: the phlegmy rattle of congested breathing. She stiffened, unable to turn around, not wanting to know who was there.

'Well, well, well.' Ed Wallis's voice crackled in his throat.

Caroline exhaled slowly as she turned, relieved it wasn't Prior. 'Hello, Ed.' She forced a smile.

'We must stop meeting like this.' He was holding a fat arm over his enormous belly, the other arm resting on top, clutching a mobile phone. He shook his head. 'Still burning the midnight oil?'

'Actually I was just off home.'

'What have you been up to?'

'Up to?' Caroline glanced towards her handbag on the desk. 'Oh you know the sort of thing – last minute packing. It's like going away on holiday, isn't it? There's always something you remember you've forgotten at the last minute.'

Ed was staring at her handbag. 'I thought Bishop's were coming in to do all the packing for you.'

As ever Ed was the most well informed security guard in the whole department.

'Oh, you know us girls – we like to fuss over that sort of thing ourselves. It's just nicer to pack your own stuff.'

'Is that what you were doing?'

Caroline nodded.

Ed shuffled over to the crate she'd just labelled. 'This is your stuff is it?' He lifted a flap and peered inside.

'No!' She took a breath and lowered her voice. 'No – I was just doing Tracy a favour. She's not back for a couple of weeks yet.'

Ed shut the flap and turned back to her. 'You haven't heard then?'

'Heard what?' Caroline took a step closer to her desk. Ed mirrored her movements and sidled sideways, somehow managing to manoeuvre himself so that he was within reaching distance of her bag. 'She's up for a disciplinary. Breach of the Code of Conduct.'

Disciplinary? Dear Christ, what have I done?

'On what grounds?'

'That I don't know.' He slipped his mobile into a pocket. 'I'm surprised no one's told you anything about it though.' He took another step sideways and glanced around the office. 'Seems like you're in the dark all ways round.' He chuckled.

'Yeah – well, that wouldn't be a first.' She took a step towards her desk and reached out a hand for her bag. 'If you'll excuse me – I really do need to get going.'

'Not sure I can, as it goes.' He quickly spread his arms and legs, completely blocking access to the desk.

'What do you think you're doing?' She took another step and stopped. Any further and she'd collide with his stomach. 'Stop playing silly buggers, Ed.'

'Does your boss know how hard you're working, how many extra hours you're putting in? Do you think I should mention it to him?'

Caroline drew in a sharp breath. 'Oh – I wouldn't bother. Doesn't cut much ice with Jeremy. You'd be wasting your time.'

'So you'd rather I didn't tell him about this evening?'

'What about it?'

'Doing your own packing. Poking through Tracy's stuff. Should I keep quiet about that then? Not mention it? Just keep it between ourselves, shall we?'

'I didn't "poke through" anything – I was doing Tracy a favour. You can tell Prior whatever you like. Right now, I'd like you to get out of my way.'

'Really? Tell him anything, can I?'

Caroline shrugged. 'I don't know what you think you saw, but you can tell Prior anything you like, and I'll explain whatever I need to.'

'You're sure?' He twisted and reached an arm behind his back, his hand on her bag. 'Maybe I could find something in here to back me up.' He lifted the bag. 'What do you ladies keep in your handbags? This thing weighs a ton.' He opened the bag and peered inside.

'Take your fucking hands off my bag!' Caroline screamed at him.

'Language!' He reached in a hand.

Caroline lunged towards him, both fists ploughing into his chest, at the same time drawing up her knee as rapidly as she could, hard and fast, right into his crotch. He let out an animal wail, dropped her bag and doubled over, clutching his balls. She scooped up the bag and staggered backwards.

'Don't threaten me, Ed.' She secured the shoulder strap across her chest and clung on tight to her bag. 'You start talking to my boss and maybe I'll report you to yours.' She backed away, towards the exit.

'Fucking bitch!' The words came out of Ed's mouth in a high-pitched squeal. 'I'll fucking get you!'

'I'd think twice about that, Ed. It's a dismissible offence... sexual harassment.'

33

'I haven't got long,' Caroline said. 'I need to get home.'

'I'm sorry I'm late. You didn't really give me much notice. I had to—'

'Don't bother inventing some excuse.'

Angela Tate collapsed onto the stone bench outside the Royal Festival Hall and squeezed Caroline's arm. 'Are you all right?' she said, fixing a smile on her face that seemed to Caroline like an afterthought. 'You look a bit weird.'

'Shall we get on we this?'

'OK.' Tate glanced up and down the river. 'It's bloody freezing sitting here. Let's walk and talk.'

With some effort, Caroline levered herself to her feet.

'West or east?' Tate pointed first towards the London Eye and the Palace of Westminster beyond, then in the opposite direction towards Waterloo Bridge.

Caroline had no intention of going back to Westminster. She'd had more than enough for one day. 'East,' she said.

They'd got as far as the painted yellow steps leading up to Queen Elizabeth Hall when Tate's mobile started to ring. She answered the call and shrugged an apology at Caroline.

Caroline lengthened her stride, forcing Tate to pick up speed. They'd reached the tables of second-hand books outside the NFT by the time Tate finished her call. The traders were packing up for the night. Tate shoved the phone back in her bag and picked up a dog-eared copy of *Scoop*.

'I haven't read this in years.' She inspected the cover, front and back. 'It was hysterical. Have you read it?'

Caroline prised the book from Tate's hands, placed it gently back on the table and steered the journalist away from further distraction.

'Did you manage to find out anything else about the contractors on the spreadsheet after I spoke to you?' Caroline glanced left and right, not entirely sure what she was expecting to see.

'Actually I did – I made a few calls, called in a few favours.' Tate looked her up and down. 'I thought you had something you wanted to tell me?'

'I will, later. What did you find out?'

'It seems each firm has a parent company registered at Companies House, but they're just empty shells. Is that even legal in government procurement?'

'Not my area of expertise.'

'I'm guessing it's some tax evasion scam.'

'And are the companies linked in any way?'

'Why? Should they be?'

Caroline shrugged. 'Is that all you could find?'

'That's quite a lot. It took a fair amount of digging around to come up with that much – especially this late in the day.' She pulled her raincoat tighter. 'I did find out that most of the contractors have been getting steady work from the Department for Education for a couple of years.' She shoved her hands under her arms. 'And other government departments before that. The Department of Health in particular. And before that Transport.'

'Health and Transport?'

Tate nodded. 'Why?'

Caroline sucked in a breath. 'You've not made the connection?'

'What connection? I only found out half an hour ago.'

'Those are the departments where William King held ministerial posts before he came to the DfE.'

'Bloody hell, you're right. You're a genius.' Tate reached out her arms then quickly drew them back. 'Is it possible Fox made the connection too and threatened to expose King?' She pulled a notepad from her bag and scribbled down a few lines.

'There's something else you should know about those companies,' Caroline said quietly.

Tate stopped writing.

Caroline tried to moisten her lips with her tongue, but her mouth had gone completely dry. 'I need a drink.' She headed towards the entrance of the NFT. Tate caught her up as she reached the door.

Caroline tried to get comfortable on a hard bench at a table by the window while Tate went to the bar. She kept her handbag on her lap and hooked an arm through the strap.

Tate came back with two large glasses of chilled white wine. Caroline took a tentative sip, then a large gulp.

'Well?' Tate said.

Caroline gazed out at the last of the booksellers loading their wares into large plastic crates. Immediately she pictured Ed in the office, stranded in a sea of brightly coloured crates, bent double, cursing her between agonised breaths. She took another big gulp of wine in an attempt to wash the memory away.

'You really did need a drink.' Tate smiled at her.

Caroline put down her glass and leaned towards the journalist. 'Those contractors...'

'Yes?'

'They may have something else in common.' Caroline picked up her glass again, suddenly uncertain how much she should divulge. Would telling Tate incriminate Pete? She couldn't do it to him.

'Come on, Caroline. If you've got something to say — something that might help us find out about what really happened to Martin... it's your duty to tell me.'

Is it? What would you know about duty?

Caroline got up quickly. 'This was a mistake.'

'What?'

'It's all gone too far.'

Tate put a hand on Caroline's arm. 'You're right, in a way. But *it* hasn't gone too far. *We* have. We've come too far to turn back. We can't just stop. Not now.'

'But the evidence has vanished. It's all been magicked away. And besides...' Caroline screwed up her eyes.

'What is it?'

'I think my boss suspects something. If he doesn't right now, he will by tomorrow.'

'What's happened?'

'You don't need to know.'

Tate gently pushed Caroline back towards her seat. 'Sit down. Finish your drink at least.'

Caroline opened her mouth, but the words wouldn't come. What could she say? She stared into Tate's eager face, her eyes searching Caroline's. It took Caroline a moment to recognise that look.

It was hunger.

She let out a stuttering breath and cleared her throat.

'I feel like something big is about to happen,' she finally said. 'The pressure's building. Not only on me.'

'The election's just over a week away — that's the big something. If you're right and the department is being cleansed of evidence, that's probably happening right across Whitehall. Everywhere that King has been. All the surfaces he's left his dirty paw prints on are being decontaminated. He's making sure he presents a blemish free version of himself to the electorate next Thursday.'

Caroline gulped another mouthful of wine without tasting it. 'OK,' she said. 'There are two things I want you to know. One needs more investigating. The other you have to handle exactly the way I tell you.'

Tate raised her eyebrows, but picked up her notebook and pen without a murmur.

'Those contractors... it might be nothing... but I know at least one of them is owned by Larson.'

Tate's mouth fell open. 'You're sure?'

Caroline nodded. 'Certain. VL Construction is run by Valerie Larson. It's quite possible others might be owned by Larson's as well. It's worth checking them all out. Call in a few more favours.'

'If some of the other companies are owned by the Larsons too... that means...'

'A possible connection between King and Larson and the likelihood of some very dodgy dealing in the procurement process.'

'But what if King knew about the health and safety record too? That's got to do serious damage to his campaign.'

'Yes – good luck with proving any of that.'

'We have the spreadsheet.'

'That may not be enough.'

'It's a bloody good start.' Tate scribbled down some notes for a few moments then stopped suddenly. She stared into Caroline's face. 'You said there were two things. What's the second one?'

'You have to promise me you'll do exactly as I say.'

'If I possibly can, I will.'

'You've got to do better than that. If this isn't done properly, if you don't work it for all it's worth... then the diabolical position I've just put myself in will have been for nothing. Promise me.'

'Christ, Caroline. What's happened?'

'Promise me!'

'OK – whatever it takes – you have my word.'

Caroline wasn't sure what Tate's word was worth. But right now she felt as if she was running out of options. She reached into her bag and left her hand inside. She stared into Tate's eyes. They were bloodshot. 'My way and my timing.'

Tate nodded and looked down at the bag.

'I'm going to give you something, something that's damaging for the department... damaging for the government, potentially.'

'Is this to do with the contractors?'

'It's something else.' She pulled the CD-ROM from her bag and glanced up at a frowning Tate. 'This disc has been missing for a while – months, most probably. Three weeks ago I was given the task of locating it. And I've spent the last three weeks getting absolutely nowhere. We'd pretty much given up any hope of finding it.'

Tate seemed transfixed. She couldn't take her eyes off the disc.

'I found it by accident this evening. It contains the personal details of over 150,000 pupils. It wasn't until someone in the department went looking for it that they discovered it had disappeared.'

'Where did you find it?'

'That you don't need to know.'

Tate pursed her lips.

'So here's all this information and it's floating around.' Caroline waved the CD-ROM in front of Tate's face. 'No one knows where it is. The powers that be are petrified it's going to turn up in the back of a cab, or left on the tube, or in a car boot sale.'

'Well it wouldn't be the first time that happened.'

'The first time it's happened this close to an election.'

Tate shifted in her seat. 'What kind of personal details? Address? Age?'

Caroline nodded. 'Free school meal and SEN status too.'

'SEN?'

'Special Educational Needs.'

'So much for child protection.' Tate kept her eyes on the CD-ROM in its plastic case.

'I haven't had a chance to wipe it,' Caroline said.

'Wipe it?'

'My fingerprints will be all over it.' She pressed it into Tate's hands. 'Make sure you clean it really well then handle it as much as you can.'

'You want me to handle it?'

Caroline nodded. 'Get some colleagues to handle it too. I don't know anything about DNA, but I would have thought the more people who handle it, the more difficult it becomes to analyse whatever traces are found.'

'Who's going to be interested in doing a DNA analysis?'

Caroline shrugged. 'I'm just trying to protect myself. Although I have a feeling it's a bit late for that.'

Tate held the CD-ROM at arm's length and squinted at it.

'I want you to write a story about the department losing such important information. I want you to write about the large amount of resources wasted looking for it. Ask questions about how the department could have such a casual attitude to data protection.'

Caroline looked at Tate's pad and pen lying on the counter next to her glass of wine. 'You're not making notes.'

'And you're not going to tell me how to write a story.'

Caroline sighed. 'OK – but you must do at least one thing for me.'

'Must I?'

'Please, Angela – this is really important.'

'What is it?'

'I want you to say you received the CD-ROM through the post. But you never thought to keep the envelope.' Caroline bit her bottom lip. 'You need to make something up about it being mislaid in your office somewhere – to explain your delay in making it public. Say that you made a note of the postmark at the time it was originally received – say it was posted from Cambridge on 25th March.'

'A month ago? It really did get mislaid. Any particular type of envelope I carelessly discarded?'

'A padded one.'

'I was joking.'

'You need to say there was no letter with it. Just a Post-It stuck to the front of the CD case with a short note scrawled across it.'

'Which I also threw away, presumably?'

'I'll leave that to you – any way you want to spin it.'

'That's very generous, thanks.'

'Can you get the story in tomorrow's paper?'

Tate rocked back in her seat. 'That's a bit of a tall order.'

'Front page.'

'You don't ask for much.' Tate flipped the package over. And what did the note say? Do I at least know who posted it to me?'

Caroline filled her lungs and exhaled slowly. A nerve in her right cheek started to twitch.

'You do. And you must make that a major part of the article.'

'And that person would be?'

'Martin Fox.'

34

A points failure at London Bridge had delayed all the trains coming into Charing Cross from southeast London and Kent. It was 8:55am by the time Caroline jumped off the number 11 bus.

She flew up Great Smith Street and ran past reception relieved to see Ed Wallis wasn't manning the desk.

Flushed and breathless, she finally reached her own desk in time to see Jeremy Prior storm out of his room, a mobile phone clamped to his ear. She watched as he marched the length of the office, shouting a stream of obscenities into the phone as he went, finally disappearing through the fire exit door at the other end.

Caroline was certain it was too early for the first edition of the *Evening News* to have hit the streets. Nevertheless, she found herself grabbing the bright pink pay-as-you-go mobile from her bag and hitting the speed dial button.

'Is it out yet?' Caroline whispered, holding a hand over her mouth.

'God no! First edition leaves the depot around eleven,' Tate said. 'I haven't even seen it yet. Is something wrong?'

Caroline thought she could detect an edge of nervousness in Tate's voice.

'My boss knows.'

'What has he said to you?'

'Nothing – he doesn't need to – I've seen the thunderous look on his face.'

'He doesn't know. No one knows. It's not even on the website yet – we've gone for shock value – hitting all our channels at once.'

'He knows.'

'That's impossible. He'd have to be so well connected…'

The fire door burst open and Jeremy Prior marched back into the office, his face twisted in a scowl.

'I've got to go.' Caroline slipped the phone into her pocket and busied herself switching on her computer and monitor. She kept her head down, finally glancing up to see Prior hurry into his room and slam the door behind him.

That morning, while Caroline had sat on the train for almost an hour in the no man's land between New Cross and London Bridge, she had decided the only sensible tactic she could adopt was one of absolute denial. If she vowed that she didn't know anything and swore she hadn't done anything, what was the worst that could happen? That thought had sent an involuntary shiver across her shoulders, and she resolved to banish the possible outcomes from her mind.

But that was easier said than done.

She turned back to her computer, hoping her access issues had miraculously remedied themselves overnight.

The door at the other end of the office opened again and Ed Wallis appeared. He limped slowly towards her, looking straight ahead. When he drew level with her desk, his mouth twitched but still he didn't make eye contact. Eventually he got to Prior's door and knocked on the glass. As he waited he glanced over a fleshy shoulder and locked eyes with Caroline for a moment. Then he smiled. Caroline's breath got trapped somewhere inside her throat as she watched him open the door and hobble inside.

She held on tight to the arms of her chair, resisting an overwhelming urge to flee, reminding herself it was Ed's word against hers. Whatever story he spun Prior she would counter it. So what if she was in the department outside normal office hours? That wasn't a crime. It wasn't even out of the ordinary.

She saw Prior offer Ed a seat. Ed waved it away, instead opting to lean his weight against the back of a chair. He seemed to be talking non-stop and, amazingly, given his earlier outburst, Prior seemed to be listening. Considering. Occasionally nodding.

Caroline swallowed, trying to force back down the rising queasiness in her throat. If Ed accused her of taking something from Tracy's box she would just remain calm and deny it. Maybe throw in a bit of indignation that the finger was even being pointed in her direction. She attempted a deep breath, but her throat felt constricted. Her heart was pumping too fast. She could see dark spots before her eyes and her head started to buzz. She pressed her fingernails into her palms and concentrated on the pain. The buzzing subsided after a few moments and a few moments after that the spots melted away. *Just. Stay. Calm.*

Ten minutes of seemingly convivial conversation later, Ed re-emerged from Prior's office. He didn't bother to shut the door. Caroline had expected a self-satisfied grin, but his face was blank. He slipped out of the main exit without saying a word.

What was going on? It wasn't Ed's style to miss an opportunity to gloat. She glanced back at Prior's room and saw Pam lumbering through the door.

Caroline sat at her desk feeling helpless, as if she was waiting to be escorted to the executioner. She couldn't just sit and do nothing. She jumped up and hurried into the lobby to discover Ed was still waiting for the lift to arrive. It wasn't until she was standing shoulder to shoulder with him that he acknowledged her presence.

'Nice little chat was it?' she said.

'Private little chat. Man to man.' He ducked sideways, shuffling away from her.

'Are you in the habit of having cosy, manly chats with the head of the academies division, then?'

'There's a first time for everything.'

The lift arrived. Ed limped inside, Caroline just behind him.

'Actually, I was thinking of having a nice little natter with your boss.' She stared into his sweating face. 'You know, woman to woman. Perhaps we could talk about you. What do you think Ed? Do you think I might need to? Just to even things up a bit?'

The lift doors pinged open onto the first floor lobby, but no one got in or out. Ed repeatedly jabbed a fat finger against the ground floor button.

'Always seem to go slow when you're in a hurry, don't they?' She smiled at him and he seemed to shrink away. 'How's the er… groin injury?'

'I don't know what you're talking about.'

Really? What was he playing at? If he had a mind to he could probably have her arrested for actual bodily harm.

The doors finally opened onto the ground floor and Ed limped out. Caroline decided to stay inside.

'I just told him everything I saw,' he said, as the lift doors started to close. 'Nothing more, nothing less. Nothing for you to worry about, if you weren't doing anything wro—'

The doors shut and cut off the end of his sentence. Caroline leaned back against the cool mirrored wall and inhaled deeply. What had Ed seen? She pressed '4', and headed back up to the hangman's rope.

When she got back to her desk she found Pam sitting on it studying her nails.

'What was that all about?' Caroline pointed to Prior's office. 'Why did he want to see you?'

Pam hesitated for a moment, just long enough to worry Caroline. 'Oh gosh, nothing,' she said. 'He's just in one of his moods. He wanted to kick the cat and I was the closest thing.' Pam smiled, then turned and walked away.

The air felt prickly with static, full of all the stuff that wasn't being said. Caroline sank onto her chair, fearing that as the day progressed things would only get worse.

35

The first thing Angela did when she got back to the office was take off her shoes. She closed her eyes and imagined submerging her feet in a bowl of warm soapy water.

'Sleeping on the job, now, is it?' Frank Carter nudged her as he walked past. 'You do know Evans-the-Editor is after your blood, don't you?'

'I've only just got in.'

'Well if you want to avoid a bollocking, you should go right back out again.'

'What's it about?'

'He wouldn't say.' Frank scratched a scabby patch of stubble on his chin. 'Where've you been, anyway? You look like shit.'

'Gee thanks, Frank.'

She opened the top drawer of Jason Morris's console and pulled out a mirror and peered into it. 'Christ, you weren't exaggerating.' She tidied the line of lipstick on her bottom lip with a little finger. 'I've just spent the best part of two hours doorstepping drug clinics, flashing Freddie Larson's mugshot at any addict who looked compos mentis enough to recognise themselves in a mirror.'

'Any luck?'

'Maybe. A bloke outside a clinic in the City told me he knew him. It's just possible he was telling the truth. But there wasn't much life left in his eyes to judge one way or the other.' She sighed. 'Mind you – he was still alert enough to prise 30 quid out of me.'

'I'd have given him good money to see that.'

'Shut up, Frank.'

'So, have you got an address for Freddie?'

She shook her head.'

'A number?'

'No.'

'That bloke must have seen you coming. What did you get in return for your hard earned?'

'Freddie's due in at the clinic tomorrow lunchtime. All I can do is go back there and wait for him.'

'Is that it?'

'It's the first positive ID I've had. I've got no choice but to follow it up.'

'Do you want me to come with – as back up?'

She looked Frank up and down. 'What – you'll protect me if he turns nasty?'

Frank shrugged. 'Something like that.'

'Please yourself.'

'I'll take that as a yes.'

Angela opened the drawer again and attempted to slide the mirror back in. Somehow it was now too big for the space. She yanked hard on the drawer below. It slid out four inches like it always did, then refused to budge a fraction more. Not in the mood to be defeated by a piece of office furniture, Angela braced her knees against the front of the console and grabbed the handle of the offending drawer with both hands. She pulled as hard as she could. The drawer shifted another half inch then stopped. She jiggled it from side to side and up and down. She pushed it in and out as fast as she could to loosen whatever was stopping it. Then she tugged again and was rewarded with another two inches of progress.

'Jesus, Ange. Are you still wrestling with that bloody thing?' He shook his head. 'That's called Karma that is. If you will jump into a dead man's drawers you've got to expect consequences.'

'Cheers, Frank – you should have been a sodding prophet. Missed your vocation there.' She grabbed the top drawer again and tried lifting it outwards and upwards. It slipped out almost effortlessly.

'Shame you didn't try that before,' Frank said.

Angela laid the drawer on the desk and peered into the console. Towards the back she spotted a bright yellow strip protruding from the runner. She reached in and pulled out a cyclist's ankle strap, Velcro tabs at both ends. She threw it onto the desk.

'Is the other one lurking in there somewhere?'

'Doesn't look like it.' She tested the second drawer. It slid in and out as if the runners had been greased with butter.

Frank picked up the fluorescent strip and tossed it into the bin. 'I thought young Jason kept all his cycling gear downstairs.'

Angela closed the drawer. 'Downstairs?'

'In the basement.'

'The basement?'

'You know, the floor beneath ground level – showers, changing rooms, lockers… gym, bike park.'

'They've got all that in the basement?'

'Where did you think people left their bikes?'

'Why would I ever trouble myself thinking about that?'

She opened the drawer again and began to decant some of the contents of the top drawer into the newly functioning middle one, fully expecting the amount of crap to double overnight. When she'd evened out the load she slotted the half-empty top drawer back into the console. As she was closing it she spotted the useless little key she'd pulled off the key ring. She plucked it out of the drawer and carefully inspected it front and back. The number 64 was stamped into the metal on one side.

'Jason's cycling stuff... you say he kept it in the basement?'

Frank nodded.

'Was it ever cleared out?'

'I've no idea.'

'In a locker, was it?'

'Yes Ange – you must have seen the sort of thing – rows of slim metal cupboards, very narrow doors.'

'Do you know which one?'

'How would I?'

'Does the lift go all the way to the basement?'

Her landline started to ring. She snatched the receiver and hollered 'Tate' into the mouthpiece.

'My God, Angela. Is that how you always answer your office phone?'

'Dennis?'

'We've got more manners here in the provinces.'

And no reason to get out of bed in the mornings.

'Actually, I'm in the middle of something right now.' She glanced down at the small key resting on her palm. 'Can it wait?'

'Depends if you want to wait for that list of students arrested at the demo.'

'You're bloody quick.'

'I like to keep on my toes. I've got that joint story credit to earn.'

'How many arrests were there?'

'Twenty-three. I'll email you the list.'

The line went quiet. Angela waited for a moment then broke the silence, just as she supposed Watson had wanted her to.

'I sense you have something else to tell me. I can feel the tension leaking out of the phone. Cough it up, Dennis, don't leave me in suspense.'

'I take it you're already sitting down.'

Angela closed her eyes and waited. There was no harm in letting Watson enjoy his moment. But he could whistle for a joint byline.

'Remember I got you this, all right?' he said.

'Dennis – what do you want me to do – dedicate my first novel to you?'

'We have an agreement. A joint byline is the least you can do. You'll be good to your word?'

'Haven't I always been? Now whatever you tell me is going to seem like such an anti-climax.'

'Guess who arrested Freddie Larson in 1979? Go on.'

'I don't know... Inspector Morse?'

'It's Cambridge, not bloody Oxford. Guess again. Think big.'

'Why are you making me do this? I don't know... Sir Ian Blair?'

'Warm. Care to have a another stab at it?'

'Warm? Please Dennis – just put me out of my misery.'

'OK, OK.' Watson cleared his throat. 'The arresting officer was none other than Deputy Assistant Commissioner—'

'Barry Flowers.'

'You guessed! How the fuck—'

'Woman's intuition.'

'If I said that you'd have my bollocks on a plate.'

'Too damn right.'

'Well here's something you don't know.' He paused again for effect. 'Sir Barry, formerly known as PC Flowers, was transferred from the Cambridgeshire force less than a month after he arrested young Master Larson.'

36

After Pam had had her little chat with Prior, he called Lisa in. Then after Lisa left Greg from IT turned up for an audience with the head of the academies division. When Greg emerged his expression was grimmer on the way out than it had been going in.

At 11:15am Caroline's pay-as-you-go mobile rang.

'Just thought I'd let you know, the paper's leaving the depot right about now.' Tate sounded almost breathless with excitement. 'I'm still waiting for copies to arrive in the office.'

Caroline couldn't think of anything to say.

'This *is* what you wanted.'

When Caroline didn't comment Tate hung up.

Was it what she wanted? There was no going back now. She buried her face in her hands.

'I do know the way.' Tracy's voice. 'I didn't actually need an escort.'

Caroline looked up to see a small procession led by a security guard she didn't recognise. He was followed by Tracy Clarke clutching a laptop to her chest. Ed Wallis was bringing up the rear. His limp seemed to be getting worse. Tracy went into Prior's office, Ed and the other guard stood sentry either side of the door. It looked as though she was under arrest.

Ed gazed unashamedly straight at Caroline. He pointed two fingers at her, shaped in the barrel of a gun. Then he pulled an imaginary trigger.

What the hell?

Caroline got up and hurried towards him. His colleague nudged him with an elbow. Caroline followed his gaze and watched as a smiling Tracy Clarke reached over Prior's desk and shook his hand. It looked for all the world as if they were concluding a deal.

'What's going on?' Caroline tried to control the waver in her voice but failed.

Ed looked at the other guard and winked at him. The door opened and Tracy emerged from the room minus her laptop.

'Jeremy's ready for you now,' she said and smiled at Caroline.

'Sorry?'

'Jeremy asked me to tell you to go straight in. I wouldn't keep him waiting.'

'What's it about?'

'Oh I think I should leave him to tell you that.'

A gathering weakness in Caroline's legs spread to the rest of her body in an instant. She tried to smile at Tracy, but Tracy was already turning away, chatting amiably with Ed's colleague as they all made their way towards the exit.

Deny everything. Plead ignorance. If all else fails, act stupid.

She cleared her throat and tapped on the open door.

'Tracy said you—'

'Yes, yes. Come in.' Prior perched on the edge of his huge desk. 'Have you seen the paper?'

Caroline hesitated. He knew already. Before the paper had hit the newsstands.

'Paper?'

Caroline looked longingly at the chair on her side of his desk. He hadn't asked her to sit down.

'Oh come now, Caroline. How long are you going to keep this up?'

For as long as it takes.

'I have no idea what you're talking about, Jeremy.'

Prior smiled. He looked her up and down. 'You know, I almost admire your bravado. Did the journalist suggest this approach, or is it a strategy you came up with all by yourself?'

Caroline shrugged. 'Journalist?'

Deny everything.

'If this is the way you want play it, fine.' His tone had sharpened. The muscles around his eyes tightened. 'I've had my diary cleared for the rest of the day. I'm all yours! We can take just as long as you want.'

She stared at him. He was leaning forward, balling his fists and breathing heavily. He had the look of a man about to take flight. Or pick a fight.

Caroline concentrated for a moment on her own stiffening muscles. She consciously willed her shoulders to relax. She loosened her arms and hands. The terror she'd felt coming into Prior's office was beginning to subside. He was getting rattled. She needed to stay calm. He was fishing for a confession. She would give him nothing. *All day? Why not?*

'Well?' Prior said, casting his arms wide.

'Well?' Caroline mirrored his open gesture.

He let out a long breath, reeled his arms back in and rested his hands, one on top of the other, on his narrow thigh. 'I had a very interesting chat with Ed Wallis – the security guard – earlier today.' He smiled. 'He's a charming chap. Salt of the earth, men like Wallis. Made this nation what it is. Always interested in the greater good, never thinking of themselves.'

Salt of the earth? Ed was obviously a much better actor than she'd given him credit for.

'He told me about your... foraging expedition last night. How he found you in the dark... rummaging, I think was the word he used, through someone else's belongings. Is that something you make a habit of?'

'I can't imagine what Ed thought he saw. But I know I certainly wasn't "rummaging" through anything.'

'Tracy's belongings, it seems.'

Admit only as much as you have to.

'Oh – that. I packed up Tracy's stuff – that's probably what he means. I put it all in a crate so it wouldn't get lost in the move.'

'Why were you in the office so late?'

'I had some personal items I wanted to pack myself. You know – women's stuff. Didn't want burly great removals men mauling them. You understand, I'm sure.'

Prior shook his head. 'I do wish you would make this easier for yourself, Caroline. Let me have the whole truth, without my having to prise it out of you piece by piece. If nothing else it's embarrassing – for both of us.'

Caroline shrugged again.

Plead ignorance.

'Very well, let me attempt to curtail the agony. As you are aware, I have also spoken to Tracy Clarke this morning.' He clasped his hands together and shifted his position, making himself a little taller. 'Tracy was deeply shocked when I told her about the story in the newspaper.'

'What story?'

'You see, she supposed the CD-ROM was safely stored in her box of belongings. The belongings she remembers specifically asking you to look after for her.'

Caroline's heart started to beat faster. *Your word against hers. Stay calm.*

'She had no idea we'd been hunting for it all this time,' he said. 'It would be almost farcical, if it weren't so desperately serious. Don't you think?'

'I don't understand. You're telling me Tracy had the CD-ROM all this time?'

If all else fails, act stupid.

'As I say – high farce.' Prior had adopted a mocking tone.

'I still don't know what this has to do with me.'

'I've joined the dots, Caroline. I've made the connections.'

He has nothing. He's bluffing. Stay calm.

'Though of course, this helped me draw my conclusions.' He reached an arm behind his back and produced a mobile phone. He hit a few buttons and turned it around so that the screen was facing Caroline. The image was not much bigger than a postage stamp, grainy and dark.

'Can you stand there and deny that's you?'

'I can't really tell what it is.'

'I'm sure technology is available to enhance the image.'

After a few seconds the tiny movie ended and froze on the last frame – an image of Caroline leaning over a plastic crate.

'Would you like to see it again?' Prior asked.

Caroline slowly lifted her gaze from the phone to his face. He was smiling.

'You know, I think it showed great presence of mind to record this for posterity,' he said. 'As I said before, Wallis really is concerned to do his bit.' He put the mobile back on his desk and reached for his landline. 'In fact,' he said, picking up the receiver and punching numbers into the keypad, 'why don't I ask him to come back up here right now? I'm sure he'd take great pride in personally escorting you from the building.'

37

Angela stepped out of the lift into a dimly lit corridor that stank of ripe sweat and stale deodorant. She followed the smell and found herself in the men's changing rooms.

Just as Frank had promised, a row of metal lockers ran the length of one wall. She checked the numbers printed on the doors until she found number 64. Before she had a chance to open it, a naked man dripping water onto the floor appeared from the gap in the wall opposite the lockers. He was towelling his hair dry as he walked towards her. She stared first at his face then his crotch then back up again to the scowling expression contorting his mouth. He stared right back at her, making no attempt to cover himself up.

'Don't mind me, love,' she said, turning back to the locker. 'Really – I'm like a nurse. There's nothing I haven't seen before.'

Angela shoved the key into the lock and pulled open the locker. A cycle helmet tumbled out and bounced across the floor.

'Well that's buggered now.'

She looked up to see Frank standing in the doorway, hands on hips. 'I don't need a minder,' she said.

'It wasn't you I was thinking of.' He smiled at the naked man who didn't smile back and scooped the helmet from the floor. 'No wonder he suffered fatal head injuries if his helmet was still in his bloody locker.'

God only knows what really happened to him.

Angela tugged at a pair of panniers wedged into the narrow space. They wouldn't budge. She removed a water bottle, a towel and a toilet bag and tried again. One of them weighed a ton. She opened it. It was full of second-hand paperback books.

Frank peered into it. 'What exactly do you think you're doing?' he said.

Angela removed several novels with no particular connecting theme. 'Maybe he was planning a trip to Oxfam.' She reached into the second bag and groped around in the bottom. She could sense Frank leaning over her, breathing his tobacco breath onto her neck.

'You know what I was saying about Karma?' he said.

'Give it a rest, Frank, for God's sake.'

'But aren't you getting a shivery feeling up your spine?' Frank said. 'Doesn't it feel a bit like walking on his grave?'

'As you so helpfully pointed out not four weeks ago, Jason Morris was cremated.' Her hand struck something solid at the bottom of the long bag. She dragged out a small digital video camera and dipped her hand back into the saddle bag. It was empty. She quickly slipped the camera into a pocket, shoved everything else back into the locker and locked the door.

'I can feel my hair frizzing in the steam,' she said. 'I've got to get out of here.'

She reached the lifts just as a flushed faced Dominic Evans, wearing snug Lycra shorts and a sweat-soaked vest, stepped out. Journalist and editor eyeballed one another for a moment, both lost for words. Unfortunately for Angela, Evans recovered the power of speech first.

'My office, fifteen minutes,' he said and pushed past her into the corridor.

Little bastard.

Angela went straight back to her desk, grabbed her handbag, coat and shoes and took the stairs down to street level. She stood in the ground floor foyer and crammed her beleaguered feet into her shoes. Sitting behind the high reception desk, the security guard was shaking his head and laughing at her.

'If anyone asks,' she said, easing her heel into a shoe, 'you haven't seen me all day.'

He gave her a conspiratorial wink and waved her out of the building. Outside, on Blackfriars Road, she considered making for the nearest pub, but quickly decided that would be the first place Dominic Evans would check after discovering she wasn't at her desk. She looked up and down the street and spotted a black cab approaching. She flagged it down, jumped in and told the driver to head south.

'I was just heading back to Camden. How far south?'

'It's all right – you won't need inoculations.'

Angela pulled the video camera from her pocket and switched it on. A half dozen film roll icons appeared on the screen, a date underneath each one. She selected the video Jason must have recorded the day before he died and immediately his worried face filled the small screen. He ran a hand over his buzz cut and stared with grim eyes into the camera. A low battery symbol blinked over his chin.

'OK,' he said, his voice distorted as it came out of the tiny built-in speaker. 'I guess this is just a bit of a sanity check. Talking to a camera makes talking to myself a bit less weird. And weird is what I've been having trouble with lately. Everything's just too fucking weird.' He paused and took a deep breath. 'Anyway, after what happened last night I think it's safe to assume that the gloves are off. Now I know who's involved...' He stopped and rubbed a hand over his face. He let out a grunt. '*Involved.* Such a fucking understatement.' He paused again. 'Now I know that I need to get some proper—'

The screen went black.

'Oh come on!'

'You all right back there?' She glanced up to see the cab driver looking at her in the rear-view mirror.

She didn't bother answering. She tried the power switch again, but all that appeared was the image of a battery with a red lightning strike running through it.

'Fuck!'

The driver glanced at her again. She collapsed back on the seat and looked out of the window. They were just approaching Southwark tube station. An *Evening News* vendor was doing very little business just outside the entrance. Angela tried to make out the headline on the poster propped up against his stand. It wasn't the one she was expecting. The cab was just pulling away from the traffic lights.

'Turn into The Cut!' she hollered at the driver.

'I'm in the wrong lane, love.'

'Do it!'

The cab swerved across the path of a double decker bus, swung right and stopped outside the pub on the corner. Angela jumped out and ran across the road to the newspaper stand. She grabbed a copy of the *Evening News.*

'That'll be 50p, darling,' the vendor said.

The front page headline was something about William King visiting a school in Dollis Hill. Angela flicked through the inside pages.

'This isn't a reading library, you know.' The vendor tried to grab the paper.

She snatched it out of his reach and eventually found what she was looking for buried on page eight. Two measly columns. Even the headline wasn't the one she'd asked for. Evans had promised her the front page and a double spread inside for the CD-ROM story. *Two columns?* She shoved the paper under her arm and ran back across the road.

'Oi!' the vendor called after her. 'I've got four kids to feed.'

She clambered back into the cab. 'Turn around.'

'Where are we going?'

'Back to Blackfriars.'

Fucking Evans.

She stared down at the heavily edited, watered-down version of her piece and shook her head. A ringtone chirruped in her bag. She grabbed it and stabbed the answer button.

'Have you seen the paper? That little bastard has pissed all over my copy.'

'Take it from me, Ange. Evans is the least of your worries. What have you got yourself into this time?' Frank spoke in an echoey urgent whisper, the sound of rushing water almost drowning out his voice.

'Frank? What's that noise in the background? You sound like you're calling from a urinal.'

'That's because I am,' he hissed.

'What's going on? I'm on my way back in right now. The fucking jumped up little—'

'You can't come back to the office.'

'What?'

'Two nasty looking blokes in cheap suits, claiming to be detectives, are waiting for you in Evans's office.'

'Why?'

'As far as I can make out they're very interested in that CD-ROM of yours.'

'What's it got to do with the police?'

'Shit! Someone's coming.'

'Frank?'

The line went dead.

38

Caroline stood in the same telephone box on the corner of Martin Fox's Street as she had nearly four weeks earlier. From her vantage point she could see the front garden and the first floor windows of his house. She'd already walked past it once and discovered, to her enormous relief, that the police guard had been stood down. In theory there was nothing to stop her marching right up the front path and knocking on the door. Nothing except the trace of self-respect she was managing to cling on to.

The previous day she'd left the department in a daze. Ed and his colleague had collected her from Prior's office. They insisted she hand over her security pass, even before she was allowed back to her desk to pick up her bag and jacket. They then marched her to the lifts, took her through the basement car park and escorted out of the side exit in St Ann's Street.

She must have stood there, disorientated in the bright sunshine, for minutes, blinking rapidly, unsteady on her feet, like a newborn lamb. As she swayed from side to side, several passers-by asked if she was all right. When finally an old woman offered to take her to the nearest police station, Caroline thanked her and set off for Charing Cross station on foot, hoping the cool breeze blowing off the river would help clear the fug from her head.

She was still in a state of shock when she got home. She turned on the television. The BBC News Channel was running a trailer for the upcoming *Question Time* special. William King's face flashed on the screen, grinning as usual. She switched over quickly to Sky News and a re-run of the story about an unknown Labour MP's defection to the Liberal Democrats. That was yesterday's news. Where was Martin Fox? Caroline flipped back to the BBC and stood in front of the TV, too stressed to sit down, until the main bulletin came on at the top of the hour. The discovery of the missing CD-ROM was the very last item before they moved on to the sports report. There was no mention of Martin. The piece focused solely on the data protection issues. It wasn't the story Tate had promised her at all.

And now, as Caroline lurked suspiciously in a telephone box, Tate still wasn't answering her phone. She shoved the bright pink mobile back in her pocket and peered out of the phone box at the first floor windows of Martin's house, checking for some sign of life, trying hard to remember exactly what had prompted her decision to travel half way across London. It felt as if she was clutching at straws. Making a desperate final lunge for the truth.

Who was she kidding? Right now all she wanted was someone to tell her she wasn't going mad.

The kiosk door swung open. Caroline jumped.

'Are you going to be long?' A sweaty bald head pushed into the phone box. 'I don't mean to rush you, but I can't hang about.'

The unshaven man filled the confined space with his halitoxic breath.

Caroline cleared her throat. 'I've just finished. If you'll excuse me.' She waited for him to step to one side, and had barely cleared the box before he sidled in. She hurried away and was half way up the street and fast approaching Martin's house, without even meaning to be. She stopped on the opposite side of the road and looked up to see the curtains at the first floor window had been drawn right back. The blinds on the ground floor jerked open. She saw a tall figure peering out between the wooden slats. Caroline could just make out blonde hair framing the narrow face – the woman from the funeral. It had to be. Caroline glanced up and down the road. The woman pulled up the Venetian blind and stared right at her, holding her gaze for a moment before turning away.

Caroline ran across the road and up the path. She pressed firmly on the doorbell before she had a chance to change her mind.

The door flew open.

'What do you want?'

The woman was taller and thinner than Caroline remembered, her body a collection of sharp angles and long limbs. Her bony tanned feet were stuffed into a pair of Birkenstocks.

'Who are you?' She was wearing skinny jeans and a tight sweater. The outline of a pair of almost spherical breasts pressed through the thin wool. Caroline couldn't take her eyes off them and for a moment was completely lost for words.

'Well?' The woman pushed a long lock of hair behind her ears. It immediately sprang back out again and fell across her face.

'I'm sorry to disturb you,' Caroline finally managed. 'I'm looking for Martin's cousin.'

'What do you want with her?'

'Is she in?'

The tall woman peered over the top of Caroline's head to the street beyond. 'Where are the others?'

'Others?'

'The other reporters.'

'Reporter? Me? God no.' Caroline smiled. 'I can't stand the press. Is Martin's cousin here?'

The woman held on to the edge of the door, ready to slam it shut at any moment. 'You'll have to get in touch with my publicist. I'm not supposed to talk to anyone unless they've cleared it with him first.'

'So you are Martin's cousin then?'

'Wait here and I'll get his business card.' She started to close the door.

'No!' Caroline forced a smile. 'Please – I'm not a reporter. Honestly. I used to work with Martin at the department.'

The woman frowned and looked down at Caroline's feet, her gaze tracking slowly back up to Caroline's face. 'I suppose you do look like a civil servant.'

Caroline tugged at the bottom of her jacket.

'Martin's colleagues were at the funeral,' the blonde woman said. 'I don't remember seeing you there.'

'I was at the cemetery. I didn't feel up to attending the wake. I was too upset. I worked with Martin for the academies—'

'Caroline?'

The rest of Caroline's sentence stalled in her throat. Suddenly her chest felt tight.

'Why didn't you say that straightaway?' The woman stood to one side. 'Come in, please. My name's Samantha, call me Sam.'

Caroline started up the narrow hall and stopped, unable to take another step. She could smell Martin's aftershave. An instant memory flooded back. Martin in the hotel lift, smiling at her.

'Are you OK?'

'Fine.'

'The living room's just on the right.'

'How did you know my name?'

'Martin's told me all about you. I'll make us coffee, shall I?'

Caroline ventured into the living room and perched on the edge of a large cream sofa. Why would Martin tell his cousin about her? She blinked and snatched another breath. All about you, the woman had said.

Not everything, surely?

No, Martin would have kept what happened between them private. She edged back on the sofa and scanned the room. It was mostly the way she'd imagined it. The beautifully finished wooden table and dining chairs were clearly handmade, the sofa was upholstered in silk, and an enormous red and green Oriental rug covered most of the wide oak floorboards. But there were no paintings or prints on the walls and no photographs on the mantelpiece. No suggestion of Martin's personality apart from the piles paperbacks and jazz CDs stacked haphazardly on the shelves either side of the fireplace. Anyone might have lived here.

Samantha returned from the kitchen with a stainless steel cafetière and two mugs balancing on a tray. She put the tray on the coffee table and lowered herself carefully onto the sofa next to Caroline.

'Did you want milk? There isn't a milk jug – but I could bring the carton through.'

'Black is fine.'

'I'm not really used to having guests.' Samantha swept a long thin arm towards the untidy shelves. 'I'm so sorry about the mess. It's taking an absolute age to get things straightened out.' She pushed down the plunger of the cafetière and half-filled both mugs with thick dark coffee. 'The police pretty much turned things upside down and didn't put anything back in the right place.'

'The police?' Caroline leaned forward and scanned the room again. 'What were they looking for?'

'They wouldn't tell me when I asked. I didn't want to make a fuss. I didn't feel it was my place to. But they have to investigate properly, don't they? Under the circumstances.' She flicked hair from her face and sighed.

'Did they take anything away?'

'It's hard to tell. Though Marty's computer has gone from his study. His laptop too.'

Caroline was disappointed, but not surprised. A small part of her hoped to find something in Martin's house that had escaped the departmental cleansing process. Some overlooked shred of evidence.

'And they still haven't returned the computers – after all this time?'

Samantha shook her head and bit her bottom lip. 'I suppose I should do something about that, shouldn't I? Chase it up?'

Caroline nodded, half smiled. She knew even if the machines were returned, they'd come back restored to their factory settings, wiped of all documents and any trace of their previous owner.

'But they were only doing their job. They have to be thorough, don't they?'

'Oh they're certainly thorough.'

'Do you know, they even interviewed me? I don't know what they were expecting to find out.'

'What did they ask you?'

230

Samantha's face darkened for a moment. 'Why do you want to know?'

Caroline sat back again; she didn't want to seem too earnest. She tried to relax the muscles in her face. 'They interviewed me too – they wanted to know about his mood, his state of mind.'

Samantha rested a beautifully manicured hand on top of Caroline's and squeezed. 'It must have been so horrible for you – finding him like that. When I read your name in the paper I literally gasped. I was so upset for you. But then I thought, of all the people to have discovered him, I'm sure Martin would rather it was someone he trusted. Better than a stranger. He really thought a lot of you, you know.'

A shiver ran across Caroline's shoulders.

Samantha squeezed her hand tighter then let go, checking her nails before folding her arms tight across her breasts. 'Is it a bit chilly? Your hands are frozen. Would you like me to put some heating on?'

'What did you tell the police about Martin's mood?' Caroline was determined not to get sidetracked.

'I'd seen Marty just the day before he...' The thin blonde woman picked up her coffee and took a sip. 'I hadn't seen him for ages before that. He did seem a little... preoccupied.'

'What did you think about the note Martin left?'

'The note? That was very weird, wasn't it? It was total fantasy, the whole thing.'

Thank God.

'And is that what you told the police?'

'They didn't ask me about the note. They only wanted to know about his will – what arrangements he'd made with the solicitor about things.'

'Did they ask you for his solicitor's details?'

'No – they had them already.' She put down the mug and stared into space. 'Actually I remember thinking at the time it was a bit strange... they asked me if Marty had given me anything to look after for him. You know – documents or computer files. That was odd, wasn't it?'

'What kind of documents?'

'They didn't say.'

Caroline could feel her pulse pounding in her ears. 'And had he? Do you still have them?'

'Oh no – he didn't give me anything. In a way it would have been so much more straightforward if he had.'

'It would?'

'A copy of the will would really have smoothed things along. At one stage I thought I might not even be able to move in here.'

'I don't follow.'

'The fire. Everything was lost.'

Caroline glanced around the room and peered out into the hall.

'Not here!' Samantha gripped the sofa cushion. 'No – the solicitor's office.' She shook her head. 'They say things come in threes, don't they? I keep waiting for the third disaster to strike. It's made me a bit twitchy.'

'There was a fire at Martin's solicitor's office?'

'I'm surprised you don't know about it. It was all across the news. The whole row of offices and shops in the street were completely burned to shells. It started in the early hours of the morning they think. Just the day after Martin... after he... died. They closed Waterloo Bridge there were so many fire engines called out.'

My God they were thorough.

Caroline picked up her coffee mug, and slowly blew across the surface of the liquid, needing a moment to consider everything Samantha had just told her. Whoever's responsibility it was to eradicate any trace of a paper trail had taken their job very seriously. Who could have organised something that big? Aware Samantha was staring at her, Caroline lifted the mug to her lips and took a sip of coffee.

'Is it OK? Not too strong? I'm never sure how many spoonfuls of coffee to put in. Marty was much more domesticated than me. I'm useless!'

'The coffee's fine. For a woman unused to visitors, you're making me feel very welcome.'

Samantha lifted a hand to her throat and smiled, suddenly embarrassed.

'Have you had many people come to the house, you know, to pay their respects?'

'No, not really. Apart from the two nice men from the party.'

'Really?'

'They were very kind, so sympathetic. They said I could ask them for help if I needed it, any time.'

'That was nice of them.'

Like a pair of circling buzzards.

'It was, wasn't it?'

Samantha bit her lip. Her teeth were dazzlingly white against the redness of her mouth. Caroline took a moment to study the woman's tanned face. For someone who obviously enjoyed sunbathing, Samantha had remarkably few wrinkles. It was impossible to gauge how old she was, but presumably she was quite a few years younger than Martin. Curiosity finally got the better of her.

'Are you Martin's cousin on his mother's or father's side?'

Samantha stared at her and tilted her perfectly sculpted chin towards her chest and let out a squeaky giggle.

'I can't really see a family resemblance.'

'Why are you teasing me?'

'What do you mean?'

'You really don't know?'

Caroline put down the coffee mug and leaned towards Samantha. There it was again, Martin's cologne. Samantha must have been wearing it. 'No,' Caroline said. 'I really don't.'

'But I thought Marty would've told you about me. He trusted you. I assumed he told you everything.'

Caroline sniffed in a breath and released it slowly.

'I'm not his cousin!' Samantha flicked her hair from her face and pulled back her shoulders, sticking out her round breasts. 'Matthew – my publicist – thought the cousin thing was a good idea. He said it'd give me some breathing space. While we worked out a strategy. You know, whether or not to wait until closer to the election. Matthew says it'll have more impact if we do.' She stopped and put a hand to her mouth. 'God that sounds so calculating, doesn't it?'

'Wait for what?'

'Marty was the closest thing to family I ever had.' She looked down at her hands. She was twisting a small silver ring around her middle finger. 'He paid for all of this.' She waved her hands up and down her body. 'And the hormone treatment before the surgery. He knew how much it meant to me.' She sniffed and lifted her head back, like a newly-crowned beauty queen who doesn't want to spoil her make-up. 'Marty was always so generous. This doesn't come cheap, you know – not if you want it done properly.'

Caroline didn't know where to look. 'Treatment? I'm sorry, I had no idea you'd been ill.'

'Oh I wasn't ill. Though I know some people think of it as a condition. God, some people even say it's a sickness, don't they? But I like to think of it as ironing out nature's wrinkles. Correcting her mistakes.'

Was she just talking about plastic surgery? Breast enhancement? A face-lift? Caroline realised her mouth was hanging open. She snapped it shut.

'I'm sorry. It must be quite a shock.' She managed a smile. 'You don't know anything about me and Marty, do you? And yet Marty told me all about you and your family and the work you were doing with him. How important it was to both of you.'

Caroline gripped the arm of the sofa. 'Were you and Martin a couple?'

'You really didn't know?'

Caroline shook her head.

'We broke up after I first started my treatment. I was going through such a big transition I needed to be… unattached… free. It's hard to explain.'

Caroline had a flash of a darkened hotel room, the awkward, embarrassed fumbling.

Oh God!

A sudden chill shivered up both arms and crept across her shoulders. How could she have been so blind? So caught up in her infatuation with Martin, when all the time… She got up and quickly fell back down again. Her legs felt like they'd been filleted by an expert fishmonger. She took a deep breath and stood slowly, testing her balance, working out if she could make it to the front door.

'I should go,' she said.

Samantha jumped up. 'I've really shocked you – I'm so sorry. That's why Matthew thought it best to leave it a few weeks. The whole gender reassignment thing is shocking for some people.'

Slowly, Caroline stepped around the sofa and into the hall. Samantha followed her to the front door. Caroline stopped, the door half open.

'Leave what?' she said.

'I'm sorry?'

'You said your publicist—'

'Going public with my story. He's thinking the *Daily Mail*. Or maybe the *Sunday Mirror*. There's a book deal in the pipeline as well. I've still got to choose the ghostwriter. It needs to be someone sympathetic. Someone who understands the process, someone—'

'What about the note?'

'What note?'

'Earlier – you said Martin's suicide note was total fantasy. But now you're telling me you were his lover.'

'Take it from me.' Samantha held out her hand and squeezed Caroline's arm. 'That note was *totally* made up. Marty was never ashamed. Of anything. He was discreet, always. Private. But he was never ashamed of who he happened to fall in love with. God no.'

'You should have said that when it was all over the newspapers. Why didn't you?' Caroline unpeeled the woman's bony fingers from her arm. 'Don't tell me – your publicist told you not to.'

'I was upset and confused. Vulnerable. I probably shouldn't have listened to him.'

Caroline stepped through the door then turned back. 'Can I ask you to do something for me? Not for me… for Martin?'

Samantha nodded, keeping her gaze locked on the ground.

'Don't listen to your publicist again. You said it yourself just now. Martin was private. Discreet. Hasn't he given you enough already?'

Samantha's nostrils flared, a tear ran down her cheek.

'Keep your revelations to yourself and let Martin rest in peace.'

39

Frank Carter's 20-year-old Mercedes had filled with smoke.

'Crack a window, will you?' Angela Tate waved a hand in front of her face, trying to coax the cigarette fumes back in Frank's direction.

'I thought we were trying to remain inconspicuous.' He wound the driver's window down an inch.

'If the car gets any smokier someone'll call the fire brigade.' She coughed. 'We won't blend into our surroundings then.'

'When did you become such an ex-smoking fascist anyway?'

'Let me think... how long have we been sitting here?'

Frank checked his watch. 'That's a good point actually, Ange. What time is Freddie Junior supposed to show?'

'Lunchtime.'

'It's 2:15.'

Angela peered towards the glossy red door of a four-storey Georgian building across the street. There had been no movement in or out of the drug rehabilitation clinic since they'd arrived – just after 11:30am.

'I think that fella saw you coming. You can't trust a junkie.'

'Ex-junkie getting treatment.'

Frank rolled his eyes.

Angela continued to stare through the windscreen, getting an uncomfortable feeling that Frank and his unstinting lack of faith in human nature might actually be proved right on this occasion. She could have sworn the man who'd told her about Freddie's lunchtime appointment was telling the truth. Maybe she was losing her touch.

'Aye, aye.' Frank tapped a finger against the rear-view mirror. 'Don't look round, but some bald bloke is heading towards us at speed.'

Angela resisted the urge to turn round and finally spotted Freddie as he ran up the flight of stone steps leading to the clinic's front door.

'Well, go on if you're going.' Frank nudged her with an elbow.

'I'm not chasing him inside. That's not the plan. Why did you think I wanted your car?'

'The car? I thought you wanted to have me around in case he got nasty. And for moral support.'

'Those things are a welcome bonus. I do appreciate you looking out for me, Frank. Really I do.' She glanced at the beer belly overhanging his belt. 'Although in hand-to-hand combat I'd fancy my chances more than yours.' She squeezed his upper arm trying to find a bicep, but only managed to grab a handful of flab. 'No – the plan is to wait for him to come out and follow him home.'

'Oh that's OK then. Simple.' He hit the steering wheel with both hands. 'How do you even know he's going home afterwards?'

'He's getting his *medicine* isn't he? He'll want to get back home with it.'

Frank was shaking his head. 'What if he lives a tube ride away? How do you propose we follow him then?'

'All right – I'll grab him on the way out. I've just got a feeling he's local. I didn't want to accost him in the middle of the street.'

'Looks like that's you're only option.'

After 20 minutes Frank started fidgeting again, adjusting his headrest, straightening the seatback, tweaking the rear-view mirror. 'There's not a back way out, is there?' He lit another cigarette.

'I didn't do a 360 degree recce – I don't know.'

A sudden rap on the glass of the driver's window jolted Frank out of his seat. His cigarette dropped into his lap.

'Jesus Christ!' He slapped frantically at his leg trying to extinguish the burning tip.

Angela saw the hairy knuckle tap the glass again. 'For God's sake, Frank, wind down your window.'

A policeman wearing a cap displaying the insignia of the City of London Police stuck his head through the gap. 'Can I ask you what your business is in this area, sir?'

'I erm… I'm just waiting'

'Waiting for what, sir?'

'It's our son – he's in the clinic over the road.' Angela leaned over and put a hand on Frank's thigh, flicking the dead cigarette into the footwell. She smiled at the police officer. 'We're just here to make sure he gets home OK after his treatment.'

'I'm sorry, madam. You can't stay here. No waiting permitted.'

'But I need to—'

'You can wait for him on foot, but the vehicle has to move. There's a multi-story a few hundred metres up the road.'

'OK, officer – will do.' Frank waited for the head to withdraw and quickly wound the window back up. 'Poxy ring of steel. It's like the bloody Gestapo.'

Angela opened her door.

'I'll get back as fast as I can. But in the meantime you're on your own with freaky Freddie.'

'I'm sure I'll cope.' She swung her legs out of the car and grabbed her bag.

'Good luck, Ange.'

She waved at Frank as he pulled away and nodded to the policeman, watching him return to his colleague still sitting in the squad car, hoping Freddie wouldn't make an appearance until they'd driven away.

She needn't have worried. It was another ten minutes before the bright red door opened again. A stocky nurse dressed in a pristine white tunic and blue trousers held a fist tight around Freddie Larson's arm. He walked him down the steps and deposited him on the pavement. Freddie looked dazed for a moment, as if his eyes were adjusting to the light. The nurse jogged back up the stairs and slipped back behind the door.

'You can't do this!' Freddie shouted up the steps, his voice croaking and cracking. 'It's illegal. I need my medicine!'

Angela hurried across the street. 'Mr Larson?'

Freddie spun round to face her. He watched her suspiciously as she reached his side of the road. 'Who wants to know?'

Angela had told herself she'd be able to decide in a split second whether to go with the truth or a lie at the outset. But as she looked into his sweating face she wasn't sure which way to play it. *When in doubt, play for time.*

'I saw what just happened. Are you OK?'

'What's it to you? How do you know my name? Do you work for that bunch of shysters?'

'The clinic? No! Not at all.' She scanned his face. The wild look he had in his eyes only moments before had almost disappeared. 'My name's Angela Tate. They can't treat people like that. Do you want me to call the police?'

'Fuck no.' He took a step towards her. 'You still haven't answered my question.'

She shrugged.

'How do you know me?'

She let out a breath. 'I'm trying to locate all the mourners who attended Martin Fox's funeral.'

'Are you a lawyer? Has he left me something in his will?' He wrapped his long arms round his body and rocked forwards and back on the balls of his feet.

'Were you expecting him to?'

'A simple yes or no would suffice. I can't be wasting time here. I'm a busy man.'

'Has the clinic refused you treatment?'

'What?'

'You've come out empty handed.'

'Who are you? Nosy bitch.'

'I work for the *Evening News.*'

'You're a fucking hack? What did you say your name was?'

'Tate.'

'Should I have heard of you?'

'Not really.' She glanced up the quiet little side road towards the traffic ploughing up and down Bishopsgate. 'Look. Why don't I call us a cab, take you home. We can talk better there.'

He hugged himself tighter. 'Why should I talk to you?'

'You might find it… financially rewarding.'

'How much?'

'Depends on what you tell me.'

'I don't want to go home. I'm going to score fuck all there.'

'I can take you wherever you want to go.' She gestured for him to follow her to up the main road.

'How do I know it's not a trap? How do I know you haven't got a fake cab waiting round the corner, ready to kidnap me?'

Paranoid bloody bastard.

'Who would want to kidnap you?'

'God botherers. Wouldn't be the first time she's tried to have me abducted.' He shook his head.

'She?'

'Doesn't matter.' He blew out a congested breath. 'Got any cigarettes?'

Angela reached into her bag and handed him a pack of ten and her lighter. 'Keep them.'

'You can't buy me off that easily.'

'I don't doubt that.' She pointed towards the streaming traffic at the end of the road. 'Shall we?'

'How much have you got on you?' He eyed her handbag. She squeezed it tighter.

'I'm not carrying anything. That's not the way it works. You talk to me, I go back to my editor, he writes you a cheque.'

'How stupid do I look?' He lit a cigarette, took a long drag and pocketed the pack. 'I'm not very popular with my bank manager at the moment.'

'Why don't you answer a couple of questions and we'll see how it goes? I can phone my editor. We can arrange something for you. In cash.'

'Why don't you walk me to the nearest hole in the wall and then ask your questions.' Freddie Larson puffed out a cloud of smoke and started walking towards Bishopsgate. 'Lots of banks round here.'

Angela hesitated.

He turned back to her. 'Do you want to talk to me or what?'

Angela caught up with him. She probably only had a couple of minutes before they reached the nearest cashpoint. 'Tell me about Martin Fox. Why were you at his funeral?'

'Paying my last respects. Why else would I be there?'

'How did you know him?'

'Went to college with him a few years back.'

'What was that, 30 years ago?'

'Give or take.'

'So you kept in touch over all those years?'

He sniffed but didn't answer.

'Were you close to him?'

Freddie Larson lengthened his stride.

'Can you slow down? I'm not as fast as you in these shoes.'

He stopped and turned back to her. 'Got to get to the bank, haven't we?'

'Only if you answer my questions.' They passed a café. 'Why don't we sit down for five minutes, have a coffee. Talk properly.'

'I still need the cash… five minutes, max.'

'Fine.'

They took a table near the door. Angela wiped a porthole in the condensation steaming up the window and spotted Frank across the road, lighting a cigarette, heading back towards the clinic.

A waitress, grubby apron wrapped around her waist, wandered over to them, took their order and came back immediately with two black coffees.

'So… Martin Fox,' Angela said once she'd gone.

'What about him?'

'Have you been close over the last 30 years?'

'Close? What are you trying to say? We weren't fucking, if that's what you're getting at. That's all you lot want to write about isn't it? Nice juicy sex scandals.'

'It's not what I meant.' Angela took a sip of coffee and wondered how she could change tack without making Freddie any more suspicious than he already was.

'I wasn't his type, anyway.' Freddie had opened a sachet of sugar and was emptying it onto the tabletop. He reached for another.

'No?'

'He liked boys.'

'Boys?'

'Don't get excited. It's not what you're thinking. Youths, I mean. Lean, smooth, hairless things. Not kids though. He wasn't a paedo.'

Angela blew out her cheeks. *Thank fuck for that.* How would she ever break the news to Caroline Barber if he had been?

'Sorry to disappoint,' Larson said and drew down the corners of his mouth in an exaggerated frown.

'You were at college with Fox?'

'Yep.'

'Did you know William King too?'

'What's he got to do with anything?' He shifted in his seat, his leg started to shake under the table.

'He was at college at the same time as Fox. They knew one another – I thought you might know both of them.'

Freddie was pushing the pile of sugar around the table.

'Come on Freddie, the sooner you answer my questions, the sooner we can get you some cash. That's what you want isn't it?'

'Fucking bastards.'

'Who's that?'

'Fucking clinic. One payment, that's all. They can't stop treating me. I'm not well. Should be some kind of law against it.'

'One payment?'

'In arrears.'

'Hopefully the money I give you might sort that out.' She smiled and looked down at the mountain range of sugary peaks Freddie Larson had sculpted on the tabletop. 'Tell me about King.'

'Don't know him.'

'But did you, at college?'

He shrugged.

'Please, Freddie.'

'It's Mr Larson to you.'

This was going nowhere.

'I'm not talking about King. Fucking bastard.'

'You didn't get on with him?'

'Did you hear what I just said?' He scraped his chair back and stood up. 'This is all a pile of shit. You're not going to give me any fucking money are you?' He pushed his face into hers. Most of his teeth were black, and smelled as though they were all rotting in his head. He pulled away and opened the door of the café. He stood on the threshold for a moment, looking up and down the street as if he was searching for something.

Angela left a five-pound note on the table and joined him at the door. 'I can help you get some medicine.' She said.

He jerked away from her. 'Fuck – you shouldn't creep up on people like that.'

'Still expecting to be abducted?' She was in danger of losing her patience with him.

'Are you laughing at me? I'm not fucking paranoid.' He hugged himself again. 'Doesn't mean they're not out to get me,' he muttered under his breath.

'Who – the *God botherers*?'

'No. Fuck – not that bunch of amateurs. These people are serious. They've been watching my place.'

'Are you saying you're under surveillance?'

'I'm going to get busted any day – I just know it. Put me away to shut me up. If I'm lucky.'

'What are you saying, Freddie?'

'Mr Larson!'

'All right!' Angela threw up her hands.

'Are you getting me that money or what?'

'It's a two way deal.'

His cheek twitched. 'Something's going to happen. Soon. I can feel it. I don't feel safe.' He stepped out onto the street, still checking up and down. 'Even at the fucking clinic.'

'Because they refused you your treatment?'

'They wouldn't even give me the results of my blood test.'

'Blood test?'

'Hep C, they said. Now suddenly they know nothing about any fucking blood test.' He dragged a sleeve across his nose and sniffed. 'It was a new nurse, but fuck – they can't even keep track of something as simple as that. It's shit. I should find a new fucking clinic.'

'My paper could help you do that.'

He turned to face her, his eyes darting about. 'Yeah?'

'I've told you – I want to help.' She started walking south down Bishopsgate, towards Liverpool Street station. 'Let's find a bank right now – prove how serious I am.'

'I'm still not talking about King. I wouldn't be in this fucking mess now if it wasn't for him.'

'I think a lot of people share your opinion of him.'

'Yeah, well… And they don't even know him like I do.' He grabbed her arm and pulled her round to face him. 'There's an HSBC just up here. Five hundred is good. Might take off somewhere. Somewhere they can't find me.'

'Sorry, I don't have that much in my account.'

'What? Haven't you got a company credit card?' He speeded up again and Angela had to jog to keep up.

'I wish I had. This is my personal account.'

They reached the bank. Angela shoved a debit card into the machine, shielded her hand as she punched in her PIN, and selected the £50 option. Freddie Larson glanced at the screen.

'Fifty will get me fuck all.'

'It would get you a train ticket somewhere, if you're so desperate to get away.' She dragged the notes from the machine, wrapped them around her business card and shoved the bundle at him. 'You haven't actually told me anything I couldn't find out somewhere else. This is just a token of good faith.'

He stuck the cash in a pocket.

'There's more,' she said. 'Potentially much more – if you actually tell me something I don't know.'

Freddie sniffed and checked up and down the street. 'How much more money?'

'I'd need to discuss that with my editor.'

'Call him, then.'

'I can't waste his time if you're just pissing me about. Answer some more questions first.'

He shifted his weight from one foot to the other. 'Fucking clinic.'

'Tell you what, why don't we take a walk around the block, you can answer a few more of my questions and we finish up back here for more cash. But only if you tell me something new.'

Freddie Larson chewed his lip, looked up and down the street again. 'OK,' he said eventually. 'But then you phone your paper to get me some proper money.'

'Let's just see how we go, shall we? Take it one step at a time.'

He started walking away.

'Tell me about Cambridge.'

'What about it?' He lengthened his stride.

Angela did her best to keep up, but at this rate they would have circumnavigated the block before he answered a single question.

'Did you enjoy your time there? Make any friends?'

He shrugged. 'Bunch of fucking wankers, most of them.'

'But some were OK?'

'Why do you want to know? What fucking story are you writing anyway?'

'I'm trying to build a picture of Martin Fox. I'm doing a major profile.'

'You mean a hatchet job?'

'Not at all.'

'What have my friends at college got to do with your profile?'

He was proving to be more suspicious than his mother.

'Did you and Martin Fox have any mutual friends?'

'I'm not talking about King – I've already said.'

'Not King.' He was really starting to piss her off now. 'Other students.'

He shrugged. 'We went to a few of the same bars – shagged a few of the same blokes.'

Angela raised her eyebrows.

'Don't look so disgusted – I didn't have any of his sloppy seconds, if that's what you're thinking. It was the other way round if anything.'

Freddie Larson was gay. Of course he was. How had she not made the connection before?

'Can you remember any of their names?'

'Why?'

'I'd like to speak to them.'

'You don't need to speak to them. You are getting me that money?' He grabbed her arm.

They'd turned down a quiet street. Angela looked left and right. There was no one about. His grip tightened.

'You're my main source – of course. But I need a bit of the flavour of Fox's student days to get the full picture.' She tried to pull her arm away. He held firm. 'You know – adventures the pair of you might have had… sexual conquests… any wild parties you went to…'

He twisted her arm and pushed his face closer to hers. 'What have you heard?'

She pulled back her head. *Heard?* It felt as if her arm would break at any moment. 'Oh – you know…' She quickly considered her options. She should be as vague as possible. 'Rumours hang around newsrooms for years. They start off as gossip, but they never really go away.'

'Well, whatever it is you think you know, you're wrong. It had nothing to do with me.'

He let go of her arm and set off again at a jogging pace. When he realised she hadn't followed him he ran back at her. 'Come on – we've got to get that money.' He started jogging on the spot and tugged at her sleeve like an overactive child demanding an ice cream. Rather than a man in his late 40s itching for his next fix.

Angela wasn't prepared to hand over any more of her own money without getting something substantial in return.

'That's not what I've heard,' she said, feet still firmly rooted to the pavement.

'What?'

'I've heard it was *everything* to do with you.'

'Who told you that?'

He grabbed her arm again and squeezed hard.

'I can't remember who first came to us with the story.'

'They're lying fucking bastards.' He started walking and pulled Angela behind him, his fingers gripping tighter. 'I need that money.'

He dragged her along the street for another 50 yards until they turned a corner onto the main road. Then he fell into step with her, making his hand on her arm look less like a threat and more like a display of affection. She considered shouting for help, but as they neared the ATM she could feel his grip slackening.

'How much can you get out in one go?'

'You're not getting a penny more until you tell me exactly what happened.'

'Fuck you!'

'How much do you need my money?'

He grabbed her jacket and pulled her close. 'Fucking bitch.'

'Who was involved, Freddie?'

'My name's *Mr Larson*.'

This approach really wasn't working. She pushed his hands from her lapel and started to walk away. She waved an arm at a passing taxi.

'Wait!' Freddie joined her at the kerb. 'It wasn't my fault.'

'Whose fault was it?'

'Get me the money and I swear I'll give you a name.'

'Give me the name and I promise to hand over the cash.'

He wrapped his thin arms around his ribs and started rocking backwards and forwards. 'Shit. None of it was ever meant to get out.' He stopped rocking and looked at her. 'How much do you know already?'

'If you want the money, I think we should stick to me asking the questions, don't you?'

'If you know so much why has your paper never printed anything about it before?'

She sucked in a deep breath. 'What? And get our arses sued?'

'At least he was good for something then.' He was half talking to himself.

'Who? Good for what?'

'Forget it.'

She pulled her debit card from her handbag and started to walk towards the cashpoint machine. 'Name, Freddie. Whose fault was it if it wasn't yours?'

He scurried after her, dragging the back of his hand across his nose. He let out a short breath. 'Then you'll give me the cash?'

She nodded.

'William King.'

Her heart sank. It felt like he was plucking King's name out of the air, just because he'd mentioned him earlier.

'Come on. Give me the cash.'

'I already knew about King.'

'Give me the cash and I'll give you the other name. They were both there when it actually happened. They were both as guilty as one another.'

Angela punched in her PIN and withdrew another £200 pounds. Freddie tried to snatch it from her but she was too fast. She shoved the cash deep into a pocket and kept her hand wrapped tight around the notes. The street was too busy for Freddie to try anything.

'Name,' she said.

'It's been too many years. You won't be able to prove anything. And you'd still get your arses sued if you tried.'

'Name!'

Fat beads of sweat had started to appear like dew drops on his bald head. He wiped a hand over them.

'Come on, Freddie.'

He stared her straight in the eye. 'Rachael Forster.'

'Is that name supposed to mean something to me?'

'It's what she was called back then, before she got married.' His gaze shifted to the hand Angela had shoved in her pocket.

'What's her married name?'

'Rachael Oakley.'

40

'The prime minister's wife?' Caroline stared into Angela Tate's face, expecting to see some sign of doubt. She couldn't detect even the slightest flicker.

'*Ex*-prime minister's wife.'

'And you believed him?'

They were sitting on a bench at the western end of Embankment Gardens. Caroline grabbed the edge of the wooden seat with both hands and shook her head.

'Why shouldn't I believe him?'

'I would have expected you to know when someone is bullshitting you.'

'I do – he wasn't. It was too random a choice for him to make up. He would have plucked some other, more credible name out of the air if he was lying.'

'He was a drug addict desperate for his next fix – he would have told you anything he thought you wanted to hear.' Caroline lifted her feet so that a street cleaner could get to a crisp packet that had fluttered under the bench.

'He knew her maiden name,' Tate said after the cleaner had moved away. 'How would he know something like that unless he knew her when she was single? Rachael Forster married Duncan Oakley in 1980.'

'OK – what exactly happened? What was this 'thing' that Freddie Larson said was her fault?'

Tate looked away. Her face twitched into a grimace. 'He hasn't told me that yet.'

'What?'

'I've got to rustle up some more money first.'

'Oh come on, Angela. He's playing you. You must see that.'

Tate reached into her bag and withdrew a packet of Marlboro Lights and a lighter. She lit a cigarette and sucked down a long first drag before she spoke again.

'I've checked it out. Assuming the 'thing' happened while Freddie Larson was in Cambridge—'

'You're basing that assumption on what?'

'We were talking about his time there when he brought up the 'thing'.'

'Do you know how ridiculous you sound right now? You're practically helping to invent the story for him.'

Tate smiled. 'It wasn't that long ago I was accusing you of having an overactive imagination.'

Caroline blew out her cheeks. 'Yes – I've got a whole new perspective now. Unemployment can do that for you.'

'You haven't lost your job.'

'Not yet, not officially.' Caroline stared blankly at the tourists strolling along the path through the gardens. 'Give it a few more days.' She turned back to Tate who was staring at the glowing end of her cigarette. 'What did your editor say about bumping the CD-ROM story off the front page?'

'I still haven't spoken to him. I haven't been back to the office. I'm keeping my head down.' She flicked the ash from her cigarette.

'I don't understand. Assuming someone leaned on your editor to downplay the story, why didn't he bury it completely? Why print any story at all?'

Tate sucked more smoke into her lungs. 'I suppose too many people knew that the CD-ROM was missing. Better to make the whole thing into a smaller story and control it than risk it coming out some other way.' She exhaled slowly. 'Damage limitation.' She turned to Caroline. 'Have the police questioned you about it yet?'

'I would imagine a visit is imminent.'

'Admit nothing – I'm going to stick to the story we agreed. The CD-ROM came in the post from the late minister, just days before his death. Let them try to prove otherwise.'

Caroline sighed. Her breath came out in a ragged stutter. She closed her eyes for a moment. 'It's all been for nothing,' she said. 'I thought going public with the CD-ROM would stir things up a bit. Start people asking questions… about the department… about Martin. But nothing's changed. We're no nearer discovering the reason for Martin's death.'

'I think Freddie's story might help us with that.'

'Really? A middle-aged junkie pointing the finger at Rachael Oakley? Blaming her for something – you don't even know what – that happened, what – 30 years ago?'

Tate took another long drag on her cigarette.

'Was Rachael Oakley even at Cambridge then?'

The journalist shifted in her seat. She ran a tongue over her teeth. 'She went to Oxford University.'

'Well then!'

'But her family's country pile is in Cambridgeshire. Not ten miles outside the city.'

'And you've decided, with very little help from Freddie himself, that there's a connection between William King—'

'There's some seriously bad blood between Freddie and King. He wasn't faking that.'

'A connection between King, Freddie and Rachael Oakley?'

Tate nodded. 'And Martin Fox. He seemed to be the one Freddie was closest to.' She threw her cigarette to the ground, stubbed it out under her boot and took a very deep breath. 'There's something I haven't told you.' She ran her fingers through her hair. 'About Martin.'

Caroline held up a hand. 'It's OK – save your breath. I already know.'

'Are we talking about the same thing?'

'He was gay. There – I've said it for you.' She looked at Tate who was carefully avoiding making eye contact.

'How long have you known?'

'Since about lunchtime.'

'Christ! You seem to be handling it very well.'

If you only knew what my insides were doing right now.

'I'm still convinced the suicide note was a fake,' Caroline said. 'I've spoken to someone close to Martin who agrees. Categorically.'

'Who?' Tate was staring intently into her face now.

'It doesn't matter who – no one for you to get your claws into.' A drop of rain fell on her cheek. The clouds were darkening. She got to her feet. 'Good luck with Freddie Larson. When are you seeing him?'

'Tomorrow night – why?'

'That should give him plenty of time to cook up a nice juicy story for you.'

Another fat raindrop hit Caroline's face. The gardens started to empty as tourists ran for cover. Caroline headed in the direction of the entrance gate. Tate followed.

'He's telling the truth,' Tate shouted after her.

'Even if he is, you won't be able to corroborate any of it. Any evidence will have been destroyed years ago.'

They passed through the gate just as a loud crack ripped through the sky. A second later the clouds unleashed a torrent of water. Caroline and Tate skirted round a flower stall and dived into the entrance of Embankment tube.

Caroline's head and shoulders were drenched. She opened her bag and fished out a packet of tissues. When she'd finished blotting the rain from her face she turned to Tate. 'With no corroboration, do you really think your editor will be happy to publish Freddie's story? Judging by his recent track record, I can't imagine he'd let it get anywhere near the *Evening News*.' She shoved the ball of soggy tissues back into her bag. 'Admit it – it's hopeless.'

Tate seemed to deflate. Her shoulders sagged. 'You're beginning to sound like a woman who's given up.'

'What more can we do, realistically?'

'I haven't worked that out yet. But we can't just throw in the towel.'

The rain was thundering down, splashing high off the pavements.

'Let's look at the sequence of events… you find Martin Fox at his desk, at around the same time Duncan Oakley resigns as prime minister, then later that evening William King becomes interim PM.'

'But you said there was no connection before – you practically ridiculed my suggestion that there might be.'

'I didn't have Freddie Larson linking all the main players together before.' Tate grabbed Caroline's arm. 'We can't give up now – we just need to dig a little deeper.'

Caroline stared at the puddle rapidly forming into a lake in the gutter outside. She shook her head.

'Come on! We still have those dodgy companies linking Larson and King. The answers are somewhere in all those documents you got for me. It wasn't in vain, Caroline, believe me.' She shook Caroline's arm. 'I can't do this on my own. We've both been cast out, one way or another. We need to fend for ourselves.'

A black cab pulled into the kerb, sending up a spray of dirty rainwater. The passengers jumped out and ran towards the entrance to the tube station. Before they got there, Tate yanked at Caroline's arm and dragged her into the downpour and across the pavement. She threw open the cab door, shouted at the driver and bundled Caroline inside. The taxi did a quick U-turn and before Caroline could get her breath back, they were heading south towards the river down Northumberland Avenue.

'Where are we going?'

'Home,' Tate said. 'I think we've got some planning to do.'

Caroline waited on the kerb while Angela Tate argued with the cab driver about how much he should write on the receipt.

The rain had stopped and the late April sun was doing its best to dry the roads and pavements. Caroline closed her eyes for a moment and lifted her face towards the sky. Her tangled shoulder muscles loosened just a fraction. Tate joined her on the pavement.

'This is me, here.' She pushed open a black metal gate and hurried down a flight of steps, pulling a set of keys from her handbag. She froze when she reached the door.

'Shit.'

Caroline was right behind her. She saw what Tate saw. The door was open a couple of inches, the wood of the doorframe splintered around the lock. Tate eased the door open and stepped inside. Caroline reached out a hand and grabbed the sleeve of Tate's raincoat.

'Shouldn't we call the police?' she said.

Tate answered with a grunt and pushed through into the hall. She was looking at the walls as she went, then down at the rucked rug beneath her feet. 'Can you smell shit?' she said quietly.

Caroline sniffed. 'No. Can you?'

'Not yet.' She carried on up the hall and paused at the first doorway. She stood there for a moment and took a deep breath.

'Wait.' Caroline stood beside her. 'Someone could still be in there.'

Tate nudged her foot against the bottom of the door. It creaked open. The room beyond contained a brass bed, an enormous wardrobe and a dressing table. Everything appeared to be intact. Tate peered behind the door.

'No one lurking there,' she said. Her voice had picked up a slight quiver.

'Anything missing?'

'Hard to say, but if there is, I've been robbed by the neatest burglars ever.' She tried a smile and failed. 'Shall we move on?'

Caroline nodded and sidestepped out of the way. She followed Tate down the hall and they repeated the process at the next two doors. Like the master bedroom, the narrow box room and windowless bathroom seemed to have been left unmolested.

At the end of the hall an archway led into a galley kitchen. Even from where she was standing, Caroline could see undisturbed work surfaces and closed wall cabinets. Which left only the final door on the right.

'Brace yourself, pet.' Tate pulled a face, her attempt at lightening the mood falling flat. She turned the handle and pushed open the door, but remained firmly on the threshold.

Caroline tried to peer over her shoulder. 'What's the damage?'

Tate rushed in and scanned the room. 'I say again – tidy burglars.' She turned towards a window at the rear. 'Ah... much as I feared.'

Caroline followed her gaze. A small wooden desk, not much bigger than a child's school desk, sat in a corner, a white and transparent keyboard on top, attached to a mouse. 'They've taken your monitor?' She leaned her hands on her knees and peered beneath the desk. A power cable was plugged into the wall at one end and thin air at the other. 'And your PC.'

'It was an iMac.' Tate screwed up her face and sucked in a breath through gritted teeth. She strode towards a tall cupboard next to the desk and yanked open the doors. The shelves inside were empty. 'Well, at least they haven't tried to make it look like an opportunistic break-in by a passing junkie. I'm not sure if that's a mark of incompetence or breathtaking arrogance.'

Caroline grabbed her phone from her bag as Tate opened the row of drawers inside the cupboard.

'I'm afraid your son won't be getting his memory stick back.' Tate shook her head.

'Where did you leave the CD-ROM?'

'In the office.' She shook her head. 'My editor asked me for it.'

'What about back-ups?'

'Also in the office.' Tate stared into the empty drawers. 'I think we're missing something here.' She stuck a hand in her hair and glanced around the room. 'There was nothing truly damaging on the CD-ROM. Highly embarrassing that personal details were lost in the first place, but the information was innocuous enough.'

'What are you saying?'

'If this was just about the CD-ROM, you'd think it would have happened yesterday. Detectives were sent to my office to question me yesterday afternoon. Presumably they recovered the disc from my editor. If they were just after any copies I'd made, they would have come here with a warrant, wouldn't they?'

'So you think this is about something else?'

'If my editor let them go through all my stuff—'

'They would have discovered all the other documents I gave you.'

Tate nodded. 'Which might explain the delay in coming here – they wouldn't have known the significance of the documents until they reported back.'

'Reported back to who?'

Tate shrugged. 'Whoever leaned on my editor to bury the story on page eight... whoever sent the police to question me... people with enough clout to keep their secrets secret.'

'King?'

Tate shrugged.

'So by now they must have joined the dots and worked out you got the documents from me?'

'Wouldn't take much detective work – would it?'

252

Caroline tapped in her home phone number. After half a dozen rings she heard her own outgoing message on the answerphone. 'Something's not right. Mum should've picked up.'

'Maybe Jean's having a nap.'

'I should get home, make sure everything's OK.' The sick feeling in Caroline's stomach intensified. 'Will you be all right on your own?'

'Be buggered if I'm staying here.'

41

Even before the cab had come to a halt Caroline could see her front door swinging wide. A wave of nausea surged upwards from the pit of her stomach as she ran into the garden. Through the open door she saw her mother sitting on the stairs cradling the phone in her lap.

'Mum!' Caroline ran to her and grabbed her hand. 'Are you all right?'

'I'm fine.'

'You don't look fine.'

'I'm all right – I got home to discover the door open. I've only been in ten minutes, less, probably. I've called the police.'

'Where are the kids?' The surging nausea made it to the back of her throat.

'Don't worry – they're not home yet.'

'Do you feel strong enough to get up? I think we should wait outside.'

'Why?'

'Someone could still be in the house,' Caroline whispered.

'Oh there's no one here.'

Caroline tugged on Jean's hand. 'You don't know that, come on.'

'Don't fuss, Caroline. I've already checked.'

'You've what?'

'I've poked my nose round every door. The house is quite empty.'

Caroline squeezed her mother's hand. 'You shouldn't take risks like that.'

'I didn't take any risks – I was armed.' Jean gestured towards a long fire iron leaning against the wall at the bottom of the stairs.

'What were you thinking?'

'Hello!' Angela Tate appeared at the front door.

'Oh God.' Caroline reached into her bag and retrieved her purse. 'The cab! How much do I owe you?'

Tate waved the purse away.

'You didn't waste any time.' Jean said. 'Surely the *Evening News* isn't interested in domestic break-ins.'

'How are you, Jean? How's the head?'

'Oh – you know, the odd headache now and then.' She narrowed her eyes. 'What are you doing here?'

Tate looked at Caroline. Caroline opened her eyes wide and shrugged.

'It's a long story, Jean. I'm sure your daughter will fill you in.' She smiled. 'At some point.' She pointed down the hall. 'Do you know what's missing yet?'

Caroline took a deep breath and turned towards the living room door. She edged closer and peeked in. She caught her breath. The sofa and two armchairs had been upended, seat cushions strewn to the four corners of the room. The contents of the sideboard cupboards and drawers – books, CDs and magazines – were scattered across the floor, the doors of the cupboards hanging off broken hinges. Jean's collection of porcelain figurines had been swept off the shelving unit above the television and lay in small piles of broken china.

'My God.' Tate joined her at the door. 'You must have got the B-team.'

Caroline crept into the room, picking her way across the mess, and checked the sideboard. It was completely empty. She turned slowly, taking in the extent of the damage. 'My laptop's gone,' she said, quietly.

'You're sure?'

Caroline nodded.

'Anything else? Files? Paperwork?'

'I don't keep anything like that in the house.' She rubbed her face with both hands and stared down at the broken CD cases and torn paperbacks at her feet.

'Shame they didn't know that,' Tate said.

Caroline squeezed her eyes tight shut and concentrated on stifling the sob that was threatening to erupt from her chest and reminded herself these were just things, broken things. She snapped her eyes open.

'Something's wrong,' she said.

'It's all bloody wro—'

'No! Something's out of place... it's just too... quiet.'

She rushed back into the hall.

'Where's Minty?' she asked her mother.

Jean stared at her daughter open-mouthed. 'You know I haven't actually seen her.'

Caroline ran through the kitchen and into the garden. 'Minty!' She clapped her hands against her thighs.

'Maybe she chased off the burglars,' Tate shouted from the hall.

'She's not that kind of dog.'

Caroline hurried through the front door and ran onto the street and shouted the dog's name again.

'She must have got out while the door was open.' She scanned the top of the street, then the bottom. 'Minty! Come on girl!'

A police car was turning in from the main road. Caroline watched as it cruised to a standstill opposite the house. Two uniformed officers climbed out – the same two policewoman who'd come when Dan went missing. Were they the only two officers ever on duty?

'You got here very fast,' Caroline said.

'We were in the neighbourhood. Mrs Henderson, is it?' The slim one stared at Caroline without a flicker of recognition.

Caroline shook her head. *Unbelievable.* 'Mrs Henderson's inside.'

The plump one joined her colleague. 'How's your son, madam? Dan, wasn't it?'

'He's fine – thanks for asking.' Caroline shot the other officer a dirty look. 'Did you see a dark grey dog wandering the streets on your way here? She's a cross between a greyhound and a Labrador.'

'Can't say I did.'

Caroline took a last look up the street and led the way back into the house. She left the police officers talking to her mother in the living room and went into the kitchen with Tate. 'I'd offer you a cup of tea only...' The kitchen counters and most of the floor were littered with the contents of the drawers and cupboards. 'Why did they wreak such havoc here and leave your place practically untouched?'

'Maybe I just got lucky.'

Caroline shook her head wearily. 'Right – maybe you should be grateful – you got robbed by burglars who cleared up after themselves.' She glanced around the room. 'Such a bloody mess.'

'I suppose it's possible you really did get the B-team. Some bunch of amateurs.'

'Who?'

'If we're assuming that King is behind all this... and that does seem to be the most likely explanation... maybe the professionals searched my place and extra help was drafted in to ransack yours.'

'From where?'

'King's only been in the job a few weeks – maybe his resources are spread a bit thin. Maybe he had to enlist the help of one of his most trusted external contractors.'

'Larson?'

'He does have an army of security personnel at his disposal.'

'And they did this?'

Tate shrugged. 'It's not beyond the realms, is it?'

'Whoever turned this place upside down, they were professional enough to get what they came for.'

'Did you make any back-ups of the documents?'

'Only on my laptop.' She let out a long sigh. 'You think the police will have taken everything away from your office?'

'The files were on the memory stick, I copied them onto my iMac at home and the one in the office.'

'No other copies? You didn't email them between your home and work accounts.'

'Why would I email them?'

'Just clutching at straws.'

Tate ran a hand through her hair and stared down at the floor. 'Bloody hell, Caroline Barber – you're a genius.' She pulled a mobile from her bag, jabbed a key and shifted impatiently from one foot to the other while she waited for someone to answer.

'Frank... I can't tell you right now.' Tate turned towards Caroline and rolled her eyes. 'Can you speak? I need you to check something with... Aleesha in the IT department. She had a copy of some files—' She switched the phone to her other ear and turned away. 'What do you mean?' She thumped a hand against the kitchen counter. 'When did this happen?'

After a few more seconds she hung up. She shoved the mobile back in her bag and retrieved a packet of cigarettes.

'Well?'

'The IT department emailed me the unencrypted versions of those password protected files.'

'And?'

'Right now they're helping the police with their enquiries.' Tate pulled a cigarette out of the packet. 'I'll be outside.'

Caroline watched Tate pick her way across the debris littering the kitchen floor and glanced up at the clock above the door. Claire should have been home by now. With Ben. The nausea rose up again. She rushed into the hall and found the home phone on the bottom step of the stairs. Claire's mobile went to voicemail after a few rings. Caroline left a short message, trying to keep her tone as casual as possible. She joined Tate on the front porch.

'So...' Tate said. 'What's next?'

'Next?'

Tate nodded and took a deep drag on her cigarette.

'We don't have any proof left. I thought it was a lost cause before. Now I know it is. There isn't anything else we can do.'

'We're not giving up that easily.'

'You're not serious?'

Tate shrugged.

'What do you suggest?'

'There'll be something. Someone's bound to have ballsed up and left some piece of evidence somewhere. It's just a question of finding it.'

'Finding it? You and me?'

'No one else is volunteering.'

Caroline glanced back into the house. She saw her ransacked kitchen, the pile of coats heaped on the floor in the hall. The poker leaning up against the wall.

'What if Mum had arrived while they were still here? What might have happened then?'

'Jean can look after herself.'

'Don't be ridiculous – she's 64. What if the kids had been home?'

'But they weren't.'

'It's my family we're talking about.' She leaned a hand on the wall.

'How can you give up now? After everything you've been through?'

'Just watch me.'

'Please, Caroline.' Tate squeezed her arm. 'You're forgetting – we still have Freddie Larson.'

'*You* have Freddie Larson. And you know what? You're welcome to him.' She let out a long breath. Every part of her seemed to be aching. She just wanted it all to be over. She pulled Tate's hand from her arm. 'Good luck with Freddie – I hope he comes through for you, I do really. But there's nothing more I can do.'

She stepped back into the house and pushed the door to behind her.

42

Claire and Ben still hadn't turned up. They were over 30 minutes late. Caroline had phoned the school and was told that Claire had collected her brother from his Tae Kwondo class at the regular time. Caroline then tried Dan, who was his usual monosyllabic self. He didn't know where his sister was and he hadn't heard from her.

'I want you to come home right now,' Caroline said.

'I'm busy.'

'Where are you?'

'Mate's house.'

'Which mate?'

Dan mumbled something incomprehensible.

'Home, Dan. Right now. I mean it.'

She slammed the phone down just as the two policewomen were coming out of the living room.

'I've left the crime reference number with your mother, you'll need it for your insurance claim,' the fat one said.

'When will your forensics people arrive? I'd like to make a start on tidying up.'

The chunky policewoman shot her colleague a glance. The other woman responded with an almost imperceptible nod. 'There's a backlog, unfortunately. They can't arrange for anyone to come out until tomorrow. Some time in the afternoon most likely.'

'As late as that?'

'There's been an incident on the Holbeach Estate. A couple of incidents, actually. Resources have been diverted over there.'

'The Holbeach?' Caroline's heart thudded in her chest. 'When was this?'

'I can't give you that information.'

'My son and daughter walk up Holbeach Road to get home. I was expecting them to be here by now.' She grabbed the policewoman's sleeve. 'I need to report them missing.'

Again the two officers exchanged a look, the fat one tugged her arm from Caroline's grasp. 'After what happened last time, don't you think it would be best to leave it a while? There's no need to panic.'

'Panic? Are you even listening to me? My daughter and my *eight-year-old* son haven't come home.'

'How old is your daughter?'

'What's that got to do with anything? They're not here!'

The policewomen started to ease past Caroline towards the front door. 'Give it an hour, then if they still haven't turned up, call the station.' The plump PC handed Caroline a card.

'Anything could happen to them in an hour. I want to report it now.'

The thin one expelled an impatient sigh. 'I'll radio it in from the car. We can't deal with it ourselves, madam. We're needed elsewhere.'

'The Holbeach estate?'

'I can't tell you that.'

'I'll walk you to your car.'

Caroline followed them to the squad car across the road and waited while the thin one sat in the front passenger seat and made a call on her mobile phone. She strained to hear what the officer was saying, but the policewoman was mumbling into the phone. She stuck her head in the car. 'Tell them they've never been late before. Tell them how serious it is. Make sure they underst—'

She was cut off by a high-pitched wail. *Ben?* Caroline ducked back out of the car and started running towards him.

'Mum!' he shouted.

Fifty yards down the road, Ben and Claire were walking slowly towards her, Claire carrying something awkwardly in her arms. She was struggling to put one foot in front of the other. Ben was holding on to his sister's arm. Caroline could see a dark smear right across his white jacket. She pumped her arms and willed her legs to move faster. As she got closer she finally made out the shape in Claire's arms.

'Oh dear God!'

Claire was sobbing as she stumbled up the road. Finally Caroline reached them. She wrapped her arms around Ben and lifted him off the ground. She turned to Claire.

'Is she...?'

Claire nodded. 'I couldn't just leave her there.'

'Of course you couldn't.'

Minty's long legs were dangling from Claire's arms. Caroline squeezed Ben tighter and pressed her cheek against his, trying to obscure his view of the dog's tangled corpse.

They walked slowly towards the house.

'We were... on our way... home.' Claire struggled to force out the words between sobs.

'It's all right, sweetheart. You can tell me later. Let's just get inside.'

When they got to the front door Caroline ushered the children straight through the hall, grabbing the dog's blanket from the cupboard under the stairs. She hurried them past the mess in the kitchen and straight out the back door.

'What's happened?' Claire said.

'Don't worry about it, love. I'll explain later.'

Caroline spread the tartan blanket across the lawn. Claire gently lowered Minty's battered body onto it. Ben wriggled out of Caroline's grasp and threw himself onto the dog. He tried to move her head, to thread his skinny little arms around her neck.

'Come on, baby. You need to let go.' Caroline grabbed his baggy jacket and tugged.

'No! Leave me alone!'

'But we have to wrap the blanket around her. We don't want her to get cold, do we?'

Ben relaxed his grip just enough for Caroline to drag him away from the bloody mess on the ground.

'Is she going to heaven?' he said.

Caroline glanced at Claire, who hadn't taken her eyes from the dog.

'I told him all about doggie heaven on the way home,' Claire said.

'Yes, of course she is, sweetheart. But first we have to make sure she's nice and warm.'

Ben yanked his arms away from his mother's and patted the dog's head, then bent down and kissed her nose. 'Bye bye Minty.'

'Why don't you go in and see your gran – she can make you your tea.'

'I don't want any.'

Jean appeared at the back door and held out her hand. 'What about a chocolate milkshake?' She put an arm around his shoulders and steered him back into the house.

When they were safely inside Claire fell into Caroline's arms. 'It was horrible, Mum. I didn't know what to do.'

'It's all right love. You did really well, carrying Minty all that way.' She squeezed Claire tighter.

'But I was so scared.' Claire started sobbing again.

'Of course you were – what you did was very brave. Picking her up when she was so badly injured. Bringing her all the way home.'

Claire pulled away and looked into Caroline's face. She wiped a sleeve across her streaming nose. 'I don't mean that.'

Caroline saw the distress in Claire's eyes. There was a terror in that look that she'd never seen before. 'What is it, love?'

'I was scared... of... the men.'

Caroline felt as if her guts had been wrenched out. She searched Claire's face and struggled to breathe in, waiting a moment before she could speak, knowing she needed to keep her voice as even and normal as possible. 'What men, darling?'

'The two men on the motorbike. It was horrible.'

Caroline's legs started to shake; she walked Claire to the bench by the back door and sat them both down. She cleared her throat. 'Where were they, these men?'

'Outside the school. Ben's school.' Claire pushed her fists into her eyes. 'I can't stop seeing it, over and over.'

'Claire...' Caroline swallowed hard. 'Did they touch you?'

Claire shook her head, her hands still hiding her face.

'Look at me, Claire. Did they hurt you?' She tugged her daughter's hands from her eyes and grabbed her cheeks, turning her head to face her.

'No.'

'Or Ben?'

'No.'

'You would tell me, if—'

'They didn't touch us!'

'All right, love – all right.' The constriction in Caroline's throat relaxed just a little. 'Tell me what happened. From the beginning.'

'But it was so horrible.'

'I know love, I know.' She wrapped an arm around Claire's shoulders, pulling her in close. Her gaze was inevitably drawn back to the uneven shape under the red and green blanket. 'Tell me what the men were doing at Ben's school.'

'I don't know. They were just sitting on the bike – I wouldn't have noticed, but it was a really big bike, a red one – and Ben pointed it out to me – you know what he's like about bikes and cars.' She swallowed.

'What did they look like – the men?'

'They were wearing crash helmets – I couldn't see their faces... they looked odd.' Claire sniffed and wiped her nose on her sleeve again.

'What do you mean?'

'They looked too smart to be riding a bike.' Claire started to shiver. 'They were wearing suits.'

'We should go inside.' Caroline edged forward on the bench, but Claire didn't budge.

'No – I want to stay out here.'

'What happened after that?'

'They started up the bike and rode away.'

'They did?' Caroline closed her eyes for a moment and allowed the air to escape from her lungs.

Claire nodded and wriggled closer to her mother. 'But then they came back.'

Caroline squeezed Claire even closer.

'We got as far as the estate when I saw them again. They were driving really fast, coming towards us. I made sure Ben was on the inside of the pavement and we carried on walking. I tried to hold his hand, but he didn't want to.' She pushed out her bottom lip. Another sob escaped. 'They were just a little way from us when the bike swerved onto our side of the street. It got really close and then swerved away again. The man sitting at the back turned round and shouted something.' Claire looked down at her hands.

'What did he say, sweetheart?'

'I don't know – I couldn't hear him over the noise of the engine.' Tears were streaming down Claire's face now. Caroline tried to wipe them away, but Claire stopped her. 'Don't fuss Mum. I'm all right.'

'I'm sorry!' Caroline shoved one hand between her knees and squeezed Claire tighter with the other. 'What happened after that?'

'We carried on walking. I grabbed Ben's jacket and dragged him along faster. He had to practically run to keep up with me. He started whining that he was getting tired.' She squeezed her eyes shut, forcing more tears onto her cheeks. Her chest heaved.

'It's OK, baby. Take as long as you need.'

'That was when we heard Minty. We were probably halfway home by then. Ben heard the barking first. He shouted her name and I told him not to be stupid – it was just some random dog. But then we saw her. Running from the other end of the street. Ben ran towards her. I tried to grab his collar but he wriggled away from me. I ran after him. Then I heard the motorbike again.' She took a deep breath.

Caroline closed her eyes, imagining what must have happened next. *Bastards.*

'The bike was coming from behind us this time. I ran as fast as I could to get to Ben – he was just about to step into the road. I grabbed his belt and yanked him back onto the kerb.' Claire took a big gulp of air. 'Ben opened his arms and shouted to Minty. She ran towards him.' Claire stopped, unable to control her voice any longer. A sob escaped from her mouth, followed by another and another. Her whole body was shaking.

'Shhh... it's all right.' Caroline tried to pull her closer, but she resisted.

'I haven't…' She snatched another breath. 'Finished.' Her chest heaved several times before she could speak again. 'The sound of the bike got louder – it must have been speeding up – then it flew right past us and smashed into Minty. She bounced up in the air and came crashing down onto the road. She was howling. I grabbed Ben's arms. I had to stop him running to her. The bike was turning round by then, I could see it was going to come back. I thought they were coming for us.' Her eyes opened wide, as if she could see the whole scene right in front of her. 'They ran the motorbike right over Minty. And then—'

'They did what?'

'She stopped howling.' Another sorrowful sob burst out of her mouth. Caroline couldn't bear to hear any more.

'That's enough love.'

'But I need to tell you. I haven't finished yet!'

Caroline shook her head, covered her mouth with her free hand.

'They came right up to us again. I shoved Ben behind me. Then the man on the back shouted, like he did before. He lifted his visor.'

'Did you see his face?'

Claire shook her head. 'He was wearing a scarf over his mouth. The thing he said… it didn't make any sense.'

'It doesn't matter what he said, love. It doesn't matter.' Caroline stroked her daughter's hair and kissed the top of her head. Claire pulled away.

'I have to tell you.'

'It's all right – you don't have to do anything.'

'He told me I had to.' She was shouting now.

'What do you mean?'

'Tell your mum… he said that… tell your mum…' Claire sobbed again.

Caroline sucked in a shaky breath. 'What did he say?'

'Tell your mum this is just a warning.'

43

Friday morning and half of Friday afternoon came and went with no sign of the police forensics people.

Caroline spent most of the day watching the street from the living room window, looking out for unfamiliar vehicles or pedestrians lingering where they shouldn't be. Every time she heard the roar of an approaching motorbike she ran into the front garden, expecting to see two besuited thugs cruising up the road. She hadn't worked out what she would do if they did appear, but kept the poker propped up against the wall by the front door just in case.

Just after 3:30pm she heard a key rattle in the lock. The front door opened and her mother stepped wearily inside.

'Where's Ben?' Caroline peered around Jean and saw the garden path was empty. 'What's happened?'

'It's all right – he's just outside.'

'You left him on his own on the street?' She pushed her mother out of the way.

'He's not on his own!' Jean hollered after her.

Caroline pulled up sharply at the garden gate when she saw Pete swinging Ben over his shoulder and spinning him round, his skinny legs flying. Ben was actually giggling. *Thank God.* He'd cried himself to sleep the night before. There was nothing she could say to console him.

Jean joined her on the path. 'He was waiting on the corner of the street when I arrived. Are you going to invite him inside?'

Should she?

'Have the police come yet – to dust for fingerprints or whatever it is they do?'

Caroline didn't take her eyes off Ben. Pete was tickling him now.

'I'm still waiting for them. I get put on hold every time I call.'

Jean clucked her tongue against her teeth. 'What do we pay our taxes for?' She moved away. 'I'll put the kettle on. Shall I make tea for him too?' She nodded at Pete. 'Is he stopping?'

Again, Caroline didn't know how to answer.

'You still haven't told me the real reason he left. That story about his sister being poorly might be OK for the kids, but you can't fool me. I could just ask him, I suppose.'

'Not now, Mum.'

Jean threw up her hands. 'All right. Keep me in the bloody dark.' She muttered something under her breath as she walked away.

Caroline wandered slowly out onto the street.

'Hello, sweetie. Gran's in the kitchen – why don't you ask her for a glass of milk and a biscuit?'

Pete stopped tickling his son and lowered him onto the ground. Ben was breathless and pink-cheeked. 'Go on,' Pete said. 'Your mum and me need to talk.' Pete pushed gently against Ben's shoulders and coaxed him towards the house. 'Ask Gran if I can have one of those biscuits.' He turned to Caroline. 'Why didn't you call me when it happened? I should have been here last night.'

Caroline looked up into his face and narrowed her eyes. 'Who told you about it?'

'Jean phoned me this morning.'

'She did what?'

'I know, it surprised me too.'

'She had no business doing that.'

'For God's sake, Caz.' He clamped his big hands on her shoulders. 'They're my kids too. I should have been here, looking after them.'

Caroline threw her head back, and sucked in a breath, trying to stay calm. She ducked away from him. 'I was going to call you later. I've had a lot on my mind.'

'That's no excuse.' He reached out a hand and held her arm. 'We can't talk out here. Let's go inside.'

'I'm not sure that's such a good idea. The kids have been through enough – I don't want you confusing them.'

'You're the one who's keeping me away.'

'Have you been drinking?'

'We're back to that again, are we?'

'Have you?'

Pete let go of her arm.

'I'll take that as a yes.'

'I haven't had a drink since you threw me out. Ask Denise.'

'Denise? Your sister would say anything you asked her to.'

'It's the truth.'

'I've only got your word for that – at the moment it doesn't count for much.'

'I want to come home, Caz. We've been through rocky patches before – we always come out the other side.'

'This is different.'

'You can't do this to us. To the family.'

'Me? You're the one who can't tell the difference between right and wrong. Not much of a role model for the kids, are you?'

Pete sniffed. 'The kids don't need to know anything about what happened at work. They won't hear it from me. Come on, Caz – we can work this out.'

He reached out for her, but she stepped quickly away and ended up stumbling into the gutter. The curtain at a window across the street jerked back and Caroline's neighbour stared right at her.

'Let's go inside. I'm not putting on a floorshow for number 24.'

Jean was emerging from the kitchen, drying her hands on a tea towel, when they reached the front door. 'Someone from your office just called... Pam I think she said her name was.'

'What did she want?'

'She asked me to ask you what you wanted to do with all your personal stuff. Whether you wanted it parcelled up and posted on. When I asked her what she meant she got a bit vague and hung up. What was she talking about?'

Caroline poked her head into the kitchen. Ben was cramming a Jaffa Cake into his mouth, staring intently at a Harry Potter DVD playing on the television on the kitchen counter.

'Best to keep him distracted, I thought,' Jean said.

Caroline plodded into the living room, gesturing for Pete and her mother to follow her. She righted an armchair and threw the cushions back on the sofa. 'You'd better sit down,' she said. 'It's a long story.'

By the time she'd finished telling them the details of her suspension and everything that led up to it, she felt exhausted.

'Have you spoken to the union rep?' Jean asked.

Caroline shook her head, unable to make eye contact with her mother.

'Really they should have been your first port of call as soon as all this blew up. It's not too late to get them involved now though. If you don't feel up to it, I can speak to them for you.'

'You don't have to fight my battles for me, Mum.'

'I just want to help. Twenty years your father was shop steward. I do have some experience in this sort of thing, you know.'

Caroline wrinkled her nose.

'What is it, don't you trust me to say the right thing?'

'Just leave it, Mum.'

'But I can help.'

'No – you can't. And neither can the union. I let my subs lapse. I haven't been a member for a couple of years.'

'What?'

Caroline finally met her mother's gaze.

'Your father would be turning in his grave. After everything he taught you. How could you?'

'For God's sake, Mum – there's no need to bring Dad into it!'

A loud bang on the front door jerked Caroline out of her seat, grateful to get away from her mother's questions. 'That'll be the forensics team, I expect.'

She ran to the door yanked it open. Her mother's friend, Albert, was standing in the front path. She led him into the living room.

'Oh my Lord,' Jean said when she saw him. 'I completely forgot you were coming.'

'Am I the first to arrive?' Albert looked around the room. 'Goodness – what happened in here? It looks like a bomb's gone off.'

Jean led Albert through to the door at the back of the living room and into her annexe. She glanced back over her shoulder. 'Don't think I've finished with you, madam.'

'God give me strength,' Caroline murmured under her breath.

The front door opened and closed. Caroline rushed back into the hall to see Claire standing by the coat rack, shrugging off her blazer.

'Could you go and sit with Ben for a while? He's in the kitchen.'

'I've got a ton of revision to do.'

'Please, Claire.'

Pete appeared in the hall. 'Come on, Claire – do what your mum says.'

'You're back! Is Dennie feeling better, now?'

'Denise?'

Caroline jabbed him in the ribs with a sharp elbow. 'Auntie Dennie's much better, isn't she?'

'Er... almost fully recovered.' Pete watched Claire disappear into the kitchen.

'What did you tell them?'

'Your sister's had an operation. You're looking after her.'

'And they believed you?'

'Just play along if they ask you. OK?'

'I can't go on lying to them. We need to sort this out. Why don't I stay over? I'd feel much better being here, keeping an eye on them.'

'Would you?'

'I can sleep on the sofa. I just want to be near.'

There was another knock on the door. Caroline reached for the latch, expecting to see a man in a paper romper suit holding a Metropolitan Police toolbox in his hand.

It was Angela Tate.

'What are you doing here? I've already told you... I can't help anymore.'

'I came as soon as I heard the news. I tried calling, but your phone must be switched off.' She marched straight into the living room. 'Still waiting for forensics to show?' She looked around the room. 'You know it's entirely possible they've got no intention of sending anyone out. Depends how far their tentacles have reached.' She turned to Pete and stuck out a hand. 'Hello, I'm Angela Tate.'

'Angela's the journalist I just told you about... this is Pete, my...'

Pete took Tate's proffered hand in his. 'The word she's looking for is *husband*,' he said.

'Pleasure.' Tate sank onto the sofa. 'I went home after I left here yesterday afternoon and called out a locksmith to fix my door. Then I threw a few things in a bag and legged it. I've set up home in a nice big anonymous Novotel in west London. They'll never find me there.'

'Who's after you?' Pete sat down next to Tate.

'How much have you told him?' Tate turned to Caroline.

'I was getting there.'

'Who's after me? Take your pick. My boss... the police... secret service, CIA...' She let out a breath. 'Any chance you could find a glass and a bottle of something comforting in this mess? I feel like I need a stiff one.'

'Pete – there's a bottle of brandy from last Christmas in the cupboard next to the cooker.'

'There isn't,' he said quietly. 'I finished it.' He smiled at Tate. 'Coffee or tea?'

'Coffee – strong, black, two sugars.'

Tate waited for Pete to leave the room before speaking. 'Haven't you seen the news?'

'What's happened?'

'The secretary of state has made a statement.'

'Mentioning me?'

'No. As far as her statement goes, you're still an unnamed senior civil servant.'

'Senior?'

'Congratulations on your belated promotion.' Tate smiled. 'No – the S-O-S has taken the opportunity to reiterate how seriously the department takes data protection. How the loss of the CD-ROM is an aberration, how it will never happen again... yadda bleeding yadda. How you can't judge an entire administration by one rogue employee—'

'Rogue... me?'

'I know – it just gets better and better, doesn't it?' She took a breath. 'Anyway she said all that and then hit the assembled hacks with the punchline none of them was expecting.'

'What?'

'She took one for the team. She's fallen on her sword.'

'You're not serious.'

'Deadly. Meanwhile William King is laughing all the way to the polls.' Tate leaned her head on the back on the sofa, then quickly lifted it away again. 'Oh... I'm not contaminating a crime scene, am I?'

'I think we may have moved beyond that by now, don't you?'

'In that case.' Tate kicked off her shoes and drew her feet up onto the cushion. 'God I'm exhausted.'

'Sitting in a hotel room watching CNN?'

'I've been working my arse off since you last saw me, trying to track down some of the families affected by the health and safety violations on that list of yours.'

'You found another copy of the document?' Caroline leaned forward in her chair.

'Alas, no. But I can still retain a few important facts.' She tapped her temple. 'Hasn't turned to mush just yet.'

'And?'

'Not much, unfortunately. I managed to get the contact details for two of the families. Both widows refused to tell me anything about the settlements they'd reached with the companies. It seems they've signed some sort of gagging order. It was the only way they could get their hands on any financial compensation. I would imagine that's true of most of the names on the list.'

'Did you explain how important it was? What's at stake?'

'They didn't want to listen. They sounded scared, Caroline. Terrified.'

Pete came back into the room balancing three overfilled mugs on a tray.

'Terrified of what Larson might do to them.' Tate shook her head. 'We can't let him get away with it.'

'We?'

Caroline looked away.

Pete lowered the tray onto the coffee table, but wouldn't look at his wife. 'I'll go and sit with Ben,' he said. 'Let Claire get back to her homework.'

'No, Pete. I think you should stay right here,' Caroline said. 'You heard that didn't you? About Larson?'

Pete chewed the inside of his mouth and stared at the carpet.

'Isn't it time for you to do something?' Caroline laid a hand on his arm.

He put a hand over hers and looked into her eyes.

'Please, Pete.'

Tate quickly swung her feet back on the floor and sat up. 'What's this? Have I missed something?'

'Come on, Caz. It'd just be me against Larson and his army of lawyers. Who's going to listen to me?'

'You've at least got to try.'

'Would you mind telling me what you're talking about?' Tate got to her feet.

'We might have another throw of the dice... maybe... with Pete's help.'

'We've already been through this, Caz.'

'What if I told you Larson... or people very close to him, were responsible for all this?' She threw a quick glance at Tate.

'The break-in?'

'And what happened to Ben and Claire yesterday.'

'I don't understand.' Pete searched her face. 'What are you saying?'

'The people who have stopped me and Angela digging up any more information.'

'They did this?'

Caroline nodded. 'They were behind it.'

'And they killed the dog?' He tipped back his head and sucked in a breath. 'That was Larson's people?'

'Most probably.'

'Fucking bastards.'

Caroline looked into Pete's face and saw some of the old fire back in his eyes. Still squeezing tightly on his arm, she turned back to Tate.

'I think my husband has something he wants to tell you about Larson.'

44

Frank Carter stubbed out his fifth cigarette and looked at his watch.

'Has a habit of being late, freaky Freddie, doesn't he?'

'Maybe he turned up, took one look at you, and scarpered.' Angela was sitting two tables away from Frank outside The Flying Horse on the corner of Wilson Street.

Frank fidgeted on the wooden bench attached to the table. 'We've been here over two hours now, Ange. I've got a strange sense he's not gonna show.' He rubbed his hands together. 'I'm freezing my bollocks off.'

'I'll wait on my own.'

'I can't just leave you.'

Frank got up and sat down at her table. He leaned forward and spoke in a whisper. 'How much did you say you had on you?'

'I didn't.'

'But you've maxed out all your credit cards – am I right?'

'If you really want to help me out...'

'Yeah?'

'Go and get me another vodka and tonic.'

Angela continued to sit at her table, Frank at his, for another 45 minutes before she reluctantly accepted Freddie Larson wasn't going to make an appearance.

'I'm sorry, Ange. I wish the feckless git had come through for you, I really do.' He stood up and stretched his arms over his head and wandered towards her. 'Do you want me to run you anywhere? I don't like the idea of you walking the streets looking for a cab with that much wedge on you.'

She blinked slowly at him.

'All right! I know you can look after yourself – nothing wrong with being a bit careful though is there?'

'You can take me to Liverpool Street Station – I'll get a taxi there.' She wearily threaded her arm through the straps of her handbag and levered herself up.

'Has him not showing totally fucked things over for you, then?'

'He wasn't my only iron in the fire.'

'Maybe the lure of Daddy's millions was just too tempting. Sir Fred can't have much life left in him, can he? Perhaps Freddie's taking the long view. He doesn't want to risk upsetting the old man talking to you.'

'I can't imagine Freddie's a big advocate of delayed gratification. My money in his hand now versus a handout from Valerie Larson when Fred finally snuffs it? There's no contest. He'd be bloody stupid to think Widow Larson would go the Lady Bountiful route.'

Frank shrugged. 'Maybe the waster was too off his tits to even remember he agreed to meet you.'

'Doesn't really matter now, does it?'

'Suppose not.'

They started walking towards Frank's car. 'Did you remember to bring that charger I asked you for?'

'I've got half a dozen of them in the car – wasn't sure which one you needed.'

'Cheers, Frank.'

'Don't tell me I've actually done something right.'

'There's a first time for everything, Frankie.'

As soon as she closed the hotel room door behind her, Angela Tate kicked off her shoes. She padded across the plush carpet and sank onto the bed, shaking a blue and white striped plastic bag from a half bottle of Three Barrels. She snapped off the cap and took a slug straight from the bottle, then forced herself off the bed again in search of a glass.

Two double brandies later, she sorted through the collection of power supplies Frank had given her and plugged in Jason Morris's digital video recorder. She flipped the camera on and was rewarded with a charging battery symbol and no way to access the welcome screen. She left it charging on the little desk in the corner of the room, switched on the television and settled herself on the bed, determined to get rat-arsed as quickly as she could.

The local news bulletin ended and she flicked over to Newsnight without even thinking. One of her mobiles rang just as she was nodding off. She emptied her bag onto the bed and flipped each phone over until she found the one with the illuminated screen.

Caller unknown.

'Hello?'

'Is that Miss Tate?' A woman's voice – for a moment she'd hoped it might have been Freddie.

'Yes – who's this?'

She heard a sharp intake of breath.

'How did you find out?' The woman sounded angry.

'Who am I speaking to?'

'You had no right to tell him.'

'I'm sorry – who is this?'

Angela pulled the phone away from her ear a couple of inches, her thumb hovering over the call end button.

'Fred didn't need to know.'

Fred?

By the accent, Angela could tell she didn't have Valerie Larson on the other end of the line. She ventured the next best guess.

'Betty Larson?'

'Why did you have to do it?'

Angela pulled herself upright on the bed and muted the television. Betty must have kept the business card she gave her. 'I'm sorry, Mrs Larson. You need to need to explain what—'

'Don't play the innocent with me. How else would he have found out?'

'Who? Found out what?' She swung her legs over the edge of the bed and eased herself to her feet, hoping a brisk walk around the room would wake her up. 'I honestly don't know what you're talking about. Can you just please tell me.'

There was a long pause, followed by a coughing fit.

'Mrs Larson? Are you all right?'

'I've just had that woman on the phone – calling me all the names under the sun. She's got such a filthy mouth. I don't know how he could ever have married her.'

'Are you talking about Lady Larson?'

'Lady? There's nothing ladylike about her.'

'Why was she phoning you? Has something happened to Fred?'

'What? I don't know! She wouldn't bother getting in touch with me if it had.'

'Why don't you give me your number and I'll call you back? This call must be costing you a fortune.'

'I wasn't born yesterday – I'm not giving you my phone number.'

Angela peered through the blinds at the night-time traffic on the Westway, the triple glazing muffling the sound from outside, making it seem as if the cars were floating along the tarmac.

'I'm really not following. What has her phone call got to do with me?'

'She called me to gloat.'

Angela let out a sigh. 'Why don't you call me back when you've calmed down?'

'I don't need to calm down! Why couldn't you leave well enough alone? All these years – he never needed to find out.'

'Please…' Angela spoke as quietly and as reasonably as she could. 'I truly don't know what I'm supposed to have done.'

'Freddie won't see a penny of his money now, you do realise that? Fred will stop paying for his treatment and he'll end up back on the street, stealing, begging, whatever it takes to get hold of that evil filth.'

Angela sank down onto the sofa next to the window and tried to catch her breath. Fred had already stopped paying for his son's treatment.

'Please tell me what's happened.'

'How can you carry on pretending you know nothing about it? How did you find out?'

'Find out what?'

'That Freddie isn't Fred's son!' Betty Larson yelled at her and set off another coughing fit.

Angela could hear Betty gasping for breath. The worst of it subsided after a few moments.

'Why couldn't you leave well alone? What has Freddie ever done to you?'

'I'm sorry, Mrs Larson – I still don't understand. Why do you think I had anything to do with it?'

'Digging around where you have no right to.'

'Please believe me – this is the first I've heard of anyth—'

The line went dead.

Angela sat very still for a moment, staring at the lifeless phone in her hand. Freddie not Larson's son? The way Betty Larson had just been talking it sounded as if she'd known all along; kept it secret from Fred for 40-odd years. Angela glanced at the contents of her handbag strewn across the bed, the envelope meant for Freddie still bulging with twenty-pound notes. Had anyone even told him?

She blinked hard and got up, grabbed the kettle from the dressing table and filled it from the bathroom tap. She emptied two sachets of instant coffee into a mug and sat back down and watched the noisy little kettle start to boil. Over the sound of gurgling, spluttering water, she heard a faint bleep. It took her a while to realise it wasn't one of her mobiles discharging, but Jason Morris's digital video camera finishing its charging process. She padded over to the desk and found the film roll icons had reappeared on the welcome screen. She selected the one she'd tried to watch before. The video resumed at the point she'd left it previously.

'Now I know that I need to get some proper evidence.' Jason Morris pointed a remote control towards the screen and the image froze on his face, fixed in a wide-eyed grimace.

'Oh come on, Jason!' She quickly navigated back to the welcome screen and selected the last film Jason must have recorded before he died.

Again his face filled most of the screen, his expression anxious.

'Tony kicked off again today.' He gulped noisily. 'He threatened to set his pit bull on me. Tried to make it seem like he was joking, for the benefit of everyone else in the room, but the way he looked at me...' Jason stared towards the light off to his left. It was casting strange shadows across his face. 'Fuck – he suspects something – I know he does. I've been watching my back all evening, making sure I'm not on my own with him.' He buried his face in his hands and made a low moaning noise. Then he took a deep breath. He pushed his hands over his head and looked up towards the ceiling.

In the background Angela could make out the sofa she'd seen through his living room window. Propped up against the wall next to it was Jason's bike. Before it got mangled under the wheels of a van.

She shuddered.

'I feel like I'm totally out of my depth now – no way did I imagine they'd have such high profile backers. They've seemed like such a bunch of amateurs all this time.' He folded his arms across his chest and shook his head. 'I wanted to get one of the meetings on video, but they've started patting everyone down as soon as we get through the door. It's too fucking risky – especially with Tony breathing down my neck.' He stood up and walked across the room, out of shot for a moment. Then he returned with an open bottle of beer in his hand. He stood behind his chair and leaned a hand on the back. 'I fucking hate to admit defeat – but I'm giving it to the end of the week then I'm out. I can't live like this anymore. Constantly looking over my shoulder, expecting a knife under the ribcage whenever I see Tony.' He drank half his beer before continuing. 'All I can do is give Evans the names of the main players, but God knows what he'll be able to do with the information.' He puffed out his cheeks. 'Arrogant bunch of wankers.' He shook his head. 'Walking around like they're untouchable. Thinking they can get away with murder.' He drank more of his beer. 'Shit! They probably can.' He stared into space for seconds, his eyes fixed on something beyond the camera. 'I bumped into the big man himself tonight,' he eventually said. 'So blasé, he was actually wearing his *uniform* under his jacket.' He ran his hand over his head and collapsed back down on the chair. 'I had a cosy little chat with the deputy assistant commissioner about the *cricket* for fuck's sake. Turns out Barry Flowers is a big Essex fan.'

45

Half a dozen mismatched suitcases and assorted sports bags were lined up in a row in the hall. Caroline squeezed an extra pair of Ben's pyjamas into his Buzz Lightyear suitcase and propped his stuffed blue rabbit with the one floppy ear between the metal uprights of the handle. She leaned over the banister and shouted up the stairs.

'Come on Claire! Everyone else is ready. What are you doing up there?'

Her daughter's face appeared over the rail on the first floor landing.

'I'm waiting for the bathroom.'

'Who's in there?'

'Dan. He's been ages.'

'Dan?' Caroline hurried up the stairs. Dan was usually in and out of the bathroom in less than five minutes. Immediately Caroline imagined the worst. She whispered to Claire. 'How long?'

'An hour, maybe?'

'And you didn't think to check on him?'

Claire shrugged.

Caroline tapped on the door. 'Dan? We're waiting to leave, love. Are you nearly finished in there?'

'Tell him to hurry up!' Claire said.

'Go downstairs and ask your gran if you can use her bathroom.'

'But my stuff is in there.' Claire thumped a fist against the door, and rattled the handle. 'Dan! Mum's here – she's right outside the door – come out!'

'Downstairs, Claire. I'll bring your stuff down.' She turned back to the door. 'Come on, sweetheart.' From inside the bathroom she heard cabinet doors slam shut. 'Is anything wrong, love? If there's something you need I can get Gran to stop off at the supermarket on the way.' She leaned her head against the door. 'Come on, love.'

What was he doing in there? She pictured him pulling out blades from Pete's safety razor... leaning over the bath... It was just too quiet. 'Dan! Is everything OK?'

The door opened suddenly and Caroline tumbled forward into the gap. Dan held out his arms and managed to stop her falling over.

'Don't fuss, Mum.' He ducked around her. 'God!'

She heard him mutter something about getting up 'so early on a Sunday morning' as he disappeared into his room. He slammed the door shut behind him.

Caroline headed straight for the bathroom cabinet and flung open the doors. A full complement of paracetamols, aspirin and ibuprofen still occupied the top shelf and a new packet of razor heads didn't look like it had been tampered with. She exhaled, told herself not to overreact, and stuffed all the painkillers into a pocket. Just in case. She flew down the stairs and ran into her mother coming in the front door.

'We're nearly ready, Mum.'

Jean huffed.

'I do appreciate what you're doing.'

'I don't see why *you* can't take them – it's not like you've got a job tying you down.'

Caroline weaved around Jean and tested one of Claire's bags for weight. She could barely lift it. 'I've already explained. I've got a few things I need to tidy up. I'll come down to the chalet on Thursday, maybe even before that. Depending on how things pan out.'

'I don't know why you're being so mysterious.'

Caroline dragged the bag to the front door and over the step.

'And why isn't Pete here helping?' Jean said. 'I thought he'd moved back in.'

'Did he tell you that?'

Jean shrugged. 'I'm not blind. I know he didn't go back to his sister's on Friday night.'

'Not that it's any of your business… he slept on the sofa.'

'I'm well aware of that. I could hear his snoring through the wall. I don't know how you put up with him for so long.'

Caroline dropped the bag and turned back to her mother, not wanting to shout her business in the street. 'Can you just drop it? Now is not the time.'

'I've got meetings planned. We're going to leaflet the polling stations on Thursday. I need to get back to organise it.'

'You can't leaflet – it's not even legal.'

'We won't be telling people who to vote for. Just letting them know which parties are supporting the academy programme.'

'I'm sure your boyfriend and the rest of your merry men will manage perfectly well without you.'

'If you're talking about Albert, he's not my boyfriend.'

'Maybe you should tell him that.'

Caroline picked up a corner of the bag and hauled it all the way to the kerb, her mother two steps behind. She opened the boot of her Fiesta. The space inside seemed smaller now she'd cleared the junk out than it did before. They'd never fit everything in. Jean grabbed one end of the heavy bag sitting on the pavement.

'After three,' she said.

'You'll do yourself an injury. I'll get Dan to help.'

'We can manage.'

Reluctantly, Caroline grabbed the other end and they heaved the bag into the boot and the little red car bounced on its creaking suspension. Caroline scrutinised the rear roadside tyre. As she prodded the tread with a knuckle, an enormous four-wheel drive roared towards her. It was going far too fast. It whooshed by, almost clipping the Fiesta's wing mirror. Caroline tried to get a good look at the driver as it sped away; only exhaling when she saw it was a grey-haired woman.

'You will drive carefully?' She turned to her mother.

Jean rolled her eyes. 'Actually, I thought I'd take the opportunity to practice my rallying skills on the M20.'

'Seriously, Mum – if you feel insecure about anything – if other drivers look like they're playing silly buggers—'

'What are you talking about?'

'If you get shaken up by anything. You know… notice any strange vehicles or feel like you're being followed – just pull over and call the police.'

'Followed? I'm not James Bond, Caroline. Who's going to be following me down to the Isle of Sheppey?' She threw her hands in the air. 'International spy rings must have fallen on very hard times if they're relocating to Leysdown.' She shook her head. 'All this nonsense at the department has addled your brains.'

'I can't believe you're saying that. You saw the state the kids were in on Friday night.'

'They were upset because of the dog – we all were. It was a terrible accident.'

'Someone ran the dog over deliberately.'

Jean muttered something under her breath.

'What if it had been Ben?'

'Don't exaggerate, Caroline.'

'Just promise me you'll be careful.'

'I'm always careful.'

Dan appeared at the front door. He pushed up his sleeves and stood scratching his arms

'Give me a hand with the other bags,' Caroline shouted at him.

He grunted and went back into the hall. He was gripping a bag in each hand by the time Caroline reached the house.

'I realise you don't want to go away,' she said. 'But you have to trust me – it's for the best.'

'Whatever.'

'You can talk to Kylie on the phone every day. The time'll flash by. You know it's OK to give her your new number?'

'What?' He looked at her as if she was speaking a foreign language.

'And while we're on the subject, you still haven't given me your old phone.' She held out a hand.

'Not possible.'

'Claire's given me hers – even your gran's handed her mobile over. Come on, Dan. I got you a new one for a reason. You can't use the old phone. It's not safe. Give it to me.'

'Don't have it.'

'You don't—'

'Lost it.' He looked away. 'Yesterday.'

'Why didn't you tell me?'

He shrugged.

'For God's sake, Dan!'

'I don't know why you're being so paranoid.'

'I've already explained. We've got to be careful.' She stared into his eyes. 'You're not lying to me, are you? If I find out you've still got it...'

Dan grunted again and struggled to the front step with the two heavy bags.

'Be careful with my stuff.' Claire ran to the door and stabbed a finger into her brother's ribs. He flinched.

'Sorry... forgot,' Claire said.

'Forgot what?' Caroline stood between them. What's going on? What's wrong with your side? Dan?'

Dan ignored her and trundled outside with the bags.

'Claire?'

She shrugged. 'He fell over or something.' She started sorting through the coats on the rack by the front door. 'Have you seen my leather jacket?'

'Can you have a word with him while you're away?'

'With Dan? What about?'

'About Kylie – he won't speak about the situation with me at all. He's got to take his responsibilities seriously.'

Claire threw a coat onto the floor, chucked hats and scarves on top. 'Dan's OK. I've got too much to think about without getting into all that.'

'Please, Claire.'

'It's bad enough I have to go away at all. Do you know how much revision I have to do?'

Caroline shook her head. 'I'm sorry. OK? I'm sorry I'm making you do this. But I don't have a choice. It's for your own good. Just have a quiet word with Dan, will you?'

'I would've thought Kylie was the least of his worries.' Claire tugged at a tan leather jacket and managed to knock the remaining coats onto the floor.

'What's that supposed to mean?'

'You'll have to ask him.'

'Do you even know if Kylie has made a decision about whether or not to keep the baby?'

'God, Mum. It's not a baby – it's a collection of cells embedded in the wall of her uterus.'

Caroline closed her eyes for a moment. 'At least try – he'll listen to you.'

Claire snorted a laugh. 'I have more meaningful conversations with Ben.' She unzipped a purple suitcase and tried to stuff the jacket inside.

'Where is your brother?'

'Haven't seen him.'

Caroline shouted up the stairs for Ben, then noticed the stuffed rabbit she'd balanced on his suitcase had disappeared. She ran into the kitchen and through the back door, calling his name as she went, a familiar queasiness blooming in her stomach. She scanned the garden and spotted him beneath the overgrown eucalyptus, kneeling by a mound of fresh soil.

'I'm saying goodbye to Minty,' he explained, without her having to ask. 'I told her not to miss us too much.'

A pile of fast-withering pansies sat at the summit of the mound. Ben must have reached a hand through the hole in the fence and helped himself from the neighbour's flowerbeds. Caroline dragged him towards her and kissed the top of his head and sniffed in a breath. His hair smelled of Vosene. She patted the mound, mumbled a goodbye to Minty and lifted Ben to his feet. 'Promise me you'll look after your brother and sister while you're away.'

He nodded.

'Just think, in a couple of hours you'll be by the seaside, making sandcastles.'

'When will you and Dad be coming?'

'I'll be down in a couple of days.'

'What about Dad?'

Caroline swallowed. 'Maybe at the weekend.'

'I have to wait a whole week?'

'We'll see.'

'Will you put flowers on Minty's grave while I'm away?'

'Of course I will.'

Fifteen minutes later all the bags had been squeezed into the boot and her three children were safely strapped into their seats. Caroline handed the car key to her mother and checked up and down the street.

'Good grief, Caroline. Stop being so jumpy.' Jean shoved the key in the ignition.

'Remember the gear stick jams a bit going from second to third?' Caroline said. 'Just make sure you've got your foot right down on the clutch. You will drive carefully?'

'I've been driving perfectly well for over 45 years, Caroline. I don't think I need any lessons from you.'

'Call me when you arrive. In fact, get Claire to call me when you're nearly there.'

'It's only the Isle of Sheppey – not a lunar expedition. I'll give you three rings when we get there. There's no need to pick up.'

46

Caroline walked up the stairs, stopping after each flight to listen for noises below. The lifts in Pete's sister's block never seemed to be working and she really didn't want to risk getting stuck in a graffiti-stained, urine-soaked metal box waiting for the fire brigade to come and rescue her.

Instead of jumping on the number 75 bus from Catford directly to Lewisham, Caroline had taken a train to New Cross then walked to New Cross Gate where she picked up the East London line. She travelled five stops north to Shadwell and eventually arrived in Lewisham via the DLR. But even after all her precautions, she still couldn't shake the feeling she was being followed.

Denise's flat was on the third floor, Caroline walked up to the fifth, waited quietly for five minutes at the bend in a stairwell, then crossed the long walkway running parallel to her sister-in-law's. She finally reached the third floor by way of another staircase.

By the time she knocked on Denise's door she felt as if she'd just finished a marathon. Pete opened the door in his boxers and an old t-shirt, shaving foam smeared across his face.

'For God's sake, Pete! Why aren't you dressed?'

He left the door open and padded back up the hall without saying a word.

'Did Denise get off all right last night?' She stood by the open bathroom door, watching him rinse the rest of the foam from his face.

'Yeah – she's really not happy spending the bank holiday with Mum though. They're probably at each other's throats as we speak.' He threw a towel onto the floor and automatically Caroline picked it up. She folded it neatly over a towel rail and wandered into the living room to wait for Pete to get dressed.

There was a gentle knock on the front door. 'I'll get it,' Caroline shouted. She opened the door to a grave-faced Angela Tate. The journalist was dressed from head to toe in black. Her hair was scraped back off her face, oversize sunglasses balancing on top of a scarf tied tight against her head. Caroline's mouth fell open.

'What?' Tate said. 'Bit too Milk Tray Man/Grace Kelly mutant Ninja?'
She plucked at the neck of her jumper. 'Is that what you're thinking?'

'We are getting there in broad daylight.'

Tate followed Caroline into the living room at the end of the hall.

'If you wanted to be inconspicuous you might have been better off in
a hard hat and a pair of dungarees. Or a boiler suit.'

'My days of ostentatious feminism are long gone.' Tate tugged the
bottom of her jumper over the waistband of her black drainpipe jeans
and lifted a rubber-soled foot in the air. 'At least I remembered the
sensible shoes.' She collapsed onto a sofa. 'When I decamped to the
hotel I didn't pack with a covert operation in mind. I left my place a bit
of hurry, if you remember.'

Pete wandered into the room, his face set in a grimace.

'Are you sure you're up for this?' Tate asked him.

'He wants to do the right thing.' Caroline rested a hand on his arm
and felt the tension in his muscles.

'I'm as up for it as I need to be,' he said.

Caroline squeezed his arm and smiled up at him. *Come on, Pete.*

Tate pulled a slim silver flask from her bag and unscrewed the cap.
'Dutch courage, anyone?'

Pete held up a hand, glancing at Caroline. Caroline shook her head.

'Drinking on my own again – it's enough to give a girl a reputation.'
She took a long slug and carefully stoppered the flask. 'Now, are we all
clear exactly what we've got to do?' She looked from Pete to Caroline. A
phone started ringing. 'Sorry. I thought I'd turned them all off.' She
pulled four mobile phones from her bag and rejected three of them.

'Who's this?'

Pete looked at his watch and shifted from one foot to the other.

'How did you get this number?' Tate looked up at Caroline and
shrugged.

Pete moved towards the door. 'I'll just check I've got all my stuff.'

'Oh… I see,' Tate said quietly into the phone. She gestured for
Caroline to join her on the sofa. 'When did this happen?' She checked
her watch. 'I didn't really know him that well at all.' She stared at
Caroline, her face darkening. 'Are you treating it as a murder enquiry?'

Caroline swallowed and watched Tate pull her notepad from her bag.

'How long will that take?' Tate turned to Caroline and raised her
eyebrows. 'Yes – yes of course.' She flipped back through the pages of
her notepad. 'Her name's Betty – yes. It's 29 Bayer House, Culver
Estate, E2 1EU.' She scribbled a note in her pad. 'Thank you officer –
I'll call you back just as soon as I can.' She ended the call and stared at
her phone.

'Bad news, I take it?' Caroline asked.

Tate unstoppered her flask and took another swig. 'I suppose we should be grateful the Met aren't as joined up as they say they are, otherwise they might be swooping down on me right now.'

'What's happened?'

'That was Bethnal Green police station.' She sniffed. 'Freddie Larson's body was discovered early this morning. The police found an empty syringe lying next to his body. And my business card in his pocket.' She pulled apart the back of her mobile phone and slipped the SIM card from its slot. 'Has your Pete got something in his toolbox I can use to smash this up?'

As planned, Pete took the slip road off the M25 at junction 28. Caroline peered through a gap in the plywood partition that separated the front of the van from the storage area in the back. Crouching uncomfortably next to Tate, wedged between reels of electric cable and panels of plasterboard, she watched as Pete conscientiously checked wing mirrors and indicated in plenty of time as he took the fourth exit on the roundabout.

'You still OK back there?' he shouted.

Caroline glanced at Tate, who shifted on her hips and gave her the thumbs up.

'We'll survive.'

'Not long now – traffic's really light. Wish it was like this every day of the week.'

Caroline pressed her back against the wall of the van and tried to get more comfortable. They'd moved from the cab into the back at Thurrock services, only two junctions ago, but already her spine was aching and she had the beginnings of cramp in both feet.

'Whatever happens,' Pete said, 'don't do anything until I thump three times on the door. If you don't hear me, just sit tight.' Pete's voice was modulating like a teenage boy's. Caroline hadn't heard him this nervous since he stood next to her at Lewisham register office 24 years ago.

'It's all right, Pete. We've been though it enough times. We'll wait for your signal.' She smiled at Tate, who had once again retrieved the silver flask from her bag. 'I'm surprised you've got any of that left.'

'I'm only allowing myself medicinal-size sips.' Tate lifted the flask to her lips and sank a mouthful.

Caroline pulled her mobile from her bag and punched in her mother's new number. After a few rings the call went to voicemail. She tried Claire's phone. Claire answered straightaway.

'Hi Mum.'

'Why isn't your gran picking up?'

'Isn't she?' Claire seemed to hesitate.

'Are you all right, love?'

'Yeah.'

'Can you put her on?'

'She's not here.'

'Where is she?'

'She er... went to the shops.'

'Is everything OK?'

'Yes. I expect she's driving – that's why she hasn't answered.'

'That doesn't usually stop her.' Caroline switched the phone to her other ear and leaned away from Tate. 'How's Ben?'

'He's fine.'

'And Dan?'

There was another hesitation.

'Claire?'

'Fine.'

'Put him on.'

'He's... still in bed.'

'Make sure he doesn't stay there all day. I love you, sweetheart.'

'Me too.'

The van broke sharply and Caroline and Tate slammed back into the partition.

'Sorry about that,' Pete shouted. 'Stupid bugger in front of me decided to slow down for no reason. Only about five minutes now.'

Caroline peered through the little gap and spotted a dark saloon bumping along the track ahead of them.

'Where does this road lead to?'

'Just the yard. And the trade entrance to the mansion.'

Caroline watched the car accelerate away. 'Mansion?'

'Yeah, the Larsons practically live over the shop.'

Caroline turned back to Tate. 'Did you know they lived so close to the office?'

Tate shrugged. 'I've only been here once before – to interview Valerie Larson. We didn't really have a chance to make small talk about her domestic arrangements.'

'That car's just turned left,' Pete said. 'It must be going to the house.'

A few minutes later the van was slowing down.

'Right – this is it,' Pete shouted. 'Radio silence until I tell you otherwise.'

'Aye aye cap'n.' Tate slipped the flask back into her bag. Caroline thought she spotted a slight shaking in Tate's hand as it re-emerged.

The van stopped and Pete was saying something Caroline couldn't make out. Then she heard the mumble of another voice quickly fade. They were on the move again. She let out a breath and Tate did the same.

'First hurdle,' Tate whispered.

The van turned in a wide circle and stopped again. This time the engine was turned off. The driver door opened and clunked shut. Caroline tensed and waited for Pete's signal. It didn't come. She glanced at Tate, who shrugged back at her. She strained to listen for movement outside and heard the crunch of feet on gravel. Then low voices. Two, maybe three men talking to Pete, standing right next to the van. More gravel crunching followed, then the driver door opened and closed again. The engine coughed into life. They were on the move, reversing. Another circle and the engine died. There was a sudden thunk against the back doors. Caroline jumped. Another two thumps and one door swung open. Pete appeared in the gap, smiling at her.

'We're all set,' he said.

'Are there many people about?'

'More than I was expecting for a bank holiday. Lots of faces I don't recognise. More security than usual too. We'll just have to be careful. Take everything nice and slow.' He dragged a heavy toolbox from the back of the van. 'Do you need a hand getting out?'

Neither of them answered. They shuffled forward, crouching low, and dropped from the back of the van without resorting to clasping Pete's outstretched hand. Pete had backed the van right up to the entrance of a single storey Portakabin. With the van doors open they were shielded from view. Caroline followed Pete and Tate through the main door.

Tate looked around the reception area. 'They've painted since I was last here.'

Pete ducked behind the desk and opened a drawer. He pulled out a big bunch of tiny keys and threw them on the desk; they landed with a clank next to a bone china mug, sending the contents slopping over the side. Caroline hurried to the desk and picked up the keys. She put the back of her hand against the mug. It was warm.

'We've got company.'

Caroline followed Tate down a narrow corridor leading to an oak door standing ajar at the other end. Tate reached the door and looked over her shoulder at Caroline. Caroline nodded back. They both waited for a moment, just listening. Then Tate pushed the door wide. The room was empty. Caroline exhaled.

'Thank God for that.' Tate whispered. 'Hopefully Valerie Larson will be too busy nursing her sick husband to come in on a bank holiday.'

Just as Caroline was easing the door back to its original position, she heard Pete's voice. He was shouting.

'Hello, Shirley!'

Too loud. Stay calm, Pete.

'They got you in on a bank holiday too?' Whatever Shirley said in reply, it was too quiet to make out. Caroline stepped away from the door and looked around the room. At the far end a bank of flat screen monitors were stacked one on top of the other. All the screens were blank. Running from the door to the monitors was a long line of wooden filing cabinets, three drawers in each. She loosened her grip on the bunch of keys Pete had given her and glanced down at them. None of the keys was labelled. She closed her eyes and inhaled slowly. Tate jabbed an elbow into her arm.

'How good is Pete at keeping sour-faced old women entertained?'

'He can turn on the charm when he has to.'

'Let's hope he's Shirley's type.'

47

Three cabinets down and ten more still to check, Caroline was beginning to lose heart. The thought of Pete chatting up some strange woman down the other end of the corridor had sparked a twinge of jealousy she was amazed still existed. She closed another drawer and pulled open the one beneath.

'So what's this Shirley woman like?' she whispered.

'Now's not the time.' Tate didn't look up. She flicked through the file she was holding and slotted it back in a drawer.

'I just want to know what we're up against.'

'She's officious and rude.' Tate pulled out another file. 'Actually, that's not strictly accurate. She was only obnoxious to me. As soon as some hulking great construction worker came in she was all smiles and batted eyelids.'

'Great.'

'Your Pete scrubs up OK. Hopefully he'll keep her distracted.' She nodded to the open cabinet in front of Caroline. 'Still no joy?'

Caroline shook her head. She leafed through another folder.

The women continued to work in silence, the only sound the gentle click of a catch as a drawer opened or closed. Caroline stretched her arms and unkinked her back. She rolled her head from one side to the other.

Then she froze.

Her phone was ringing, loud and insistent. She ran across the room and leapt onto her bag to muffle the sound and located the mobile in an outside pocket. She stared at the flashing message on the little screen telling her Dan was calling and looked desperately at the keypad trying to remember which was the call answer button. She found it and lifted the phone to her ear. There was no sound from the other end.

'Dan?'

Tate was waving at her from the other side of the room. She pointed at the door and dragged a finger across her throat. Caroline threw up her free hand and desperately scanned the room for a nook or niche to hide herself in. She could hear Pete's voice, begging Shirley to come back. Then footsteps thundering down the corridor.

The door swung open. Caroline stood facing the receptionist, her phone still clamped to her ear.

'Who the hell are you?' The receptionist took a step into the room towards Caroline, then turned abruptly at the sound of Tate clearing her throat. 'What is this?' She stared hard into Tate's face. 'I know you.'

The door slammed shut. Pete edged himself towards Shirley, blocking off her exit.

'What's going on, Pete?' The receptionist took a step backwards.

'Sorry, Shirley. You should have stayed in reception.' He moved in closer. Again Shirley backed away from him.

Tate dragged a chair from the other side of the room. 'Sit down, Shirley.'

The woman spun round to face her. 'What do you think you're doing with those files? That's confidential information.'

'I should bloody well hope it is.' Tate gestured to the chair. 'Come on, play nice and we can all get along splendidly. Sit down!'

Shirley glanced at Pete, who was still covering the door, and made a quick lunge towards the desk, stretching out an arm for the telephone on the far side. Tate got to it before her and yanked the cord from its base. She shook her head.

'I do so wish you hadn't done that.'

Pete grabbed Shirley's arms from behind. She tried to wriggle free. 'Please, Shirley,' he said. 'I don't want to hurt you.' He looked up imploringly at Caroline. 'I can lock her in one of the other rooms, if you like. Keep her out of the way.'

Shirley stamped hard on Pete's foot and tried to pull away.

Tate moved the chair closer. 'No – I want her where I can see her.'

Pete returned to guard duty on reception and between them Caroline and Tate secured the receptionist to the metal-framed chair with a combination of computer cables and phone leads. Tate tugged hard on the final cable.

'You're going to be in so much trouble for this.' Shirley was practically snarling at her.

'I'll jump off that bridge when I come to it. Now where was I?' She turned round and faced the bank of lifeless television screens. 'How do you switch this lot on?' She spun back to Shirley. 'Where's the power button?'

The receptionist turned her face away.

'OK, fine – I'll find it for myself.'

While Tate inspected the panel of monitors, Caroline went back to the files. She'd reached as far as the L's. Before she tucked her phone away in a pocket, she punched in Dan's number. After half a dozen rings the voicemail service kicked in. She hung up without leaving a message, not wanting to be accused of fussing. She lifted out the next hanging file from the run and leafed through the contents.

'Finally!' Tate said.

Caroline looked up to see the monitors had all flickered into life. Tate stood back and scanned them. 'Good God – there's an army of security out there.' She shuddered. 'Come and have a look at this. Jean's mob haven't organised another demo, have they?'

Caroline hurried over to the five rows of CCTV screens and checked each one. All but two of the 20 displays seemed to be monitoring various parts of the yard, including the gates at the entrance and the outside of the reception block. Each image featured at least two heavy-set security guards, sipping hot drinks from polystyrene cups or smoking cigarettes. The two monitors on the right in the middle row were displaying images from somewhere outside the complex. One showed another set of gates, these ones made of ornately decorated ironwork, rather than the galvanised steel of the yard gates, and the other featured a columned portico around a grand front door. The bonnet of a dark green car was just visible in the bottom corner of the screen.

'The Larson mansion?' Caroline said.

Tate nodded. 'I can't imagine what else it could be. I'm surprised there isn't a camera set up right next to Sir Fred's sick bed, just so Valerie can keep her beady eye on him.'

On another of the screens Caroline noticed a guard with his arms outstretched. He play-punched his colleague on the arm and set off in the direction of the camera.

'We should get back to it,' Caroline said and returned to the open drawer.

'Now, Shirley.' Tate approached the receptionist. 'Where can I find information about all of Sir Fred's subsidiary companies? Would it be under 'S' for sub-contractors? Or 'T' for tax evasion?'

The receptionist huffed out a breath.

'Please yourself – I'll just carry on working through the alphabet until something turns up.'

'You should leave now – while you've still got the chance.' The woman glanced at the security system monitors.

'Thanks for your concern – but I think we've got it under control.' Tate returned to the cabinets and plucked out a handful of files. 'These don't seem to be labelled using any kind of logic.'

Caroline was making good progress. She was already halfway through the O's. She lifted out a thick folder from the back of the drawer and peered at the label: *Out of court settlements*. She quickly scanned the contents.

'OK – this is something,' Caroline said. Tate stopped what she was doing. 'Records of all the compensation requests for the workers who were injured and the families of the men who died.'

Tate hurried over to her and glanced at the paperwork. 'Fantastic! See what I mean, though? You would have thought that'd be filed under 'C' for compensation.' She went back to her own drawer. 'Oh fuck this.' She wrenched open a random drawer and stared down at the files inside. 'Looks like I wasn't so far off the mark after all.' She lifted out an armful of folders. 'Seems 'T' *is* for tax.' She dumped the folders on top of the cabinet and fanned them out.

Caroline heard a scuffling noise behind her. She turned to see Shirley trying to get to her feet, the chair lifting off the ground like an awkward pack attached to her back.

'Sergei!' the woman shouted.

Caroline followed her gaze and spotted a security guard running up the steps to their building. She shoved a hand over the receptionist's mouth and forced her to sit back down. Then she held her breath and listened.

'Hello, mate.' Pete's voice, too loud again. 'No, I'm waiting for Shirley to come back. I'd try again later if I were you.'

Shirley screamed into Caroline's hand. The sound came out as a muffled groan.

'There's nothing to see down there.' Pete sounded panicked.

There was a crash followed by a thud. Caroline and Tate looked at one another, unable to move. Caroline sucked in a breath and let it out again, she pressed harder against Shirley's mouth. Then she heard a loud grunt. It sounded like Pete. A scraping noise followed, getting louder, approaching the office. Caroline braced herself. Then let out another breath.

Pete appeared at the door, bent over, gripping a thick ankle of meaty security guard in each hand. 'He weighs a ton.' Pete dragged him through the doorway and into the room, finally dumping him against the wall opposite the filing cabinets. 'He shouldn't get in your way there.'

'What did you do to him?'

Pete screwed up his face. 'It was a rubber mallet – he should be all right. He's still breathing.' His hands were shaking as he bent over and checked the man's pockets. 'God almighty.' Pete stretched a sleeve over his hand and pulled something from inside the guard's jacket. He held out his hand, a heavy revolver dangling from his fingers.

'Oh my God! Put it down!'

He scanned the room. 'Where?'

Caroline ran to a cabinet she'd already searched and yanked open a drawer. Pete laid the gun carefully inside and she locked the cabinet, slipping the key into a pocket. 'We should leave,' she said.

Shirley started to rock her chair from side to side; she took a deep breath and screamed.

'For fuck's sake.' Tate wrenched the scarf from her hair, tied a thick knot in the middle of it and marched over to Shirley. 'Pete! Hold her still.' She waited for Pete to steady the back of the bucking chair and shoved the knot into Shirley's mouth, then secured both ends behind the woman's head. Shirley moaned and saliva seeped through the material.

'Hermes.' Tate shook her head. 'What a terrible bloody waste.' She hurried back to the files on top of the cabinet. 'Pete – you stay outside in reception. We'll keep an eye on the monitors and shout if anyone gets anywhere near.' She flicked through the first two files then discarded them. The third she took more time over. Caroline was trying to simultaneously watch Shirley, Tate, and the monitors, while checking more files herself.

'Bloody hell.' Tate flicked through a thick pile of paperwork. 'Details of donations and loans made to political parties going back ten years. I'll leave you to guess which party got the bulk of the money. I'm sure not all of that was officially declared.' She reached the bottom of the stack of papers. 'Oh this just gets better. One of Larson's companies has donated funds to England for the English.'

Caroline stopped what she was doing. 'That's enough now, isn't it? We should call it a day.' She glanced up at the monitors then down at the unconscious security guard. She watched him until she was certain he was still breathing. 'We shouldn't push our luck.'

Tate leafed through more pages. 'Shame there's nothing here proving Barry Flowers' connection with the gang of Nazi thugs. Jason's investigations seem to have been in vain.'

'Come on,' Caroline said. 'Let's just go.'

'Ten more minutes. We can't walk away from all of this.' Angela Tate turned back to the open drawer. 'There's still so much stuff we haven't even touched.'

The security guard started to moan. Tate stuck her head into the corridor and shouted for Pete. 'And bring something to tie him up with.' She walked the length of the cabinets and stopped at the last one. She kicked the bottom of the drawer. 'There wasn't a key for this one, was there?'

'No – 12 keys and 13 cabinets.'

Tate marched over to the gagged receptionist. 'Where's the key, Shirley?'

Shirley turned her face away.

'I don't have time for this.' She barged past Pete coming through the door, and disappeared down the corridor. She returned a few moments later wielding a crowbar and a hammer.

'What are you going to do to her?' Caroline put herself between Tate and Shirley.

'Nothing!' Tate said. 'I'm getting the bloody drawers open.'

Caroline stepped back and watched Tate go at the cabinet, keeping an eye on the monitors at the same time. Pete's offer of help was dismissed, Tate sending him back out to reception with a wave of her hand.

There was movement on one of the television screens. Then the one next to it. The dark green sedan that had been sitting on the gravel drive outside the Larson mansion was on the move. The wrought iron gates opened and the car swept out. Caroline couldn't make out who was inside. The car disappeared from view.

Tate let out a loud grunt. The crowbar flipped into the air and clattered onto the floor. The top drawer was open. Caroline peered inside as Tate shoved in a hand. The hanging files inside took up only half the space, but each one was stuffed with paperwork. Tate pulled out all the files and spread them across the floor. Caroline closed the drawer and quickly checked the ones beneath. They were both empty.

Shirley started moaning, her eyes wide as she stared down at the files.

Tate flung open the first file and handed another to Caroline. Caroline laid the paperwork on the desk and continued to glance up at the monitors every few seconds.

'Bloody hell.' Tate waved a sheet of paper at her. 'Freddie Larson's blood test wasn't for Hep C after all. These are DNA results requested by Valerie Larson.' Tate shoved the sheet to one side.

Caroline blew out a breath and stared down at the uppermost piece of paper on the desk. It was a formal letter printed on expensive thick paper, from a pastor in Kentucky. She scanned the contents quickly and moved on to the sheet below. Both documents were letters of gratitude thanking Sir Fred for his generous donations to their ministries. She checked a third and a fourth, again both expressed enormous gratitude, both were sent from churches in America.

'I think we may have found proof of Sir Fred's creationist tendencies,' she said. 'We should definitely go now. We really do have enough.'

Tate didn't respond. She was sitting on her haunches staring open-mouthed at a collection of black and white ten by eight inch photographs spread across the floor.

Caroline crouched down next to her.

'What is it?'

Still Tate said nothing.

Caroline peered at the photos. She blinked and sucked in a breath. One of the pictures showed a naked man half submerged at the end of a large swimming pool, his mouth gaping. In another the same man lay stretched out on a towel or blanket by the side of the pool. A uniformed policeman was standing next to the body.

Caroline pointed towards the image. 'Is that...?'

Tate nodded. 'PC Barry Flowers.' She slipped a photograph from a stack. 'Look at this.'

The picture was taken from another angle, lower down. The stark white corpse was clearly visible in the foreground. Just behind the body, sitting on the edge of a sunlounger, was a wide-eyed man. Next to him a woman gripped tightly onto his arm. Caroline peered more closely at the photograph.

'Oh my God.' She looked up at Tate, who nodded again. 'I don't believe it,' she said. Caroline sucked in a breath and let the photograph of a terrified Rachael Oakley and William King fall out of her hands.

48

Pete cheerily shouted goodbye to someone and eased the van through the yard gates. They drove along the bumpy track for five minutes before he said another word.

'Are you all right back there?'

Tate answered for them both. 'We'll survive. Just stop as soon as it's safe to let us out.'

They bounced down the road for another ten minutes before the van finally turned and came to a halt.

'Bloody hell! I'll have to stop somewhere else. Just sit tight.'

The engine started up again and Pete crunched the gear stick into reverse, backed up a few feet then stopped again.

Caroline heard him winding down his window. She eased out a breath and closed her eyes. As soon as she did the scenes captured in the black and white photographs crowded in on her.

'Sorry, officer,' Pete said. 'Took a wrong turn. What's going on?'

'What have you got in the back?'

Caroline clenched her fists and held her breath.

'Just some building gear.'

'Working on a bank holiday?'

'Actually I'm just on my way home – I'm running a bit late.'

An agonising few seconds of silence followed.

'All right, sir. Move along.'

The van accelerated backwards, the engine complaining all the way. Pete swung back round and they were bouncing along the track again. Caroline finally released the breath she'd been holding.

'What was all that about?' Tate shouted after a few moments.

'Field full of police vans – must have been a dozen of them – riot gear, the lot.'

'In the middle of Essex?' Tate turned to Caroline. 'Maybe Jean's little gang have got a demo organised and someone's tipped off the police.'

Caroline shrugged.

After another ten minutes the van stopped again and Pete opened up the back.

Tate waited by the passenger door for Caroline to slide onto the seat next to Pete. She was clutching a thick pile of files close to her chest, another few were stuffed into the bag over her shoulder. Caroline stared at the bag.

'Oh!' She lifted a hand to her mouth. 'I left my bag in the office.'

'We can't exactly go back for it,' Tate said.

'It had my purse inside – my house keys, my mobile.' She pressed a hand against her pocket and lifted out a mobile phone. 'The other phone, the one you gave me, was inside.'

'Shirley knows Pete, she knows me. It's not like we were anonymous in there. Leaving your bag's not going to make any difference either way.'

The phone in Caroline's hand started to ring.

'Claire?'

There was silence the other end.

'What is it, sweetheart?'

'Gran's gone.'

A cold wave of dread swept up Caroline's back and across her shoulders.

'What do you mean, love?'

'She went out and she hasn't come back.'

Thank God. 'Have you tried calling her?'

'She's not answering.'

'Maybe she got stuck in a big queue at the supermarket.'

'She didn't go to the supermarket.' Claire's voice was barely audible. 'She went out to look for Dan.'

'What do you mean?'

'Dan's gone too.'

'Where did he go?'

'He wouldn't say. He got a text and then stormed off.'

'From Kylie? She's the only one with his new number.'

'He's still got his old phone.'

Caroline closed her eyes. *Oh Dan.* 'Think, Claire. Where would he have gone?' She could hear her daughter breathing noisily into the phone.

'I'm really worried. Gran was really in a mood this morning – she said she hadn't slept all night, because she'd forgotten her tablets.'

'Her tablets?'

'Her sleeping pills.'

Caroline's breath caught in her throat. 'Forgotten them or lost them?'

'She left them at home. Dan said he'd go back and get them for her – take the train. She told him not to worry about it, she said she'd have a glass of wine tonight instead.'

'Do you think that's where he's gone – to get Gran's pills?'

'Are you at home now? I tried phoning but nobody answered.'

'Your dad and me are on our way.'

'You need to hurry. I think he might be… I don't know.'

'What is it, Claire?'

Pete glanced at her. He put a hand on her leg.

'There's stuff going on with him at the moment…'

'Has something happened with Kylie?'

Claire was breathing noisily into the phone again. 'I promised him I wouldn't say anything. He told me he was going to sort it out on his own.'

'The baby? Is she going to have the baby?'

'Oh Mum! You didn't really believe any of that, did you?'

Caroline put her hand over Pete's and squeezed his fingers tight.

'Dan and Kylie aren't together. Not like that, anyway. He hangs around with her, but that's just because he fancies her boyfriend.'

She must have misheard. 'What was that?'

'He fancies Chris – Kylie's boyfriend.'

'Of course he doesn't. Dan's not like that.' Caroline took a moment longer to process the information. 'I'd be able to tell.'

'Well you didn't. And he is.'

Caroline squeezed Pete's hand harder. She stared through the windscreen without really seeing anything. How could Dan be gay?

'Mum? Are you still there?'

'I can't… I can't take it in. If you're right, why did Kylie say the baby—'

'Because her boyfriend's black and her dad's the biggest racist ever. Kylie's really scared of him.'

'I'm not surprised she's scared.' *I'd be bloody scared.* 'Claire – do you know anything about the cuts and bruises Dan's been picking up recently?'

Claire didn't reply.

'Claire?'

'Sorry… I can't…' She let out a long sigh. 'I promised not to say—'

'He's missing again, Claire – don't you think you need to tell me everything you know?'

Claire sucked in a rattling breath.

'Come on, Claire. You're not betraying Dan. You're helping him.'

'He's being bullied.' Claire blurted out the words. 'Online, mostly. And boys from his school are sending him gross photos on his mobile and calling him a paedo. Some of the girls too.'

'Paedo?'

'He went out with a boy in year nine last year. God – he was only a couple of months younger than Dan. I didn't realise anyone was actually beating him up until yesterday.'

'Beating him up?'

'Oh God – he's gonna go mad when he finds out I've told you.'

'Why didn't you tell me before?'

'Dan made me swear not to.'

'For God's sake, Claire. Can't you make your own decisions?' Her voice was louder and harsher than she'd meant.

Pete looked at her again. 'Do you want me to pull over?' he said.

'It's not my fault – don't shout at me.' Claire sobbed.

'I'm sorry. Listen – you've got to be honest with me now. Do you think Dan is going to do something... anything—'

'He might... I don't know.' Claire sobbed again. 'If he finds Gran's pills...'

'It'll be all right, I promise. I'm going to call Dan now. I want you to dial 999 and tell the police about Dan and your gran. Can you do that?'

Claire sniffed. 'Yes.'

'Are you sure Dan's headed back home?'

'I think so.'

'I want you to stay right where you are, in case Dan or your gran comes back. Just sit tight. OK?'

The line went quiet.

'Claire? Are you still there?'

'I thought I heard a noise.'

'Is it Dan? Is he back?'

Claire let out a loud shriek.

'Claire! What is it?'

'A window smashed. I think someone's trying to get in.'

She screamed again.

'Call the police, Claire – right now!'

The line went dead.

'Claire!'

'What is it?' Pete was indicating and slowing down.

'Don't stop!' Caroline punched Dan's number into her phone. It went straight to voicemail. 'You've got to get to the chalet. I need to get home. Is there somewhere round here I can pick up a cab?' She jabbed three nines into her phone.

'The mainline station – we're probably ten minutes away. What's going on, Caz?'

'Police.' Caroline shouted into the phone. 'Hello? An intruder is trying to attack my children. 14 Sheridan Court, Leysdown… What? I don't know the fucking post code.'

The van lurched forward as Pete stamped on the accelerator.

'No – I'm not calling from that address. For God's sake – you've got to get someone out there right now. Thank you.'

She hung up and dialled again, this time telling another police dispatcher about Dan. Pete leaned over the steering wheel, as if he was willing the van to move faster.

'We can't get stopped for speeding,' Tate said.

Caroline had almost forgotten the journalist was in the van with them. 'She's right – we don't want to get pulled over. Stick to the limit.'

'Fuck that.' Pete checked his mirrors. 'I know these roads. I'll slow down when I have to.'

The Nokia ringtone chimed from inside Tate's bag.

'What the…? No one has that number except you,' Tate said.

'The mobile you gave me was in my bag… back in Larson's office.'

Tate pulled the files from her bag and fished around inside. 'I thought I'd switched it to silent.' She stared at the screen then glanced at Caroline.

'Answer it!' Caroline urged.

'Hello. Who is this?'

Caroline leaned her head towards Tate's ear. There was silence at the other end. Then a clanking sound. A muffled voice started to speak.

'I'm calling from er… what's her name?' A woman's voice. 'Mrs Barber's phone. Who am I speaking to?'

'I asked you first.' Tate hit a button and held the mobile in front of her mouth. The hiss and crackle of heavy breathing rattled out of the phone's tiny speaker.

'I'm trying to contact Mrs Barber? Or her husband? He was a recent employee of ours.'

Caroline glanced at Pete who mouthed the word 'Larson'.

'They have some property of mine,' Valerie Larson said.

'I don't know what you're talking about.'

'Perhaps you could pass on a message?'

'Sorry, I've never heard of them.'

'Oh that's a shame. You see, I really need to speak to one of them. Quite urgently.'

Caroline locked eyes with Tate.

300

Valerie Larson cleared her throat. 'If you do happen to run into them, would you tell them something for me?'

'You're wasting your time.'

'Oh I doubt that.'

There was mumbling in the background. Caroline couldn't make out what was being said.

'If you see them, tell them their children say hello... Ben... and ... Claire, is it?'

The line went dead.

Caroline snatched the phone from Tate and hit the redial button.

'She's bluffing,' Tate said and clutched the files closer to her chest.

The call was answered before it even rang out.

'Oh good – I have your attention now.'

'Let me speak to my children.'

'Mrs Barber? Bring those files back and I'll consider your request.'

Caroline looked at Pete. 'OK – we're about 30 minutes away from you, less than that, maybe. We'll bring all the files back. Just don't hurt them – please.'

The line went dead again.

Tate hadn't released her grip on the files.

'We've got to get back there.'

'She's bluffing,' Tate said again.

'For God's sake, Angela. I don't fucking care. I'm not prepared to take that chance.'

'But think of all the stuff we've found. We can finally get some justice for Martin. We can't just give back the evidence.'

'They have my children.'

'We don't know that.'

'For fuck's sake! I heard Claire screaming! Someone was breaking into the chalet.'

'Please, Caroline, you've got to trust me. Valerie Larson would try anything to—'

Caroline ignored her. 'How long before we get to the station?' she asked Pete.

'Five minutes.'

'OK – drop me there first. You take the files back, then get to the chalet. Keep trying Claire's phone. I'll keep trying Dan's.'

'Where are you going?' Tate had gathered up all the files in her arms and was clutching them even tighter.

'Home. Dan needs me.'

'Caroline – you're overreacting.'

The phone rang again – the number had been withheld. Caroline answered. 'Yes?'

'Mum?'

'Oh Claire, sweetheart. Are you OK? Have they hurt you? Is Ben all right?'

There was a pause. Then a man's voice.

'If I don't hear from my boss in half an hour, confirming her property is back safely, you won't get another chance to say goodbye.'

'For God's sake – we'll get there just as fast as we can! Please – don't hurt them.'

'Don't think about calling the police – if we see them anywhere near...'

The line died again. Caroline punched three nines into the phone.

'What's happening now, what are you doing?' Pete said.

'I've got to stop the police before they get to the chalet.'

Pete yanked the steering wheel hard and they swerved down another lane. Caroline saw a signpost for the station.

It was a mile and a half away.

49

Two uniformed security guards waved the van through the gates into the yard and Pete parked in the same spot he'd used earlier. Half a dozen thickset men in smart suits emerged from the building to greet them.

'No need for you to come in, Pete,' Angela said.

Caroline's husband swivelled in his seat and stared at her. 'You're fucking joking. No way. *You* stay in the van.' He reached for the files.

Angela held on to them. 'There's no telling what they might do to you. They could make it look like an accident.' She glanced at the small army surrounding the van. 'If anything happens to me while I'm in there it'd be much harder for them to explain.'

Come on, Pete. Trust me.

'Let me do this,' she said and grabbed the door handle.

Pete quickly leaned over and snatched her wrist. 'We'll go in together.'

Angela and Pete were escorted into reception, another six wide-necked men were waiting for them inside.

'I've never seen so many guards here before,' Pete whispered to her. 'Feels like something else is going on.'

'Maybe they are expecting another demo,' Angela whispered back.

Three men stepped to the left of the corridor leading to Valerie Larson's office, the other three to the right, creating an intimidating channel for Angela and Pete to walk through. Angela followed as slowly as she could behind Pete, still desperately trying to formulate a contingency plan.

Second rule of journalism – always have a Plan B.

She clung on to the files, wishing she'd thought to hide one or two in the back of the van without the Barbers noticing.

Two more muscle-bound giants in Armani suits flanked the oak door at the end of the corridor. One of them reached across and levered down the door handle. The thick panel of wood swung aside to reveal Valerie Larson at the far end of the room, sitting behind her desk, Shirley standing beside her. Larson looked at Pete and shook her head.

'Peter Barber?'

He nodded.

'Shirley tells me you're one of our best workers.'

Shirley was staring at him too, rubbing her wrist where the computer cables had bound her to the chair.

'One of our most *loyal* employees, apparently. Where did it all go wrong Peter?'

A guard drove a meaty fist into the small of Pete's back. He staggered into the middle of the room. Angela stayed just inside the door, clutching the files behind her back. Another guard grabbed her by the arm and dragged her forward, next to Pete.

Larson jumped out of her seat. 'Where's Mrs Barber?'

The two guards shrugged almost comically at one another.

Larson strode towards them. 'Where's your wife, Peter? Hiding out in the van? Did you think you could protect her from this?' She prodded a guard. 'Go and get her.'

'She's not here,' Pete said.

'What?'

'She had to deal with a family emergency.'

'A family emergency? Is she planning to single-handedly overpower the four men currently babysitting your children?' She snatched the files from Angela's arms and threw them on the desk. 'Is that all of them?'

Shirley sifted carefully through the pile and nodded.

'How do I know you haven't taken copies? How do I know that Mrs Barber doesn't have them on her right now?'

'Copies?' Angela said. 'When have we had time to make copies, for fuck's sake?'

'There's absolutely no need to use that kind of language with me.' She shook her head. 'Gutter mouth from the gutter press.'

'The *Evening News* is not—'

'Oh shut up! Don't you think your loyalty is a little... misplaced? I can't imagine it will save you from redundancy.'

'What?'

'I know all about your current... employment situation.'

Larson pointed towards a guard. 'Search the van.'

'You're wasting your time – there's nothing in there,' Pete said. 'There aren't any copies.'

'Give me your bag,' she barked at Angela.

Angela held on tight to her bag.

'Do you want to do this the painful way?' Valerie Larson nodded to one of the guards. A hand grabbed either side of the bag and wrenched it from Angela's arm, the straps scraping across her sweater and dragging at the flesh beneath.

'Easy!' Pete lurched towards the guard. Another came at him from behind and pinned his arms behind his back.

The first security man handed Angela's bag to his boss. Valerie Larson marched back to her desk, upended the bag and shook the contents free. Notebook, pens, wallet, glasses, hip flask and mobile phones all came clattering onto the desk. Larson flicked through the notebook of shorthand squiggles then discarded it. She snatched up each phone in turn and inspected it front and back.

'Check his pockets,' she shouted.

Immediately two guards started pawing at Pete. Reflexively, he threw up an elbow and caught one of the men in the face. The guard staggered back, holding his cheek. Pete swung quickly round and buried a fist into the other's stomach. Angela watched the action unfold as if it was happening in slow motion. What did he think he was doing? There were too many of them. She glanced up at the files on the desk. If she could just reach one document... slip it under her jumper.

It was too late.

Two more men ploughed into Pete, knocking him to the ground. A sharp-tipped boot struck him under the chin, snapping his head back.

'That's for Sergei,' the guard said.

The guard Pete had hit in the face moments before raised a fist and brought it thundering down into his chest.

'That's enough!' Larson yelled.

At once the men froze. One of them completed the task of checking Pete's pockets and deposited a wallet and mobile phone onto the desk, like a gun dog obediently dropping a grouse. Larson checked the back of Pete's phone.

'If you've been lying to me...' She hit a few buttons on the keypad, staring intensely at the small screen. 'How touching – so many portraits of his children.' She threw the phone on the desk. 'What about Mrs Barber's phone?'

'What about it?'

'How many of the documents did she photograph?'

Angela stared at Valerie Larson for a long moment. She had no idea Pete's phone had an in-built camera. If only she'd known that 40 minutes ago... She looked down at his body lying inert at her feet. A trickle of blood had oozed from his nose. She watched him until she was sure she saw his chest rise and fall.

Thank God.

'Did you hear me?' Larson strode towards her. 'His wife's phone?'

Angela pointed towards the desk. Her hand was shaking. 'You've got it. She left her phone behind, remember? You used it to call me.'

Larson snatched the bright pink phone from the desk and turned it over in her hands.

Shirley, who'd said nothing for the last five minutes, suddenly piped up. 'That's not her phone.' She waved a hand at her employer. 'I saw her with another phone when she was here. A black one.'

'So what?' Angela stepped forward. A restraining arm on her elbow held her back. She shook it free. 'I gave the other phone to Caroline – it's exactly the same as the one in your hands – just a different colour. It's a throwaway cheap phone. It doesn't have a camera. We didn't photograph the documents. Dear God, I only wish we had.' She took a step closer to Valerie Larson.

'You think I'm going to take your word for it?' Valerie Larson shook her head. 'Give me her number.'

Caroline was sitting in the back of the cab, willing the driver to go faster, when her mobile rang.

'Hello?' she said.

'Mrs Barber, where are you?'

'Has Pete arrived with the files? Are Ben and Claire all right? Tell me you've let them go.'

'I'm afraid I can't.'

'What? Where's my husband? He was on his way to you, I swear. Maybe he's had an accident.'

'I rather fear he has.'

Caroline's heart lurched upwards into her throat.

'What's happened? They were bringing the files back to you, honestly.'

'Oh they brought them back.'

'Then I don't understand. If you have—'

'What they didn't bring was you. Where are you, Mrs Barber?'

Caroline peered out of the cab window. 'It's hard to tell. We haven't crossed the QE2 bridge yet...' She leaned forward and stuck her face into the gap between the front seats. 'Where are we?'

'Just coming up to Thurrock services,' the driver said.

'Thurrock,' Caroline shouted into the phone. 'What does it matter where I am? You have your files back. Call off your men.'

'If only it were that simple.'

'I want to speak to my husband.'

'That won't be possible.'

'Why? What have you done to him?'

'I need you to come back here right now.'

'I can't – I've… I've got to get home.'

'A family emergency, I've been told.'

'That's right – my son… he's—'

306

'I'm not interested in the details, Mrs Barber. You come back here right now, or I'll tell my men in Sheppey to take care of your children. Permanently.'

Valerie Larson hung up.

Caroline stared at the phone for a moment, unable to do anything else, her head so full she couldn't concentrate. She drew in a long breath. Exhaled. She quickly tapped in Dan's number. His mobile rang and rang until the call was diverted to voicemail.

'Stop the car!' she shouted.

The driver looked at her in his rear-view mirror.

'I said stop the car!'

'I can't just—'

'Pull over onto the hard shoulder. Now!'

The car indicated and pulled in.

'If you're going to be sick—'

'For fuck's sake, shut up. I need to think.'

Caroline put a cold hand across her forehead and closed her eyes. She tried to assemble the facts as calmly as she could. But her mind wouldn't settle. How could she choose between going home to Dan or saving Ben and Claire? She called Valerie Larson.

'I do hope you're phoning to let me know you're on your way. Otherwise you're wasting precious time, Mrs Barber.'

'Why do you need me there?'

'It's a matter of trust, and quite frankly, I don't trust you, your husband or the people you choose to associate with. Especially not them.' Valerie Larson let out a long sigh.

'Please – you don't understand. I can't come back. Not right now. I need to get home. My son... I have to make sure he's safe.'

'What about your daughter, Mrs Barber? What about your other son? What about their safety?'

'Please. Don't make me choose like this. I can't... I can't choose.' Caroline stared out of the window. A lorry thundered past. The cab rocked.

'You have 30 minutes to get back here.'

'Please – please don't do this. You would understand if you...' She swallowed. 'I am begging you. Please. Don't make me do this. I'll come back just as soon I can. You have my word.'

'Your word means nothing to me. Do you understand? You're wasting time. Don't call again – not if you want to see your children alive.'

She hung up.

'It's dangerous just parked up like this, you know.' The cab driver turned awkwardly in his seat. 'We're like sitting ducks. Anything could ram into the back of us.'

'Shut up!'

Caroline's mobile rang again. A number she didn't recognise.

'Mrs Barber?'

'Yes – who is this?'

'I'm the duty sergeant at Lewisham police station.'

Caroline swallowed. *Thank God.* 'Did you find Dan? Is he OK?'

'The officers we sent to your home have just called in. There's no sign of your son at the premises.'

'They went inside?'

'The officers were unfortunately obliged to force entry into the property. You did agree to that, I believe?'

'Yes, yes. Did they check all the rooms?'

'A thorough search was completed, madam. The house was unoccupied.'

'Unoccupied? When was this?'

He hesitated; she heard the rustling of paper. 'About 20 minutes ago.'

'But Dan might have turned up in the last 20 minutes. Get them to check again – they need to stay there until—'

'We don't have the resources for that kind of operation, madam.'

'But I think he's going to harm himself.'

She heard an exasperated sigh on the other end of the line.

'I'm sorry, madam, with the best will in the world—'

Caroline hung up. She swallowed down a sob, her chest heaved.

The driver was staring at her again. 'If you are going to be sick, you should—'

'Shut up!'

She redialled the police station. 'Put me through to Ralph Mills – it's urgent.'

'Can I take your name, madam?

'Caroline Barber. Please hurry.'

'I'm afraid DC Mills is not available at the moment. He's not due back in until later this afternoon. Can I take a message?'

'Please tell him to go to my house. As soon as he can.'

Caroline ended the call and sank back into her seat. She took a deep breath and closed her eyes. Her chest shuddered as she exhaled. After a few moments she opened her eyes and met the cab driver's gaze in the rear-view mirror.

'Start the car.'

50

'He needs an ambulance.' Angela Tate knelt down next to Pete. The blood oozing from his nose had turned into a steady trickle. His breathing was shallow. Too shallow. 'I said he needs an ambulance!'

Valerie Larson ignored her.

'Do you want another death on your premises? Call a fucking ambulance!'

Shirley moved towards them then stopped. She turned and looked at her boss. When the almost imperceptible nod came from Valerie Larson, the receptionist rushed to Pete and sank to her knees. She lowered her head to his mouth and held a finger up to Angela to stop her talking.

'His airways aren't blocked – he's still breathing.' She looked up at one of the security guards. 'Help me turn him.'

'Stop! You might do even more damage.' Angela pulled the woman's hand away from Pete's chin.

'I'm St John Ambulance trained – I know what I'm doing.' Shirley wrangled her wrist from Angela's grasp.

'Trained… you? Is that the company's one concession to health and safety?'

'I don't know what you're talking about,' she said.

Between them, Shirley and the gorilla in the suit turned Pete onto his side into the recovery position.

'You know exactly what I'm talking about. How can you live with yourself? Turning a blind eye to every cut corner, to every accident and incident. How do you sleep at night?' Angela stood over her. 'What has Larson promised you? Eh? Whatever it is, it can't be enough.'

The woman dusted down her skirt as she got to her feet, taking great pains to avoid eye contact with Angela.

'Do you have kids, Shirley?'

She didn't answer.

'What if it was one of them? What if a son of yours lost his life because of the sloppy work practices here?'

Shirley froze. Finally Angela seemed to be getting to her.

'Imagine that for a moment and see how easy it is to carry on lying for them, covering up their crimes.'

The receptionist grabbed Angela's arms and shook her. 'You don't know anything, so why don't you just shut your mouth?' She hurried behind the desk and stood beside her boss.

'I don't know what you hoped to achieve with that little tirade, Miss Tate.' Valerie Larson opened a file on her desk. 'But I think we can assume you've failed.' She glanced up at the trembling woman standing next to her. 'For your information, Shirley lost her only child in Iraq five years ago.' She shook her head. 'Perhaps you should just sit down, keep your mouth shut and wait for your accomplice to return.' She peered at the clock. 'Although she is rapidly running out of time.'

One of the gorillas dragged a chair across the room and shoved Angela onto it.

'If my men don't get a call from me in the next 20 minutes—'

'Call your men now – Caroline needs more time.'

'Oh I don't think they'd appreciate being interrupted.'

Valerie Larson studied the contents of the file then snapped it shut. 'Freddie's DNA results are that interesting to you, are they?'

'Obviously not as interesting as they are to you.' Angela pointed to the file. 'I expect you've already had Sir Fred make a new will?'

'You're assuming Freddie was due to inherit in the first place.'

'Why else would you go to the trouble of getting a test done?'

'Well it's all academic now, isn't it? Given the fate that has befallen the little ingrate.'

'What? How do you know about that?'

Larson stared at Angela as if she was emitting a noxious smell and shifted in her seat. 'Merciful release, by all accounts.' She smiled.

Angela stood up and was quickly pushed back down by a guard. 'Arrogant bitch! You think you can get away with anything.'

'You know – I think I probably can.'

'I won't let that hap—'

A rasping, choking gurgle cut her off. Bubbles of blood foamed from Pete's mouth. Angela dropped off her chair and knelt beside him.

'For God's sake! He's dying. Now will you call an ambulance?'

Pete's chest heaved and the gurgling noise stopped.

'Do something!'

Shirley shoved her out of the way and hauled Pete over onto his back. She pressed her hand against his neck. 'Please, God,' she whispered. 'Not again.' She raised a hand and slammed it into his chest.

Angela watched helplessly as the slight receptionist pumped Pete's chest, four, five times, then pressed her mouth over his. Angela staggered back, her legs weak, her head buzzing. She got as far as the desk and sank onto the edge. In the distance, she thought she could hear the faint hum of an engine. 'Thank God.' She turned to Valerie Larson. 'Thank you.'

'What are you talking about?' Larson snapped at her, her expression one of irritation rather than concern.

'For calling the ambulance.'

'What ambulance?' Valerie Larson turned to the CCTV monitors.

The engine hum turned into a roar. Angela could make out two, maybe three separate vehicles. Then the sirens started up.

Three police vans appeared at the top left of the bank of monitors. Angela watched as they burst through the gates into the yard. Another two were parked up on the road outside the gates to the mansion.

'Sweet Christ... What the fuck?' Valerie Larson lunged towards the desk and snatched her bag and an armful of files, then flew across the room, knocking Pete's head with her foot as she went. She got as far as the door and stopped.

'Shirley! Leave him. We need to get out of here.'

Shirley stopped pumping Pete's chest, stared at her employer for a moment then pinched his nose between finger and thumb. She blew air into his mouth.

The clatter of boots on floorboards thundered up the corridor. Two uniformed police officers arrived at the door, their sheer bulk forcing Valerie Larson back into the room.

'Shit,' she said.

The officers stepped to one side to allow a man in a fluorescent jacket to pass. He flashed ID at Valerie Larson.

'Brian Nicholls, Her Majesty's Revenue and Customs.' He scanned the room.

'Please,' Angela said. 'We've got to get this man to hospital. He needs help.'

More uniformed policemen arrived at the door.

'Seize the documents. I need to speak to all Larson employees. No one leaves the premises.'

'Look at him!' Angela, with some effort, pushed herself off the desk, in the process slipping a file behind her back. 'We've got to get him proper medical attention.' She looked at Shirley. 'Is he breathing?'

'Barely,' Shirley said quietly.

'Can I borrow two of these officers?' Angela turned to the man in the fluorescent vest. 'We don't have time to wait for an ambulance now. I need help getting him into a van. I'll take him to the hospital myself.'

'I'll still need to speak to you.' The man from the Inland Revenue scrutinised her through his designer spectacles.

'Fine – you'll find me in A&E.'

Angela watched three policemen struggle to lift Pete off the floor and into the corridor. She followed them out. Someone coughed noisily behind her.

'Madam? I think you're forgetting something. No documents to leave the premises...'

Angela pushed the file at the nearest policeman without breaking her stride.

51

Police tape stretched right across Brownhill Road, flapping in the wind, beyond that two parked squad cars formed a roadblock. The whole of the high street had been cordoned off.

'This is as far as I can take you.' The cab driver swivelled in his seat. 'Sixty-eight quid.'

Caroline pulled all the notes she'd taken from Pete and Tate from her pocket and shoved them towards the driver. She jumped out of the cab and ran towards the cordon. She was still at least half a mile from home. A policeman held up his hands as she approached.

'Sorry, madam – I can't let you though.'

'I live here. I've got to get to my house.'

'We've evacuated the area. A major gas leak has been reported.'

'You don't understand – my son... he's ill. He needs me.'

Caroline tried to squeeze between a wooden barrier and the policeman. She felt a firm hand wrap round her arm, pulling her back.

'Please, madam. I don't want to have to arrest you.'

'I've got to get home.'

His grip tightened.

'Give me your address – I'll see if I can free up a couple of officers.'

'OK – I'll take them there.' She looked across the street and back again. 'Where are they?'

'I don't have the resources to do it right now.'

Caroline threw up her hands. 'There's no time.' She shook off his arm and ran back down the street, away from the cordon. She reached the junction and saw a line of stationary traffic blocking the next road. It looked like the whole area had been shut off. For a moment she imagined Dan lying in the kitchen, the oven door open, gas seeping through the whole house and out into the street.

Please God no.

She sucked in a breath and scanned the houses opposite. An old woman peered from her living room window at her. Caroline stared at her for a moment, then jabbed a finger towards the woman's front door. She ran to it and leaned on the bell. When the woman didn't respond straightaway she pounded her fist against the wood.

'All right, all right,' a voice muttered from inside.

The door opened slowly.

Caroline looked down to see the woman was leaning heavily on a walking stick.

'Police!' She flashed her mobile phone at the woman, hoping her eyes were as bad as her legs, and rushed down the hall towards a door at the end. The house was laid out just like hers. She flew through the kitchen and stopped at the back door. It was locked.

'What do you want?' The woman was making her way painfully slowly down the hall.

'Got to check all the gardens. I'll need the key for back door and the garden gate.'

Caroline lost precious seconds waiting for the old woman to find the keys. She grabbed them from her, unlocked the back door, darted across the lawn and unpadlocked the wooden gate. She left the key in the padlock and shouted over her shoulder.

'Don't forget to lock up after me!'

She hurtled down the alley that ran behind the houses, punching in the number of Dan's mobile as she went. For the first time, instead of going straight to voicemail, the call was answered after a single ring.

'Dan!'

All she could hear were the blasts of her own breath as she ran.

'Dan – are you all right?'

She reached the end of the alley and stopped. A faint rasp sounded in her ear. Then a louder, sharper noise, as if Dan was clucking his tongue against his teeth.

'Too late!'

A man's voice. *Him*? Her hand flew up to her mouth.

'Where's Dan?' she hollered into the phone. 'What have you—'

The line went dead.

Caroline willed her shaking legs forward, picking up speed until she got to the opening that led to her road. The street was empty. She ran right up the middle, past the abandoned houses, gasping for air with every step.

Finally her house came into view. She saw two figures standing in the front garden. She flew up the garden path and threw herself at the thick-necked man blocking the front door. He brushed her off like an annoying insect.

'Let me in!' She turned to the smiling man slouching against the window ledge.

'For fuck's sake, Prior! Let me into my house!' She pounded a fist into his chest. Immediately an enormous arm slipped across her throat, a crushing weight squeezing out the air.

'I'm so glad you could make it, Caroline,' Prior said. 'I'd almost given up on you.' He sniffed. 'Can you smell gas?' He sniffed again. 'No? That's strange, isn't it?'

Caroline struggled to free herself. She couldn't breathe.

'I gather a lot of reported gas leaks are false alarms. The general public does tend to overreact. Though it is an extremely efficient method of clearing an area of unwanted onlookers.'

Prior had a mobile phone in each hand, weighing one against the other. Caroline recognised them. They were both Dan's.

'Terrible worry aren't they – teenage boys.' He smiled at her. 'You just never know what they're getting up to. Who they're mixing with.' He stared at one of the phones. 'They can make all sorts of unsuitable friends nowadays of course. They do love to reach out on these dreadful social networking sites.' He smiled again. 'Such a worry.'

Caroline tried to speak, but her words came out in a muffled moan.

'For God's sake,' Prior said. 'Don't strangle her.'

The huge arm slipped away from her throat. Caroline bent over and tried to drag air into her lungs.

'Social networking can be so dangerous in the wrong hands. It's incredibly easy to remain completely anonymous. And untraceable. There are countless predators pretending to be someone they're not. And teenagers are so suggestible at that stage in their development. Don't you think?'

Caroline looked up at him. He was smiling again.

'I must admit, young Daniel did seem particularly receptive.'

Caroline thrust forward a hand, ramming it into Prior's crotch. She squeezed as hard as she could and grabbed his jacket, pulling herself upright.

A moment later she was flying backwards, her feet off the ground, more suffocating pressure against her windpipe. Prior stepped towards her, tears in his eyes. She kicked out and caught him in the shin.

He cleared his throat. 'Were you aware *just* how troubled Daniel has been lately, Caroline? Judging by my little online chats with him, it seemed he had no one else to turn to. Perhaps a little more time spent at home and fewer late nights in the office and none of this would have happened. In fact – I'm sure it wouldn't.' He smiled at her.

Caroline tried to kick him again, but he was out of reach. The pressure on her throat increased.

'A little gentle coercion goes a very long way with such a vulnerable boy.'

Black dots started to appear at the edge of Caroline's vision. She blinked. Prior's smiling face was blurring, fading into blackness.

52

'After a quarter of a mile, turn left.'

Angela glanced at the sat nav screen. 'Pete?' She reached over a hand and nudged his arm. 'Pete!'

Pete was lying across the double seat next to her. He moaned.

'Jesus, Pete! Are you still with me?'

He moaned again.

'We're almost there.'

Don't die on me, you stupid big bastard.

Pete opened his eyes wide and started to cough. A mess of bloody saliva sprayed across the windscreen. Angela slammed on the brakes. A noisy wheeze blew out of his mouth. He wheezed a second time and she realised he was trying to say something.

'What is it?' She leaned over, stuck her ear by his mouth. A moist breath blasted against her cheek.

'Drive.' Pete gripped the door, white knuckles showing through the purple and blue bruises.

Angela put her foot down. Less than a minute later they reached a set of temporary traffic lights. She stared at the red light for what seemed like minutes. Pete let out another groan.

'Go!' he managed.

'All right!'

She eased past the red light and prayed nothing would appear from beyond the curve in the road. On the other side of the blind bend she saw what was causing the problem. A small red car blocked half the carriageway, a scaffold pole protruding from its windscreen.

'Jesus that looks nasty.' She couldn't help staring into the car as they drove past.

'Caz!' Pete said.

'What?'

He swallowed and tried to draw down a breath. 'Caz's… car.'

Angela looked at the wreck as it receded in the wing mirror.

'Caroline's car?'

Pete nodded.

Dear God.

Pete closed his eyes.

'Pete?' Angela pressed on the gas and stared through the windscreen, concentrating on the road, trying not to think about what might have happened to Jean.

'Turn right.'

The sudden interjection of the sat nav made her jump.

'You have reached your destination.'

She spun the steering wheel and the van squealed into the next turning. Suddenly they left the country behind and entered suburbia.

A white clapboard chalet stood apart from its prefab neighbours, as if it had been picked up in some mid-western American town and dropped clumsily onto a square of scabby lawn. An outsized '14' had been painted on the door.

'Looks like we're here.'

Angela stopped the van across the street from the chalet. It was the only vehicle parked on the road. She wasn't sure if that was a good or a bad sign. Was it possible Larson's men had already left? She leaned over to Pete. With each outward breath he seemed to be deflating, his big chest shrinking as she watched.

'Hang in there, Pete.'

She swung her legs out of the van and dropped to the ground, then heaved open one of doors at the back and pulled out a 12-inch wrench. It felt reassuringly heavy in her hand. She crept along the fence leading to the chalet, the blood rushing in her ears. Her hands had started to sweat and the wrench was slipping from her grasp. She slipped it into her other hand and wiped her palm across the leg of her trousers. Her legs were trembling.

When she reached the front porch she sank to her knees and crawled along the wooden veranda until she reached the first window. She raised her head and peered through the glass, holding her breath. There wasn't enough light inside the chalet to distinguish one dark shape from another. She looked back out at the lawn. Her heart thudded painfully fast. A set of tyre marks ran all the way along the edge of the grass and disappeared into a track at the side of the building. She switched the wrench from her left hand to her right and wiped the other sticky palm down her jumper. She took a deep breath and tried the front door. The knob turned and the door clicked open. She puffed the breath back out and drew in another, gripping the wrench tighter in her fist. She pushed against the door and stood back.

She waited.

Nothing stirred inside. She slipped through the doorway and strained to focus in the gloom. Her eyes adjusted gradually, each looming shape materialising slowly into heavy pieces of furniture. She was standing in a square living room, the floral curtains, cushions and carpet swirling in a sickening pattern all around her. A door, half glazed with rippled glass, was open on the other side of the room. She gulped down the saliva that had pooled under her tongue and moistened her parched lips. She crept over to the door and waited again, listening for movement coming from the other rooms.

Then she heard it. A crack, the sharp splintering of something brittle snapping in two.

The wrench started to slip from her hand; she grabbed at it but fumbled. It clattered to the floor.

She froze.

A klaxon blasted outside. Angela ran back out onto the porch. She saw Pete slumped over the steering wheel in the van, his face squashed against the windscreen, the horn blaring. She ran towards the van, suddenly aware of another noise – the roar of a revving engine.

Getting closer.

She spun round too late to get out of the way. The motorbike sped by, the pillion passenger's knee thumping into her thigh as it passed. She staggered sideways and landed awkwardly on her hip. The bike weaved around the van and accelerated away. The blaring horn stopped. Pete was trying to open the van door.

'For God's sake, Pete – stay there!' Angela struggled to her feet and discovered she must have twisted her ankle as she fell. She hobbled back to the chalet, through the living room and into a narrow hall. She flung open doors on either side and quickly inspected the cramped rooms beyond. She limped back into the hall, heading for a rear door at the end.

She stopped.

Men's voices. Coming from somewhere outside. How many men had Valerie Larson sent? She felt suddenly exposed, standing in the middle of the hall unarmed. Why hadn't she picked the wrench back up? She stood listening for a moment, trying to make out what they were saying. The talking ceased. Then she heard the sound of metal hitting metal. A sliver of light appeared at the end of the hall as the back door started to open. She tensed.

A man shouted something and the door stopped moving. Then an engine roar erupted outside. An exhaust spluttered and the sound was on the move. She peered through one of the bedroom doorways off the hall and saw a blur of crash helmets speed past the window.

She let out a breath and staggered towards the back door.

She hollered for Ben and Claire as soon as she got outside. She shouted again and headed for a stone outhouse at the far end of the garden.

'Claire! Ben!'

There was a faint whimper coming from the little building. Angela lifted the latch and flung open the door. Claire was sitting on a plank lying across a broken toilet bowl. Ben was curled on his sister's lap, his arms wrapped around her neck. He turned slowly and blinked at Angela.

'Where's my Mum?'

53

Caroline opened her eyes and saw nothing but black. She lay curled, her knees tucked under her chin, on a cold, rough surface. Her legs felt heavy, as if they'd been pinned to the floor. She pressed a hand against the floor and lifted herself up into a sitting position. Hot needles exploded all over her scalp. She collapsed back to the ground and a solid mass of pain radiated through her whole body. She drew in a tight breath.

There was a smell. Something familiar and completely unexpected. She sniffed in another breath and detected the musty tang of dog.

Minty?

It took her another moment to realise she'd been dumped in the cupboard under the stairs. She pressed her fist into the floor again, pushing up through the pain, through the buzzing in her ears. She reached out her hands in the dark, feeling for the door catch. She located it, threw open the door, and fell out into the hall. She blinked, trying to adjust to the brightness.

'Dan!' Her voice was no more than a whisper, a fire burning in her throat.

She leaned heavily on the banister and dragged herself down the hall, grabbed the newel post and propelled herself up the stairs.

'Dan!'

She pushed into his room.

It was empty.

Oh please no.

She checked the bathroom, then the other rooms on the first floor. She hollered up the stairs leading to Claire's bedroom in the loft. She pulled in a breath through gritted teeth and took the steep steps to the attic as fast as she could. Claire's room was empty too.

She clattered back down both flights of stairs, numb now to the pain, and checked the living room and the kitchen. She rested a hand on the kitchen table and stood lost and hopeless as the room swirled around her. She tried to focus her attention on something that wasn't moving and spotted an old note her mother had written on the back of an envelope.

Why hadn't she thought of it before? She threw herself into the hall and across the living room and flung open the door to her mother's annexe.

Dan's arms and legs were stretched over Jean's bed, his head twisted awkwardly to one side, facing the window.

'Dan!' She grabbed his shoulders and shook him. Hard. 'Dan!' She slapped his face. 'Please! Dan.'

She dropped to her knees and landed on something. It shattered under her weight. A plastic bottle. Jean's pills. *Please God.* She pressed her fingers into Dan's neck, groping the flesh, digging in deep. Was there a faint pulse? She shook him again.

'Dan!'

She pounded his chest with a fist, tipped back his head and blew into his mouth. She leaned into his chest with one hand, released, pushed again and felt her pockets for her mobile. It wasn't there. She blew into his mouth again and saw his chest rise out of the corner of her eye. She blew again. He needed an ambulance. She didn't dare leave him to fetch the phone. She pumped his chest again.

'Somebody help me! Please!'

She called again, even though she knew no one would hear. The whole street had been abandoned.

Please God help me.

She moved back to his mouth, his face slick now with her tears. Again she massaged his narrow chest, her strength faltering, her arms numb and heavy. She knew she mustn't stop. She was so tired.

'Dan, please, come on, sweetheart.'

She kissed his forehead and filled his lungs with her breath again. She heard a noise – a scraping at the front door. She puffed out another breath into Dan's mouth, then turned towards the door and hollered.

'In here! We're in here. Hurry!'

The noise stopped.

Caroline pummelled Dan's bruised and battered chest again.

'Don't go! Please. In here!'

There was a bang. Then another, followed by the splintering of wood.

'In here!' she shouted.

Ralph Mills froze in the doorway for a moment, his eyes fixed on Dan.

*

The A&E nurse guided Caroline out of the emergency room and onto a plastic chair in the corridor.

'Please, Mrs Barber, Dan's in good hands.'

Caroline tried to get back on her feet. The woman in blue scrubs held her firm.

'I promise I'll let you know as soon as he's stabilised.'

'Will he?'

'Stabilise?' the nurse said, holding Caroline's gaze.

Caroline nodded and hot needles exploded in her head.

'We're doing everything we can. He's in the right place.' The nurse disappeared behind the swing doors.

Caroline closed her eyes and let out a straggly breath.

'I think I may have gone a bit mad with the sugar.'

She looked up to see Ralph Mills's sad smile staring down at her. She took the steaming polystyrene cup from him with trembling hands.

'Any news?' he asked.

'There are so many doctors and nurses in there with him.'

'He's in good hands.' Mills sat down.

'But it's been so long.'

'Trust me – that's a good sign.'

Caroline stared at the vapour rising from her cup, unable to blink.

'Oh – before I forget,' Mills said. 'I found this in your front garden.' He waved a mobile phone at her. 'Is it yours?'

She handed back the tea and snatched the phone. She had a voicemail message and five missed calls, all from the same number. She jabbed a bruised thumb against one button, then another and pressed the phone to her ear.

'Thank God!' Tate said. 'I've left you so many messages. Where are you?'

'Angela – I can't speak to you now. I need to try Claire again…'

'Haven't you listened to the messa—'

'And Mum. Is Pete with you?'

The emergency room doors burst open and a nurse ran out. Caroline shoved the phone in a pocket.

'What's going on?'

The nurse ignored her and ran to the end of the corridor. Caroline heaved herself up off the chair.

'You stay here,' Mills said. 'I'll find out what's happening.' He pushed through the swing doors into the emergency room.

Caroline forced out another frayed breath and retrieved her phone. She punched in Claire's number.

'Caroline?' It was Tate again.

'What are you doing with Claire's—'

'I was just trying to tell you.'

Caroline squeezed her eyes shut. She chose Dan. *Christ.* She chose Dan and sacrificed Ben and Claire. She couldn't take another blow.

'What's happened?' she said, not wanting to hear the answer.

'Don't panic!' Tate mumbled something away from the phone. 'Sorry – had to deal with—'

'What is it?'

'Are you sitting down?'

'Please tell me what's happened to my children.'

A man wearing a plastic white apron over his scrubs pushed Ralph Mills back into the corridor. The constable put a hand on her shoulder.

'Still no news,' he said. 'Which is good news. Absolutely.' He nodded to himself and sat back down.

'Caroline? Are you still there?' Tate was shouting.

'Please. Just tell me.'

'Claire left her phone with me in case you tried to call – she's on the ward with Pete at the moment.'

'What's wrong with Pete?'

'He'll be fine. The doctors seem very confident.'

'What do you mean, "seem"?'

'He's a fighter, your Pete.'

'You haven't mentioned Ben. What's happened to Ben?'

'Ben's good – he's fine. The nurses said it was OK for him to sit with Jean. As soon as I finish this call I'm going to visit her myself.'

'Visit? What's happened to Mum?'

'She had a... a little prang in the car.'

'She's had an accident?' Caroline's heart thudded against her ribs. 'How serious was it?'

'The car might not recover, but you know Jean, she bounces back quicker than anyone. She'll be flirting with the doctors before you know it.'

'Can I speak to her?'

'I'm not sure she's up to that.'

'Ben and Claire aren't hurt? Did Larson's men—?'

'They're a bit shaken up, naturally. But they are quite unharmed.'

Caroline really wasn't sure Tate was giving her the whole story. It sounded as if she was holding something back. 'Will you ask Claire to call me as soon as she can?'

'Of course. When did you get back to Larson's?'

'I... I didn't...'

'But I thought you were coming back... God, I haven't even asked you? Did you manage to get in touch with Dan? Is he OK?'

The fear and dread that Caroline had managed to control by squeezing them into a tight space between her chest and her throat suddenly burst upwards and out. She wretched a mix of bile and tears from her mouth and nose.

Mills snatched away the phone, put an arm around her shoulders and squeezed tight. He shoved a handkerchief into her hands.

'I know...' he said. 'I know. Just let it out.'

54

Caroline climbed out of the cab and looked up at the house. All the curtains were drawn.

'Hang on a minute, love. I'll get the door.'

She ran around the back of the cab and eased open the rear passenger door. She held out her hand, but it was ignored.

'I'm not an invalid.'

'Nope – course you're not.' Caroline clenched her fists and said nothing as she watched her son struggle out of the car. After some effort he finally made it onto the pavement outside the house. Caroline slammed the taxi door and waited. She followed Dan as he inched slowly up the path. He stopped at the front door and turned to face her.

'No one's going to make a fuss, right?'

'Don't worry – everyone's under strict instructions to completely ignore you. Just like they normally do.'

'Good.'

Dan's face was even paler than usual. His clothes seemed baggier, even though he'd only been three days in hospital.

Caroline shoved her key in the lock and stepped to one side. Dan grabbed the doorframe and slowly eased himself over the low step as if it was a Grand National hurdle. She followed him in, shrugged out of her jacket and watched helplessly as Dan wrestled his arms out of his, knowing any offer of assistance would be quickly rejected.

'Come through to the kitchen, Dan. I'll make you something to eat.'

'Not hungry,' he said and finally managed to escape from the confines of his coat.

'Come and keep me company, then, while I make a cup of tea.'

'I just wanna go to my room.'

'Sit with me – just for a while.'

Dan puffed out a weary sigh and dragged himself into the kitchen. He lowered himself slowly onto a chair, rested his elbows on the table and his head on his hands.

'What about a slice of toast? I bought a fresh jar of Nutella. Just a little slice.'

'You said no fuss.'

'You're right – I'm sorry, habit of a lifetime.' She filled the kettle and flipped it on.

Dan lifted his chin from his hands. 'Where's my mobile?' He glowered at her. 'I had it just before... before I...' He looked away.

'It's all right Dan – it's OK to talk about what happened.' She crouched down by the side of his chair. 'You can tell me.' She put a hand over his. 'You know you can talk to me about anything? Anything that's worrying you.'

He pulled his hand away.

'Have you got my phone?'

Caroline leaned on the tabletop and levered herself up.

'The doctor told me it'd be best if you didn't use it for a while.'

'But people might have been trying to get in touch.'

The kettle boiled. 'I think that's the point.' She collected two clean mugs from the draining board. 'Do you want a hot drink?'

'I'm going to my room.'

'Dan, please.'

He struggled from his chair and Caroline watched him shuffle into the hall. 'I can't leave you on your own, Dan.' She hurried after him.

'Look, I'm tired. I want to lie down.'

'There's pillows and a duvet on the sofa,' Caroline said. 'You can rest in the living room.'

Dan hung his head and edged closer to the foot of the stairs.

There was sound from the front door. A light tapping. Through the glass panel, Caroline saw a brightly coloured shape bouncing up and down on. She reached for the handle and slowly pulled the door towards her a few inches.

On the doorstep, dressed in a bright orange hooded cardigan and a short pink skirt, was Kylie. Pregnant Kylie. Caroline peered over the girl's shoulder and down the path, expecting Kylie's father to appear. But instead she saw a boy wearing low-crotch baggy jeans and a dark hoodie, the hood pulled down over his head. He was shifting from one foot to the other.

'Is Dan there, yeah?' Kylie said.

'Dan's not well enough to see anyone today.' Caroline spoke in a half whisper.

'We heard he was coming out the hospital today, though.'

Caroline gripped the door. 'Don't you think you've done enough damage already?'

Dan edged towards the door. 'Let her in,' he said to his mother.

'I'm sorry about all that,' Kylie said to Caroline. 'I panicked, innit.' She glanced back at the boy still loitering by the front gate. 'We got it all sorted now. Me and Chris are gonna have our own little family.'

'Congratulations,' Caroline said. 'I'm very pleased for you both.'

'Mum, please... let her in.'

Caroline sighed and reluctantly opened the door. 'You can't stay long – Dan needs to rest.' As Kylie stepped over the threshold, Caroline scowled at the boy at the end of her front garden. 'Are you coming in? Or are you happy to stay there?'

The boy rocked up the path, swinging a large brown paper bag in his hand. As he got closer Caroline noticed his top lip was split, a scab crusting over it. His left eyelid was swollen shut. It was the colour of overripe avocado. Caroline shut the door and followed him into the living room.

Kylie sat next to Dan on top of the duvet on the sofa. Her boyfriend stood by the mantelpiece. The shifting from foot to foot started up again.

'What they did to you was well out of order.' Kylie brushed a lock of hair from Dan's face.

Caroline opened her eyes wide, shocked by the display of unselfconscious intimacy. Dan always pushed her away if she tried to do anything like that.

'They're just a bunch of cowards, innit, Chris?'

Chris nodded his head but didn't say anything. He was staring at Dan. Dan looked slightly embarrassed.

'Hang on.' Caroline took a step towards the girl. 'Are you saying you know who's responsible for bullying Dan at school?'

Kylie shrugged. A moment later, Chris shrugged too.

'You've got to go to the police. Do you understand how serious bullying is?'

'Don't stress.' Chris spoke for the first time. Even Kylie seemed surprised. 'I sorted it. Me and my crew.' He stepped forward and handed Dan the brown paper bag. 'They won't be doing no more of that shit now.'

Caroline looked on in horror, wondering what Dan would discover when he opened the bag. He smiled at Chris and shoved his hand in the bag.

'Cheers, Chris. Fanks, Kylie. 'Preciate it. I'm starving, innit?' He pulled out a fist-sized object wrapped in greaseproof paper. He carefully unwrapped the paper and sank his teeth into a cheeseburger oozing tomato ketchup.

55

'When is the first result expected?' Caroline hesitated in the doorway of the living room, not sure she wanted to commit herself to the best part of six hours glued to the television screen.

'Before eleven – it's likely to be one of the Sunderlands. Safe for Labour.' Jean spoke without turning her head, her neck brace making all unnecessary movement a luxury. 'We won't get any of the interesting results through until one or two in the morning.'

'Any news on the exit polls?'

'You could just come in and watch with us.' Jean gestured to the sofa. Ben was fast asleep at one end, in Pete's normal position, like a faithful dog waiting for his master to return. Claire sat cross-legged next to him, stroking his hair, one eye on a chemistry textbook.

'I'm not sure I want to watch William King win,' Caroline said.

'Exit polls predict a reduced majority.' Jean awkwardly shifted her leg on a footstool. The plaster cast that started just above her toes and ran all the way up to the middle of her left thigh was already covered in scrawled messages. Most of them courtesy of Ben and his vast palette of felt tip pens.

'I think I may run myself a bath,' Caroline said, glancing at the spread of potato-based snacks ranged across the coffee table. 'Can I get you any more carbohydrates before I go upstairs?'

'We're all fine, love. You go and have a long soak. I'll let you know if you miss anything.'

When Caroline reached the landing she stopped outside Dan's door and listened, holding her breath.

'S'all right. I'm still alive.'

Dan was standing in the doorway of Ben's room at the other end of the landing.

'I was just…' she said.

'Really, Mum. It's OK.' He smiled at her. 'Ben wanted to borrow the Nintendo. I've left it on his toy chest.' He walked slowly down the hall and opened his door.

'You don't have to explain your every move,' Caroline said and smiled back.

'And you don't have to worry so much. I'm fine. Really I am.'

Caroline raised her hands in surrender. 'Not saying another word about it. I'm planning on monopolising the bathroom for the next two hours. I'll put everyone's toothbrush on the hall table. You can use your gran's bathroom.'

'Whatever.' Dan disappeared into his room and quietly closed the door.

Caroline stood staring at the floor, for a moment contemplating just how bad a mother she was. She filled her lungs with air and exhaled slowly and resolved to try harder.

She wandered into the bathroom, stoppered the plughole and turned the hot tap full on. The selection of bubble baths crammed into the corner of the bath didn't look very promising. Somehow the thought of luxuriating in Ben's Matey or Sainsbury's Basics orange and banana didn't appeal.

She padded into her bedroom and pulled open her underwear drawer – the only place she could safely stash her precious Issey Miyake shower gel without Claire finding it. She shoved a handful of knickers and tights to one side, sure the gel was somewhere underneath.

It wasn't.

What she found instead sent a strange mix of guilt and nostalgia rushing up from somewhere in the pit of her stomach into her chest.

She plucked out the birthday and Christmas cards and laid them flat on top of the chest of drawers. The CD Martin had given her at Christmas lay at the bottom of the drawer. She'd tried to listen to it once before, on her headphones in the office, but after a minute the squawking violin and honking saxophone had become unbearable. She plucked out the CD and scooped up the cards and marched the whole lot over to the wicker bin in the corner of the room.

She hesitated.

That really would be every last trace of Martin Fox gone forever. She remembered the lengthy apologetic message he'd written inside the Christmas card. She folded it in four and shoved it in a pocket, deciding to safely dispose of it somewhere else. She looked down at the CD, its cover decorated with a swirl of colours, musical notes rising out of the end of a saxophone. Martin's face used to light up like a small child's when he tried to describe the wonders of Thelonious Monk or Miles Davis. He must have realised he was wasting his time. It was all just random noise to Caroline. She could feel a swell of tears rising. She sniffed hard.

329

For God's sake.

Maybe she could try to listen to the CD one last time – just while she waited for the bath to fill. She checked the inlay card. Ten tracks in total. Getting through two or three of them would be her tribute to Martin – a final farewell.

She carried the portable stereo into the bathroom, slipped the CD into the top and pressed *play*, bracing herself for the first track. It was pretty much as she remembered it – trumpets squealing like nails down a blackboard.

She checked on her bath. The water level had risen all of two inches. At this rate all the election results would be in before she even got her toes wet.

A percussive ringing, completely out of time with the rest of the track, started up. How could people listen to this stuff? It took her a moment to realise the irrhythmic little blasts were coming from outside the bathroom. She stood on the landing and shouted down the stairs.

'Claire! Can you get the door?'

There was no sign of movement from the living room. She trundled down the stairs, huffing as she went, and flung open the door. Angela Tate removed her hand from the bell push and waved a large bottle of Jack Daniel's in Caroline's face.

'I thought we could commiserate the election results together.'

'I wish you'd phoned first – it's not really convenient – I'm just running a bath.'

'Cut a woman some slack. I've only just been released from police custody.'

'You were arrested?'

'Not exactly. I went in voluntarily. I had to do something – the hotel bill was getting out of hand, so I've been helping the police with their enquiries.' She started towards the kitchen. 'Except I wasn't exactly helpful.' She put the whiskey on the kitchen table and looked around the room. 'Where will I find glasses?'

Caroline reached up and retrieved two tumblers from a shelf. 'It'll be just you and me. Mum's on antibiotics.'

'How's Jean coping on crutches?' Tate pulled out a chair and sat down.

'Oh fine – but she's really shaken up, though she'd never admit it.'

'And how's Pete?' She poured them both two generous measures.

'He's been transferred from the hospital on Sheppey to Queen Elizabeth's in Lewisham.'

'So he's out of intensive care?'

Caroline nodded. 'He's on the mend.' She joined Tate at the table.

'And is he coming back here when they discharge him?' She sipped her whiskey.

Caroline shrugged. 'We've got some stuff to work on.' She could hear the distant warble of discordant notes drifting from the stereo in the bathroom. *And I've still got the last of Martin to expunge.*

'How are the kids coping?'

'Claire and Ben really seem to be OK. They're seeing a counsellor next week – to talk things through. The police don't hold out much hope of finding out who broke into the chalet.'

'There's a surprise.' Tate topped up her own glass. 'And how's Dan?'

'Dan?' She let out a long breath. 'I can't tell. Better, I think. He won't say much to me. I can't even broach the whole gay subject.'

Tate raised her eyebrows.

'Claire jokes about the big pink elephant in the room.'

'Is he at least talking to his sister?'

Caroline nodded. 'And he's booked in for a course of counselling sessions. Talking therapy.'

Tate smiled. 'They'll have their work cut out. I'm not an expert on teenage boys, but I would guess they're not renowned for their verbosity.'

'We'll see how it goes. I'd rather try that first than getting him started on anti-depressants. Which was the other option.' She took a sip of whiskey. It reminded her of Christmas liqueurs. She sighed. 'Bloody hell – all my kids are in therapy. I *am* the worst mother in the northern hemisphere.'

'And apart from that, how are you?'

'I'll survive.'

'That's the spirit.'

Tate lifted her glass. 'To justice and the greater good. Whatever the fuck that is.'

'Cheers.'

'Talking of justice, given the questions the police asked me, I would guess they're relying on one or both of us to cave in under interrogation and admit everything.' She took another sip. 'They can't prove anything without actual evidence of the information you passed on to me. And that's never going to be made public.'

'So?'

'So sit tight and say nothing.'

'But I've been captured *in the act* on Ed Wallis's mobile phone.'

'Inadmissible.'

'Really?'

Tate shrugged. 'Probably. I don't suppose the image quality is good enough to tell exactly what you were doing. The worst they could get you for is stealing a five-month-old copy of *heat*. Might be certifiable, but it's not *actually* criminal.' She knocked back another mouthful. 'I didn't mention your name. I stuck to my post room story.' She stared into her glass. 'I quite enjoyed watching them get frustrated.'

'I haven't spoken to anyone yet.'

'Well don't – I reckon you'll get your old job back in a couple of weeks.' Tate screwed up her face. 'Ah yes – that's a bit of news I should share.'

'What's happened?'

'According to my sources, your boss... Prior?'

Caroline nodded.

'He's been moved out of the DfE.'

'No doubt he's been promoted.'

'You could say that. He's now William King's assistant chief of staff.'

'Bloody hell.'

'Exactly. On the plus side, at least you won't have to face him when you finally go back into the office.'

Caroline took another sip of Jack Daniel's. 'Actually, I'm not sure I'm going back.'

'Oh... fair enough. Well just enjoy being on full pay while they drag their heels.'

'Maybe I could take voluntary redundancy.'

Tate clinked her glass against Caroline's. 'Here's to a fresh start.'

Caroline managed a smile.

'I do have some good news to impart.'

'Really?'

'My sources also tell me the Larsons are being done for tax evasion and some kind of VAT fraud.'

'That's very handy for King – just before the election.'

'Yep – all the evidence Larson had been holding over King wiped out in a single raid. Though I'm pretty sure none of those policemen would have known anything about it.'

'We know how easily evidence boxes disappear.'

'We do.'

'King really did have it all mapped out.' She shook her head. 'First he forces Duncan Oakley to resign by threatening to expose Rachael's part in whatever happened in that swimming pool.' A reflexive shiver ran across her shoulders. 'Then he worms his way into Number 10 – God knows how many favours he had to promise to make that happen.'

'Or how many threats he made.'

'Then he completely covers his tracks by destroying every last bit of evidence.' She puffed out a breath. 'And later tonight he'll secure a massive election victory. Five more bloody years.'

'You're forgetting the other loose ends he had to deal with.' Tate topped up their glasses, even though Caroline had barely touched hers. 'Freddie Larson and—'

'Martin.' Caroline lifted her glass and put it down again. 'Oh I hadn't forgotten. But I would like to.'

They both stared into their glasses.

'What *is* that noise?' Tate looked around the room.

'Oh, it's just a CD I'm playing upstairs. I should go and switch it off.'

'I can't hear music. No – it's a rushing noise – like flowing water.'

'Oh bugger.' Caroline scraped back her chair.

Outside water was gushing out of the overflow pipe above the kitchen window. 'I left the bath taps running. I need to get back to the bathroom. Go through to the lounge.' Caroline rushed into the hall. 'Drag Claire off the sofa and make yourself comfortable. I'll be down in a bit.'

The bathroom was as foggy as a Turkish bath. Caroline screwed the water off, pulled out the plug and opened a window. She stood quietly for a moment. The music had stopped. She listened instead to the water gurgling down the plughole. She found it almost soothing.

She heard a voice right next to her and started. She turned to the stereo. Martin's voice was coming out of the speakers. She hit the pause button. According to the display, the fifth track was still playing. She rewound a few seconds and pressed *play*.

Martin Fox cleared his throat. 'Hello, Caroline. I do hope that is Caroline, or all my careful planning has come unstuck somewhere along the line.' He paused.

Caroline sank down onto the side of the bath.

'Assuming it is you listening to this, and given how much you hate jazz – you really don't know what you're missing – I'm guessing that you've only made it all the way to track five because you're indulging in some mawkish act of remembrance. And if that is the case then I suppose something rather terminal has happened to me.' He took a deep breath and exhaled. 'Which is a sobering thought, I can tell you.'

The CD played silently for a few seconds. Caroline jumped up and closed the bathroom door.

Martin Fox cleared his throat again. 'So... assuming the worst, that means William King is trying to manoeuvre himself to the very top. He has some extremely powerful friends – but you must know that by now.'

I've left special instructions with my solicitor. In the event of...'
Another pause. 'My death... he is to provide you with all the evidence I
have amassed over the years. Enough to stop King in his tracks and very
probably send him to prison. Along with Fred Larson, his wife Valerie,
his son Freddie and Barry Flowers. Oh and your favourite and mine...
Jeremy Prior. But I'm telling you things you already know. It must be
tedious for you.' He let out another slow breath. 'The actual reason for
this intrusion into an otherwise perfect collection of modern jazz classics
is more personal than that. Not something I want you to discover sitting
in a solicitor's office in Waterloo.'

Caroline lowered herself onto the side of the bath again and held her
breath.

'I just want to let you know how much you mean to me.'

She jumped up and hit the pause button, aware that Dan was in the
room next door. She turned the volume right down and hit *play* again,
leaning her head close to the speaker.

'And I'm not talking about the night in the Marriott. I've probably
already apologised for that more times than you needed to hear anyway.
I think we both regret what happened... I promised myself I wouldn't
apologise again... By now you no doubt know more about my... *private
life* than I'd previously disclosed. I expect you've met Sam. I do hope
she's coping OK.

'I didn't set out to keep secrets from you, but given how much
information I've been withholding for the past 30 years, I suppose I've
felt more secure keeping my worlds entirely separate.' He paused again.
'What I'm trying to say in my desperately ham-fisted way, is that I hope
you have valued our friendship as much as I have. You're a beautiful
woman, Caroline, and I hope your husband reminds you of that fact
every day. He's a lucky man.'

Caroline reached for the pause button again, trying hard to control
the pressure building in her chest. She opened the window wider and
took a few deep breaths before she felt able to continue. She leaned
close to the speaker and restarted the CD. Seconds of silence played
before Martin Fox spoke again.

'If you're listening to this CD-ROM via a computer, you'll no doubt
be wondering why I've copied all of the evidence I've given to my
solicitor onto this disc. Overly cautious, perhaps, but I see this as a
worst-case scenario insurance policy.'

Again Caroline paused the disc. She swallowed. Evidence?

You wonderful man, thank you, thank you, thank you.

She restarted the CD, trying very hard to concentrate and to resist
punching the air.

'It's possible – perhaps even likely – that King's sphere of influence is even greater than I suspect and he has somehow managed to intercept and destroy all the other evidence I have prepared. If that is the case, then under no circumstances should you trust the police.' He swallowed noisily. 'There are a handful of journalists I still trust. In the first instance try Paul Richardson at *The Guardian*. Failing that, you should make contact with Angela Tate at the *Evening News*.'

Caroline let out a long breath. She watched the LCD counter tick through seconds of nothing except the sound of Martin Fox breathing. Finally he cleared his throat.

'The other thing I need to do is apologise. I've written a letter to Stephen Cole's parents trying to explain. By the time I found him in the pool it was too late – there was nothing I could do to save him.' Another pause. 'Nevertheless, I could have told his parents what happened. Instead I let Fred Larson *deal* with the situation and kept quiet about it just like everyone else. But make no mistake; no matter how he may try to extricate himself from blame, William King was responsible for Stephen's death. He forced so many drugs on him he may as well have held the poor boy's head under the water.'

Caroline stopped the CD. She closed her eyes and took a deep breath. Immediately the black and white image of William King and Rachael Oakley staring open mouthed at the pale corpse lying next to the pool flashed into her mind. Somewhere in that pile of photographs there must have been a picture of Martin doing exactly the same thing. He'd been a part of the conspiracy all along. Surely that made him as guilty as King. How could he have stayed quiet for so many years?

Caroline stuck her head through the open window and gulped down cool air in an attempt to control the nausea rising in her stomach.

How could he?

She stared up at the starry sky. Moments ago she'd had an overwhelming urge to scoop up the CD and hug it to her chest. Now she wasn't sure she could go on listening to it. The sob she'd been trying to trap in her chest finally escaped and she could do nothing to hold back the tears.

All this time.

She really hadn't known him at all.

After a few moments she turned back to the blinking LCD counter and pressed the play button once again. Her hand was shaking.

'I've felt so ashamed, Caroline. Not just because of what happened 30 years ago – I am ashamed of the silence I have kept ever since. I've watched King's progress over the years and after each new victory I vowed it would be his last. But still I stood back and did nothing.' He blew out a noisy breath. 'Exposing King means exposing myself and I have been too afraid to confront that truth.

'As you're listening to this, it can only mean my hand has been forced and I've taken the final step I've resisted for so many years. I expect King must have coerced Duncan Oakley into resigning and replaced him as PM. King simply cannot be allowed to continue. I have to stop him, yet I know I can't survive the personal humiliation that will inevitably follow.'

Caroline continued to stare at the counter on the stereo, unable to take her eyes off it as the seconds passed.

'I'm so sorry, Caroline. By now you've had the chance to read the note I left with my solicitor trying to explain my actions. I hope that's helped you understand why I made this decision. Why I felt taking such a dramatic step was my only option. You may see it as the coward's way out, but believe me, it will take all the courage I can muster to commit the final act.'

More seconds of silence followed.

'I'm so sorry I have disappointed you.'

The CD finally stopped playing. Caroline removed the disc from the stereo and put it back in its protective case. She grabbed a handful of toilet paper, dabbed her damp cheeks and blew her nose. She checked her face in the mirror and wiped away the smudges of mascara from under her eyes.

Disappointed? You have no idea.

She took a deep breath and unlocked the bathroom door, the sick feeling in her stomach finally subsiding. She stepped carefully down the stairs, clutching the CD tightly in her hand. When she reached the hall she stood outside the living room for a moment and tried to compose herself, willing her heartbeat to slow.

After another deep breath she pushed open the door.

'Get your coat, Angela,' she said. 'We've got a government to bring down.'

About the author

Eva Hudson was born and raised in south London and now splits her time between rural Sussex and central London. She's been a local government officer, singer, dot com entrepreneur, portrait artist, project manager, web designer and content editor.

In 2011 she won the inaugural Lucy Cavendish fiction prize for her first novel, *The Loyal Servant*. The novel was also shortlisted for ITV's People's Novelist Award.

Find out more about Eva at evahudson.com

Acknowledgements

I would like to thank my early readers, Angela, Linsay and Annabelle for pointing out all the things I was too close to see; and all those at Lucy Cavendish College, Cambridge, for spotting the potential in this story, especially Sophie Hannah, Professor Janet Todd and Beverley Yorke.

Thanks to all of my former colleagues at the Department for Education – my years in Sanctuary Buildings were truly inspirational.

Finally, enormous thanks to FC, the best editor in the world. I couldn't have done it without you.

Printed in Great Britain
by Amazon.co.uk, Ltd.,
Marston Gate.